DISCOVERING IRELAND

AN EXPLORER'S GUIDE

TRAVEL. DISCOVER. EXPLORE.

WORLD OF WUNDER

CONTENTS

May *the road rise up to meet you.*

May *the wind be always at your back.*

May *the sun shine warm upon your face;*

The *rains fall soft upon your fields and until we meet again,*

May *God hold you in the palm of His hand.*

— TRADITIONAL IRISH BLESSING

INTRODUCTION

A View of the Coastline and the Classiebawn Castle (in the distance) in Sligo, Ireland

Have you ever woken up at the crack of dawn, not because you had to, but because the outside world was too intriguing to miss? Imagine one such morning, the air crisp and expectant, as you stand amidst the majestic rolling hills of Ireland, where the first light of day transforms the dew into a shimmering blanket, and the ancient, whispering voices of the landscape seem to beckon you into a world less seen. This, my friends, is not your run-of-the-mill Ireland guide; this is the raw, mystical, and utterly breathtaking Ireland that awaits the curious and the adventurous.

My name is Adam Schreifels, and I'm here to be your somewhat quirky guide on this journey. With "World of Wunder: Discovering Ireland," my vision, or rather our collective daydream, is to peel back the layers of this Emerald Isle, guiding you to the treasures hidden beyond the well-trodden paths. We'll dive into local haunts where the food tastes like magic, explore activities that get you in tune with the true rhythm of Irish life, and uncover spots that even some locals whisper about in hushed tones of reverence.

This guide invites you on an immersive journey to experience Ireland like never before. This guide isn't just about places to visit; it's about delving into Ireland's soul, from its rugged coasts to its ancient forests, and uncovering hidden treasures beyond the usual tourist trails. Designed for anyone with a sense of adventure, whether tracing your ancestry, seeking thrills, or simply soaking in the culture and nature, this guide is your doorway to a more profound connection with Ireland.

I'm leading a team at World of Wunder, driven by a passion for exploring the unseen corners of Ireland. We bring you insights from local experts, ensuring authenticity in every experience shared. This book is more than a guide; it's a shared adventure among friends packed with stories, cultural insights, and historical nuggets, making your journey as enriching as possible. Every new year promises new adventures, and this guide is your essential companion for exploring Ireland deeply. We're offering not just the highlights but the hidden gems, with practical advice for navigating like a local. It's time to move beyond mere sightseeing to live the Irish experience truly.

Thank you for choosing this guide. While it offers a wealth of information in digestible bits, including destinations, festivals, and places to eat and stay, along with practical details like addresses and prices, it's not an exhaustive encyclopedia. We want you to experience Ireland, not read about it. Designed for everyone, from first-timers to seasoned travelers, it aims to prevent the overwhelming feeling of planning fatigue without sacrificing the joy of discovery. Note that the paperback version features black and white photos for a nostalgic feel, but if you prefer color, the Kindle version is your go-to.

This guide has been meticulously crafted with original content to make planning easier and more enjoyable. It's not just about saving weeks of research; it's about providing you with a curated, practical tool to explore Ireland's wonders. We even have downloadable maps for you compliments of Google Maps, to make navigating your journey much easier. So, let's embark on this adventure together, discovering not just a place, but a world within Ireland. Let the journey begin!

IRELAND: A BRIEF HISTORY

(BRIEF BEING THE OPTIMAL WORD)

To understand Ireland's present identity, one must understand its past. For you history buffs, Ireland won't disappoint.

In the chronicles of Ireland's past, each entry is woven with stories of magic, conflict, and profound cultural identity. The earliest of these takes us back to a time shrouded in mystery and legend—the age of the Celts. Their legacy, etched into the very landscape of Ireland, invites us on a voyage not through space but time to uncover the origins and essence of what many consider the soul of Irish identity.

1.1 THE DAWN OF CELTIC MYSTIQUE

Emerging in Central Europe around 1200 BC, the Celts, a group of tribes linked by shared language and culture, profoundly influenced Ireland from their arrival in 500 BC, establishing its Celtic identity. They introduced the Irish language, rich traditions, and vibrant arts, and built complex social structures. Druids, central to their culture, were seen as connectors between the physical and spiritual, venerating nature, especially oak trees, and fostering a belief in life's interconnectedness. Their rituals and myths, celebrating deities and heroes, defined Celtic festivals like Samhain and informed their understanding of the universe.

Celtic art featured spirals and symbols like knots, illustrating concepts such as eternal life and existence's interconnectivity, evident in the Newgrange spirals and the Book of Kells. These motifs, appearing in various artifacts, emphasized their strong bonds with nature, and cultural beliefs.

The clan-based society, governed by progressive Brehon laws, prioritized restorative justice to maintain harmony and covered diverse life aspects, reflecting a community-oriented, nature-respecting culture. Today, Ireland's landscapes and monuments invite exploration of this heritage, highlighting the importance of connection, respect for nature, and storytelling, revealing insights into a society where nature and community are deeply linked.

Celtic and Viking Art

1.2 VIKING FOOTPRINTS ON IRISH SOIL

Beginning in the late 8th century, the Viking era marked a pivotal transformation in Ireland. Initially raiding for wealth, Norse warriors evolved into settlers, profoundly influencing Irish society, culture, and geography. They established permanent settlements, including Dublin as a major trading center, followed by Waterford, Wexford, and Limerick, which were crucial in developing Ireland's urban structure and promoting trade.

This period sparked a dynamic cultural exchange, impacting architecture, language, and lifestyle. Norse urban planning and artistic influences merged with Celtic traditions, enhancing Ireland's cultural fabric. The Vikings' lasting legacy includes robust trading networks that linked Ireland to Europe, shifting from a rural, clan-based society to an urban, cosmopolitan one. Dublin thrived as a commercial and political hub under Norse influence.

The complex Norse-Irish relations, characterized by conflict and cooperation, were epitomized by the Battle of Clontarf in 1014. Alliances, often through marriage, fostered cultural synthesis, forming a shared history that shaped modern Ireland. The Viking presence, spanning over two centuries, left a significant imprint on Ireland's physical and cultural landscape, marking a major chapter in its history.

1.3 TALES FROM THE HIGH KINGS AND HEROES

Irish history brims with the exploits of High Kings and legendary heroes, whose tales blur the lines between mortal and divine, weaving a rich blend of cultural identity filled with lessons and a sense of belonging. Central to these narratives is the Hill of Tara, the coronation site of High Kings, believed to be chosen by the gods themselves. The Lia Fáil, or Stone of Destiny, signifies the divine approval of these monarchs, highlighting the sacredness and spiritual depth of their leadership.

Among the epic sagas, the Táin Bó Cúailnge shines. It features the hero Cú Chulainn defending Ulster against Queen Medb's forces with extraordinary valor, embodying themes of loyalty, honor, and the tragic nature of the conflict. Characters like Fionn mac Cumhaill enhance these stories with their heroic deeds, reflecting the values and struggles of the people.

The interplay between history and mythology in these stories enriches the narrative, offering insights into a worldview where the natural and supernatural coexist seamlessly. This blend of myth and history has deeply influenced modern Irish culture, inspiring artists, musicians, and writers to draw upon these ancient themes, connecting past and present and continuing to resonate with audiences today.

1.4 THE NORMAN CONQUEST: CASTLES AND BATTLES

The late 12th century saw Ireland's historical trajectory pivot dramatically with the Norman arrival, transforming more than just the landscape but embedding a profound shift in the nation's destiny. The Norman invasion, spurred by Diarmait Mac Murchada's appeal to Henry II of England, was initiated in 1169 with Norman knights setting foot on Irish soil, marking the beginning of a significant transformation.

This era introduced the widespread construction of castles, not merely as military bastions but as symbols of Norman authority and administrative hubs. These castles exemplified the Norman's architectural brilliance and strategic military planning. Trim Castle and Dublin Castle are enduring symbols of this era, each playing pivotal roles in consolidating Norman control and influence across Ireland.

The Normans also instigated profound changes in Irish society, law, and land ownership. Their introduction of the feudal system upended the traditional Irish clan system, redefining social and economic structures by centralizing land ownership under the crown and redistributing it under a vassalage system. This shift not only diluted the power of native chieftains but also gradually supplanted the Brehon laws with Norman legal codes, marking a gradual erosion of Irish legal traditions.

Resistance to Norman encroachment was inevitable, with figures like Hugh de Lacy leading campaigns exploiting Ireland's terrain. Yet, over time, the distinction between Norman and Irish began to fade, with Normans integrating into Irish society, adopting its language, customs, and laws, and becoming "more Irish than the Irish themselves."

The Norman period in Ireland is a testament to conflict, adaptation, and integration, leaving a legacy of castles and changed societal structures that tell stories of power, resistance, and eventual assimilation. This era reflects the complexity of cultural exchange and the capacity of societies to evolve while maintaining their identity. It underscores the enduring nature of Irish culture and resilience, illustrating how the descendants of Norman settlers have woven themselves into the fabric of Irish identity, contributing to its rich and nuanced history.

1.5 RELIGIOUS CHRONICLES: MONASTERIES AND MARTYRS

Ireland's pivotal monastic tradition earned it the title "Island of Saints and Scholars." Monks in these monasteries, dedicated to prayer, labor, and study, turned these centers into European educational hubs. Figures such as Patrick, Brigid, and Columba spread Christianity and founded monastic schools that taught arts, sciences, and classical studies, marking a golden era.

However, this era faced Viking and Norman invasions, leading to monastic sacking and the construction of round towers for protection. The Normans introduced new monastic orders like the Cistercians and Franciscans, revitalizing monastic architecture and life. Monasteries played a crucial role in preserving Western knowledge during the Dark Ages, exemplified by the creation of the Book of Kells.

The Tudor era, particularly under Henry VIII's Reformation, brought significant upheaval, dissolving monasteries, and deeply impacting Irish society. Resistance to Tudor policies, like Hugh O'Neill's Nine Years' War, symbolized Irish defiance against English rule. The plantation system introduced by the Tudors aimed to Anglicize Ireland, creating deep-seated sectarian divisions.

Despite attempts to suppress Gaelic culture, Irish resilience maintained their language and traditions, preserving a rich cultural identity. The Tudor period, with its reforms, rebellions, and upheavals, left a complex legacy in Irish history, reflecting both conflict and the enduring spirit of the Irish to protect their heritage. This narrative of transformation and resistance shapes Ireland's current and future identity.

1.7 REBELLION AND THE QUEST FOR INDEPENDENCE

Ireland's history is rich with rebellion, reflecting its people's steadfast resolve for autonomy. The 1798 Rebellion, ignited by global revolutionary zeal, marked a significant attempt by the Society of United Irishmen, uniting Catholics, and Protestants, to shed British domination. Despite the brutal suppression and tragic outcomes, it laid the groundwork for Ireland's relentless pursuit of freedom.

The Easter Rising of 1916 further epitomized this quest. Orchestrated by leaders like Patrick Pearse and James Connolly, it was a bold declaration for independence, turning Dublin into a fierce battleground. Although swiftly subdued, resulting in the execution of its leaders, the uprising kindled a nationwide call for sovereignty, immortalizing those who led it as martyrs.

This momentum ushered in the Irish War of Independence, where the Irish Republican Army, under Michael Collins' tactical guidance, engaged in guerrilla warfare against British forces. This shadow war, punctuated by ambushes and espionage, culminated in the Anglo-Irish Treaty of 1921, which granted Ireland dominion status but controversially partitioned the island, leading to a civil war. This internal strife underscored the deep ideological rifts within the emerging Irish Free State, leaving enduring wounds.

These epochs of conflict and defiance are central to Ireland's complex narrative of independence. They exemplify a nation's indomitable will to forge its destiny, navigating through triumphs and sorrows. The journey towards self-rule was marred by internal discord yet driven by a collective spirit of rebellion, showcasing the resilience and unity of the Irish people in their quest for a sovereign nation.

1.8 THE FAMINE LEGACY: EMIGRATION AND EVOLUTION

In the mid-19th century, the Great Famine drastically altered Ireland's path. From 1845 to 1849, a potato blight, coupled with poor harvests, British government neglect, and food exportation, devastated Ireland's main food source, resulting in up to 1.5 million deaths and sparking massive emigration that significantly reduced Ireland's population over the following century.

This emigration not only transformed Ireland but also impacted global communities, especially in America. Irish immigrants, despite facing hostility and harsh conditions, significantly contributed to their new communities, and preserved Irish culture. Cities like Boston and New York became hubs of Irish diaspora culture, nurturing Irish traditions in new settings.

Back in Ireland, the famine and resulting emigration profoundly influenced the cultural and social landscape, making emigration a norm and transforming agricultural practices and community life. The economic and societal shift led to diversification away from subsistence farming.

The post-famine era saw changes in land ownership and a strong push for land reform and home rule, driven by the resolve to prevent future tragedies. The famine tested human endurance and forced significant changes in Ireland's trajectory.

The legacy of the Great Famine is a complex tale of loss, resilience, and transformation, underscoring the indomitable spirit of the Irish people. It prompted major economic and social reforms within Ireland and influenced the cultural fabric of its global diaspora, highlighting Ireland's capacity to overcome adversity and evolve. This impacted both Ireland and its global community deeply.

1.9 MODERN IRELAND: A PHOENIX RISING

In the latter half of the 20th century, Ireland began to write a new chapter in its storied history. From the ashes of centuries-old conflicts and economic struggles, the nation emerged vibrant and buoyant, marking its place on the world stage with remarkable resilience and innovation.

Economic Development

Following independence, Ireland's economy was primarily agrarian, with limited industrialization compared to its European neighbors. However, the late 20th century heralded a period of unprecedented economic growth, famously dubbed the Celtic Tiger era. Beginning in the mid-1990s, Ireland transformed into one of the fastest-growing economies in the world, driven by a boom in high-tech industries, favorable corporate tax rates, and significant foreign direct investment, particularly from technology and pharmaceutical companies. This era saw a dramatic improvement in living standards, a sharp decrease in unemployment, and a surge in construction and property markets.

Despite facing a severe recession in 2008, which tested the resilience of its economy and people, Ireland bounced back with commendable swiftness. Strategic economic policies, coupled with a focus on education and innovation, have since positioned Ireland as a hub for technology and innovation in Europe. The country has also become known for its significant contributions to the global pharmaceutical and information technology sectors, embodying a successful transition from a traditional agrarian economy to a modern knowledge-based one.

Peace Process in Northern Ireland

The latter part of the 20th century also saw significant strides towards peace in Northern Ireland, culminating in the Good Friday Agreement of 1998. This historic accord marked the end of decades of sectarian violence, known as "The Troubles," which had claimed thousands of lives and deepened divisions within the community. The agreement, reached after protracted negotiations, laid the groundwork for power-sharing between unionists and nationalists, establishing a devolved legislature in Northern Ireland. It also set the stage for disarmament and the normalization of relations between the Republic of Ireland and the United Kingdom.

The peace process not only brought an end to widespread violence but also initiated a period of reconciliation and healing. It opened avenues for dialogue and cooperation, fostering a sense of shared identity among the people of Northern Ireland. The transformation from conflict to peace has been remarkable, with cities like Belfast and Derry becoming vibrant centers of culture, tourism, and economic activity, symbolizing the possibilities of reconciliation and the strength of the human spirit in overcoming division.

Cultural Renaissance

Parallel to its economic revival and peace-building efforts, Ireland has experienced a cultural renaissance that has seen its arts and literature flourish. The country has long been renowned for its contributions to literature, with giants like James Joyce, W.B. Yeats, and Samuel Beckett. This rich literary tradition has continued into the modern era, with Irish writers like Seamus Heaney, Anne Enright, and Colm Tóibín gaining international acclaim. Irish literature, with its deep explorations of identity, memory, and the complexities of the human condition, has continued to captivate and resonate with readers around the world.

Music and art have also seen a resurgence, with traditional Irish music gaining a new lease of life alongside contemporary genres. Bands and artists have blended traditional Irish elements with rock, pop, and other modern genres, creating a unique sound that has garnered a global following. Similarly, Irish cinema has risen to prominence, with filmmakers telling diverse stories that range from intimate personal narratives to larger social commentaries, further enriching Ireland's cultural landscape.

Ireland on the Global Stage

In recent decades, Ireland has also carved out a significant role for itself on the global stage. Its membership in the European Union has been a central aspect of its foreign policy and economic strategy. Ireland has been a proponent of the EU, benefiting from access to the single market and structural funds, which have been instrumental in its economic development. The country has also played an active role in EU affairs, contributing to discussions on issues ranging from data protection to agricultural policy.

Beyond Europe, Ireland has established itself as a voice for peace, human rights, and sustainable development. Its engagement in international organizations, including the United Nations, highlights its commitment to multilateralism and global cooperation. Ireland's foreign policy, characterized by neutrality and a focus on peace-keeping and humanitarian aid, has earned it respect on the world stage.

This modern iteration of Ireland, marked by economic dynamism, cultural vibrancy, and an active engagement in global affairs, stands in stark contrast to the Ireland of the past. It's a country that has navigated its way through economic upheavals, social changes, and the long shadow of conflict, emerging stronger and more resilient. Ireland today is a testament to the power of transformation and the enduring spirit of its people, a phoenix that has risen with a new sense of identity and purpose on the global stage.

Dublin Concrete Bridge

WHEN TO WANDER: MASTERING IRELAND'S MOODS

Now that you know a little of Ireland's history, let's get down to business. That's why you're here, to find out where to go in Ireland. Now, imagine you're tuning into your favorite radio station, but instead of music, it's broadcasting the whims of Irish weather. One moment, sunbeams dance across green fields; the next, a curtain of rain sweeps in, turning the world misty and mysterious. Ireland's weather is a live show, unpredictable yet profoundly beautiful, setting the stage for an adventure that changes with the seasons. Understanding this rhythm is key to planning a trip harmonizing with Ireland's natural cadence, ensuring every moment is savored, rain or shine. In other words, it will prevent you from being a miserable crab because of the weather.

2.1 DECIPHERING IRELAND'S WEATHER PATTERNS

Ireland's climate plays a symphony of variations, influenced by the Atlantic Ocean, making it a land of moderated extremes and surprising shifts. The following graph shows the average temperature and precipitation by month:

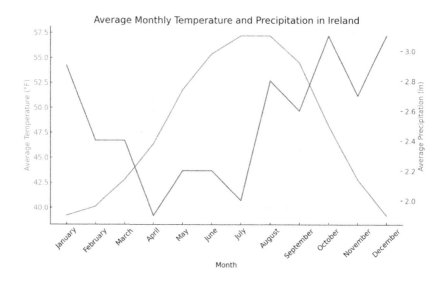

Varied Climates

East and South: These areas bask in the most sunshine, thanks to the country's westward mountains, which shelter them from the Atlantic winds. Dublin, in the east, enjoys relatively drier and warmer conditions, ideal for city tours and coastal walks.

West and North: Here, the weather sings a different tune, with more rainfall and warmer winters from the Atlantic currents. Galway, with its bohemian vibe, offers lush landscapes that are especially vibrant after a rain shower.

Best Times to Visit

May to September: These months hit the sweet spot of warm weather and longer days, perfect for exploring city streets and rural trails. June stands out with its blend of mild weather and the buzz of cultural activities.

September to November: For those looking to capture the essence of Ireland's autumnal hues, this period offers a cooler yet enchanting experience, with fewer tourists and a riot of colors in the countryside.

Rainy Season Insights

Rain is a constant companion, but rather than dampening spirits, it adds a layer of enchantment to Ireland's landscapes. The key to enjoying Ireland, even under a shower, is adopting the local mantra: "There's no bad weather, only the wrong clothes."

Outdoor enthusiasts can rejoice in the fact that rain often comes in swift, light showers, making activities like hiking and cycling still enjoyable with brief pauses to let the rain pass.

Ominous Skies Over Ireland

Packing Essentials

A checklist to match Ireland's weather moods:

- **Layers:** They are the cornerstone of smart packing, allowing you to adjust to Ireland's quicksilver weather. Think of breathable fabrics for sunny days and cozy jumpers for cooler evenings.

- **Waterproof Gear:** A lightweight, waterproof jacket is indispensable, as it doubles as a windbreaker along the coastal cliffs.
- **Sturdy Footwear:** Waterproof boots or shoes are a traveler's best friend, ensuring comfort whether you're navigating cobblestone streets or embarking on a muddy trail.
- **Sun Protection:** Sunglasses and sunscreen are must-haves, even on overcast days, to protect against UV rays that sneak through the clouds.

This list gives you the tools to understand Ireland's weather. You'll be prepared for sunshine or rain, enriching your journey with every weather-driven experience, and making sure you're not left out in the rain. Ha!

2.2 THE BEST SEASONS FOR CULTURAL FESTIVITIES

Ireland doesn't just wear her seasons; she celebrates them, each with its own festival, like turning pages in a vast, vibrant storybook. These festivities, each a spectacle of tradition and joy, invite you to step into the heart of Irish culture, where the past and present dance together in the streets. They are sure to make your travels memorable. No matter where or when you go, you'll find a festival to attend somewhere.

Spring Festivals

The first whispers of spring bring with them the green tide of St. Patrick's Day, a day when the entire island seems to bloom in fifty shades of green. Cities and villages alike come alive with parades, music, and the clinking of glasses, celebrating Ireland's patron saint with a contagious fervor. Picture this: streets thronged with locals and visitors, all united in a jubilant display of Irish pride, the air thick with the melodies of fiddles and flutes, and everywhere, the infectious cheer of a nation in celebration. (Heck even those who aren't Irish celebrate!)

St. Patrick's Festival:

- **What is it?** Established in 1996, it is Ireland's premier St. Patrick's Day celebration. Expanding from a one-day event to a four-day festival, it showcases a dynamic mix of music, dance, theater, literature, visual arts, food, wellness, and community activities. As the world's largest celebration of Irish culture and heritage, it reaches over 700 million people globally. Remember to wear green!
- **Where is it?** Dublin, Ireland
- **When is it?** March 17th and the days preceding.
- **How much is it?** Most of the events are free except for some ticketed events. Tickets must be pre-purchased and vary according to the day. Check out their website for more details.
- **Web:** stpatricksfestival.ie/
- **Instagram:** @stpatricksfestival

A Barman Serving a Drink During St. Patrick's Day Festival

Revelers Outside Temple Bar in Dublin During St. Patrick's Day

Easter in Ireland is a time for reflection, renewal, and family gatherings. Rooted in Christian tradition, it also features outdoor activities and community events, celebrating the season's first warm days. From Good Friday's solemnity to joyful Easter markets offering crafts, chocolates, and spring flowers, the season embodies Irish hospitality and the promise of new beginnings. Here are some non-religious festivals that celebrate Easter:

The Fairyhouse Easter Festival

- **What is it?** Dubbed the "Irish Kentucky Derby", it is a celebrated three-day event featuring elite horse racing, comprehensive hospitality, live music, and entertainment for all. This glamorous occasion offers over €1.25 million in prize money and includes premier National Hunt Racing. Highlights are Ladies Day, the WillowWarm Gold Cup, Family Day, and the Boylesports Irish Grand National, attracting racing fans and those seeking festive vibes.
- **Where is it?** Fairyhouse Racecourse in Ratoath, Co. Meath, Ireland
- **When is it?** Easter bank holiday weekend
- **How much is it?** $22 for a day pass. $55 for a flex 2-day pass.
- **Web:** fairyhouse.ie/
- **Facebook:** facebook.com/FairyhouseRC/

If food and drink are more your thing, with a side of music, then about 2.5 hours to the west of Fairyhouse Racetrack there is another festival that will suit your fancy. Venture to the vibrant and bohemian coastal city of Galway to celebrate Easter with food, drink, and music all provided by local artists, cafes, bars, suppliers, and producers.

Westend Easter Street Festival

- **What is it?** A festival that brings the local community together to celebrate with local producers and suppliers. The festival features live music, face painting, and a chance to sample offerings from local restaurants, cafés, and bars. It's a vibrant event that showcases the best of Galway's Westend area, with Ravens Terrace closed off to traffic to accommodate the festivities.

- **Where is it?** Galway, Ireland
- **When is it?** Easter weekend
- **How much is it?** Free to enter. Food and beverages are for purchase.
- **Web:** galwaytourism.ie/event/westend-easter-street-festival/
- **Facebook:** facebook.com/westendgalway/

Ireland's Easter celebrations are diverse, featuring everything from thrilling horse racing to community street festivals. Easter Sunday, central to the festivities, includes jubilant church services and the exchange of Easter eggs symbolizing rebirth. The day often starts with a hilltop sunrise, representing the resurrection, and concludes with a traditional roast lamb feast. Easter Monday extends the celebrations with family gatherings and community activities, also commemorating the 1916 Easter Rising, which adds historical depth to the holiday.

Traditional foods like hot cross buns and simnel cake highlight the spirit of renewal. For a unique spiritual experience, Knock Shrine in County Mayo, and St. Patrick's Cathedral in Dublin, among other places, hold special Easter ceremonies. Due to their popularity, those interested in attending should check church schedules in advance.

Summer Gatherings

As the days stretch longer and the countryside dresses in its summer best, the solstice beckons. Ancient stones align with the stars, and across Ireland, people gather to celebrate the longest day of the year. One of the most magical places to witness this is the Hill of Tara.

The Summer Solstice at the Hill of Tara

- **What is it?** The Summer Solstice at Tara draws a diverse crowd, including locals, tourists, historians, and spiritual enthusiasts. This ancient celebration, marking the year's longest day, has been important for agricultural and ceremonial purposes for millennia. It features a blend of modern and traditional activities like dawn ceremonies, music, storytelling, and guided tours of ancient monuments. A highlight is watching the sunrise, a symbolic moment that aligns Tara's ancient structures with celestial movements, underscoring its astronomical and natural significance.
- **Where is it?** County Meath
- **When is it?** Usually around June 21st. Confirm before going.
- **How much is it?** Free
- **Web:** taracelebrations.org/celebrations
- **Instagram:** @taracelebrations8

Then, as summer unfolds, the air fills with the lilting tunes of traditional music festivals. From the spirited sessions of the Willie Clancy Summer School to the lively streets of Galway during the Arts Festival, music is the heartbeat of an Irish summer. These gatherings are not just concerts but communal experiences, where the air vibrates with the strumming of guitars, the beat of bodhráns, and the warmth of shared stories and laughter.

Willie Clancy Summer School Festival

- **What is it?** If you love music and dance, the Willie Clancy Summer School is for you. This week-long festival celebrates traditional Irish music and dance, starting in 1973 to honor legendary uilleann piper Willie Clancy. It's the largest festival of its kind in Ireland and is renowned globally for its focus on Irish cultural traditions, featuring traditional tunes, songs, and dances.

- **Where is it?** Miltown Malbay in County Clare
- **When is it?** Starts on the first Saturday in July
- **How much is it?** Costs vary depending on the event.
- **Web:** scoilsamhraidhwillieclancy.com/
- **Facebook:** facebook.com/profile.php?id=100089673309995

Autumn Traditions

Autumn in Ireland is a golden season of harvest and storytelling, highlighted by Halloween, which originated from the Celtic festival of Samhain. Communities celebrate with bonfires, pumpkin carving, apple bobbing, and ghost stories, keeping ancient traditions alive. The harvest also brings festivals celebrating Ireland's agricultural roots, with family outings to apple orchards and pumpkin fields, and town fairs showcasing seasonal produce, music, dance, and livestock auctions. This time celebrates the land's bounty and community spirit, echoing the natural cycles of the world.

The Púca Festival

- **What is it?** It's named after a shape-shifting spirit from Celtic folklore. The festival aims to reclaim Halloween's traditional Irish roots. It features an array of events, including spectacular light shows, live music, storytelling, and traditional Samhain rituals. The festival's highlight is the lighting of the Samhain fires, marking the start of the Celtic New Year.
- **Where is it?** County Meath and County Louth
- **When is it?** Three to four days around October 31st
- **How much is it?** Depends on the event. $20-25
- **Web:** pucafestival.com/
- **Instagram**: @PucaFestival

The Banks of the Foyle Halloween Carnival

- **What is it?** This festival is one of the largest Halloween celebrations in Europe. Derry's historic walls provide a dramatic backdrop for the festivities, which include parades, fireworks, ghost tours, workshops, and performances. The carnival attracts tens of thousands of visitors, many of whom participate in the celebration wearing creative and elaborate costumes.
- **Where is it?** Derry (Londonderry)
- **When is it?** Four days and nights around October 31st
- **How much is it?** A mix of free and paid events.
- **Web:** derryhalloween.com/
- **Instagram:** @derryhalloween

Bram Stoker Festival

- **What is it?** Celebrating the life and legacy of Dublin-born Bram Stoker, the author of "Dracula," this festival blends the gothic, the mysterious, and the supernatural through a variety of events. From spooky theatrical performances and horror film screenings to literary events and night-time adventures, the festival offers something for fans of all ages and interests.
- **Where is it?** Dublin
- **When is it?** Four days and nights around Halloween. Check for exact dates.
- **How much is it?** A mix of free and paid events.
- **Web:** bramstokerfestival.com/
- **Instagram:** @bramstokerfestival

The Spirits of Meath Halloween Festival

- **What is it:** Various events take place under the umbrella of the Spirits of Meath Halloween Festival. This festival is family-friendly and includes a range of activities from haunted houses and spooky tours to traditional Samhain celebrations and pumpkin carving contests.

- **Where is it?** Throughout the entire County Meath
- **When is it?** October (Check for exact dates)
- **How much is it?** A mix of free and paid events
- **Web:** spiritsofmeath.ie/
- **Instagram:** @spiritsofmeathhalloweenfest

Galway Aboo Halloween Festival

- **What is it?** Held in the medieval streets of Galway's Latin Quarter, this festival claims to be the country's largest Halloween Festival. It features a mix of family-friendly events, including parades, storytelling, workshops, and a range of street performances, all celebrating the Halloween spirit in a uniquely Irish manner.
- **Where is it?** Galway
- **When is it?** Last week of October through Halloween
- **How much is it?** A mix of free and paid events.
- **Web:** galwaytourism.ie/event/galway-aboo-halloween-festival/
- **Web:** thelatinquarter.ie/
- **Instagram:** @galwayaboohalloweenfestival

Winter Warmth

As winter wraps Ireland in its chilly embrace, the country glows with the warmth of Christmas markets. Ireland is truly magical around Christmas. These markets are a wonderland of handmade crafts, local delicacies, and festive cheer, offering a glimpse into the heart of Irish Christmas traditions.

Winterval

- **What is it?** It's celebrated for its expansive offerings including 40 events, many of which are free, and is Ireland's largest Christmas festival.
- **Where is it?** Waterford
- **When is it?** December (Check for exact dates)
- **How much is it?** A mix of free and paid events
- **Web:** winterval.ie/
- **Instagram:** @winterval_waterford

Aerial View of Galway Christmas Market

Galway Christmas Market

- **What is it?** A long-standing tradition that transforms Eyre Square with over 50 wooden chalets offering food, drink, and festive fun.
- **Where is it?** Galway
- **When is it?** December (Check for exact dates)
- **How much is it?** Free to walk around. Food and beverages are for purchase.

- **Web:** galwaytourism.ie/event/galway-christmas-market/
- **Web:** christmasmarketgalway.com/
- **Instagram:** @galwaychristmasmarket

Belfast's Christmas Market

- **What is it?** It's a continental-style affair attracting over a million visitors and one of the largest in Europe.
- **Where is it?** Belfast, Northern Ireland
- **When is it?** Mid-November to right before Christmas
- **How much is it?** A mix of free and paid events.
- **Web:** visitbelfast.com/ (search Christmas Market)
- **Instagram:** @visitbelfast

Kilkenny Christmas Festival

- **What is it?** A festive market, with unique attractions like artisan stalls, food vendors, and entertainment.
- **Where is it?** Kilkenny
- **When is it?** End of November through before Christmas
- **How much is it?** A mix of free and paid events.
- **Web:** yulefestkilkenny.ie/
- **Instagram:** @kilkennyyulefest

Ireland celebrates the New Year with a blend of reflection and celebration, marking the occasion with fireworks, music, and joy. It's a moment to say goodbye to the old year and embrace the new with hope. Across Ireland, from small towns to big cities, there's a shared excitement for the new beginnings that midnight brings. Ireland's cultural tapestry, rich with tradition and festivities, invites you to join in, dance, and become part of its ongoing, vibrant story. If you're looking to bring in the New Year with fun and excitement, then Ireland is the place to do it.

2.3 HIDDEN GEMS: WHEN LESS IS MORE

Ireland, with its lush landscapes and vibrant culture, holds countless treasures waiting to be discovered by those willing to stray off the beaten path. Are you willing? Away from the hustle and bustle of popular tourist spots, the island reveals its quieter, more intimate side, where authentic experiences and breathtaking views provide a deeper connection to this enchanting land. You're sure to discover why they call this the Emerald Isle by visiting some of these destinations!

Off-the-Beaten-Path Locations

Loop Head Peninsula:

- **What is it?** Far from the crowds of the Cliffs of Moher, Loop Head offers equally stunning vistas without the tour buses. Here, you can stand at the edge of the world, where lighthouses guard the coastline, and dolphins play in the waves below.
- **Where is it?** County Clare (West)
- **Web:** loveloophead.com/
- **Instagram:** @loopheadtourism

Beara Peninsula

- **What is it?** Skip the Ring of Kerry for its quieter cousin, Beara. Drive or cycle along winding roads, discover stone circles and take a cable car to Dursey Island for a day of exploration in solitude. Great for hikers and cyclists.
- **Where is it?** It straddles County Cork and County Kerry in the southwest
- **Web:** bearatourism.com/
- **Instagram:** @beara.cork

Slieve League Cliffs

- **What is it?** These cliffs soar even higher than their famous counterparts but see only a fraction of the visitors. The views are breathtaking, and the sense of serenity is unparalleled.
- **Where is it?** County Donegal
- **Web:** slieveleague.com/
- **Instagram:** @slieveleaguecliffs

Slieve League Cliffs, County Donegal

Quiet Season Travel

Winter and early spring wrap Ireland in a unique tranquility not found in summer's hustle. The landscapes, free from crowds, reveal their serene beauty. For a peaceful, charming Irish experience, these months are ideal. You'll swap warm weather for quiet and no waits. For activities in these quieter times, consider exploring:

Winter walks in Connemara

- **What is it?** With the mountains dusted in snow and the lakes reflecting the stark beauty of bare trees, Connemara becomes a wonderland for those who dress warmly and dare to explore. It's famous for Connemara National Park, Kylemore Abbey, and its distinctive ponies. The region's beauty and cultural heritage make it a popular destination for tourists seeking to experience the natural and historical richness of Ireland.
- **Where is it?** County Galway
- **Web:** ireland.com/en-us/destinations/regions/connemara/
- **Instagram:** @tourismireland

Spring blooms in the Burren

- **What is it?** Before the tourists arrive, the Burren awakens with wildflowers blooming amidst its limestone cracks. It's a unique ecosystem, where Mediterranean, alpine, and Arctic plants grow side by side. Great for botanists and naturists!
- **Where is it?** County Clare
- **Web:** ireland.com/en-us/destinations/regions/the-burren/
- **Instagram:** @tourismireland

Local Festivals

To truly embrace the Irish way of life, you absolutely must immerse yourself in local festivals. These gatherings are a testament to Ireland's enduring traditions and community spirit, offering a glimpse into the local culture through music, dance, and storytelling.

Matchmaking Festival

- **What is it?** For those looking for love or just a good time, this is Europe's largest singles festival. It is a quirky celebration of romance, with music, dancing, and the world's only traditional matchmaker, Willie Daly, at work.

- **Where is it?** Lisdoonvarna, County Clare
- **When is it?** The month of September
- **How much is it?** A mix of free and paid events.
- **Web:** matchmakerireland.com/
- **Instagram:** @matchmaking_lisdoonvarna

Puck Fair

- **What is it?** One of Ireland's oldest festivals, where a wild goat is crowned king for three days of food, drink, music, parades, and market stalls, showcasing the playful side of Irish heritage.
- **Where is it?** Killorglin, County Kerry
- **When is it?** August
- **How much is it?** Mostly free.
- **Web:** puckfair.ie/
- **Instagram:** @puck_fair

Secret Beaches and Coastal Walks

Ireland's coastline has a string of hidden coves, sandy stretches, and cliffside paths, many of which remain largely untouched by the tourist trail. These secret spots offer tranquility and a deep connection to nature.

Silver Strand Beach, Malin Beg

- **What is it?** Nestled at the base of cliffs, this horseshoe-shaped beach is a haven of peace, with crystal-clear waters and fine, white sand.
- **Where is it?** County Donegal
- **Web**: donegalbeaches.com/beaches/silver-strand/
- **Instagram:** @SilverStrandBeachDonegalIreland

Silver Strand Beach

The Sheep's Head Way

- **What is it?** Far less trodden than the Kerry Way, this walking trail offers stunning coastal scenery, lighthouses, and ancient sites, with the Atlantic Ocean as your constant companion. Make sure you have a comfortable pair of shoes!
- **Where is it?** County Cork
- **Web:** thesheepsheadway.ie/
- **YouTube:** youtu.be/l4OlbSTyHGU
- **YouTube:** youtu.be/ND-ssr1juxY
- **YouTube:** youtu.be/jA_MtJzbGQo

Each of these hidden gems invites you to experience Ireland in a personal and profound way. Away from the crowds, you'll find the island's soul. In these quieter moments, Ireland whispers its secrets, sharing with you the magic that lies just off the beaten path.

2.4 REGIONAL HIGHLIGHTS THROUGH THE SEASONS

Spring in the South

As the cold grip of winter loosens, Ireland's southern counties awaken with a burst of life, making spring a delightful time to explore this region. The mild climate nurtures a variety of blooming gardens, turning the landscape into a canvas painted with a multitude of colors. Perfect for the nature enthusiast!

Bantry House

- **What is it?** Bantry House and Garden, overlooking Bantry Bay in southwest Ireland, has been the residence of the White family since 1739 and opened to the public in 1946. It offers Bed and Breakfast in the East Wing from April to October and serves as a sought-after venue for weddings and events. Visitors can tour the formal gardens, explore the house, enjoy a picnic or Afternoon Tea in the Library, and take inviting strolls through the historic grounds, enjoying the air filled with the scent of flowers.
- **Where is it?** County Cork
- **How much is it?** $5-$35 depending on age and desired activity
- **Web:** bantryhouse.com/
- **Instagram:** @bantryhouse

Kinsale

- **What is it?** It is a town located at the start of the Wild Atlantic Way and is famous for its colorful streets, rich history, and beautiful landscapes. In the spring, seafood starts to feature prominently on local menus, celebrating the season's fresh catch. Outdoor cafes start setting up, offering spots to bask in the gentle sun with a view of the bustling harbors. Seafood lovers delight!

- **Where is it?** Kinsale, County Cork
- **Web:** kinsale.ie/
- **Instagram:** @kinsale.ie

The Beara Peninsula's walking trails have become a hiker's paradise for those with a penchant for adventure. The moderate weather conditions are ideal for exploring the rugged beauty without the summer crowds.

Beara's Peninsula

- **What is it?** The Beara Peninsula in southwest Ireland extends 30 miles into the Atlantic, featuring breathtaking scenery, historical sites like stone circles and ancient tombs, and charming towns such as Castletownbere, Kenmare, and Glengarriff. Highlights include the Beara Way, a scenic walking route, and abundant outdoor activities like hiking and fishing, making it ideal for experiencing Ireland's natural beauty and tranquility.
- **Where is it?** It borders the County of Cork and the County of Kerry
- **Web:** bearatourism.com/
- **Instagram:** @beara.cork

Summer in the West

Come summer, the West of Ireland calls out to those who seek the embrace of wild nature. For those who like the outdoors, your paradise awaits!

Wild Atlantic Way

- **What is it?** The Wild Atlantic Way is a long-distance touring route on the west coast of Ireland, stretching over 2,500 kilometers (about 1,550 miles) from the Inishowen Peninsula in the north to Kinsale in the south. It's renowned for showcasing the raw beauty and dramatic landscapes of Ireland's Atlantic coastline, including cliffs, beaches, headlands, and bays, alongside vibrant towns, and villages. It's a great route for scenic driving or cycling enthusiasts!

- **Where is it?** The route passes through nine counties (Donegal, Leitrim, Sligo, Mayo, Galway, Clare, Limerick, Kerry, and Cork) and three provinces, offering visitors a chance to experience the rich cultural heritage and natural beauty of the Irish coast. Along the way, travelers encounter numerous attractions, such as the Cliffs of Moher, the Skellig Islands, Connemara National Park, and the Ring of Kerry, to name just a few.

- **Things to do:** The Wild Atlantic Way is designed to be explored in segments or, in its entirety, appealing to different interests and time frames. It's marked by distinctive blue and white signage, making it easy for travelers to follow. The route is popular among drivers, cyclists, and walkers, offering a plethora of activities, including hiking, cycling, surfing, kayaking, and fishing, along with opportunities to engage with local history, music, and cuisine.

- **Web:** thewildatlanticway.com/

- **Instagram:** @thewildatlanticway

Wild Atlantic Way

Connemara

- **What is it?** With its collection of boglands, lakes, and mountains that make it majestic during winter, it shines under the summer sun. Kayaking on Killary Fjord offers serene waters and panoramic views of Ireland's only fjord, a memory made more profound by the setting sun coloring the sky. It's a region where you can get much more bang for your buck.
- **Where is it?** County Galway
- **Things to do:**
- **Visit Connemara National Park:** Explore over 2,000 hectares of scenic mountains, bogs, heaths, grasslands, and forests. The park offers various walking trails for all levels, including the famous Diamond Hill Walk, which provides stunning panoramic views.

Connemara National Park

Kylemore Abbey, County Galway

- **Kylemore Abbey and Victorian Walled Garden:** Discover this historic abbey set against a lush, green backdrop. The Victorian Walled Garden is a must-see, beautifully restored to its former glory.

- **Enjoy the beaches:** Connemara boasts some of the most beautiful beaches in Ireland, such as Glassilaun Beach, Dog's Bay, and Gurteen Bay, perfect for swimming, picnicking, and relaxing.
- **Take a scenic drive on the Sky Road:** This drive offers breathtaking views of the Atlantic Ocean, Clifden town, and the islands off the coast. It's one of the most scenic routes in the Connemara region.
- **Boat trips to the Aran Islands:** Departing from Rossaveal, a trip to these islands offers a glimpse into traditional Irish culture and language, along with ancient sites like Dún Aonghasa.
- **Fishing and water sports:** With its lakes and coastal areas, Connemara is ideal for fishing, kayaking, stand-up paddleboarding, and more. Equipment rental and guided tours are available.
- **Horse riding:** Take a guided horseback ride through Connemara's stunning landscapes, suitable for all experience levels.
- **Visit the Connemara Giant:** Stop by for a photo with this fun, quirky statue, which is part of local folklore.
- **Explore the market town of Clifden:** Known as the "Capital of Connemara," Clifden is lively in the summer, with shops, cafes, art galleries, and restaurants. If you're there in August, don't miss the Connemara Pony Show.
- **Hiking and walking trails:** Apart from the national park, there are numerous other trails and walks throughout Connemara, suitable for casual walkers and serious hikers alike.
- **Web:** ireland.com/en-us/destinations/regions/connemara/
- **Instagram:** @connemara.ie

The Aran Islands

- **What is it?** A short ferry ride from the mainland offers a glimpse into a way of life that has preserved the essence of Irish culture. They consist of three islands: Inishmore (Inis Mór), the largest; Inishmaan (Inis Meáin), the middle island; and Inisheer (Inis Oírr), the smallest. Known for their stark beauty, unique limestone landscapes, and rich cultural heritage, the Aran Islands are a popular destination for visitors interested in experiencing the Irish language and tradition, ancient historical sites, and the rugged natural environment of Ireland's west coast.
- **Where is it?** At the mouth of Galway Bay. They are accessible by ferry from Rossaveal (Ros an Mhíl) in County Galway and Doolin in County Clare
- **Things to do:** Rent a bike and pedal along stone-wall-lined roads, which lead to ancient forts and breathtaking cliff views, all under the watchful eye of the Atlantic.
- **Web:** aranislands.ie/
- **Instagram:** @aranislands.ie

Aran Island Coastline

Galway

- **What is it?** Known as the "City of The Tribes." It's a coastal city that comes alive with street performers and festivals during the summer. The Galway International Arts Festival, happening in July, transforms the city into a stage for artists from around the globe, showcasing a blend of music, literature, and visual arts.
- **Where is it?** West Coast, County Galway
- **Things to do:**
- **Explore Galway City's Latin Quarter**: Wander through the cobblestone streets of the Latin Quarter, brimming with shops, pubs, and cafes. This area is alive with the buzz of street performers and musicians, especially during the summer. It's the perfect place to soak up Galway's lively atmosphere, enjoy live music, and maybe catch an impromptu street performance.

- **Attend the Galway International Arts Festival**: This is one of Europe's most vibrant and exciting arts festivals, taking place in July. The festival brings together a fantastic mix of theater, music, street art, dance, visual arts, and comedy from artists all over the world. It's a cultural highlight not to be missed.
- **Enjoy Galway's beaches**: Galway boasts several stunning beaches, perfect for relaxing, swimming, or even trying your hand at surfing. Salthill, just a short walk from the city center, offers a lovely promenade and beaches with views across Galway Bay. For a more adventurous outing, head to Silver Strand or Dog's Bay for beautiful scenery and watersports.
- **Sample local seafood**: Galway is famous for its seafood, and summer is the perfect time to enjoy the freshest catch. Visit one of the city's many seafood restaurants or take a trip to the nearby village of Barna or to Clifden in Connemara to taste locally sourced oysters, mussels, and other sea delights. The Galway Oyster Festival in September, marking the end of summer, is a terrific opportunity to celebrate Galway's seafood heritage.
- **Web:** galwaytourism.ie/
- **Instagram:** @galwaytourism

Stone Tower, County Galway

Autumn in the East

Autumn casts a spell over Ireland's Eastern region, draping it in hues of gold and amber. It's a time when history and harvest intertwine, offering unique experiences rooted in the area's rich heritage.

Brú na Bóinne

- **What is it?** Brú na Bóinne, a UNESCO World Heritage Site, hosts significant Neolithic passage tombs, including Newgrange, Knowth, and Dowth, dating back to 3200 BC. These tombs, older than Stonehenge and the Egyptian pyramids, feature intricate carvings and astronomical alignments. Newgrange is famous for its winter solstice event, where sunlight illuminates its inner chamber. The Visitor Centre provides guided tours, offering insights into the ancient builders' lives and the site's ceremonial significance, showcasing the ingenuity of Neolithic society.
- **Where is it?** County Meath
- **Things to do:**
- **Tour Newgrange:** Newgrange is famous for its winter solstice phenomenon. A guided tour lets you enter the tomb and see the ancient carvings up close. Due to the limited space inside the passage tomb, it's advisable to book in advance.
- **Explore Knowth:** It's home to the largest collection of megalithic art in Europe. The site consists of one large central tomb and several smaller ones. Guided tours provide insights into the construction and purpose of these structures.
- **Visit Dowth:** Unlike the others, Dowth is not accessible for internal tours, but you can walk around the site and admire the exterior of the tomb and its carvings. It's a quieter location, often less visited, offering a more contemplative experience.
- **Take a Walking Tour:** The area is scenic, with walking paths that offer picturesque views of the river Boyne and the surrounding countryside. It's a peaceful way to appreciate the landscape that has been significant to humans for over 5,000 years.
- **Web:** ireland.com/en-us/things-to-do/attractions/bru-na-boinne/
- **Instagram:** @newgrangeandknowthopw

Apple orchards around County Wicklow

- **What is it?** Known as the Garden of Ireland, they open their gates for apple picking. The crisp air is filled with the laughter of families gathering apples, a prelude to the making of ciders and pies.
- **Where is it?** County Wicklow
- **When is it?** The best time for harvest is the end of July through October
- **Things to do:** Visit one of many apple orchards in the region.
- **Web:** highbankorchards.com/stockists-regions/county-wicklow
- **Instagram:** @highbankorchards

Dublin Theatre Festival

- **What is it?** Established in 1957, the Dublin Theatre Festival is a premier European event each fall, featuring top Irish and international theater. It presents plays, musicals, and dance performances in diverse venues, from historic theaters to modern spaces. The festival also includes workshops, talks, and discussions, fostering engagement between artists and audiences. A cultural highlight, it attracts theater enthusiasts, professionals, and critics worldwide, offering a chance to experience innovative theater.
- **Where is it?** Dublin
- **When is it?** September and October
- **How much is it?** A mix of free discussions to paid performances.
- **Web:** dublintheatrefestival.ie/
- **Instagram:** @dublintheatrefestival_

Winter in the North

The North of Ireland, wrapped in winter's chill, offers a landscape of stark beauty and celebrations that light up the dark days.

The Mourne Mountains

- **What is it?** The Mourne Mountains, a granite range in Northern Ireland, are known for their scenic beauty, rich history, and outdoor activities. Slieve Donard, the highest peak at 850 meters, and the surrounding area are designated as an Area of Outstanding Natural Beauty. Popular among hikers, climbers, and nature lovers, the Mournes feature extensive trails and the 35-kilometer Mourne Wall, which crosses fifteen summits to enclose water reservoirs for Belfast. Rich in folklore, the mountains have inspired artists like C.S. Lewis, influencing his vision of Narnia. Activities include **rock climbing, fishing, cycling**, and **bird watching**, making the Mournes a sought-after destination for both tranquility and adventure in the Northern Irish countryside.
- **Where is it?** County Down, Northern Ireland
- **Web:** discovernorthernireland.com/things-to-do/outdoors-nature-and-wildlife/mourne-mountains
- **Instagram:** @discoverni

Mourne Mountains, Northern Ireland

Belfast

- **What is it?** "Home of the Titanic" Belfast is the capital and largest city of Northern Ireland, part of the United Kingdom. Situated at the mouth of the River Lagan on Belfast Lough, low hills surround it. Belfast is known for its rich history, cultural heritage, and role in the Industrial Revolution as a major port and industrial center, particularly famous for its shipbuilding industry—the Titanic was built here, in the

Harland and Wolff shipyard. The Christmas Market at City Hall invites you to warm up with hot mulled cider as you browse through stalls of crafts and local delicacies. It's a place of joyous gathering, where the spirit of the season is palpable.

- **Where is it?** Northern Ireland, United Kingdom
- **Things to do:** Attractions include the **Titanic Belfast Museum**, an iconic structure located on the former shipyard where the RMS Titanic was built. The museum tells the story of the ship's construction, maiden voyage, tragic sinking, and legacy. Other points of interest are the historic City Hall, the **Ulster Museum**, and the **Belfast Botanic Gardens**. The city also serves as a gateway to exploring the natural beauty of Northern Ireland, including the **Giant's Causeway** and the **Mourne Mountains**.
- **Web:** ireland.com/en-us/destinations/experiences/belfast/
- **Instagram:** @visitbelfast

For those chasing the ethereal beauty of the Northern Lights, the northern coast near Malin Head, Ireland's northernmost point, becomes a stage for nature's light show. The dark, clear nights of winter offer the best chances to witness this celestial dance, a moment where time stands still.

Malin Head

- **What is it?** Located on the Inishowen Peninsula, it's the northernmost point of the Irish mainland. Known for its rugged landscape, dramatic cliffs, and breathtaking coastal scenery, Malin Head is a place of natural beauty and historical significance. It is famed for its wild, natural charm, offering panoramic views of the Atlantic Ocean, including dramatic sea cliffs and rock formations.
- **Where is it?** County Donegal
- **Things to do:** The area around Malin Head is dotted with various points of interest, including **Hell's Hole**, a deep chasm

where the sea surges with great force, and **Banba's Crown**, the northernmost tip of Ireland, where a weather station and a World War II lookout tower can be found. The lookout tower, part of Ireland's coastal defense system during the war, is marked with the word "ÉIRE" to signify Ireland's neutrality.

- Malin Head is a popular spot for **bird watching**, **hiking**, and **photography**, especially due to its unique flora and fauna and the occurrence of the Northern Lights (Aurora Borealis), which can sometimes be seen from here during periods of high solar activity. The area's natural beauty and its significance as a point of both geographical and historical interest make Malin Head a must-visit for those exploring the Wild Atlantic Way or the broader natural landscape of Ireland.
- **Web:** ireland.com/en-us/destinations/regions/malin-head/
- **Instagram:** @tourismireland

Every region of Ireland presents a unique seasonal experience, from the South's spring blooms and the West's summer wilds to the East's autumn harvests and the North's winter festivities. Ireland's seasonal journey uncovers its heart and soul, leaving lasting memories.

2.5 NORTHERN LIGHTS AND SOUTHERN CHARMS

Chasing the Aurora

The Northern Lights' mesmerizing display is a rare global spectacle, with Ireland's northern coast offering a prime viewing spot. The best time to see this natural wonder is from October to March, with Malin Head in Donegal providing an almost magical view. Vibrant green and purple lights dance across the sky, captivating all who see them. Armagh's Observatory and Planetarium can offer predictions and advice for those seeking the aurora, making the experience more accessible. Successful viewing requires patience and a clear, dark sky away from urban light pollution.

Northern Lights, Dunree, Donegal County

Armagh's Observatory and Planetarium

- **What is it?** Armagh Observatory is a historic astronomical research institute and is one of the UK and Ireland's leading astronomical research institutes. Its primary focus is on astrophysics, solar system astronomy, and climate change.
- **Where is it?** Armagh, Northern Ireland
- **When is it?** Year-round, but October through March offers the best viewing.
- **How much is it?** Prices vary. Check for pricing.
- **Web:** armagh.space/
- **Instagram:** @armaghplanet

Southern Hospitality

In Ireland's south, warmth becomes more than just a feeling. Towns like Cobh and Kinsale in County Cork, or Waterford's historic lanes, offer rich, storied experiences filled with friendly faces. Here, strangers quickly become friends, inviting you into conversations in pubs or markets. Southern Ireland's residents openly share stories, directions, or hidden gems unknown to guidebooks. It's often in these shared meals or impromptu music sessions that visitors truly discover Ireland's heart.

Cultural Differences

Irish culture changes distinctly from north to south, each part marked by its history, landscape, and traditions. In the north, Ulster Scots heritage shapes music, dance, and dialect. Places like Derry/Londonderry, with their historical walls and murals, showcase a legacy of resilience and creativity. In contrast, the south thrives on Gaelic sports and the Irish language, with festivals like Wexford's Opera and Cork's Jazz Festival showing a strong arts heritage. Appreciating these differences enriches the experience, unveiling a land not just of scenic beauty but of rich diversity and tradition.

Wexford's Opera

- **What is it?** Wexford's opera refers to the Wexford Festival Opera, an annual opera festival that takes place in the town of Wexford, Ireland. Founded in 1951 by Dr. Tom Walsh, the festival has gained international acclaim for its focus on presenting rare, neglected, and sometimes premiere operas. It has become one of the leading opera festivals worldwide, celebrated for its unique programming and the opportunity it provides to hear lesser-known works performed.
- **Where is it? Wexford, County Wexford**
- **When is it? October and November**
- **How much is it? Prices vary. Check for pricing.**
- **Web:** wexfordopera.com/
- **Instagram:** @wexfordfestivalopera

Cork Jazz Festival

- **What is it?** The Cork Jazz Festival, officially known as the Guinness Cork Jazz Festival, is an annual music festival held in Cork City, Ireland. It is one of the largest and most significant jazz festivals in Europe. Since its inception in 1978, the festival has grown in popularity and stature, attracting jazz musicians and fans from around the world.

- **Where is it?** Cork City, County Cork
- **When is it?** Last weekend in October usually
- **How much is it?** Prices vary. Tickets sell out fast. Check for pricing.
- **Web:** guinnesscorkjazz.com/
- **Instagram:** @guinesscorkjazz

Iconic Landmarks

Both the north and south are guardians of landmarks that are not just sights but symbols of Ireland's enduring legacy.

In The North:

The Giant's Causeway, with its interlocking basalt columns, whispers tales of giants and folklore. It's a place where myths feel tangible, and the rugged coastline challenges the imagination.

- **What is it?** The Giant's Causeway, on Northern Ireland's northeast coast, is known for its unique formation of about 40,000 interlocking basalt columns, created by an ancient volcanic eruption. These mostly hexagonal columns form stepping stones from the cliff to the sea, with the tallest standing around 12 meters high. A UNESCO World Heritage Site since 1986, it is protected as a natural reserve and managed by the National Trust.
- **Where is it?** Near Bushmills, Northern Ireland
- **How much is it?** $20 for adults and $45 for families
- **Web:** nationaltrust.org.uk/visit/northern-ireland/giants-causeway
- **Instagram:** @nationaltrust

Giant's Causeway, Northern Ireland

The Dark Hedges, a dramatic avenue of beech trees, feels like stepping into a storybook. Its appearance in pop culture has only added to its allure, making it a must-visit for fans and nature lovers alike.

- **What is it?** The Dark Hedges, a scenic avenue of beech trees in Northern Ireland, was planted in 1775 by the Stuart family to enhance the approach to their Gracehill House. This road has become one of Northern Ireland's most photographed sites, with its dense canopy creating an ethereal look, particularly in mist or dusk. Its fame increased after being featured as King's Road in HBO's "Game of Thrones" second season.
- **Where is it?** County Antrim, Northern Ireland
- **How much is it?** Free
- **Web:** discovernorthernireland.com/things-to-do/the-dark-hedges-p703291
- **Instagram:** @discoverni

In The South:

Blarney Castle, home to the famed Blarney Stone, is enveloped in gardens that beckon explorers. Kissing the stone, as the legend suggests, bestows the gift of eloquence, but it's the castle's history and the beauty of its grounds that truly enchant it.

- **What is it?** Blarney Castle is renowned for the Blarney Stone, which is believed to grant eloquence to those who kiss it. Dating back to 1446 and built by Dermot McCarthy, the castle stands on a site used for fortifications since the 10th century. A major attraction, it offers visitors a rich history, stunning gardens, and the chance to gain "the gift of the gab" by kissing the stone, a feat achieved with assistance for safety.
- **Where is it?** Blarney, County Cork
- **How much is it?** $20 to $70 depending on the day. Check for pricing.
- **Web:** blarneycastle.ie/
- **Instagram:** @blarneycastleandgardens

Blarney Castle, Near Cork

Sheep Grazing Near the Rock of Cashel

The Rock of Cashel, with its medieval buildings set against a stark landscape, stands as a testament to Ireland's complex history of kings, saints, and conquests. Its silhouette at sunset captures the essence of Ireland's mystical past.

- **What is it?** The Rock of Cashel, or St. Patrick's Rock, is a significant archaeological site on a limestone hill, once the seat of Munster's kings. It houses medieval structures including a 12th-century round tower, a Romanesque chapel, a 13th-century Gothic cathedral, and a 15th-century castle. Notably, St. Patrick converted the Munster King here using a shamrock to explain the Holy Trinity, marking it as a symbol of Irish heritage and Christianity.

- **Where is it?** Cashel, County Tipperary
- **How much is it?** Prices vary depending on the date. Check pricing as tickets are limited.
- **Web:** heritageireland.ie/places-to-visit/the-rock-of-cashel/
- **Instagram:** @therockofcashelopw

2.6 EAST TO WEST: A JOURNEY THROUGH TIME

In Ireland, every road tells a story, winding through landscapes rich with history and folklore. From the historic East with its ancient tales carved in stone to the Wild West, where the land kisses the sea under the watch of the setting sun, a trek from coast to coast is nothing short of a journey through time itself.

Historic East

The eastern shores of Ireland are guardians of the dawn and keepers of the beginning chapters of this island's story. Here, the past is not just remembered; it's etched into the very landscape.

Newgrange

- **What is it?** Newgrange is a prehistoric monument dating back to 3200 BC, older than Stonehenge and the Egyptian pyramids, and is part of the Brú na Bóinne UNESCO World Heritage Site. It consists of a circular mound with a stone passageway and chambers inside. Known for the winter solstice phenomenon, sunlight streams through a special roof box into the main chamber, illuminating ancient carvings. This indicates Newgrange's dual role as a tomb and ceremonial site, reflecting the Neolithic people's advanced knowledge of astronomy and spirituality. It is a major attraction for those interested in ancient history and

archaeology.
- **Where is it?** Boyne Valley, County Meath
- **How much is it?**
- **Web:** heritageireland.ie/places-to-visit/bru-na-boinne-visitor-centre-newgrange-knowth-and-dowth/
- **Instagram:** @newgrangeandknowthopw

Dublin's Viking Legacy: The capital, with its cobbled streets and towering cathedrals, holds within its heart the saga of Viking invasions and Norman conquests. The Dublinia Museum offers a visceral plunge into this era, where history leaps off the pages, and the air is thick with the spirit of warriors and kings.

Dublinia Museum

- **What is it?** It's an interactive museum dedicated to the city's Viking and medieval history. It features exhibitions on Viking Dublin, Medieval Dublin, and History Hunters, offering insights into life during these periods through reconstructions and interactive displays. Visitors can explore a Viking ship and a medieval street and learn about archaeology's role in uncovering Dublin's past. The museum is popular among families and educational groups, providing a vivid journey through Ireland's historical development.
- **Where is it?** Near Christ Church Cathedral in Dublin, Ireland
- **How much is it?** $8 to $15. Family pricing is available.
- **Web:** https://www.dublinia.ie/
- **Instagram:** @dubliniaviking

Glendalough

- **What is it?** Glendalough is a picturesque valley known for its 6th-century monastic site founded by St. Kevin. The name means "Valley of the Two Lakes," and it's set in a scenic landscape with ancient ruins, including a round tower, stone churches, and crosses. It's part of the Wicklow Mountains National Park, drawing visitors for its historical depth, walking trails, and serene beauty. Glendalough is a significant site for those interested in Ireland's early Christian history and natural scenery.

- **Where is it?** County Wicklow, Ireland
- **How much is it?** Free and ticketed, depending on desired activity.
- **Web:** ireland.com/en-us/things-to-do/attractions/glendalough/
- **Instagram:** @tourismireland

Wild West Adventures

Moving from the historic East to the Wild West is like starting a new chapter, where the focus moves from history to the powerful presence of the wild Atlantic. These are just a few of the many wonderous sites to see in the West:

- **Cliffs of Moher:** Here, the land dramatically ends, dropping into the sea in a breathtaking display of nature's power. Standing tall against the crashing waves, the cliffs offer a view that stretches out into infinity, where the sky and sea merge into a canvas of shifting blues.
- **Connemara National Park:** Venture deeper into the west, and you'll find Connemara, where mountains, bogs, and woodlands paint a scene of rugged, untouched beauty. It's a place where the hustle of modern life fades, replaced by the tranquility of nature and the occasional company of wild ponies grazing.
- **The Burren:** This lunar landscape, with its limestone pavements and rare flora, feels like stepping onto another planet. The Burren is a paradox, its stark, barren appearance belies a delicate ecosystem where alpine, Mediterranean, and Arctic plants bloom side by side.

O'Brien's Tower

Cliffs of Moher, County Clare

Cultural Crossroads

The journey from east to west is not just a physical one but a passage through Ireland's cultural landscape, which shifts and blends like the colors of the sky at dusk.

- **Music:** In the east, traditional tunes might fill the air in a cozy Dublin pub, while in the west, a session in a Galway bar could have you tapping to a rhythm that's been the heartbeat of the region for centuries. Music migrates and evolves but always carries a piece of its origin.
- **Language:** The Irish language, with its lyrical quality, finds a stronger voice in the west, in places like the Gaeltacht regions

of Galway and Mayo, where it flows freely in conversation, signage, and music, a living link to Ireland's Gaelic heritage.

- **Craftsmanship:** The craft markets of Dublin's Temple Bar area showcase innovative designs and modern twists on traditional crafts, while the West, with its remote villages, holds artisans who keep ancient techniques alive, weaving, knitting, and crafting as their ancestors did.

Scenic Routes

The paths that crisscross from the east coast to the west are threads in the fabric of Ireland's landscape, each route a story, each turn a discovery.

- **The Wild Atlantic Way:** This legendary route skirts the western coastline, offering vistas that steal your breath and moments that capture your heart. It's a journey where every stop, from the majestic Cliffs of Moher to the tranquil beauty of Killary Harbour, is a highlight.
- **The Ancient East:** For those tracing the timeline of Ireland's history, the roads through the Ancient East unravel centuries of stories. From the Hill of Tara, once the seat of the High Kings, to the medieval city of Kilkenny, each site is a chapter from the past.
- **Coast to Coast:** For an epic adventure, start your journey in Dublin, heading west towards Galway. This route takes you through the heart of Ireland, from historic landmarks to modern cities, through changing landscapes that showcase the diversity of this beautiful island.
- **The Shannon River Drive:** Follow the meandering path of the River Shannon, Ireland's longest river, which cuts a swath through the heart of the country. This drive offers a mix of natural beauty, historic towns, and the tranquility of river life.

Traveling across Ireland from east to west mixes the old with the new, combining history and innovation, nature, and culture. This journey, from ancient sites in the east to the wild Atlantic coast in the west, offers a lot to see and do, and with it comes new experiences. Ireland's stories, adventures, and the warmth of its people make every mile memorable and every moment valuable.

2.7 CITY BEATS AND RURAL RETREATS

Ireland, a land of contrasts and harmonies, invites travelers to experience its dual nature: the lively pulse of its cities and the serene soul of its countryside. Each offers a distinct rhythm and a unique way of living the Irish experience.

Urban Exploration

Stepping into the heart of Dublin, Cork, or Galway, you're greeted with a vibrant tapestry of culture, history, and modernity. With its distinct personality, each city offers a playground for the curious.

- **Dublin** thrums with literary history and pub culture, its streets a living museum where Joyce and Yeats once roamed. With its cobblestone streets, the Temple Bar area is a hive of activity, offering a taste of Dublin's famed nightlife.
- **Cork**, set on the river Lee, is a culinary haven. The English Market, a feast for the senses, offers locally produced delicacies. Cork's maritime heritage shines on its waterfront, inviting leisurely strolls.
- **Galway, the 'City of Tribes,'** is a melody of traditional music and contemporary arts. Its yearly calendar is dotted with festivals celebrating everything from film to oysters, encapsulating the spirit of the West.

Each city invites you to delve into its unique culture through a traditional music session, a historical walking tour, or simply by engaging with the locals, who are always ready to share their stories.

Rural Escapes

Beyond the city limits, Ireland's countryside unfolds in a panorama of tranquility. Here, time slows, and the land speaks of ancient rhythms and enduring beauty.

- **The Kerry Way** winds through emerald landscapes, past lakes that mirror the sky, and quaint villages where life moves at a gentler pace.
- **The Dingle Peninsula** offers a retreat into a world where the sea crashes against rugged cliffs, and Gaelic is still spoken, a reminder of Ireland's deep cultural roots.
- **In Connemara**, the wild beauty of the landscape is a balm to the soul, with misty mountains and silent lakes that have inspired poets and painters.

These rural retreats are not just escapes but invitations to connect with a more introspective side of the Irish experience, where solitude becomes a pathway to inner peace.

Best of Both Worlds

Crafting an itinerary that weaves the vibrancy of city life with the tranquility of the countryside allows for a journey that captures the essence of Ireland. Here are a few strategies to blend these experiences seamlessly:

1. **Start in the city**. Immerse yourself in the cultural whirlwind of museums, galleries, and nightlife. Let Dublin's history, Cork's culinary delights, or Galway's arts scene be your introduction to Ireland.

2. **Transition to the countryside.** Consider taking day trips to places like Howth, just outside Dublin, or Cobh, near Cork. These short excursions offer a taste of rural beauty and history without straying far from urban comforts.
3. **Choose a rural base for exploring a region**. Stay in a country B&B or a cottage in Kerry or Connemara, using it as a launchpad for hiking, cycling, or simply soaking in the natural beauty.
4. **Mix activities to keep the pace varied**. Combine city walking tours with outdoor adventures like kayaking on the Liffey in Dublin or horseback riding in the hills of Kerry.

This approach lets you savor Ireland's contrasts, from the energetic streets of its cities to the contemplative quiet of its countryside.

Community and Solitude

Ireland's essence lies in its mix of community and solitude. City life buzzes in pubs and cafes, showcasing the Irish love for socializing, where a strong sense of unity shines through every celebration.

Yet, the countryside offers a contrast with its peaceful landscapes, perfect for introspection and connecting with Ireland's history and natural beauty. This blend of social interaction and personal reflection characterizes the Irish journey, inviting you to both connect with others and find yourself. Whether amidst city vibrancy or rural tranquility, Ireland encourages you to navigate your path and appreciate its diverse experiences.

2.8 OFF-PEAK PERKS: LESS CROWDS, MORE AUTHENTICITY

Venturing into Ireland during the off-peak seasons unfolds like a secret chapter of a well-loved book, revealing quiet streets, landscapes resting in their natural beauty, and a rhythm of life that moves to a more authentic, local beat. The cooler months or times outside the summer rush are when you can truly absorb the essence of Irish life, finding joy in the unexpected and uncovering the genuine warmth of its people.

Traveling Off-Season

Choosing to explore Ireland when tourist footfalls are lighter does more than just offer a break from the queues at famous landmarks. It opens spaces for more spontaneous encounters with locals or nature. Imagine having the Cliffs of Moher almost to yourself, the wild Atlantic winds your only companion, or wandering through the medieval streets of Kilkenny where every turn reveals a piece of history without the distraction of crowds. This time also presents a chance to see Ireland's cities in a new light, where the hustle of daily life is on full display, unmasked by the veneer of tourism. There are a multitude of reasons why traveling during the off-season has its advantages. Here are some:

- **Cost Savings.** Your travel fund stretches further during these months, with many accommodations and even some attractions lowering their prices to attract visitors. It's a time when deals surface, making that dream stay in a castle hotel suddenly within reach or allowing for longer stays. Car rental prices often dip, giving you the freedom to explore at your own pace without breaking the bank. Dining out, too, becomes a less expensive affair, with many eateries offering special rates or off-season menus that still showcase the best of Irish produce.
- **Local Interactions.** With the summer rush over, locals have more time to share their stories, whether it's the owner of a B&B in Cork recounting tales of the sea or a Dublin barista explaining the nuances of Irish coffee. These interactions weave a richer narrative of your travels, offering insights that no guidebook can. Participating in local activities, perhaps

joining a community clean-up day on a beach, or attending a workshop in a small town, fosters a deeper connection not just with the place but with its people, making you, for a moment, part of the local culture.

- **Unique Experiences:**
- **Foraging for Wild Foods:** Autumn opens Ireland's hedgerows and woodlands for foraging. Wild garlic, berries, and mushrooms offer a bounty for those willing to explore, with local experts often guiding the way.
- **Storm Watching:** The wilder weather brings a dramatic spectacle to the West Coast. Watching Atlantic storms from the safety of a coastal inn, with waves crashing against cliffs, is a memorable experience that contrasts with the calm beauty of summer.
- **Fireside Music Sessions:** As evenings draw in, music finds its way back to the heart of many pubs. These sessions, more intimate during the off-season, allow for a genuine appreciation of Ireland's musical heritage.
- **Winter Walks:** With the right gear, walking trails offer solitude and beauty, from snow-dusted forests to quiet beaches. The Killarney National Park, with its lakes framed by mountains, is particularly enchanting in the quiet of winter.
- **Samhain Celebrations:** Halloween in Ireland, especially in more rural areas, retains a connection to its ancient roots. Samhain festivals, with bonfires, traditional music, and storytelling, invite a deeper understanding of this centuries-old tradition.

Ditch the crowds and dive into Ireland's real charm when the tourist hordes have gone home. It's like having a backstage pass to the Emerald Isle, where you get to mingle with the locals, peek into their daily lives, and become one with Ireland's stunning landscapes. Imagine having those lush, green hills all to yourself! In these quiet moments, Ireland isn't just a destination; it becomes a narrative, rich with tales and vistas, offering memories that are all yours to keep, no sharing required.

2.9 CALENDAR OF EVENTS: PLANNING AROUND FESTIVALS

Ireland, a land where the calendar is as colorful as its landscapes, offers a parade of festivals that span the year, each painting a vivid stroke on the canvas of Irish culture. These festivals, steeped in tradition, music, and mirth, invite travelers to enter the rhythm of Irish life.

The Temple Bar, Dublin

The Temple Bar, Dublin

Year-Round Festivities

A month-by-month guide ensures you won't miss out on the festivities that dot the Irish calendar, each offering a unique glimpse into the country's cultural heart.

January: Kick off the year in Dublin with the **Temple Bar TradFest**, a celebration of traditional Irish music and culture set against the backdrop of one of the city's most iconic areas.

- **What is it?** TradFest is a vibrant celebration of Irish music and culture. Enjoy live music performances in Dublin's finest pubs and music venues across the city center and beyond.
- **Where is it?** Dublin, Ireland
- **When is it?** Every January
- **How much is it?** Free and ticketed, depending on the event.
- **Web: tradfest.com/**

- **Instagram:** @tradfestdublin

February: Witness the transformation of Derry into an illuminated wonderland during the **Illuminating Ulster Festival**, where light installations and performances brighten the winter gloom.

- **What is it?** The Illuminating the Walled City Festival in Derry showcases the city through light installations, music, and art. Aimed at promoting culture and boosting the evening economy, the festival involves local businesses and artists, transforming iconic buildings with spectacular light art. Scheduled for two weeks in February, it aims to attract visitors with its diverse program.
- **Where is it?** Derry (Londonderry), Northern Ireland
- **When is it?** February
- **How much is it?** Free to paid events.
- **Web:** https://visitderry.com
- **Instagram:** @visitderry

March: St. Patrick's Day needs no introduction. Across Ireland, cities, and villages don green, with parades, music, and dance celebrating Ireland's patron saint. If you're going to be in Ireland around this time, Dublin is the largest and the most spectacular. (Don't tell anyone in Galway that.)

April: Experience the **Cork International Choral Festival**, an aural feast where voices from around the world converge in harmony.

- **What is it?** Celebrated since 1954, is one of Europe's leading international choral festivals. It features a variety of events including Gala concerts, competitions, and performances from choirs around the world. The festival is noted for its eclectic program, high standards, and the warmth of its hospitality. Highlights include competitions for the Fleischmann International Trophy and performances in unexpected locations throughout Cork, enhancing the city's cultural life. It attracts around 5,000 participants each year, including up to 100 adults, youth, and school choirs participating in national competitions.

- **Where is it?** Cork, County Cork
- **When is it?** Annually held before the first Monday in May
- **How much is it?** Prices vary for location and event. Check for pricing.
- **Web:** corkchoral.ie/
- **Instagram:** @corkchoral

May: The Burren in Bloom in Clare is a festival that celebrates the unique flora of the region with walks, talks, and music.

- **What is it?** It celebrates the region's vibrant wildlife, showcasing its seasonal splendor with orchids, gentians, and an array of insects. The festival features a variety of activities, including nature walks, educational talks, hands-on workshops, demonstrations, and access to private gardens across the Burren. While many events are free or offer discounts to Burrenbeo Trust members, advanced booking is recommended for some activities due to limited space.
- **Where is it?**
- **When is it?** Throughout May
- **How much is it?** A mix of free and paid events.
- **Web:** burreninbloom.com/
- **Instagram:** #burreninbloom

June: Bloomsday in Dublin pays homage to James Joyce with readings, performances, and merriment inspired by "Ulysses."

- **What is it?** Every year on June 16th, people around the world, particularly in Dublin, celebrate Bloomsday to honor James Joyce and his iconic character Leopold Bloom from the novel Ulysses, set on this date in 1904. The day is filled with various events like reading sessions, performances, pub visits, and dressing up in styles from the early 20th century, all reflecting the book's themes and characters.

- **Where is it?** Dublin, Ireland
- **When is it?** Annually on the week leading up to June 16th.
- **How much is it?** A mix of free and paid events.
- **Web:** bloomsdayfestival.ie/
- **Instagram:** @bloomsdayfest

Acrobats performing during the Galway International Art Festival

July: Galway International Arts Festival takes over the city with visual arts, live performances, and music.

- **What is it?** Since its start in 1978, the Galway International Arts Festival has become a key yearly event in Galway, Ireland. It showcases a mix of theater, music, and visual arts, among other things. It now draws in more than 250,000 people and presents the talents of over 600 artists across 200 events. This festival not only highlights the best of Irish and worldwide creativity but also puts on performances that travel across the globe.
- **Where is it?** Galway, County Galway
- **When is it?** Usually the last two weeks in July
- **How much is it?** A mix of free and paid events.
- **Web:** giaf.ie/
- **Instagram:** @galwayintarts

August: The Puck Fair in Kerry, one of Ireland's oldest festivals, brings together music, market stalls, and the crowning of a wild goat as king.

- **What is it?** One of Ireland's oldest festivals, where a wild goat is crowned king for three days of food, drink, music, parades, and market stalls, showcasing the playful side of Irish heritage.
- **Where is it?** Killorglin, County Kerry
- **When is it?** August
- **How much is it?** Mostly free
- **Web:** https://puckfair.ie/
- **Instagram:** @puck_fair

September: Lisdoonvarna's Matchmaking Festival offers dancing, music, and the chance to find love in the traditional Irish way.

- **What is it?** For those looking for love or just a good time, this is Europe's largest singles festival, a quirky celebration of romance, with music, dancing, and the world's only traditional matchmaker, Willie Daly, at work. Single and ready to mingle?

- **Where is it?** Lisdoonvarna, County Clare
- **When is it?** The month of September
- **How much is it?** A mix of free and paid events.
- **Web:** matchmakerireland.com/
- **Instagram:** @matchmaking_lisdoonvarna

October: The Bram Stoker Festival in Dublin celebrates the author of "Dracula" with spooky events and Gothic fun.

- **What is it?** Celebrating the life and legacy of Dublin-born Bram Stoker, the author of "Dracula," this festival blends the gothic, the mysterious, and the supernatural through a variety of events. From spooky theatrical performances and horror film screenings to literary events and night-time adventures, the festival offers something for fans of all ages and interests.
- **Where is it?** Dublin, Ireland
- **When is it?** Four days and nights around Halloween. Check for exact dates.
- **How much is it?** A mix of free and paid events.
- **Web:** bramstokerfestival.com/
- **Instagram:** @bramstokerfestival

November: The Cork Jazz Festival fills the city with the sounds of jazz from international and local musicians.

- **What is it?** The Cork Jazz Festival, officially known as the Guinness Cork Jazz Festival, is an annual music festival held in Cork City, Ireland. It is one of the largest and most significant jazz festivals in Europe. Since its inception in 1978, the festival has grown in popularity and stature, attracting jazz musicians and fans from around the world.
- **Where is it?** Cork City, County Cork

- **When is it?** The last weekend in October and usually into November.
- **How much is it?** Prices vary. Tickets sell out fast. Check for pricing.
- **Web:** guinnesscorkjazz.com/
- **Instagram:** @guinesscorkjazz

December: Close the year with the magic of **Christmas markets in Belfast**, offering crafts, foods, and festive cheer. **(See Belfast Christmas Festival at the beginning of this chapter for details)**

Planning Your Visit

Aligning your travel dates with major festivals can turn a simple visit into an unforgettable adventure. Here's how:

- **Book Early:** Popular festivals mean busy travel periods. Secure accommodation and tickets well in advance to avoid disappointment.
- **Local Advice:** Check with locals or at visitor centers for festival tips – they might share hidden gems or events within the festival that aren't widely advertised.
- **Transport:** Consider how you'll get to and from festival locations. Public transport can be busier during these times, so plan accordingly.

Cultural Immersion

For a deep dive into Irish culture, some festivals stand out for their immersive experiences:

The Fleadh Cheoil: Held in different locations each year, this festival is the pinnacle of Irish traditional music, offering sessions, competitions, and impromptu jams.

- **What is it?** The Fleadh Cheoil is a major Irish festival celebrating traditional music and dance, featuring competitions, concerts, and cultural events. It gathers musicians from around the world to showcase and celebrate Irish heritage, making it essential for those interested in Irish music traditions.
- **Where is it?** One of the biggest is in Wexford, County Wexford
- **When is it?** Usually runs at the beginning of August for a week.
- **How much is it?** A mix of free and paid events.
- **Web:** fleadhcheoil.ie/
- **Instagram:** @fleadhcheoil

Oysters Served During Galway Oyster Festival

Galway Oyster Festival: Celebrate the start of the oyster season with tastings, shucking competitions, and plenty of Guinness.

- **What is it?** Starting in 1954, the festival is an iconic celebration marking the beginning of the oyster season. This festival is known for its oyster opening competitions, both Irish and World Championships, and serves as a hub for culinary and cultural festivities. It's a key event for food enthusiasts and those curious about Ireland's rich heritage, offering a blend of traditional celebrations and international participation. It usually starts with music! Bring your appetite!
- **Where is it?** Galway, County Galway
- **When is it?** Last weekend in September
- **How much is it?** Depends on how many oysters you can eat and how much Guinness you can drink. Results may vary. Ha!
- **Web:** galwayoysterfestival.com/
- **Instagram:** @galwayoysterfest

Wexford Opera Festival: Offers a mix of classic and contemporary opera performances in a charming town setting.

- **What is it?** Founded in 1951 by Dr. Tom Walsh, the festival has grown from a small-scale event into an internationally acclaimed opera festival. Performances are held at the National Opera House, which is Ireland's first custom-built, multi-purpose opera house, known for its excellent acoustics and intimate setting.
- **Where is it?** National Opera House, Wexford
- **When is it?** October and November
- **How much is it?** Prices vary according to performance and seating choice.
- **Web:** wexfordopera.com/
- **Instagram:** @wexfordfestivalopera

Lesser-Known Celebrations

Venturing off the beaten path to smaller, local festivals can reveal the heart of Irish culture in ways the larger ones might not:

The Cuckoo Festival in Kinvara welcomes the arrival of summer with traditional music, dance, and storytelling.

- **What is it?** Traditionally known as Fleadh na gCuach (it is spelled correctly), it happens during the May Bank Holiday weekend. This festival, rooted in traditional Irish music and community arts, draws musicians and artists from all over. Expect a vibrant mix of music sessions, dancing, crafts, and poetry readings in local pubs and venues, making it a perfect family-friendly event that embraces Ireland's rich cultural heritage.
- **Where is it?** Kinvara, County Galway
- **When is it?** The May Bank Holiday weekend preceding the 1st Monday of May.
- **How much is it?** A mix of free to paid events.
- **Web:** galwaytourism.ie/event/fleadh-na-gcuach-festival/
- **Facebook:** facebook.com/fleadhnagcuach

Metal Man Monument Waterford, County Waterford

The Harvest Moon Festival in Waterford celebrates the autumn equinox with lantern parades and fire shows.

- **What is it?** Celebrated around the Harvest Moon, the Waterford food festival showcases the area's rich culinary heritage and sustainable food practices. Local producers, chefs, and food lovers gather to enjoy markets, special dining experiences, workshops, and live entertainment, emphasizing local produce and culinary expertise. The festival highlights the importance of food sustainability and offers a taste of Waterford's dynamic food scene in a community-centered setting.
- **Where is it?** Waterford, County Waterford
- **When is it?** Around the Autumn Equinox
- **How much is it?** A mix of free and paid events.
- **Web:** visitwaterford.com/vw_news/waterford-harvest-festival/
- **Instagram:** @harvest_fest

Imbolc Festival in Sligo marks the beginning of spring with ancient rituals, crafts, and fire dances, rooted in Celtic tradition.

- **What is it?** Typically, this early spring festival celebrates Celtic traditions with music, dance, and various ceremonies. Also called Saint Brigid's Day, it's a time for embracing new beginnings and community spirit. It signifies a period of transition from winter to spring. This point, nestled between the winter solstice and the spring equinox, heralds the end of the darker half of the year and the arrival of brighter, longer days ahead, embodying hope and renewal.
- **Where is it?** Sligo, County Sligo
- **When is it?** February 1st and 2nd
- **How much is it?** Mostly Free.
- **Web:** ireland.com/en-us/destinations/county/sligo/sligo-

town/ **and** mallonireland.com/blogs/news/the-celtic-festival-of-imbolc-1

- **Instagram:** @tourismireland

Ireland's festivals, spanning from Imbolc to Christmas, showcase its vibrant culture, deep traditions, and community spirit. These events invite active participation and offer a taste of Irish life. They enrich the cultural landscape, making each visit memorable with lively and immersive experiences. Don't be afraid to try something new!

The true spirit of travel lies in these moments, turning visits into cherished memories that capture Ireland's charm. As we continue exploring Ireland's cultural and natural beauty, we find places where history, nature, and a sense of belonging intertwine.

NAVIGATING WHERE TO STAY

I magine tossing a coin into a wishing well, the ripples spreading out, touching edge to edge. Now, picture that well as Ireland, and your coin's journey as your own through this land of stories, music, and unspoiled landscapes. The places you choose to rest your head at night aren't just stops along the way; they're experiences, chapters of your own Irish tale waiting to unfold. These unique accommodations, while pricey, will make your Ireland trip one to remember.

3.1 CASTLE STAYS: LIVING LIKE IRISH ROYALTY

Historic Castles

Staying in one of Ireland's historic castles is like stepping into a story-book. Each castle with the option for overnight stays has its unique tale, steeped in centuries of history.

Ashford Castle, once home to the Guinness family, offers a blend of medieval grandeur and modern luxury. Imagine waking up in a four-poster bed, with views of a lake where legends seem to come alive in the misty mornings.

- **Interesting Fact:** It dates to 1228. Ashford Castle's School of Falconry, the oldest in Ireland, offers guests the chance to fly a Harris hawk in the woodlands, offering a unique amenity.
- **Where is it?** County Mayo
- **How much is it?** It starts at $450 and goes up, depending on the time and room type.
- **Web:** ashfordcastle.com/
- **Instagram:** @ashfordcastle

Dromoland Castle, with its ancestral heritage dating back to the 16th century, allows guests to roam its 450-acre estate as if they were the lords and ladies of old.

- **Interesting Fact:** It was originally the ancestral home of the O'Briens, whose lineage traces back to one of the last High Kings of Ireland, Brian Boru. It boasts golf courses set against the backdrop of historic stone and lush landscapes fit for a king (or queen).
- **Where is it?** County Clare
- **How much is it?** $700 and up depending on date and room type.
- **Web:** dromoland.ie/
- **Instagram:** @dromolandcastlehotel

Dromoland Castle, County Clare

Booking Tips

Securing a room in these sought-after destinations requires some planning.

Book Early: Reservations should be made well in advance, especially for the summer months or holidays.

Special Packages: Look for off-season packages or mid-week deals that often include a stay and experiences like dining in the castle's gourmet restaurants or spa treatments.

Cultural Significance

Staying in an Irish castle offers more than luxury; it's a bridge to Ireland's rich history. Landmarks like Cahir and Kilkenny Castle bring you closer to centuries of dramatic events, from Norman invasions to sieges. As a guest, you become part of this historical continuum, surrounded by the custodians of Ireland's legacy. These castles, echoing the era of chieftains and legends, provide a unique glimpse into Ireland's essence.

Opting for a castle stay means diving into Ireland's past, enveloped in modern comfort. It's an opportunity to explore ancient halls, dine like royalty, or enjoy the Irish landscape from a historic vantage point, making it a key to understanding Ireland's storied heritage.

3.2 COZY COTTAGES AND QUAINT B&BS

Nestled in the heart of Ireland's picturesque landscapes, an array of charming cottages and quaint B&Bs await to offer you a slice of Irish life. These are places where the pace slows, hosts greet you by name, and the warmth extends beyond the hearth. It's here, amidst the rolling hills, rugged coastlines, or vibrant villages, that you find a home away from home.

Charming Accommodations

Imagine waking up to the sound of birds chirping outside your window, the aroma of fresh-baked scones wafting through the air, and the sight of dew-kissed landscapes greeting you good morning. Ireland's cottages and B&Bs are more than just places to sleep; they are sanctuaries that capture the essence of Irish charm. Each one, whether it's a thatched cottage in Galway or a Victorian B&B in Cork, is a doorway to an experience that's intimate and authentic. These accommodations will provide you with a more affordable way to experience Ireland's charm.

The Thatched Cottages of Adare: With their whitewashed walls and traditional thatched roofs, these cottages offer a picturesque retreat that feels like stepping back in time.

- **Interesting Fact:** These cottages have been preserved to maintain the village's historical charm. They date back to the 1820s and were originally built for workers employed by the Earl of Dunraven's estate.
- **Where is it?** The Village of Adare, County Limerick

NAVIGATING WHERE TO STAY | 95

- **How much is it?** The price depends on the date and length of stay.
- **Web:** adarevillage.com/2020/03/14/the-origin-of-adares-thatched-cottages/
- **Facebook:** adarevillage

Sea Winds B&B: Perched on cliffs or nestled in coves, this B&B provides a front-row seat to the Atlantic's ever-changing moods, a perfect backdrop for a tranquil escape.

- **Interesting Fact:** It boasts a unique setting opposite the harbor and fishing boats, providing guests with stunning views of the activity in the harbor and the sea beyond.
- **Where is it?** Killybegs County, Donegal
- **How much is it?** Prices vary depending on date and room type. Check the website.
- **Web:** seawindsireland.com/
- **Facebook:** seawindsbedandbreakfastseawindsbe-dandbreakfast

Ardlenagh View is another sea-view B&B in Donegal. It is known for its beautiful and peaceful setting overlooking Donegal Bay and the Bluestack Mountains.

- **Interesting Fact:** The B&B is situated just 2kms south of Donegal Town, making it a convenient base for exploring the Northwest leg of the Wild Atlantic Way.
- **Where is it?** Near Donegal Town, County Donegal
- **How much is it?** $70 to $100. Email confirmation is required.
- **Web:** ardlenaghview.com/
- **Facebook:** facebook.com/ArdlenaghView/

Cliffs of Moher on Wild Atlantic Way

Local Hospitality

The heart of Ireland's B&B experience beats with the warmth of its hosts. These are folks who treat guests like family, ready with a cup of tea, a fireside chat, or invaluable tips on local hidden gems. It's in these interactions that the true spirit of Irish hospitality shines, turning a stay into a memory that's cherished long after you've left. Here are some benefits to staying in a local B&B:

- **A Warm Welcome:** Many hosts greet guests with traditional Irish treats, be it a freshly baked loaf of soda bread or a pot of tea served with homemade jam.
- **Insider Tips:** From the best local hiking trails to the coziest pubs for live music, hosts are a fountain of knowledge, eager to share their love for their locale.
- **Scenic Locations:** The allure of Ireland's cottages and B&Bs is undeniably linked to their settings, each offering a window to the soul of the surrounding landscape. Whether it's the pastoral serenity of the countryside or the lively pulse of a

NAVIGATING WHERE TO STAY | 97

small town, these stays are perfectly positioned to offer guests an immersive experience.

- **Rural Retreats:** Tucked away in the countryside, cottages like those in Kerry's Dingle Peninsula offer solitude amidst scenery that's lush and wild.
- **Village Charm**: B&Bs located in the heart of villages like Kinsale provide an opportunity to experience local life, from farmers' markets to festivals.
- **Culinary Delights**: One of the highlights of staying in a cottage or B&B in Ireland is the promise of delicious, home-cooked meals, often featuring local ingredients and traditional recipes. Breakfasts become a feast, not just of food, but of flavors that tell the story of the region.
- **Farm-fresh breakfasts:** Eggs from the backyard hens, sausages from the local butcher, and bread baked that morning, offer a taste of the land's bounty.
- **Local Specialties**: Depending on the region, you might be treated to smoked salmon from Connemara, black pudding from Cork, or freshly caught seafood on the Wild Atlantic Way.

In these cozy corners of Ireland, every meal is an opportunity to savor not just the food but the care and tradition that go into preparing it. It's a taste of Ireland's culinary heritage, served with a side of conversation, making each bite a deeper dive into the culture and community.

B&Bs embody warmth and authenticity, offering more than just a bed —they connect you to the land, its people, and their lifestyle. In Ireland, quiet moments like morning walks through dewy fields or evenings by the fire capture the essence of the country. It's in these settings that the true magic of the Emerald Isle unfolds. If you're looking to live life like a local this is a good place to start.

While the aforementioned were just a sampling, for a complete directory of Ireland's B&Bs we recommend using their official B&B locator at bandbireland.com/bandb-locator .

3.3 BOUTIQUE HOTELS: LUXURY AND LOCALITY

In the heart of Ireland's bustling cities and quaint towns lie boutique hotels, each with a story to tell. These aren't your standard stopovers; they're curated experiences, where luxury meets locality, and every room, every meal, whispers tales of Ireland's rich tapestry. Here, in these havens, you're not just a guest; you're a traveler being woven into the vibrant narrative of Irish culture and history.

Unique Finds

The Merchant Hotel

- **Interesting Fact:** This hotel, nestled in the Cathedral Quarter, stands as a testament to Belfast's maritime history. Its Victorian architecture nods to the city's industrious past.
- **Where is it?** 16 Skipper St, Belfast BT1 2DZ, United Kingdom
- **How much is it?** $300-$600 depending on date and room type.
- **Web:** themerchanthotel.com/
- **Instagram:** @merchantbelfast

The Dean

- **Interesting Fact:** The Dean captures the essence of contemporary Irish artistry. With rooms adorned with works from local artists and vinyl records to set the mood, it's a gateway to the creative soul of the capital, all the while offering a rooftop view that brings the city's tales right to your doorstep.

- **Where is it?** 33 Harcourt St, Saint Kevin's, Dublin 2, Ireland
- **How much is it?** $200-$2500 depending on date and room type.
- **Web:** thedean.ie/
- **Instagram:** @thedeanirl

Ireland's boutique hotels offer a unique blend of luxury, comfort, and Irish charm, catering to travelers seeking an intimate and memorable lodging experience. These hotels are often situated in picturesque locations, from bustling city centers to serene countryside settings, providing guests with an authentic taste of Irish culture and hospitality. Each boutique hotel in Ireland tells its own story, with meticulously designed rooms, bespoke services, and a warm welcome that ensures a stay is nothing short of extraordinary. Here are just a few benefits of staying at a boutique hotel:

- **Design and Décor:** The magic of boutique hotels lies in their ability to tell stories through design and decor, blending elements of Ireland's past with the flair of modern design. From the handwoven blankets that grace the beds to the locally sourced wood that frames the windows, the textures you'll find are a homage to Ireland's artisanal heritage.
- **Color and Light:** Taking cues from the Irish landscape, interiors are bathed in the greens of the rolling hills, the blues of the crashing waves, and the golden hues of the setting sun. Lighting casts a warm, inviting glow, mimicking the country's ever-changing skies.
- **Personalized Services:** Boutique hotels stand out for the personalized touches that make each stay unique. Service is not just about meeting needs but anticipating desires and creating experiences that linger in the heart long after departure.
- **Tailored Itineraries:** Concierges at these establishments pride themselves on crafting itineraries that showcase

Ireland's hidden corners, be it a private tour of a local distillery or a guided hike to a secluded waterfall.

- **Local Flavor:** From the kitchen to the spa, the emphasis is on local. Think breakfasts crafted from ingredients sourced from the nearby market and spa treatments that use seaweed harvested from Irish shores, all designed to immerse you in the land's bounty.
- **Central Locations:** Choosing a boutique hotel means not just selecting a place to stay but picking a key to unlock the heart of Ireland's cities and towns. These hotels serve as perfect bases from which to explore the vibrant streets, the murmuring pubs, and the historic landmarks that define the Irish experience.
- **City Hearts:** In Dublin, hotels like The Wilder offer tranquility within the buzz of the city. A stone's throw from the green expanses of St. Stephen's Green and the lively strips of Grafton Street, they allow for days spent exploring and nights wrapped in the comfort of luxury.
- **Town Charms:** In towns like Kinsale, known for their culinary prowess, boutique hotels are nestled among gastronomic delights, offering a taste of local cuisine just steps from your room. Here, days are for savoring, whether it's the catch of the day or the story of a local fisherman.

Shoppers on Dublin's Grafton Street

Boutique hotels in Ireland offer more than just accommodation; they provide an immersive experience. Each aspect, from design to service, enriches your journey through Ireland, allowing you to connect deeply with local life and culture. These hotels prioritize memorable experiences and personal connections over traditional luxury, making your stay a key part of exploring Ireland's essence.

While we only provided a sampling of some of Ireland's distinguished boutique hotels, you'll find a complete directory here at boutiquehotel.me/ .

3.4 ECO-FRIENDLY LODGINGS: GREEN AND SERENE

For those seeking accommodations close to rugged and natural landscapes, in the heart of Ireland, surrounded by sprawling green landscapes, there's a lesser-known path. This path takes you to accommodations dedicated to sustainability and eco-friendliness. These eco-friendly places to stay are set against beautiful natural backdrops, providing more than just lodging. They allow you to reconnect with nature, live more harmoniously with the environment, and minimize your impact on the planet.

- **Sustainability Practices:** In these special corners of Ireland, sustainability isn't merely a buzzword; it's woven into the very fabric of everyday life.
- **Solar Panels and Rainwater Harvesting:** Many eco-lodges harness the power of the sun, turning Ireland's daylight into energy, while rainwater harvesting systems capture the frequent rains, repurposing them for everything from irrigation to flushing toilets.
- **Zero Waste Initiatives:** These lodgings strive to minimize their environmental impact, from composting organic waste to encouraging guests to reduce plastic use by providing refillable water bottles.
- **Local and Organic:** The kitchens here pride themselves on sourcing ingredients locally, reducing food miles, and supporting the community's farmers and artisans. The result? Meals that are not just delicious but deeply entrenched in the local terroir.
- **Nature Immersion:** Staying in eco-friendly lodgings in Ireland is like stepping into a living, breathing work of art, where every window frames a masterpiece, and every door opens to a symphony of natural wonders.
- **Treehouses and Yurts:** Imagine spending the night perched among the branches, lulled to sleep by the whispers of the wind, or cozied up in a yurt, the stars your only ceiling. These unique accommodations offer an unparalleled closeness to nature.
- **Wildflower Meadows and Organic Gardens:** Many eco-lodges are nestled within wildflower meadows or boast their own organic gardens, inviting guests to wander, touch, and smell, to reconnect with the earth in the most tactile of ways.

For a complete directory of eco-friendly hotels go to greentravel.ie/ to find your accommodations.

Eco-Tours and Activities

The invitation to explore and engage with the natural world extends beyond the boundaries of these eco-friendly lodgings.

Guided Nature Walks: Led by knowledgeable locals, these walks delve into the flora and fauna, the cycles of life that paint Ireland's landscapes in broad strokes of color and life.

- Contact: vagabondtoursofireland.com/blog/guided-hikes-ireland
- Contact: hilltoptreks.com/

Conservation Workshops: Some lodgings offer workshops that range from building birdhouses to planting native trees. Each activity is a lesson in conservation and a chance to contribute positively to the local ecosystem.

Eco-Adventure Sports: For the thrill-seekers, eco-lodges often collaborate with adventure sports providers that adhere to sustainable practices, offering everything from kayaking on crystal-clear lakes to cycling through verdant valleys. For a complete list of Eco-friendly things to do go to ireland.com/en-us/things-to-do/themes/sustainability/sustainable-ireland/

Contribution to Conservation

Choosing to stay in these eco-friendly lodgings offers more than a serene escape; it's a declaration of commitment to preserving the beauty and integrity of Ireland's natural heritage.

- **Supporting Local Wildlife:** Many of these lodgings are involved in projects aimed at protecting local wildlife, from creating habitats for endangered species to supporting marine conservation efforts. Guests are often invited to partake in these initiatives, turning a holiday into a meaningful contribution.

- **Promoting Sustainable Tourism:** By choosing eco-friendly accommodations, you're voting with your wallet, encouraging the growth of sustainable tourism in Ireland. This not only helps preserve the natural beauty but also fosters a tourism model that benefits local communities and the environment alike.
- **Educational Impact:** Staying in these lodgings is an educational journey, one that opens eyes and minds to the importance of sustainable living. From learning about renewable energy sources to understanding the principles of permaculture, guests leave not just rested but enlightened, carrying the seeds of change back to their communities.

In these eco-friendly retreats across Ireland, guests are immersed in a unique experience that blends seamlessly with nature's harmony. These places offer not just accommodation but an opportunity to engage in environmental preservation. Beyond a mere stay, they represent a chance to learn, grow, and connect with a community dedicated to safeguarding the planet's future. Here, visitors become part of a larger conservation effort, turning each moment into a chance to contribute positively to the environment. One of the best ways to experience Ireland is through Nature.

3.5 HOSTELS AND BUDGET ACCOMMODATIONS

In the land where every stone tells a story and every glen holds a melody, the adventure shouldn't have to end when the day does. For the traveler with an eye on their budget but a heart yearning for the richness of Ireland, hostels and budget accommodations provide a haven. These spaces aren't just about saving pennies; they're about enriching experiences, making new friends, and finding yourself amidst the laughter and stories of fellow wanderers. Some of my most memorable times while traveling have happened at hostels! They're not just for twenty-somethings!

Abbey Court Hostel, Dublin

Budget-Friendly Options

Ireland's hostels and budget accommodations are scattered like gems across the landscape, each promising a stay that's light on the wallet but heavy on experience.

The Generator Hostel lights up the historic Smithfield area, offering not just beds but a cultural hub where travelers meet.

- **Interesting Fact:** It offers a jacuzzi suite, a shared room that comes with its very own hot tub.
- **Where is it?** Chimney Viewing Tower, Arran Quay, Smithfield, Dublin, D07 F2VF, Ireland

- **How much is it?** Starts at $15 for shared to $100 depending on the date and room type.
- **Web:** staygenerator.com/hostels/dublin
- **Instagram:** @staygenerator

Bru Bar & Hostel

- **Interesting Fact:** Live music fills the evenings, and the city's charm is just a step away.
- **Where is it?** 57 MacCurtain Street, Centre - North, Victorian Quarter, Cork, T23 CD00, Ireland
- **How much is it?** Check the website. Rates vary according to date and room type.
- **Web:** bruhostel.com/
- **Instagram:** instagram.com/explore/locations/244648881/bru-bar-hostel/

Kinlay Hostel

- **Interesting Fact:** It is housed in a historic building that was once part of the Eyre Square Shopping Centre and offers convenient keyless entry.
- **Where is it?** Merchants Rd, Eyre Square, Galway, H91 F2KT, Ireland
- **How much is it?** Prices vary depending on room type and date. Check the website.
- **Web:** kinlaygalway.ie/
- **Instagram:** @kinlayhostelgalway

These locations offer more than just a place to sleep; they serve as gateways to the soul of Ireland, ensuring that the adventure continues even as you rest. For a more complete guide to Ireland's hostels go to hostelworld.com/ or ireland.com . While you'll be trading in some privacy or luxury while staying in a hostel you will gain this:

- **Social Atmosphere:** The true wealth of staying in hostels lies in their vibrant social tapestry. Here, the world comes to you, bringing stories from every corner of the globe, all converging under a single roof.
- **Communal Kitchens:** become stages for culinary exchanges, where a recipe shared is a friendship formed.
- **Common Rooms** hum with the energy of planning and reflection, as travelers swap tales and tips over cups of tea or pints of stout. You may meet a lifelong friend at a hostel I have.
- **Organized Events,** from pub crawls to city tours, foster a sense of community, turning solo journeys into shared adventures.
- **Location Advantages:** Nestled in the hearts of cities, perched on the edges of cliffs, or tucked away in quaint towns, the strategic locations of hostels and budget accommodations in Ireland ensure that you're never too far from the action.
- **City Center Hostels** put you amid the urban dance. Like the one in Dublin's city center, with its labyrinth of history, pubs, and culture, is just outside your door.
- **Rural Hostels,** like those near the Cliffs of Moher or the Ring of Kerry, offer an escape to nature, where the landscapes of legends beckon just beyond.
- **Coastal Hostels** like Finn McCool's Hostel along Northern Ireland's Causeway Coast, invite you to fall asleep to the lullaby of waves and wake to the embrace of ocean air, with the wild Atlantic as your companion.
- **Amenities for Travelers:** Hostels most always offer Free Wi-Fi to stay connected. Secure Lockers provide peace of mind, safeguarding your belongings as you explore. Bike Rentals offer an eco-friendly way to discover the nooks and crannies of towns and the countryside. Laundry Facilities ensure that the road doesn't wear on you. Book Exchanges invite you to leave a story behind and take a new one with you.

In the world of hostels and affordable places to stay, laughter fills the walls, and each room brings people from different cultures together. Your time here adds to your story of visiting Ireland. The experience gets richer as you connect with a community of travelers, all united by a love for exploring. These places don't just give you a bed; they welcome you into a circle of like-minded individuals, all set against the backdrop of Ireland's captivating scenery. I recommend doing at least one hostel stay during your trip. You won't regret it. Age doesn't matter.

Rural Irish Cottage

3.6 FARM STAYS: RURAL IRISH LIFE

Nestling into the rhythm of rural Irish life offers an experience quite unlike any other, where the connection to the land and its cycles becomes as comforting as a familiar melody. On a farm stay, the verdant landscapes of Ireland serve not just as a backdrop but as an integral part of daily life, inviting you into a world where the bond with nature is tangible, and the pace of life flows with the seasons. If you don't mind getting your hands dirty this stay is for you!

Immersive Experiences

Stepping onto a working farm in Ireland, you cross a threshold into a realm where every task, from tending to livestock to harvesting crops, is steeped in tradition yet vibrantly alive. These stays peel back the layers of Irish rural life, offering a hands-on introduction to the customs and work that have shaped the countryside for generations.

This immersion into the ebb and flow of farm life not only offers a break from the rush of modern living but also fosters a profound appreciation for the work that goes into tending the land and its inhabitants.

- **Morning Chores:** With the dawn chorus as your alarm clock, you might spend mornings helping to milk cows or feed chickens, an authentic slice of farm life that's both grounding and enlightening.
- **Sheepdog Demonstrations:** Watching a skilled shepherd and their dog work in seamless unity to herd sheep is to witness a living art form, one that speaks of harmony with the natural world.
- **Daily Life and Activities:** Haymaking and Harvest, depending on the season, you might find yourself amid haymaking, where the fields come alive with activity, or helping to harvest everything from potatoes to apples, a direct link to the land's bounty.
- **Nature Walks:** Farms often have trails that meander through fields and woodlands, offering peaceful strolls where the only company might be a curious cow or a flock of sheep.
- **Culinary Adventures:** The meals are at the heart of the farm stay experience, where the farm-to-table concept is not a

trend but a way of life. Here, food tells a story, one of care, community, and connection to the land.

- **Breakfasts with a View:** Imagine starting your day with a hearty breakfast made from ingredients just gathered from the farm, enjoyed at a table with views of the fields where those very ingredients were grown.
- **Cooking with the Hosts:** Many farm stays offer cooking sessions, where you can learn to make traditional Irish dishes using the farm's produce, a hands-on way to dive into the country's culinary heritage.
- **Family-Friendly:** For families, a farm stay is a treasure trove of experiences, offering adventures and learning opportunities that are as enriching as they are entertaining.
- **Animal Encounters:** For children, the chance to interact with farm animals, from petting lambs to watching pigs wallow, is not just fun but also educational, offering lessons in empathy and responsibility.
- **Outdoor Fun:** A farm's expanse provides a natural playground, where kids can run free, explore, and engage in activities like treasure hunts or nature crafts, all under the watchful eye of the countryside.

Get ready to plug into nature and reconnect with your crew in Ireland's countryside, where the simple pleasures of life aren't just observed—they're lived. Opt for a farm stay, and you're not just visiting; you're part of the family. Here, amidst rolling fields and the honest-to-goodness rhythms of rural life, each day feels like a homecoming. It's all about embracing those deep-rooted traditions and the warm, hearty welcome of Irish hospitality. As you become part of centuries-old tales woven through the community and the land, a farm stay isn't just a getaway; it's stepping into a beloved, enduring lifestyle.

3.7 HISTORICAL HOTELS: SLEEPING WITH STORIES

In the heart of Ireland, where every lane whispers secrets of yore and every stone is a silent witness to ages past, there exists a special kind of sanctuary for the traveler. These are historical hotels, and grand dames of lodging, each with a soul crafted through centuries. Here, the night is not just for rest but for a journey through time, where dreams intertwine with the tales of those who walked these halls before.

The Shelbourne

- **Interesting Fact:** A Renaissance hotel that has stood gracefully since 1824, offering a glimpse into Dublin's Georgian era. Its walls have hosted literary giants, political figures, and stars of the screen, making it a living museum of Irish history.
- **Where is it?** 27 St Stephen's Green, Dublin, Ireland
- **How much is it?** $300 and up depending on date and room type.
- **Web:** marriott.com/en-us/hotels/dubdt-the-shelbourne-autograph-collection/overview/
- **Instagram:** @theshelbournedublin

Glenlo Abbey Hotel

- **Interesting Fact:** Once an 18th-century abbey, this hotel near the shores of Lough Corrib invites guests into a world where luxury and history blend seamlessly. Each room tells a story, be it of the monks who once sought solace here or the nobles who later called it home.
- **Where is it?** Bushypark, County Galway, H91 XD8K, Ireland
- **How much is it?** $300 and up, depending on room type and date.
- **Web:** glenloabbeyhotel.ie/

- **Instagram:** @glenlo_abbey

Ghostly Tales

The rich tale of Irish history is not without its shadowy threads, and these historical hotels often have tales that send a delightful shiver down the spine. Don't worry—the ghosts are all friendly... (I think).

Ballygally Castle Hotel, Northern Ireland

Ballygally Castle, County Antrim:

- **Interesting Fact:** This 17th-century castle-turned-hotel is known for its resident ghost, Lady Isabella Shaw. Guests might hear the rustle of her dress along corridors or feel a gentle touch at night, a reminder of the castle's storied past.
- **Where is it?** Coast Rd, Ballygally, Larne BT40 2QZ, Northern Ireland, United Kingdom
- **How much is it?** $90 and up, depending on date and room type.

- **Web:** ballygallycastlehotel.com/
- **Instagram:** @ballygally_castle_official

Kilkea Castle, Kilkea

Kilkea Castle

- **Interesting Fact:** Dating back to 1180, this castle is said to be haunted by the Wizard Earl, an ancestor who dabbled in alchemy. His presence is felt in the eerie yet fascinating atmosphere that envelops the castle after sundown.
- **Where is it?** Kilkea Demesne, Castledermot, Co. Kildare, R14 XE97, Ireland
- **How much is it?** $150 and up, depending on date, room type, and promotion.
- **Web:** kilkeacastle.ie/
- **Instagram:** @kilkeacastle

Luxurious Preservation Efforts

Maintaining the historical character of these properties while integrating modern amenities is a careful and respectful endeavor. The focus is on authentic restoration, from detailed woodwork to decorative ceilings and stained glass, to preserve the hotel's historical essence.

Additionally, these hotels adopt sustainable measures, such as eco-friendly products and energy-saving lighting, showing a commitment to historic preservation and environmental care. Their prime locations offer easy access to Ireland's cultural and scenic highlights, combining heritage charm with convenience.

The Westbury

- **Interesting Fact:** Just a stone's throw from vibrant Grafton Street, this hotel offers easy access to Dublin's museums, galleries, and the famous Temple Bar area, making it a perfect base for explorers keen to uncover the city's treasures.
- **Where is it?** Balfe St, Dublin 2, Ireland
- **How much is it?**
- **Web:** doylecollection.com/hotels/the-westbury-hotel
- **Instagram:** @westburydublin

The Granville Hotel

- **Interesting Fact:** Overlooking the River Suir, this hotel is a gateway to the Viking Triangle. It stands close to medieval treasures, artisan shops, and the Waterford Greenway, inviting guests to step out and step back in time.
- **Where is it?** Meagher's Quay, Trinity Without, Waterford, Ireland
- **How much is it?** $125 and up, depending on room type and time of year.
- **Web:** granvillehotel.ie/

- **Instagram:** @granvillehotelwford

In these hotels, every corner tells a story, and every room is part of a grand tale from the past. They're more than just a place to sleep; they're gateways to history. Under the same roofs that once sheltered historical figures, the night carries tales of romance, mystery, and bravery. With the dawn, you awaken not just rested but enriched, carrying tales that connect past and present, tales that stay with you like vivid dreams.

3.8 SELF-CATERING SANCTUARIES: YOUR HOME IN IRELAND

In Ireland's lush surroundings, self-catering accommodations let travelers create their own experiences. These places offer more than just a place to stay under the stars—they provide a home. Here, cooking meals, sharing laughs, and welcoming each day bring you closer to the essence of Ireland. There are a multitude of benefits these accommodations offer, such as:

- **Independence and Flexibility:** The allure of self-catering stays lies in the freedom they bestow. Here, the day's rhythm is yours to command, from the moment you rise, perhaps to the gleam of a dew-swept dawn, to the evenings that wind down under a ballet of stars. It's this independence that beckons families seeking adventure without the constraints of scheduled meals or travelers on extended stays, craving a routine that mirrors life at home yet is imbued with the novelty of Ireland.
- **Create Your Schedule:** Wake up to the sun or sleep till noon; your time is unequivocally yours here.
- **Personal Touches:** Decorate the space with finds from local markets, turning a house into your home, even if just for a while.

- **Living Like a Local:** Shop at nearby stores, chat with neighbors, and become a part of the community, even if temporarily.

Ballygally Holiday Apartments Self catering Co Antrim Coast Northern Ireland

Variety of Options

From quaint cottages tucked away in verdant valleys where the morning mist rolls in like a soft blanket, to modern apartments in the heart of bustling towns where history and modernity dance in harmony, Ireland's self-catering options are as varied as the landscapes that cradle them.

- **Country Cottages:** These are ideal for those seeking solace in nature, surrounded by trails that beckon and night skies that dazzle.
- **City Apartments:** Perfect for urban explorers, these apartments are a stone's throw from the vibrant tapestry of Irish city life.
- **Coastal Havens:** For lovers of the sea, where the soundtrack of your stay is the serene lullaby of the waves.

Each option offers a unique lens through which to experience Ireland, tailored to your tastes, your dreams, and your wanderlust.

Cooking Local Produce

Embracing self-catering is an invitation to dive into the heart of Irish cuisine and explore the bounty that this land generously offers. Cooking with local produce, whether it's seafood freshly plucked from the Atlantic's embrace or vegetables cradled by the fertile soil, is not just about nourishment but connection.

- **Farmers' Markets:** Visit local markets to gather ingredients, each a mosaic of the region's flavors.
- **Sea to Table:** Indulge in the freshest catch in coastal areas, cooking up a storm with recipes shared by fishermen.
- **Seasonal Delights:** Let the seasons guide your menu, celebrating the land's offerings from spring's first greens to autumn's hearty harvest.

This journey through taste and tradition enriches your palate and weaves you into the story of Ireland, one meal at a time.

- **Cost-Effective:** For the mindful traveler, self-catering accommodations unfurl as a tapestry of cost-effective wonders. They stand as proof that the richness of an Irish adventure need not be tethered to a lavish budget. With the freedom to cook, dining becomes an affordable joy rather than a costly necessity.
- **Extended Stays:** The longer you stay, the more cost-effective these accommodations become, turning a holiday into an expedition.
- **Shared Costs:** For groups or families, sharing a space means shared expenses, making the dream of an Irish odyssey attainable for many.

In self-catering accommodations, you have the freedom to choose your stay and meals, unbound by schedules. In these moments, like enjoying a morning coffee or reflecting in the evening, Ireland becomes more than just a visit; it becomes a home. Surrounded by inspiring landscapes and historic towns, you don't just find a place to stay, but a life filled with laughter and love, creating a story that's entirely yours, part of Ireland's enchanting narrative.

3.9 UNIQUE AIRBNB'S ACROSS THE EMERALD ISLE

Across Ireland, hidden gems are waiting to make your visit extraordinary. Airbnb offers a unique glimpse into Ireland's spirit, from ancient lighthouses to cozy spots in lively cities, inviting you to explore Ireland's core up close.

One-of-a-Kind Stays:

Consider staying in a converted lighthouse on the wild coast, a beacon in the night, or a treehouse in an ancient forest where the sound of leaves replaces the world's noise. In Ireland, Airbnbs are more than places to stay; they're doorways to unforgettable moments, like the cozy embrace of a peat fire on a chilly evening.

Lighthouses & Treehouses: Ireland's Airbnb offerings, like the Wicklow Head Lighthouse or the enchanting treehouses in Cork, provide just that for those who dream of nights under stars or atop waves.

Historic Homes: Step back in time with stays in centuries-old cottages and grand manors. Each room is a page from history, inviting you to live out tales of yesteryear.

Some benefits to staying at an Airbnb:

- **Local Hosts:** Airbnb's soul lies in its hosts, those who open their doors and hearts, guiding you to the authentic pulse of

Ireland. They're not just providers of keys but keepers of local lore, ready to share the secrets that guidebooks overlook.

- **Insider Tips:** From the best-hidden pub in Dublin to the quietest beach on the Wild Atlantic Way, hosts offer insights that turn a good trip into an extraordinary adventure.
- **Personalized Experiences:** Many hosts go beyond, arranging experiences like a day with a local fisherman or a private tour of a nearby castle, crafting moments that become the highlights of your stay.
- **Diverse Locations:** Ireland's landscapes are as varied as the tales that thread through them, and Airbnb's are nestled in every imaginable setting, promising the perfect backdrop for every traveler's dream.
- **Urban Escapes:** In the heart of cities like Belfast and Galway, find apartments that offer a sanctuary amidst the buzz, where history and modern life dance in the streets outside your window.
- **Rural Hideaways:** Out in the countryside, amid the emerald hues, cottages, and barn conversions sit in solitude, offering peace and a deep breath of fresh, Irish air.
- **Seaside Retreats:** Along the coast, homes cling to cliffs and nestle in harbors, where the rhythm of the tide marks the time, and the horizon stretches into infinity.
- **Unique Amenities:** The little things transform a stay into a story, and Airbnb's across Ireland is dotted with amenities that do just that. Each unique feature or experience adds a layer of wonder to your journey, like a brushstroke of magic on the canvas of your travels.
- **Hot Tubs with Views:** Imagine soaking in a hot tub as the sun sets over the Cliffs of Moher or under the stars in a secluded garden, the world at peace around you.
- **Historical Tours:** Stays in properties with rich histories often come with the chance to explore their past, led by hosts eager to share their knowledge.

- **Artistic Workshops:** In the creative haven that is Ireland, some Airbnb's offer workshops right on the premises, from pottery to painting, each an invitation to tap into your creative spirit.

Small Cottage House in Doolin, Co. Clare

If you're looking for an epic trek across Ireland, crashing at some standout Airbnbs will really plunge you deep into the heart of this enchanting land. Every stop is more than just a stay—it is a full-on dive into dramatic vistas, historical hotspots, and the warmest welcomes you could imagine. These experiences paint a truly authentic and wondrous picture of Ireland, at least they did for me. It's not just a place to visit; it's a world to live in, love, and pass on. For your own slice of Irish magic, hit up Airbnb's site and search for stays in Ireland at airbnb.com/s/ireland/ .

TASTING IRELAND

Picture this: you're wandering through a bustling Irish market, the air rich with the mingling scents of freshly baked bread, savory stews, and the earthy tang of local cheeses. Your stomach rumbles, a clear sign that while sights can dazzle and sounds can entertain, it's the taste of a place that anchors memories deep within us. Ireland's culinary landscape, with its blend of hearty tradition and innovative flair, invites you to observe and taste, savor, and indulge in the stories each dish tells. So, grab a fork (or a pint!), and let's explore the delicious diversity of Irish cuisine.

4.1 TRADITIONAL IRISH DISHES AND WHERE TO FIND THEM

Staple Foods

The backbone of any cuisine is its staple ingredients, and in Ireland, potatoes, bread, and meat hold court. The humble spud, introduced in the 16th century, quickly became a staple, while bread, from soda to wheaten, accompanies nearly every meal. Meat, especially lamb and beef, features prominently stewed, roasted, or boiled, each preparation a testament to both necessity and craft.

Tip: For an authentic taste, visit a local farmer's market like the **English Market in Cork**. Here, you can sample artisanal cheeses, freshly baked soda bread, and, if you're lucky, some homemade potato farls.

Iconic Dishes

Ireland's culinary fame may rest on a few iconic dishes, but what amazingly delicious dishes they are.

Irish Stew: Originally a peasant dish, it has been perfected in its simplicity: tender meat, potatoes, and onions slow-cooked to comfort food heaven. **O'Neill's Pub and Kitchen** serves a version that's both traditional and heartwarming...basically to die for.

- **What is it?** This expansive venue features a complex layout that includes a rooftop beer garden and carvery, complemented by antique decor.
- **Where is it?** 2 Suffolk St, Dublin 2, D02 KX03, Ireland
- **How much is it? $$**
- **Web:** oneillspubdublin.com/
- **Instagram:** @oneillssuffolkstreet

Irish Stew with a Pint of Stout

Traditional Boxty Dish

Boxty: A potato pancake that's part of the culinary trinity: boiled, mashed, and grated potatoes mixed and fried. **Gallagher's Boxty House** in Temple Bar, Dublin, is the go-to spot.

- **What is it?** Opened in 1988 by Pádraic Óg Gallagher, The Boxty House is celebrated for bringing genuine Boxty recipes to the table, using locally sourced Irish ingredients. The menu showcases three traditional Boxty varieties from Leitrim, Cavan, and Fermanagh, including Pancakes, Dumplings, Bread, and Fries, complemented by an array of Irish drinks.
- **Where is it?** Temple Bar District, Dublin, Ireland.
- **How much is it?** $$$
- **Web:** boxtyhouse.ie/
- **Instagram:** @boxtyhouse

Colcannon: A soulful mix of mashed potatoes, kale, or cabbage, and a knob of butter. It's Irish comfort on a plate. Try it at **The Brazen Head**, in Dublin.

- **What is it?** Dublin's oldest pub. Established in 1198. Now that's old.
- **Where is it?** Dublin, Ireland
- **How much is it?** $$
- **Web:** brazenhead.com/
- **Instagram:** @brazenheaddublin

Pub Grub

Pubs are the heart of Irish social life, and their food reflects Ireland's culinary soul: hearty, comforting, and generously served.

Pub Classics: Think beef, Guinness pie, fish and chips, and bangers and mash. **The Stag's Head** in Dublin not only offers these classics but also offers them in an atmosphere that is quintessentially Irish.

- **What is it?** It's a renowned pub distinguished by its Victorian elegance, warm welcome, and its famous pint of Guinness. (Make sure to order early because it takes a bit for the foam to settle.) Situated in Dublin's vibrant center, it's a favorite among both locals and tourists for its authentic Irish pub experience.
- **Where is it?** Dublin, Ireland.
- **How much is it?** $$
- **Web:** stagshead.ie/
- **Instagram:** @stags_head_dublin

Traditional Guinness Pie

Traditional Irish Fish and Chips

Modern Twists: Many pubs, like **The Ballymore Inn**, have elevated the pub grub game, introducing local ingredients and modern techniques to traditional dishes.

- **What Is It?** An upscale gastropub.
- **Where is it?** Ballymore Eustace, County Kildare
- **How much is it? $$$**
- **Web**: ballymoreinn.ie/
- **Instagram:** @ballymoreinn
- **Make sure to try:** Everything! It's all good!

Culinary Tours

The best way to understand a cuisine is to dive in, hands first. Culinary tours and cooking classes offer an immersive way to explore Irish cooking traditions.

Dublin Tasting Trail

Wander through Dublin's streets, sampling artisanal cheeses, Irish whiskies, and traditional snacks while learning about the city's food history.

- **What is it?** It's an award-winning experience led by local guides who are passionate about food and the city. These guides take participants to the best food spots, offering a mix of history, culture, and, of course, delicious tastings. The trails are designed to introduce both visitors and locals to Dublin's culinary treasures, with a focus on artisan food producers, markets, and other hidden gems. Foodies delight!
- **Where is it?** Dublin and Cork
- **When is it?** Fridays and Saturdays in Dublin, and only Saturdays in Cork. Subject to change.
- **How much is it?** $80
- **How long?** 2.5 to 3 hours
- **Web:** fabfoodtrails.ie/ **Pre-booking is a must!**
- **Instagram:** @fabfoodtrails

Cooking Classes

At **Ballymaloe Cookery School**, you can learn to cook traditional Irish dishes using ingredients from their organic farm.

- **What is it?** Nestled in County Cork, the Ballymaloe Cookery School, established by Darina Allen in 1983, is a cornerstone of Irish culinary tradition. Committed to slow food and sustainable farming, it operates on a 100-acre organic farm. Students learn the intersection of Irish cooking and organic farming from top chefs like Rachel Allen. More than just a school, Ballymaloe celebrates Ireland's food heritage with a farm-to-fork approach, appealing to enthusiasts of genuine Irish cuisine.

- **Where is it?** Cork, County Cork
- **When is it?** Year round. Depends on the length and type of class. Check the calendar for dates.
- **How long is it?** Ranging from a few hours to 12 weeks.
- **How much is it?** $70-$16,750, depending on type and length of class.
- **Web:** ballymaloecookeryschool.ie/ **Pre-booking is a must!**
- **Instagram:** @ballymaloecookeryschool

In every bite of Ireland's traditional dishes, you're tasting more than just food; you're savoring history, culture, and the love of a good meal shared. Whether it's in the bustling atmosphere of a crowded pub, the intimate setting of a local eatery, or the fresh air of a farmer's market, the flavors of Ireland speak of a land rich in tradition and ripe with innovation.

4.2 FARM-TO-TABLE: THE ORGANIC MOVEMENT

In the lush, verdant lands of Ireland, a revolution is quietly unfolding in the fields and on the tables. It's a movement that's turning back the clock while simultaneously pressing fast forward on sustainability and health. This is the farm-to-table movement, a celebration of the best that Ireland's soil has to offer, served up in a manner that's as fresh as the morning dew, or a freshly poured pint of Guinness.

Sustainability in Irish Cuisine

Sustainability isn't a new concept in Irish cuisine; it's a tradition that's being rediscovered and embraced with newfound vigor. Across the country, chefs, farmers, and food enthusiasts are championing a return to organic farming practices and locally sourced ingredients. This movement isn't just about reducing carbon footprints or supporting local economies (though it does both admirably); it's about rediscovering the rich flavors and nutritional benefits of foods grown and prepared with care.

Restaurants and cafes now proudly trace their ingredients back to the fields from which they were harvested, highlighting the journey from soil to plate. Menus change with the seasons, reflecting the natural cycles of growth and harvest, ensuring that diners enjoy the freshest produce at its peak.

Featured Farms and Producers

Ireland's green landscape is dotted with farms and producers who are leading the charge in the organic movement. Each has its own story of sustainability and passion for the land.

Ballymaloe Farm in County Cork is a beacon of organic farming. The Allen family practiced environmentally friendly agriculture long before it became fashionable. Their farm supplies the legendary Ballymaloe House with fresh, organic produce, a testament to their commitment to quality and sustainability.

- **What is it?** Ballymaloe Farm in Cork, closely linked with the esteemed Ballymaloe House and Cookery School, stands as a beacon of Irish cuisine and hospitality. This family-owned establishment is renowned for its luxurious stay and farm-to-fork dining across 300 acres. Internationally recognized as the cradle of modern Irish cuisine, it champions the Allen family's sustainable food ethos. Daily menus feature seasonal farm produce, offering guests an authentic Irish Country House experience.
- **Where is it?** Shanagarry, County Cork
- **How much is it?** $$ to $$$$. Lunch is the cheapest option at around $20-$30 per person. Sunday brunch is $75, and dinner is over $100 per person. We recommend that you treat yourself here. The food is phenomenal so splurge at least once on your trip.
- **Web:** ballymaloe.com/ **Reservations are recommended.**
- **Instagram:** @ballymaloe_house

The Little Milk Company

- **What is it?** Founded in March 2008, The Little Milk Company is a cooperative of organic dairy farmers across Ireland, pooling together 3 million liters of milk annually for the country's organic sector. Initially focusing on high-quality cheddar cheese from local organic ingredients, the company has won numerous awards for its cheese range. Central to its mission is promoting sustainable agriculture, using eco-friendly farming practices to support the local economy.
- **Where is it?** Dungarvan, County Waterford, Ireland
- **How much is it?** Prices vary.
- **Web:** thelittlemilkcompany.ie/
- **Instagram:** @thelittlemilkcompany

These producers aren't just growing food; they're cultivating a legacy of sustainability and respect for the land that feeds the body and uplifts the spirit.

Restaurant Highlights

The farm-to-table movement has given rise to a new breed of restaurants across Ireland, places where the connection between the land and the dining table is celebrated in every dish.

Sage Restaurant

- **What is it?** Sage is a casual neighborhood restaurant led by Chef/owner Kevin Aherne. It focuses on a "hyper-local" ethos, sourcing ingredients within a 12-mile radius. The menu, showcasing local vegetables, fruits, herbs, meats, poultry, and fish, changes weekly based on seasonal availability. Sage also features The Greenroom, a café, and a wine bar for more casual dining options.
- **Where is it?** Midleton, County Cork

- **How much is it?** $$ **Reservations required.**
- **Web:** sagerestaurant.ie/
- **Facebook:** facebook.com/Sage2.0RestaurantFoodstore

The Tannery

- **What is it?** Since opening in 1997 by Paul and Máire Flynn, The Tannery in Dungarvan has been celebrated for its fresh, local Irish cuisine and Paul's culinary innovation. It offers a warm atmosphere, a vibrant wine bar, and exceptional service, ensuring a delightful dining experience amidst the coastal charm. The establishment also features a Cookery School for culinary enthusiasts.
- **Where is it?** Dungarvan, County Waterford, Ireland
- **How much is it?** $$$$
- **Web:** tannery.ie/ **Reservations required.**
- **Facebook:** facebook.com/TheTanneryDungarvan

Each meal at these restaurants is a journey through Ireland's culinary landscape, a celebration of the bounty that the land offers. Make sure to try at least one!

Agricultural Events

Numerous agricultural shows and events throughout the year offer a firsthand look at Ireland's rich agricultural heritage for those looking to immerse themselves fully in the country's farm-to-table scene.

The Burren Slow Food Festival

- **What is it?** Annually, Burren's culinary festival brings everyone together to explore artisanal foods from local creators, offering a unique chance to meet the producers, mingle with food enthusiasts, and watch cooking demonstrations by renowned chefs. It's an opportunity to savor County Clare's genuine flavors and witness the community's commitment to preserving their culinary heritage.

- **Where is it?** Lisdoonvarna, County Clare
- **When is it?** Usually in May
- **How much is it?** Free
- **Web:** slowfood.com/festival
- **Instagram:** @slowfoodclare

The Ploughing Championships

- **What is it?** While primarily an agricultural competition it has become a showcase for Ireland's food scene. Stalls and demonstrations highlight the best of farm-to-table dining, from organic meats to artisanal cheeses.
- **Where is it?** Ratheniska, County Laois
- **When is it?** September
- **How much is it?** Free
- **Web:** npa.ie/
- **Instagram:** @nationalploughing

These gatherings aren't just about digging into the smorgasbord of Irish flavors; they're a full-on celebration of community ties, the lush land, and the green practices that sustain them. Pack your appetite and your chattiest self!

Every crunch of an organically grown carrot or tender slice of grass-fed beef tells Ireland's story—a narrative woven from its history, it's here and now, and its aspirations. But this farm-to-table buzz? It's far from just a fad. It's a heartfelt return to the basics, a joyful rediscovery of eating food nurtured with devotion and whipped up with a sprinkle of love. Dive into this movement that serves up Ireland in its truest form, one scrumptious morsel at a time. So, who's hungry?

4.3 SEAFOOD SPLENDORS ALONG THE COAST

Ireland's coast, where the Atlantic meets the land, is rich in seafood. The coastline, with its mix of bays and ports, is the setting for Ireland's long-standing seafood culture. Here, seafood is a big deal (huge), from salmon making their way upstream to oysters found in underwater beds. This part of the book takes you through the flavors of the sea, highlighting the traditions, community spirit, and the experience of enjoying freshly caught seafood.

Fresh Catch:

The seas that embrace Ireland's shores are generous, offering a variety of seafood that's fresh, abundant, and utterly delectable.

- **Salmon**: Revered both in river and sea, Irish salmon is a culinary icon. Whether smoked gently over oak or served fresh, its flesh is tender and rich.
- **Oysters**: From the beds of Galway Bay, oysters are a delicacy that captures the essence of the sea. They are best enjoyed with a dash of lemon or a pint of stout.
- **Mussels and Lobsters**: Nestled in the waters of Bantry Bay and along the Wild Atlantic Way, these shellfish are harvested with care, promising a taste that's both sweet and salty, like the ocean breeze.

These sea offerings are not just meals; they're an invitation to taste the wild, unbridled spirit of Ireland's coastal waters, each bite a journey through waves and tides. When in these regions, make sure to try their specialties—you won't regret it!

Historical Fishing Villages:

Dotting the coastline, Ireland's fishing villages are the heartbeats of maritime life, where tradition sails alongside modernity. If fishing is your jam, check these out.

- **Kinsale**: Once a medieval fishing port, now a gourmet capital, Kinsale's narrow streets and colorful facades echo with tales of seafarers and fishermen. Here, seafood isn't just on the menu; it's a way of life.
- **Dingle**: In this Gaeltacht town, boats bob in the harbor, bringing in their catch as they have for centuries. Dingle's charm lies not just in its scenic beauty but in its culinary prowess, where seafood is served with a side of history.

In these villages, seafood is more than sustenance; it's a story of survival, of communities holding fast to their heritage while navigating the tides of change.

Fishing boats off the coast of Dingle

Fishing boats off the coast of Northern Ireland

Seafood Experiences:

Beyond the plate, Ireland offers immersive seafood experiences that draw you closer to the source, celebrating the ocean's bounty with hands-on adventures.

Oyster Shucking Classes

- **Galway Oyster Festival** A festival where oysters are the star. Peruse the various booths, or go to local eateries, where you can learn the art of shucking oysters, each shell opening to reveal not just a delicacy but a tradition that dates back centuries. Web: galwayoysterfestival.com/
- **Flaggy Shore Oyster Experience** in County Clare, along the Wild Atlantic Way. This 90-minute journey is both educational and tasty, taking you through the history of oyster farming in the area, and the life cycle of an oyster, and includes a hands-on shucking lesson followed by oyster

tasting paired with organic wine. Tours are available every Wednesday, Friday, and Saturday from noon, with tickets priced at €55 per person. Web: flaggyshoreoysters.ie/oysterexperiences/

- **Connemara Wild Escapes** hosts an Oyster Farm Tour & Tasting in Letterfrack, Connemara. This one-hour guided tour takes you through the oyster farming process from seed to plate, allowing you to shuck your oysters and learn about their growth. The tour is designed to excite all senses, combining the taste of fresh oysters with stunning views along the Wild Atlantic Way. It's available every day from 11h00 in June to September, with extended tours during Spring tides that include a walk to the oyster beds. Web: connemarawildescapes.ie/oyster-farm-tour-oyster-tasting-letterfrack-connemara-guided-1-hour

Sea Foraging Tours:

Along the wild shores, experts guide foragers in search of seaweed, mussels, and other edible treasures, teaching not just the how but also the why and weaving tales of survival and cuisine.

- **Orchards Near Me** in County Mayo, offers coastal foraging treks where you can learn to gather mussels, periwinkles, seaweed, and more, followed by a session on cooking these finds into delicious dishes. They emphasize the importance of sustainable foraging, advising on weather considerations, appropriate attire, and the necessity of understanding tidal movements for a safe and rewarding experience. Web: orchardsnearme.com/
- **Atlantic Irish Seaweed** in Kerry offers seaweed discovery workshops, where participants can learn about various seaweeds along the pristine Irish coastline on the Wild Atlantic Way. This immersive tour, praised by global visitors,

teaches the sustainable harvest and culinary uses of seaweed. Web: atlanticirishseaweed.com/

- **Wild Atlantic Cultural Tours**, based in Killala Bay along the Wild Atlantic Way, provides guided tours with Denis Quinn. These tours involve wild food and seashore foraging, including cockles, mussels, and seaweed. Denis shares his extensive knowledge of local flora, fauna, and the area's heritage. Web: northmayo.ie/wild-atlantic-cultural-tours-killala/

These experiences aren't just about tasting; they're about understanding, about connecting with the sea in a visceral and real way, with salt on your lips and the wind in your hair. Remember, water is your friend.

Must-Visit Restaurants:

Ireland's seafood restaurants are sanctuaries of flavor, where chefs turn the ocean's harvest into plates that are as beautiful as they are delicious.

Moran's Oyster Cottage

- **What is it?** Nestled by the water, this thatched cottage beauty has been serving oysters for over 250 years. It's a place where time slows, and the simple joy of fresh oysters and Guinness feels like a nod to eternity. If you like oysters, this is a gem! Heck, it's a gem, even if you don't like oysters.
- **Where is it?** Kilcolgan, County Galway
- **How much is it?** $$
- **Web:** moransoystercottage.com/
- **Instagram:** @moransoystercottage

The Fish Box

- **What is it?** This family-run establishment brings the sea's freshness directly to your table, with dishes that sing of the ocean's depth and the family's fishing legacy. It doesn't get much fresher than this!
- **Where is it?** Dingle, County Kerry
- **How much is it?** $$
- **Web:** thefishboxdingle.com/
- **Instagram:** @thefishboxdingle

Fishy Fishy Café

- **What is it?** Helmed by Chef Martin Shanahan, this restaurant is a testament to the town's gourmet status. Here, seafood is elevated to an art form, and each dish is an homage to the fishermen and the sea.
- **Where is it?** Kinsale, County Cork
- **How much is it?** $$$
- **Web:** fishyfishy.ie/
- **Instagram:** @fishyfishyrestaurantkinsale

As you cruise along Ireland's coast, every meal becomes a bit of magic —a chance to kick back and toast the sea, the salty old souls who fish it, and the culinary wizards who spin these sea tales onto your plate. Packed with rich seafood gems, charming villages, and seriously good eats, the Irish coastline offers up a flavor-filled, soul-stirring journey. With the soundtrack of crashing waves and seagull calls, you'll savor the real taste of Ireland's ocean affair. It's more than just scrumptious dishes; it's a celebration of stories from the sea, each bite a tribute to the island's longstanding love affair with the vast, blue deep.

4.4 MODERN IRISH CUISINE: CHEFS AND INNOVATORS

In the world of Ireland's culinary scene, a new flavor is emerging, vibrant and bold, by chefs who dare to dream and innovate. This is a story not of tradition, bound by the past but of tradition reimagined and reborn. It's a narrative where the rich heritage of Irish cooking meets the excitement of global flavors and techniques, creating a culinary landscape that's as dynamic as it is delicious.

Innovative Chefs:

In the bustling kitchens of Ireland's most forward-thinking restaurants, chefs are playing with fire—and ice, and smoke, and modernist cuisine techniques—to redefine what Irish food can be. These culinary artists aren't just cooking; they're questioning, experimenting, and crafting dishes that challenge and delight in equal measure.

JP McMahon

- **Where is it?** Aniar in Galway
- **Known for:** McMahon champions a terroir-based approach, where local ingredients are the stars, transformed through a lens of creativity and respect. His dishes, often inspired by the rugged Irish landscape, bring out the essence of each ingredient in surprising ways. This restaurant is a Michelin-starred restaurant. If you want a fantastic fine dining experience you won't forget, don't miss this!
- **How much is it?** $$$$
- **Web:** https://www.aniarrestaurant.ie/
- **Instagram:** @aniargalway

Aisling Moore

- **Where is it?** Elbow Lane Brew & Smokehouse in Cork, County Cork.

- **Known for:** She combines her passion for local produce with an innovative approach to cooking that incorporates elements of fire and smoke, infusing traditional dishes with new life and flavor.
- **How much is it?** $$
- **Web:** elbowlane.ie/
- **Instagram:** @elbowlanecork

These chefs, among others, are the architects of a new Irish cuisine, one that respects its roots while reaching for the stars.

Contemporary Restaurants:

Across Ireland, restaurants are emerging as bastions of culinary innovation, spaces where the boundaries of traditional Irish cooking are expanded with each plate served. These Michelin-starred restaurants are the epitome of this.

Liath

- **What is it?** This small yet mighty Michelin-starred restaurant has quickly become a beacon of culinary creativity, offering a constantly evolving menu that's as thoughtful as it is thrilling. Their seasonal approach to their cuisine means their menu is ever-changing.
- **Where is it?** Nestled in the Blackrock Market, Dublin
- **How much is it?** $$$$
- **Web:** liathrestaurant.com/
- **Instagram:** @liathrestaurant

The Muddlers Club

- **What is it?** This Michelin-starred restaurant is making waves with its bold approach to flavor and presentation, weaving local ingredients into a tapestry of dishes that are both familiar and utterly new.

- **Where is it?** In the heart of Belfast's Cathedral Quarter, Northern Ireland
- **How much is it?** $$$$
- **Web:** themuddlersclubbelfast.com/
- **Instagram:** @themuddlersclubbelfast

In these spaces, dining is not just an act of eating but an experience, a journey through tastes, textures, and tales that captivate and inspire. Expect to be dazzled! The price is worth it!

Culinary Awards and Recognition

The world has noticed Ireland's culinary renaissance, with accolades and awards aplenty shining a spotlight on the talent and innovation that define modern Irish cuisine.

- **Michelin Stars:** Ireland's contemporary restaurants have earned their stars not just for the quality of their ingredients or the skill of their chefs but for their daring in pushing the envelope of what Irish cuisine can be.
- **Global Recognition:** Beyond the Michelin guide, Irish chefs and restaurants are being celebrated on the global stage, with awards and mentions in everything from the World's 50 Best Restaurants to James Beard nominations, heralding Ireland as a must-visit culinary destination.

This acclaim is more than just recognition; it's a testament to the passion, creativity, and hard work that fuel Ireland's culinary fire.

Trends in Irish Cooking

As the landscape of Irish cuisine evolves, several trends have emerged, each reflecting the dynamic interplay between tradition and innovation.

- **Foraging:** Chefs are looking to the wild, rediscovering the bounty of Ireland's forests, fields, and shores. Foraged ingredients, from sea herbs to wild mushrooms, are finding their way onto plates, adding depth and a sense of place to dishes.
- **Fusion Flavors:** Ireland's culinary scene is increasingly global, with chefs drawing on the flavors and techniques of cuisines from around the world. This fusion approach has led to exciting combinations, where Irish ingredients meet Asian spices or South American heat, creating flavors that are entirely new yet unmistakably Irish.
- **Sustainability:** At the heart of modern Irish cooking is a commitment to sustainability, from nose-to-tail eating to zero-waste kitchens. This trend is about more than just good food; it's about respect for the environment and the future of the planet.
- **Tech in the Kitchen:** Modernist techniques and technologies, from sous vide to dehydrators, are becoming common tools for Ireland's chefs, allowing for precision, experimentation, and the creation of dishes that defy expectations.

These trends show the future of Irish cuisine, one that's rooted in the past yet eagerly reaching for what's next. It's a cuisine as diverse as the people who call Ireland home, a delicious mosaic of flavors, stories, and dreams. This is modern Irish cooking: bold, innovative, and utterly irresistible.

4.5 STREET FOOD AND MARKETS: LOCAL FAVORITES

In Ireland, the streets and markets are alive with a culinary vibrancy that tells the tale of a nation's love affair with food. It's here, among the hustle and bustle, that the heart of Irish cuisine beats strongest, offering a taste of the country's soul one bite at a time.

Street Food Scene

The aroma of grilling meats, the sizzle of frying fish, and the sweet scent of baking dough weave through the air in Ireland's street food scene. This is where tradition meets innovation, with food trucks and stalls serving everything from classic fish and chips to fusion tacos filled with locally sourced ingredients.

- **Fish Tacos on the Go:** At the edge of Galway's market, a food truck serves up a storm with its signature dish: fish tacos. Fresh catch from the day, lightly battered, served in a soft tortilla with a dollop of homemade salsa and a squeeze of lime, encapsulates the essence of Irish seafood with a global twist.
- **Boxty Reimagined:** In Dublin, a stall breathes new life into the traditional boxty, offering it with a variety of fillings, from spicy lamb to vegetarian options, showcasing the versatility of this beloved potato pancake.

These mobile eateries not only satiate hunger but also kindle curiosity, drawing locals and travelers alike into the fold of Ireland's evolving food narrative.

Farmers' Markets

Farmers' markets are the backbone of local communities, serving as gathering places where the bond between land and table is celebrated.

They're where you'll find the freshest produce, artisanal goods, and a sense of camaraderie that's as nourishing as the food on offer.

- **The English Market, Cork:** An institution since 1788, this covered market is a feast for the senses, offering everything from artisan cheeses to fresh seafood. It's a place where you can chat with the producers, learn the story behind your food, and leave with a basket full of Ireland's best. **Web:** corkcity.ie/en/english-market/
- **St. George's Market, Belfast:** Every weekend, this market comes alive with the smell of fresh bread, the vibrant colors of seasonal vegetables, and the sound of local musicians. It's a celebration of Northern Ireland's culinary diversity and community spirit. **Web:** belfastcity.gov.uk/stgeorgesmarket

Farmers' markets are not just places to shop; they're experiences that connect you to the heart of Irish food culture.

Food Markets

The resurgence of food halls and covered markets has brought a new dimension to Ireland's food scene. They offer a communal space where a variety of cuisines and cultures converge under one roof.

- **The Temple Bar Food Market:** This modern food hall in Dublin brings together some of the city's best culinary talents in one space, offering everything from gourmet burgers to sushi. It's a place to explore new flavors, meet friends, and enjoy the buzz of Dublin's dynamic food scene. **Web:** templebarmarkets.com/foodmarket
- **The Milk Market, Limerick:** With its origins dating back to 1852, this weekend market has evolved into a vibrant food hub, where local produce, freshly baked goods, and international cuisines create a tapestry of tastes that reflect the diversity of modern Ireland. **Web:** milkmarketlimerick.ie/

Food halls and covered markets are not just about convenience; they're about community, offering a place for people to gather, share meals, and celebrate the joy of eating together.

Seasonal and Regional Specialties

Ireland's culinary landscape is shaped by its seasons and regions, with each area offering specialties that reflect the local environment and heritage.

- **Spring in Orchard County:** In Armagh, known as Orchard County, spring brings a bounty of apples. Local markets overflow with apple-based products, from crisp ciders to tangy chutneys, celebrating the region's apple-growing heritage.
- **Autumn Seafood in Donegal:** As autumn winds sweep the coast, Donegal's markets and food stalls brim with the bounty of the sea. From mussels harvested in local bays to smoked mackerel caught off the coast, the season's catch showcases the region's rich seafood traditions.
- **Winter Warmers in Kerry:** When winter's chill descends, Kerry's street food vendors offer comfort in the form of hearty stews and rich, creamy hot chocolates. These dishes, made with local ingredients and a touch of Kerry's culinary magic, provide warmth from the inside out.

Every nook of Ireland whispers a unique tale with its food, which drew me into its vast culinary world. Roaming from the lively food trucks on crowded streets to the bustling markets filled with local farmers and artisans, I found myself wrapped in Ireland's rich palette of flavors and narratives. Amid the laughter and spirited talks, Ireland's true essence reveals itself in every bite, a blend of history, innovation, and the heartfelt warmth of its community.

4.6 WHISKEY AND BREWERIES: A SPIRITED JOURNEY

Ireland, with its rolling green landscapes and rich history, offers more than just a feast for the eyes and the palate—it's also a haven for those who appreciate the art of distillation and brewing. Can you say Jameson with a side of Guinness? This section is your guide to the spirited side of Ireland, where every sip tells a story of tradition, craftsmanship, and the sheer joy of sharing a good drink.

Irish Whiskey Distilleries

Whiskey, or "uisce beatha" in Irish, meaning "water of life," is more than a beverage in Ireland; it's a cultural emblem woven into the fabric of the nation's history and social life. Distilleries dot the landscape, each offering a unique insight into the craft of whiskey making.

- **Old Bushmills Distillery in County Antrim:** Bushmills claims the title of the oldest licensed distillery in the world. It offers a deep dive into the craft of making triple-distilled malt whiskey. Tours and tastings here are a journey through time, with a glass in hand. **Web:** bushmills.com/distillery/
- **Jameson Distillery Bow St. in Dublin:** This distillery offers an immersive experience into the world of Jameson, blending history with modern storytelling techniques. The tasting sessions are not just educational; they're a celebration of the spirit's versatility. **Web:** jamesonwhiskey.com/en-us/visit-our-distilleries/jameson-bow-street-distillery-tour/

Jameson Distillery, Dublin

Visiting these distilleries, you'll learn about the intricate process of whiskey making, from malting and fermentation to distillation and aging, gaining an appreciation for the patience and skill that goes into every bottle. You'll also get to sample. Please drink responsibly.

Craft Beer Revolution

Craft beer mania isn't just big in the United States, the craft beer scene in Ireland is bubbling with creativity and passion. Across the country, small breweries are redefining Irish beer, experimenting with local ingredients, and drawing on a variety of global influences to create brews that are distinctly Irish yet universally appealing.

- **Galway Bay Brewery:** Known for pushing the boundaries of brewing, Galway Bay Brewery has become a staple of the craft beer scene in Ireland. Their range includes everything from robust stouts to hoppy IPAs, each with its unique character. Try the Foam and Fury IPA. **Web:** galwaybaybrewery.com/
- **The White Hag Irish Brewing Company:** Located in County Sligo, this brewery draws inspiration from ancient Irish

mythology to create award-winning beers that are rich in flavor and story. The Ninth Wave Pale Ale is a treat! **Web:** thewhitehag.com/

- Beer festivals, such as the **Galway International Arts Festival**, often feature craft beers, offering a platform for breweries to showcase their creations and for enthusiasts to discover new favorites. **Web:** giaf.ie/

Pairing Food and Spirits

The synergy between food and spirits can elevate a dining experience, creating combinations that are memorable and flavorsome. Here are a few tips for pairing Irish food with whiskey and beer:

- **Whiskey and Cheese:** A smooth Irish whiskey pairs beautifully with the sharpness of aged cheddar, balancing the richness of the cheese with the warmth of the spirit.
- **Stout and Seafood:** A stout's deep, roasted flavors complement the brininess of oysters and mussels, enhancing the taste of the sea with each sip.
- **IPA and Spicy Food:** An IPA's hoppy bitterness can cut through the heat of spicy dishes, refreshing the palate, and readying it for the next bite.

Exploring these pairings, you'll discover how the right drink can turn a meal into an experience, highlighting and harmonizing flavors in delightful ways.

Pub Culture

I remember back to the time when I studied Pub Culture while in London. (No really, it was a class for credit). Ireland is no different. In Ireland, pubs are more than places to drink; they're the heart of community life, where stories are shared, friendships are forged, and the craic is always mighty. The culture of the pub is integral to the whiskey and beer experience, offering a warm, welcoming space to enjoy Ireland's spirits and brews. The pubs in Ireland are like the coffee shops in the United States.

- **The Traditional Music Session:** Many pubs host live traditional music sessions, where the tunes flow as freely as the drinks. Enjoying whiskey or craft beer in this setting is to experience Irish culture in its most vibrant form.
- **The Literary Pub:** Dublin, with its rich literary heritage, boasts pubs frequented by some of Ireland's most famous writers. Sipping craft beer or whiskey in these pubs is a way to experience history and inspiration.

In these pubs, every glass shared is an invitation to connect, to join in the laughter, the music, and the stories that make Ireland uniquely enchanting.

Diving into Ireland's distilleries and breweries, experiencing its pub culture, and mastering the art of pairing food with spirits, I discovered that I'm not just tasting Ireland; I'm living it. Each sip took me further into the Irish lifestyle, where the joy of a good drink is always enhanced by friends and the tales we shared.

4.7 TEATIME: CAFES AND AFTERNOON TRADITIONS

Traditional Irish Teatime

Teatime isn't just for the Brits! In Ireland, the ritual of teatime unfolds like a well-loved story, familiar yet filled with delightful surprises at every turn. This isn't just a pause in the day; it's a tradition steeped in history, offering a moment of connection over a cup of warmth. The scent of brewing tea, the clatter of fine china, and the comfort of a freshly baked scone are the simple pleasures that define this cherished custom.

Afternoon Tea Tradition

The roots of afternoon tea stretch back to the 19th century, blossoming into a cherished institution over time. In Ireland, this tradition takes on a character all its own, blending the classic elements of tea, sandwiches, and sweets with a touch of Irish hospitality. The typical fare might include:

- Delicate finger sandwiches filled with cucumber, smoked salmon, or egg mayonnaise.
- Warm, buttered scones served with thick clotted cream and homemade jams.
- A selection of pastries and cakes, from the light-as-air Victoria sponge to the rich, decadent chocolate cake.

Gathered around the table, stories are shared, and laughter flows as freely as tea, making this more than a meal—it's a moment of joy.

Best Tea Rooms

Across Ireland, tea rooms and cafes serve up this afternoon tradition with their unique flair. Here are a few spots where the tea and the setting are equally enchanting:

- **The Merrion Hotel, Dublin:** In the heart of the city, The Merrion offers an afternoon tea that's as elegant as it is delicious, set against the backdrop of their stunning Georgian drawing rooms. **Web:** merrionhotel.com/
- **Adare Manor, County Limerick:** For those seeking luxury, Adare Manor's afternoon tea is a lavish affair, served in a grand gallery overlooking the formal gardens. Don't forget your manners! **Web:** adaremanor.com/

Each venue offers a distinct experience, inviting you to linger over your cup and savor the art of slowing down. I recommend trying to fit this into your itinerary to have an authentic Irish experience truly.

Modern Takes on Teatime

While tradition forms the heart of teatime, contemporary cafes, and tea rooms infuse this ritual with fresh energy and creativity. These modern takes might include:

- **The Blind Pig, Dublin:** This speakeasy-style bar offers a 'Tipsy Tea' where cocktails inspired by classic teas add a spirited twist to the afternoon tradition. **Web:** theblindpig.ie/
- **Clement & Pekoe, Dublin:** Focusing on quality and simplicity, Clement & Pekoe takes a minimalist approach to teatime, showcasing exceptional teas and coffee alongside artisanal baked goods. **Web:** clementandpekoe.com/

These spots prove that tradition can evolve, offering new ways to enjoy this timeless ritual.

Tea and Scones

At the heart of any Irish teatime are tea and scones, a duo that's simple yet sublime. The scone is a study in perfection—crisp on the outside, tender, and warm on the inside. Here are a few variations and their companions:

- **The Classic:** A plain scone, buttered, with strawberry jam and a dollop of cream, is a testament to the beauty of simplicity.
- **The Savory Twist:** Cheese or herb scones offer a savory counterpoint to the sweetness of the tea and are often served with butter or cream cheese.
- **Regional Specialties:** In some areas, scones might feature local ingredients like seaweed or blackcurrants, adding a unique flavor profile that speaks of the land.
- **Tea,** whether a robust **Assam or a delicate Earl Grey,** is the ideal accompaniment, its warmth and bitterness providing the perfect balance to the rich, sweet scone.

Every cup of tea and scone embodies the essence of home, tradition, and the simple pleasures of Irish culinary culture. Teatime merges history and hospitality, providing a pause that transcends refreshment —it's about connection, sharing stories, and creating memories. Whether in a grand historic hotel, a quaint tearoom, or a modern cafe, this cherished ritual remains a vital part of daily life in Ireland, continually inspiring and delighting as a core thread in the nation's cultural fabric. Make time for tea, you won't regret it.

4.8 VEGAN AND VEGETARIAN DELIGHTS

In a land historically celebrated for its lush pastures and hearty meat-based fare, a vibrant revolution is quietly simmering. Ireland's culinary scene is witnessing a green surge, with vegan and vegetarian cuisine gaining ground, reflecting a shift towards more conscious eating habits. This transformation speaks volumes about the nation's evolving palate and its openness to embracing plant-based goodness without forsaking its rich culinary heritage.

Growth of Plant-Based Eating

The roots of this green movement run deep, fueled by a growing awareness of health, sustainability, and ethical considerations. It reflects Ireland's adaptability and willingness to blend tradition with innovation. From bustling cities to serene countryside locales, eateries and households alike are reimagining meals, proving that plant-based eating in Ireland can be as hearty and fulfilling as its traditional counterparts. This shift is more than a trend; it's becoming a way of life, with Ireland's culinary landscape richer for it.

Vegan and Vegetarian Restaurants

Ireland offers more than meat and potatoes. Navigating its cities, one discovers havens of plant-based cuisine that delight the senses and challenge culinary norms.

- **The Happy Pear, Greystones:** What started as a small veggie shop by twin brothers has blossomed into a community offering mouthwatering vegan fare that emphasizes whole, organic foods. **Web:** thehappypear.ie/our-cafe-and-shop/

- **Cornucopia, Dublin:** A trailblazer in the vegetarian scene, this restaurant serves wholesome, innovative dishes that draw both locals and tourists eager for a taste of plant-based creativity. **Web:** cornucopia.ie/
- **Paradiso, Cork:** With an ever-evolving menu that highlights seasonal produce, Paradiso has elevated vegetarian dining to an art form, showcasing the potential for plant-based cuisine to star on the culinary stage. **Web:** paradiso.restaurant/

These establishments are just the tip of the iceberg, with more popping up each year. Each contributes its unique flavors and flair to Ireland's dining scene.

Local Ingredients

At the core of Ireland's vegan and vegetarian revolution is a celebration of local, seasonal ingredients. Chefs and home cooks alike are tapping into the bounty offered by Ireland's fertile lands.

- **Foraged Wild Foods:** From nettles and wild garlic in the spring to berries and mushrooms in the autumn, foraging adds a wild, nutritious twist to plant-based dishes.
- **Organic Produce:** Farmers' markets and organic co-ops are treasure troves of fresh produce, with everything from kale and carrots to apples and pears, all contributing to a vibrant vegan plate.

This focus on local and seasonal ingredients enhances the flavors of vegan and vegetarian dishes, supports the local economy, and minimizes environmental impact, creating a culinary cycle that benefits all.

Food Festivals

Ireland celebrates the diversity and creativity of vegan and vegetarian cuisine by hosting a variety of food festivals and events that cater specifically to plant-based diets.

- **Dublin Vegfest:** As Ireland's largest vegan food event, Vegfest is a vibrant celebration of vegan living. It features talks, cooking demonstrations, and a plethora of vegan food stalls that showcase the innovation and passion driving this movement. **Instagram:** @dublinvegfest
- **Cork Vegfest:** A Day-long feast for the senses, Cork Vegfest brings together vegan food producers, chefs, and enthusiasts, creating a space to share, learn, and indulge in the finest plant-based cuisine Ireland has to offer. **Web:** facebook.com/corkvegfest/

These festivals are not just about food; they're about community, education, and the joy of discovering that plant-based eating in Ireland is not just possible but utterly delicious.

In the green fields of Ireland, where tradition and innovation dance a lively jig, the vegan and vegetarian movement is blossoming, painting the culinary landscape with vibrant new colors. It's a testament to the adaptability and openness of the Irish spirit, proving that even in a land famed for its stews and dairy, there's plenty of room at the table for green delights. With each plant-based dish crafted from local ingredients, Ireland is writing a new chapter in its culinary story, one that's inclusive, conscious, and bursting with flavor.

4.9 FOOD FESTIVALS: A FEAST FOR THE SENSES

Throughout Ireland, food festivals are a big part of the calendar, celebrating life and community through cuisine. From coast to city, these festivals are more than just events; they're where people come together to enjoy food and share in the country's culinary heritage. They showcase Ireland's food culture, blending tradition with new ideas under the open sky. You won't go hungry, that's for sure!

Major Food Festivals

- **Galway International Oyster & Seafood Festival:** As autumn paints the landscape, Galway celebrates the oyster, a jewel of the sea, with a festival that's as much about camaraderie as it is about cuisine. Shucking competitions, tastings, and gala events make this a must-visit for seafood aficionados. **Web:** galwayoysterfestival.com/
- **Taste of Dublin:** In the sun-dappled days of summer, Dublin's Iveagh Gardens transform into a foodie wonderland. Top chefs, restaurants, and food enthusiasts gather for four days of tastings, demonstrations, and culinary delights, offering a bite-sized experience of Dublin's dynamic food scene. **Web:** tasteofdublin.ie/

These festivals are more than events; they're jubilant declarations of Ireland's love affair with food, inviting everyone to partake in the bounty and creativity that define Irish cuisine. They're a great and fun way to try new things and experience the culture and cuisine in a relaxed and more affordable way.

Beach BBQ Festival in Bray, County Wicklow

Regional Culinary Events

Nestled within Ireland's scenic landscapes, regional culinary events shine a spotlight on local specialties and traditions, offering a taste of the place and its people.

- **A Taste of West Cork Food Festival:** This festival is a tribute to the region's rich culinary heritage and abundant natural resources. From farm visits and foraging walks to chef-led dinners, the event stitches together the fabric of community, landscape, and cuisine into a tapestry of regional pride. **Web:** tastecork.ie/food-producers/a-taste-of-west-cork
- **Donegal Food Festival:** Set against the backdrop of the Atlantic, this festival celebrates Donegal's rugged beauty and culinary bounty. Local chefs, artisan producers, and musicians create an atmosphere as hearty and welcoming as a Donegal hearth, making it a highlight of the culinary calendar. **Web:** govisitdonegal.com/festivals-and-events/food

These events offer a window into the soul of Ireland's regions, each with its flavor and flair. They invite visitors to savor the unique tastes that make up the Irish culinary mosaic.

Interactive Experiences

Beyond the tastings and demonstrations, food festivals in Ireland often feature interactive experiences, inviting attendees to roll up their sleeves and dive into the world of Irish cuisine.

- **Cooking Demonstrations:** Renowned chefs share their secrets, turning cooking into a spectator sport where the aromas and flavors leap from the stage into the audience.
- **Food and Whiskey Pairings:** Experts will guide attendees through the nuanced world of pairing. The right whiskey can elevate a dish to new heights, offering a symphony of flavors that sing of Ireland's culinary diversity.

These hands-on experiences not only entertain but educate, offering insights into the art and science of Irish cooking. Each festival is a learning opportunity as much as a culinary celebration. This is a great way to make your trip memorable!

Cultural Significance

Food festivals in Ireland do more than just feed the body; they nourish the soul, fostering a sense of community and shared heritage. They're a testament to Ireland's evolving food landscape, where the past is honored, the present celebrated, and the future embraced with open arms and empty plates.

- **Promotion of Irish Cuisine:** These festivals serve as platforms for showcasing the richness of Irish food, from farm-fresh produce to innovative dishes that push culinary boundaries.

- **Community Building:** At their heart, food festivals are gatherings of people united by a love for food. They strengthen bonds, forge new connections, and celebrate the communal spirit that's a hallmark of Irish culture.

In these gatherings, Ireland's story is told through its food, a narrative of resilience, creativity, and warmth that welcomes all to the table.

When the tunes wind down, and the final bites of our feast disappear, the buzz of Ireland's food festivals still hangs in the air. Here, food is more than just grub—it's a slice of culture, a community bash, and a way to really get each other. With satisfied bellies and happy hearts, we're all geared up for the next round of Ireland's food scene, hungry for more tastes and tales.

THE CRAIC BY NIGHT

I magine strolling down a cobblestone lane, the echoes of your footsteps mingling with the distant strum of a guitar. A warm glow spills from the windows of a nearby pub (or maybe a patron who had too many pints), the laughter and music floating out the door promising an evening filled with the kind of stories you'll recount for years. In Ireland, nights are never just about heading out; they're an invitation to become part of a centuries-old tradition where music and camaraderie reign supreme. This chapter doesn't just open the door to Ireland's night scene—it pulls up a chair and offers you a pint.

5.1 TRADITIONAL MUSIC SESSIONS IN LOCAL PUBS

Music and Culture

In the heart of every traditional Irish pub, there's a rhythm beating that's as essential to Ireland as its rolling green hills. This music, played in sessions that can spring up spontaneously or fill a weekly schedule, is the lifeblood of Irish culture. Far from being mere performances, these sessions are communal gatherings where musicians circle tables, playing sets that meander from jigs to ballads, telling Ireland's story through melody and verse.

Where to Find Sessions

For anyone looking to immerse themselves in this quintessential Irish experience, certain pubs are known far and wide for their commitment to traditional music.

Traditional Irish Music Session in Northern Ireland

- **The Cobblestone in Dublin** stands out not just for the quality of its music but for its welcoming atmosphere, where beginners play alongside legends. **Web:** cobblestonepub.ie/
- **Gus O'Connor's Pub in Doolin** is a pilgrimage site for traditional music lovers. Nestled in a village known as the heart of Irish music, the pub is a stone's throw from the Cliffs of Moher, making it the perfect stop after a day of exploration. **Web:** gusoconnorsdoolin.com/

- **De Barra's Folk Club in Clonakilty** offers a cozy setting for some of the best folk and traditional music in County Cork. Legends like Christy Moore have graced its stage, adding to the pub's storied history. **Web:** debarra.ie/

Participation and Etiquette

Diving into a traditional music session is to become part of a living tradition. Here are a few tips to ensure the experience is joyful for everyone:

- **Listen First:** Spend some time soaking in the atmosphere and understanding the flow of the session. It's about unity, not solos. This isn't the time to channel your inner Bono or Sinead O'Connor.
- **Respect the Musicians:** While it's a communal space, remember musicians are sharing their art. Applause after a set is always appreciated, but save the chatter for the breaks.
- **Joining In:** If you play an instrument, it's polite to wait for an invitation from the session leader. Sessions are incredibly welcoming, but they thrive on a certain musical synergy.

Famous Musicians and Bands

Sessions can surprise you. On any given night, you might find yourself sharing a pint with musicians who've toured the world. Bands like The Chieftains and Altan, and artists like Sharon Shannon and Mundy, have been known to join in or even start a session in a cozy pub corner. It's a reminder that in Ireland, music is a circle—ever-expanding, always inclusive.

In these pubs, under the warm glow of hanging lanterns, every strum and note brings the past alive, connecting everyone in a timeless celebration of Irish culture. The music here isn't just heard; it's felt, a pulsating reminder of the island's soul, inviting everyone to tap their feet and lose themselves in the melody.

5.2 LITERARY PUBS: FOLLOWING THE FOOTSTEPS OF GIANTS

Under the dim glow of lamplights, Ireland's oldest pubs hold the stories of literary legends who once visited. These places, rich in history, offer more than just a pint of Guinness—they're gateways to the past, where famous writers and poets once found inspiration. These pubs honor Ireland's literary tradition, making every visit feel like stepping into a piece of history.

Literary Heritage

Ireland's pubs have long been sanctuaries for the creative mind, providing a haven where words could flow as freely as the drink. It's in these settings that literary legends like James Joyce, Samuel Beckett, and W.B. Yeats gathered, debated, and sometimes even penned their next masterpiece on a napkin. These pubs, rich in atmosphere and history, continue to honor their legacy, serving as custodians of Ireland's storied literary tradition.

Pub Tours

For those eager to tread the same floors as their literary heroes, several curated pub tours offer a guided journey through these iconic locales.

- **Dublin's Literary Pub Crawl** weaves through the city's historic streets, stopping at pubs famed for their literary associations. Guides, often actors or writers themselves, bring the tales of literary lore to life, making the experience as educational as it is entertaining. **Web:** dublinpubcrawl.com/

THE CRAIC BY NIGHT | 165

- In Belfast, the **C.S. Lewis Tour** explores the haunts of the renowned author, delving into his inspirations amidst the city's vibrant pub scene. **Web:** discovernorthernireland.com/things-to-do/c-s-lewis-trail-p709901

These tours not only illuminate the past but also highlight the ongoing relationship between Irish pubs and the literary community.

Themed Nights and Readings

The tradition of storytelling, a cornerstone of Irish culture, thrives in the modern pub setting through organized themed nights and readings.

- **The Stag's Head** in Dublin often hosts evenings dedicated to the works of local poets and authors, allowing contemporary voices to echo through its historic rooms. **Web:** stagshead.ie/
- **The Sunflower Pub** in Belfast offers a stage for spoken word performances, where both established and emerging writers share their work, fostering a new generation of literary talent. **Web:** sunflowerbelfast.com/

These events serve as a reminder of the pubs' role as communal spaces where creativity is not just remembered but actively nurtured and celebrated. You're sure to have a memorable experience taking part in one of these events.

Historic Pubs

Several pubs stand out for their indelible link to Ireland's literary past. Each has stories etched into its fabric, perhaps even its walls. Ha!

- **Davy Byrnes in Dublin**, famously mentioned in Joyce's Ulysses, remains a pilgrimage site for fans of the novel. Its walls, adorned with memorabilia, whisper tales of the past to those who listen closely. **Web:** davybyrnes.com/ (See I wasn't kidding about the walls.)

- **The White House in Limerick**, known for its weekly poetry nights, has welcomed poets and writers for decades, solidifying its place in Ireland's literary landscape. It also holds the title of being Limerick's oldest bar. **Web:** thewhitehousebar.ie/
- **Tigh Neachtain in Galway**, with its cozy corners and eclectic decor, has long been a gathering spot for the artistic community. It offers a welcoming space for discussion, debate, and the occasional impromptu performance. **Web:** tighneachtain.com/

These pubs aren't just places to drink; they preserve Ireland's cultural history, keeping the influence of its literary greats alive. Here, literature is held in high esteem, and the influence of famous Irish writers is tangible. Entering these pubs feels like being part of a living story, where each corner has its tales, and each visitor could be a character from a book. The ambiance suggests that even a regular night out here might turn into something remarkable.

5.3 CLUBBING IN IRELAND: BEATS BEYOND TRAD MUSIC (AKA IRISH FOLK MUSIC)

Ireland's music scene extends beyond its historical roots into vibrant city nights filled with contemporary sounds. From electronic dance music's deep bass to rock's electric guitar riffs, the country's music landscape is constantly evolving. It invites everyone not just to listen, but to truly experience the music and share in the night's lively atmosphere.

Diverse Music Scene

The music scene in Ireland's clubs is as varied as the landscape of the country itself. On any given night, you can find yourself lost in the hypnotic beats of a world-class DJ, headbanging to a live rock band, or swaying to the soulful melodies of an indie artist. It's this diversity that defines Ireland's club scene—a place where every musical taste finds its home, and every night offers a new soundtrack.

- In Dublin, clubs like **The Workman's Club** have become institutions known for showcasing a wide range of music that spans genres and eras, ensuring there's something for everyone. **Web:** theworkmansclub.com/
- **Cyprus Avenue** in Cork offers a more intimate setting. The connection between the artist and the audience is palpable, making every performance feel personal. **Web:** cyprusavenue.ie/

Top Clubs

For those ready to dive into the heart of Ireland's clubbing scene, there are a few spots that stand out for their commitment to great music and unforgettable nights. (Assuming you don't overindulge in the spirits.)

- **District 8 in Dublin**, a beacon for electronic music lovers, where top DJs from around the world spin tracks that keep the dance floor moving until the early hours. **Web:** district8dublin.com/
- **Róisín Dubh in Galway**, known for its eclectic lineup, from rock bands to electronic acts, has cemented its place as a cornerstone of the west's nightlife. **Web:** roisindubh.net/
- **The Limelight in Belfast**, with its multiple rooms catering to different music tastes, from chart-toppers to alternative rock, ensures every visitor finds their groove. **Web:** limelightbelfast.com/

Dancers Party to the Music

DJ Culture

The heartbeat of Ireland's club scene is undoubtedly its DJs, local and international, who bring their decks to life each night. These artists, through their skill and passion, have the power to transform a room of strangers into a unified body, thumping in rhythm to the same beat. It's a dynamic culture, one that celebrates innovation and respects the artistry behind the turntable.

DJs like Or:la and Krystal Klear, who have roots in Ireland, have gained international acclaim, showcasing the depth of talent within the country's borders.

Clubs often host guest DJ nights, where stars from the global scene come to play, offering club-goers in Ireland a taste of the world's best beats.

DJ Spins Via Laptop at a Club

Nightlife Districts

For anyone looking to explore the depths of Ireland's nightlife, certain districts stand out as the stars of evening entertainment. These areas, alive with the glow of neon signs and the promise of memorable nights, and perhaps some people stumbling drunk, are where stories begin, and legends are born.

- **Temple Bar in Dublin** might be known for its traditional pubs, but as night deepens, it transforms, with clubs and bars offering everything from live DJs to themed dance parties.
- **The Cathedral Quarter in Belfast** offers a contrast of the historic and the modern. Cutting-edge clubs nestle among cobbled streets, providing a backdrop as intriguing as the music.

- **Galway's West End** is a testament to the city's reputation as a cultural hub, with venues that blur the lines between pub and club, offering live music and DJ sets in spaces filled with character.

Temple Bar, Dublin

Diving into Ireland's club scene is an experience that goes beyond a typical night out. It's about getting swept up in an atmosphere where the music sets the tone. The nightclubs pulse with the latest beats, showcasing the vibrant spirit of modern Ireland. As the bass thumps and the lights swirl, the nightlife really kicks off, inviting you to be part of an electrifying vibe that keeps going until dawn. If you're a traveler looking to capture the essence of Ireland after dark, these clubs are where you'll find it.

Molly's Dance & Music Club, Killaloe

5.4 COZY PUBS: FIRESIDE CHATS AND PINTS

In Ireland's winter, with its cold air and misty landscapes, a warm pub offers a perfect escape. Imagine sitting by a crackling peat fire, warming up as you relax in a comfy chair with a stout in hand. Dim candlelight, quiet talks, and the scent of peat shape the ambiance, creating a space for unwinding, thinking, and connecting with others. Depending on where you are in the country, this might be more of a necessity to stay warm than an ambient circumstance.

Warm Ambiance

The allure of a traditional Irish pub in the winter months lies in its promise of warmth—not just the physical warmth provided by the fireside but the warmth of welcome that greets every patron. These pubs are havens from the cold, their interiors a cozy cocoon of wood paneling, dim lighting, and shelves laden with bottles of whiskey that catch the light like amber. Here, the world outside slips away, replaced by an ambiance that nurtures the soul and fosters a sense of belonging.

Conversation and Community

What truly sets these cozy pubs apart is the role they play as the heart of community life. They are places where conversation flows as freely as a drink, where stories are shared, and where laughter resounds. In the glow of the fire, strangers become friends, bound by the shared warmth of the pub. It's a setting where the art of conversation is cherished, where people lean in to listen, and every tale told adds another layer to the rich vibrance of community life.

In an age where digital connections often supersede physical ones, these pubs stand as bastions of genuine interaction, reminding us of the value of face-to-face conversation. Some pubs may even forbid you to use your cell phone. (Okay, maybe only in jest.)

If you're in Ireland during winter, don't miss the chance for a relaxing, romantic evening at the pub, either with friends or the newfound friends you're about to meet. You're sure to have stories to share.

Pubs with History

Across Ireland, some pubs have weathered many years, rich with history and stories from countless visitors. These places are more than just spots for a drink; they are guardians of history, each carrying its unique tales from the past.

- **Sean's Bar in Athlone** lays claim to being the oldest pub in Ireland, with a history dating back over a thousand years. Crossing its threshold is like stepping back in time, the air thick with tales of yore. **Web:** seansbar.ie/
- **The Brazen Head in Dublin**, reputed to be Ireland's oldest city pub, has been a meeting place for rebels, rogues, and royalty alike. Its fireside is a coveted spot, where the past and

present merge in the warmth of its embrace. **Web:** brazenhead.com/

Visiting these historic pubs is to touch Ireland's living history, sit where legends once sat, and raise a glass to those who've passed through their doors. 1000 years old…that's old!

5.5 CRAFT BEER HAVENS

In the land where tradition flows as richly as the River Shannon, a new wave of brewers is stirring the pot, or more accurately, the brew kettle. Ireland's craft beer scene is flourishing, transforming the beer landscape with innovative flavors that challenge the stout and ale dynasties of old. This movement is not just about brewing; it's about crafting stories, one batch at a time, stories that are as diverse as Ireland itself.

The Craft Beer Movement

Gone are the days when the term 'Irish beer' evoked images of just a few well-known stouts and ales. Now, the craft beer scene in Ireland is buzzing with creativity, driven by passionate brewers who are not afraid to experiment. They blend traditional techniques with modern flair, producing everything from hoppy IPAs to fruity sours, each beer a reflection of its maker's dedication and the local ingredients from which it's crafted. This shift towards craft brewing is more than a trend; it's a renaissance, redefining Ireland's beer identity. Watch out, Guinness!

Brewpubs and Taprooms

For those eager to sample the frothy fruits of this beer revolution, Ireland's brewpubs and taprooms are the places to be. Here, you're not just a customer; you're a guest, invited to taste and appreciate the labor and love poured into every pint.

- **The Black Sheep in Dublin** is a cozy spot where the taps are always changing. Here, you can sample not only local Dublin brews but selections from across Ireland and beyond. **Web:** galwaybaybrewery.com/blacksheep/
- **Galway Bay Brewery** has several venues across the country, each with an impressive lineup of their own craft creations alongside guest brews, ensuring every visit offers a new tasting adventure. **Web:** galwaybaybrewery.com/
- **Rising Sons Brewery in Cork** provides a firsthand look at the brewing process, with their tanks just a stone's throw from the bar. The brewpub's atmosphere is as inviting as the beers are diverse, making it a must-visit for enthusiasts and novices alike. **Web:** risingsonsbrewery.com/

These venues are more than just places to drink; they're community hubs where conversations flow as freely as the beer, and where the vibrancy of Ireland's craft scene is on full display.

Beer Tastings and Tours

For those looking to dive deeper into the craft beer experience, many of Ireland's breweries offer behind-the-scenes tours and tastings. These experiences provide a glimpse into the art and science of brewing, from the selection of malts and hops to the fermentation process that brings the beer to life.

- **Wicklow Wolf Brewery in Newtown Mount Kennedy** invites visitors to explore its eco-conscious brewing approach, followed by a guided tasting that highlights its range of sustainable beers. **Web:** wicklowwolf.com/
- **The White Hag Brewery in Sligo** offers an immersive tour that delves into the mythology that inspires their beers, coupled with a tasting session that's as informative as it is enjoyable. **Web:** thewhitehag.com/

These tours are a chance to meet the makers, hear their stories, and understand the passion that fuels their craft, all while sipping on the result of their hard work.

Beer Festivals

The true spirit of Ireland's craft beer scene comes alive at the many beer festivals scattered throughout the year and across the island. These festivals are a celebration of the craft, bringing together brewers, connoisseurs, and casual drinkers alike in a shared appreciation for good beer.

For an extensive guide to Ireland's food and beer festivals throughout the year check this website out: thelifeofstuff.com/food-and-drink-festivals-ireland-2024/

These festivals are a testament to the thriving craft beer community in Ireland, a place where tradition and innovation merge in the name of great beer.

Ireland's craft beer scene is lively, blending innovation with tradition and mixing local flavors with global influences. It's all about celebrating the brewers' creativity, the sense of community in pubs, and the adventure of exploring unique beers. Craft beer in Ireland tells its own story, adding a new chapter to the country's legacy of literature and rebellion, one beer at a time.

5.6 HISTORIC PUBS: DRINKING WITH GHOSTS

The walls of Ireland's most storied pubs whisper of ancient tales and ghostly presences, their foundations rooted deep in history and mystery. These pubs, guardians of Ireland's past, serve not just pints but portals to a time when legends roamed the land. Here, every creak of the floorboards and flicker of candlelight hints at stories waiting to be told, inviting patrons to sip on a bit of history with their stout.

Pubs with Stories

In the heart of these historic pubs, the air is thick with tales of yore, and each pint is served with a side of lore. Okay, maybe that's a bit much.

- **Grace Neill's in Donaghadee**, claimed to be Ireland's oldest licensed pub (There are a lot of pubs that claim to be the oldest if you didn't notice), has quenched the thirst of pirates and smugglers. The ghost of Grace herself is said to roam the bar, ensuring the hospitality she was known for in life continues in death. **Web:** graceneills.com/
- **Kyteler's Inn in Kilkenny** tells the darker tale of its original owner, Dame Alice Kyteler, accused of witchcraft in the 1300s. Patrons might come for the brews but stay for the stories of Alice's escape and the spirits left behind. **Web:** kytelersinn.com/

These pubs stand as silent witnesses to centuries of history, their stories passed down like precious heirlooms, enriching each visit with the weight of ages.

Haunted Pubs

For those drawn to the spine-tingling allure of the supernatural, Ireland's haunted pubs offer thrilling encounters with the other-worldly.

- **The Brazen Head in Dublin**, while known for its literary connections, also hosts spectral visitors from its long past. Guests have reported sightings of Robert Emmet, the Irish patriot, whose love story ended in tragedy. **Web:** brazenhead.com/
- **Durty Nelly's by the Bunratty Castle** is home to more than just traditional music. The spirit of Nelly herself is rumored to

linger, a reminder of the pub's origin as a tollhouse and her dubious methods of collecting. **Web:** durtynellys.ie/

A night spent in these pubs might offer more than just a drink; it could include a brush with the past, as the veil between worlds grows thin in the glow of the hearth.

Architectural Gems

Beyond their spectral residents, these historic pubs are also celebrated for their architectural beauty, preserving the craftsmanship of bygone eras.

- **Sean's Bar in Athlone** features wattle and wicker walls dating back to its founding, offering a glimpse into medieval construction techniques. Its sloped floors and low ceilings speak of centuries of gatherings. **Web:** seansbar.ie/
- **The Old Thatch in Killeagh** claims the title of Ireland's oldest thatched pub. Its roof, a testament to traditional building methods, shelters a space that has welcomed travelers since the 1600s. **Web:** discoverireland.ie/cork/the-old-thatch-bar

These pubs are architectural time capsules, their structures as much a part of their charm as the legends that haunt them.

Preserving Traditions

In Ireland's historic pubs, the warm glow of candlelight keeps the nation's traditions of music, storytelling, and hospitality vibrantly alive. These places are not just venues for drinks; they're where Ireland's cultural heartbeats, from haunting tales and lively traditional music to the welcoming spirit that treats every guest as a friend. It's here that the past and present merge, offering a delightful taste of Irish life and history with each pint served, making every visitor part of Ireland's ongoing story.

5.7 THE BEST LIVE MUSIC VENUES

In Ireland, you'll find a lively scene for live music, where venues buzz with the energy of performances. It's a place where melodies fill the air, offering a welcoming atmosphere for everyone. The music here bridges gaps, connecting people through shared songs. Whether it's the soft sounds of strings or the bold blast of electric guitars, these venues showcase a wide range of musical styles that make any night out vibrant and memorable. If you're traveling to Ireland and love live music, these spots are a must-visit for an enjoyable evening.

Live Music Venues

Across the Irish landscape, certain venues have etched their names in the hearts of music lovers, becoming synonymous with unforgettable nights and groundbreaking performances.

- **Vicar Street in Dublin** has solidified its reputation as the go-to spot for a wide array of musical genres. Its stage has seen everything from the soulful serenades of folk artists to the pulsating beats of rock bands, making every visit a unique auditory adventure. **Web:** vicarstreet.com/
- **The Crane Bar in Galway** offers an intimate setting where the connection between artist and audience feels almost tangible. Here, the focus is on acoustic and indie performances, providing a platform for soul-stirring music that resonates in the quiet spaces of the heart. **Web:** thecranebar.com/

Each venue, with its distinct atmosphere, invites you to lose yourself in the music, to let the melodies carry you away to a place where only the song exists.

Up-and-Coming Bands

Ireland's music scene thrives not just on its established acts but on the fresh energy of emerging talents who bring new sounds to the stage. Venues across the country play a crucial role in showcasing these burgeoning artists, offering them a spotlight to shine.

- **Whelan's in Dublin** is revered as the cradle of new talent, its stage a steppingstone for artists on the brink of their breakthrough. Bands and singers who grace its space often find themselves on the cusp of national, if not international, acclaim. **Web:** whelanslive.com/
- **Connolly's of Leap in West Cork,** with its quirky charm and welcoming vibe, has become a haven for indie bands and musicians. It's a place where the unexpected becomes the norm, and every performance is a chance to discover your next musical obsession. **Web:** connollysofleap.com/

These venues serve as landmarks that bring together artists and audiences to celebrate the latest in music.

Iconic Concerts

Over the years, certain performances have transcended the ordinary, becoming etched in the memory of venues and the hearts of those who witnessed them. These iconic concerts are a testament to the power of live music to create moments of transcendence.

- **U2 at Slane Castle** became more than just a concert; it was a cultural phenomenon, a gathering that showcased the band's undeniable connection to their Irish roots, set against the backdrop of the historic castle. If you're a U2 fan check this out for sure! **Web:** slanecastle.ie/concerts/
- **Sinéad O'Connor at The Olympia Theatre** offered an evening of raw emotion and incredible talent, reminding

everyone in attendance of her impact on the music scene, both in Ireland and beyond. **Web:** 3olympia.ie/

These performances, among countless others, have contributed to the lore of the venues, making them pilgrimage sites for music lovers seeking to connect with the echoes of the past.

Music Festivals

Ireland's calendar is also dotted with music festivals that transform historic and unique venues into stages for unforgettable live performances. These festivals not only highlight the depth of talent within the country but also draw artists from around the globe.

- **Electric Picnic in Stradbally** melds the charm of the Irish countryside with a lineup that spans genres and generations. The estate becomes a living, breathing entity, pulsating with beats and melodies that echo through the trees. **Web:** electricpicnic.ie/
- **Other Voices in Dingle** turns the picturesque town into a nexus of musical innovation. Intimate gigs in St. James' Church and impromptu sessions in local pubs capture the essence of connectivity that lies at the heart of music. **Web:** othervoices.ie/

In Ireland, festivals offer a dynamic mix of music and scenery, turning into lively music scenes as the evening sets in. These events are more than just performances; they're opportunities to create lasting memories and experience music history in the making. Night after night, each song and performance adds to a collective experience that captures the vibrant essence of Irish nightlife.

5.8 NIGHT TOURS: GHOSTS AND LEGENDS

When the sun dips below the horizon, and shadows stretch across the cobblestones, Ireland transforms. The night air, charged with mystery, invites the brave and the curious to explore its darker side. Here, ghost tours and nighttime explorations of haunted castles are not merely about the thrill; they're an homage to a land where history and folklore are intertwined, where every ancient stone and whispering wind might hold a story.

Ghost Tours

The allure of uncovering the mysteries that lurk in the shadows draws many to the ghost tours peppered across Ireland. These are not your average strolls; they are immersive experiences that weave together the historical and the supernatural, making the past feel startlingly present. Not for the faint-hearted or those with a heart condition. Ha!

- In Dublin, the cobblestone streets come alive on the **Dublin Ghost Bus Tour**, a journey that takes you through the city's most haunted spots, from eerie graveyards to abandoned buildings, all while a guide recounts tales of the macabre. **Web:** ghostbus.ie/
- **Cork Ghost Tour** brings a lighter touch to its tales of the paranormal. Guides blend humor with horror as they lead you through the winding streets, revealing the city's ghostly inhabitants and their spine-tingling stories. **Web:** corkghosttour.ie/

These tours offer a unique lens through which to view the city, one shrouded in darkness and mystery, where every corner holds a story, waiting to be told. For those looking for an otherworldly adventure and don't mind some spine-tingling surprises, these tours are for you!

Haunted Castles and Buildings

The ancient castles and historic buildings of Ireland are not just monuments to the past; they are keepers of secrets, many believed to be home to spirits from centuries gone by. Night tours of these haunted locales invite the daring to step into a world where history meets the supernatural.

- **Leap Castle in County Offaly**, known as Ireland's, most haunted castle, opens its doors to those wishing to encounter its infamous spirits, including the malevolent Elemental. The castle's chilling atmosphere is enhanced by the tales of its bloody past, recounted by the current owner. **Web:** leapcastle.net/
- **Charleville Castle**, also in County Offaly, offers night tours that explore its Gothic architecture and resident ghosts. The stories of playful spirits and tragic deaths add layers to the experience, making the castle's beauty even more haunting in the moonlight. **Web:** charlevillecastle.ie/

Exploring these ancient structures at night, when the shadows deepen and the past feels close enough to touch, is an unforgettable experience. It is a journey through time and into the heart of Ireland's ghostly legends.

Storytelling Traditions

The essence of Ireland's night tours lies in storytelling, a vital tradition where guides skillfully mix history with folklore, bringing to life stories of ghosts and legends handed down over time. Their storytelling talent lies in making the past feel immediate and vividly drawing listeners into the narratives, offering both entertainment and the occasional chill. These narrated tales, set against the backdrop of a moonlit night, aim not only to spook but also to keep Ireland's rich folklore and history alive, linking the past with the present.

Family-Friendly Options

For those traveling with younger adventurers, Ireland offers ghost tours that capture the imagination without causing nightmares or heart attacks. These tours are crafted to be spooky yet suitable for all ages, ensuring that the experience is enjoyable for everyone.

- **The Ghosts of Kilkenny Tour** balances the eerie with the educational, making it a hit with families. The guides, with their knack for storytelling, engage audiences of all ages, ensuring that the tales of ghosts are more fascinating than frightening. **Web:** kilkennyghosttours.com/
- **Belfast's Ghost Walk** takes a similar approach, offering a family-friendly route through the city's haunted spots. The stories, while full of mystery, are told with a light touch, captivating children, and adults alike. **Web:** ghostwalkbelfast.com

These tours offer a way to see Ireland's scarier side, making it fun for all ages. They show that everyone loves a good ghost story, enjoying the mystery and the supernatural together. On these tours, through dim streets and old castles, you'll hear about Ireland's ghosts and legends. It's a chance to dive into the night and be captivated by stories from the dark side of Ireland's history, where the real thrill of these tales comes to life.

5.9 LATE-NIGHT EATERIES AND STREET FOOD

After a night of music or storytelling in a pub, Ireland's streets come alive with the promise of delicious food. This is when a different magic happens, catering to late-night hunger with a variety of flavors. As we explore the late-night food scene, we find a showcase of Ireland's diverse tastes and culture through its eateries and street food, offering something for everyone.

After-Hours Dining

The night owls and the merrymakers need not worry about where their next meal will come from. A constellation of late-night eateries lights up the Irish nightscape, offering everything from piping hot fish and chips wrapped in paper to gourmet burgers that demand both hands and full attention.

- **Eddie Rocket's in Dublin** (I wonder if he's related to Johnny Rocket), a diner that seems to borrow from a time when rock 'n' roll ruled the airwaves. It serves American-style burgers and shakes until the wee hours. **Web:** eddierockets.ie/
- **Zaytoon in Dublin**, known for its mouth-watering Persian dishes, becomes a sanctuary for those seeking sustenance with a side of spice. Their kebabs have achieved almost legendary status among Dublin's night revelers. **Web:** zaytoon.ie/

These spots, and many like them, provide not just food but a place to relax, to reflect on the night's escapades, and to share in the universal joy of a meal enjoyed together.

Diverse Cuisine

Gone are the days when late-night food meant choosing between a kebab and a slice of pizza. Now, the night markets and eateries of Ireland boast a culinary diversity that mirrors the nation's changing demographics and evolving tastes.

- **My Goodness in Cork City** offers vegan delights that dazzle the palate, proving that late-night food can be both nutritious and delicious. **Web:** mygoodnessfood.com/
- **Boojum** captures the flavors of Mexico, serving burritos and tacos as vibrant and colorful as the streets of Guadalajara. Its food satisfies cravings for something fresh and full of zest. Their guacamole is to die for. **Web:** boojummex.com/

This diversity in late-night dining options is a nod to Ireland's growing multiculturalism. It is a delicious mélange of flavors from around the globe, each adding its unique note to the country's culinary palate.

Food Trucks

As the moon climbs high and the night progresses, food trucks light up, drawing in those looking for a late meal. These trucks have become key to Ireland's culinary landscape, serving up creative dishes that add an interesting twist to the night.

- **The Big Blue Bus**, parked at the back of The Bernard Shaw in Dublin, serves pizzas with toppings ranging from the classic to the creative, all cooked in a wood-fired oven that's as quirky as the bus itself. **Web:** facebook.com/thebigbluebus/
- **Julia's Lobster Truck in Galway** brings the taste of the sea to the streets, serving lobster rolls that are a symphony of flavor, each bite a reminder of Ireland's rich seafood heritage. **Web:** instagram.com/juliaslobstertruck/

These trucks, with their ever-changing locations and menus, add an element of serendipity to the night, turning the search for food into an adventure all its own.

Cultural Melting Pot

Ireland's late-night food scene is an exciting blend of tradition and innovation, showcasing how classic Irish flavors merge with international influences to shape a modern culinary identity. International dishes have expanded local palates and fostered a deeper appreciation for culinary diversity. Food festivals and events throughout the year spotlight this range, offering everything from traditional Irish fare to contemporary global dishes. The evolving scene is particularly evident in street food stalls and night eateries, which celebrate Ireland's cultural and culinary diversity. For foodies, an evening out in Ireland is a chance to enjoy a rich mix of tastes in a welcoming atmosphere.

BEYOND THE BEATEN PATH

Picture this: You're wandering through an Irish landscape so lush, it's like something straight out of a fantasy novel. But here's the twist - you're miles away from the usual tourist spots, surrounded by the kind of raw beauty that few travelers get to witness. That's the heart of this chapter; it's about those secret corners of Ireland that are whispered about like folklore but are as real as the ground under your feet.

We're not just talking about avoiding the crowds. It's about connecting more deeply with Ireland's soul by exploring places that even some locals hold sacred. These are the spots where you can hear the whisper of the past in the wind and see the untamed beauty of the land stretch out before you. Let's peel back the veil on Ireland's best-kept secrets.

6.1 UNCOVERING IRELAND'S BEST-KEPT SECRETS

Exclusive Locales

You might think you've seen all Ireland has to offer, but there are still pockets of untouched beauty that remain under the radar. Take, for example, the **Beara Peninsula**. While the Ring of Kerry gets all the limelight, Beara offers a tranquility and beauty that can make you feel like you've stepped into a world forgotten by time. **The Healy Pass** alone, with its winding road through rugged mountains, offers views that can rival any postcard picture of Ireland you've ever seen.

Web:

- bearatourism.com/
- discoverireland.ie/cork/the-healy-pass

Personal Stories

Talk to a local in a quiet pub in Clonakilty or a café in Kenmare, and you might hear about the time they stumbled upon a **hidden beach along the Copper Coast**, a stretch less frequented but no less stunning than the Cliffs of Moher. Or they might share tales of **Lough Hyne, a saltwater lake near Skibbereen known for its bioluminescence** - a magical night swim surrounded by glowing water. Incidentally, I didn't do this here but did do it in Puerto Rico. I highly recommend it. It's truly magical. Check the weather for overcast skies, as they allow for the best viewing.

Web:

- visitwaterford.com/copper-coast-greenway-mahon-falls/
- thewildatlanticway.com/sight/lough-hyne/

Travel Tips

Respect goes a long way. These spots are cherished not just for their beauty but for their serenity. When you visit, leave no trace. Stick to paths, take your rubbish with you, and keep the noise down. It's about preserving the magic for the next wanderer. For places like the **Sliabh Liag cliffs**, higher and less crowded than Moher, check the weather beforehand. The best views come on clear days.

Web:

- sliabhliag.com/

Cultural Insights

Understanding the stories behind these hidden gems adds layers to your experience. Before you set off for the **Grianan of Aileach, a hilltop fort in Donegal**, read up on its history as a seat of power dating back to 1700 BC. Knowing its past makes standing within its ancient walls feel like stepping back in time.

Web:

- discoverireland.ie/donegal/grianan-of-aileach

Interactive Maps: You can find an interactive curated map highlighting Ireland's hidden gems compliments of Google Maps here: **World of Wunder's Map of Ireland's Hidden Gems**: https://qrco.de/bf79eG .

To ensure these places are around for everyone to enjoy in the future, here's a checklist of tips for responsible exploration. Tick them off as you prepare for your adventure to ensure you leave these places as beautiful as you found them.

1. Respect the Environment:

- Leave no trace: Pack out all trash and litter.
- Stay on designated trails to avoid damaging fragile ecosystems.
- Follow any posted guidelines or regulations for conservation areas.

2. Support Local Communities:

- Patronize local businesses, accommodations, and eateries to contribute positively to the local economy.
- Respect local customs and traditions and engage with locals in a friendly and respectful manner.

3. Learn About the Area:

- Research the history, culture, and natural features of the places you plan to visit.
- Take guided tours led by knowledgeable locals to gain deeper insights into the area.

4. Practice Responsible Photography:

- Avoid trampling vegetation or disturbing wildlife to get the perfect shot.
- Use a telephoto lens to capture distant wildlife instead of approaching too closely.

5. Minimize Your Impact:

- Use public transportation, walk, or bike whenever possible to reduce your carbon footprint.
- Choose eco-friendly accommodations and activities that prioritize sustainability.

6. Be Prepared:

- Check the weather forecast and dress accordingly.
- Carry a map, GPS device, or mobile phone with offline maps in case you get lost.

7. Leave Wildlife Alone:

- Observe wildlife from a safe distance and avoid feeding or touching them.
- Keep noise levels down to avoid disturbing animals.

8. Practice Water Safety:

- Obey warning signs and advisories at beaches, lakes, and rivers.
- Only swim in designated swimming areas and follow any safety instructions provided.

9. Leave Cultural Heritage Untouched:

- Avoid climbing or touching historical structures, monuments, or ancient ruins.
- Refrain from removing any artifacts or souvenirs from archaeological sites.

10. Be Mindful of Noise:

- Keep noise levels down, especially in natural areas, to avoid disrupting wildlife and other visitors.
- Respect quiet zones or designated areas for meditation or reflection.

Aerial View of Beach in Dogs Bay, Connemara, Galway

These less-traveled paths invite you not just to see, but to engage with Ireland in a way that's deeply personal and utterly unforgettable. They're a reminder that sometimes, the true essence of a place lies beyond the well-marked roads, waiting quietly for those willing to look a little closer. So, dare to take the road less traveled!

6.2 ANCIENT SITES AND RUINS RARELY VISITED

Ireland, a tapestry woven with threads of history and myth, is dotted with ancient sites that whisper tales of a time long past. Beyond the famed ruins that gather crowds, hidden relics shrouded in mystery lie waiting for the keen explorer to uncover their stories. These sites, set against the backdrop of Ireland's breathtaking landscapes, offer a glimpse into the island's rich and tumultuous history.

Historical Mysteries

Each stone and artifact found in Ireland's less visited ancient ruins holds a piece of a puzzle stretching back thousands of years. From the early **Neolithic tombs hidden in the lush valleys of the Wicklow Mountains** to the **forgotten ring forts that dot the western coastline**, these sites are chapters of history left open, inviting you to ponder the lives of those who came before. For instance, the **Carrowmore Megalithic Cemetery in Sligo**, one of the oldest such sites in Ireland, contains dolmens and passage tombs that predate even the Pyramids of Egypt, yet it remains a tranquil spot, often missed by those sticking to the main tourist trails.

Web:

- atlasobscura.com/places/seefin-passage-tomb-2
- dublinevents.com/ring-forts/
- heritageireland.ie/visit/places-to-visit/carrowmore-megalithic-cemetery/

Accessibility Information

Discovering ancient treasures, often found off the beaten path, is part of the adventure. Some sites require effort to reach but offer scenic landscapes. Detailed maps and local guides provide insights into the best times to visit. Check with the tourism office or your hotel for maps and tours beforehand.

Planning is key for the more remote sites, such as the early Christian monastic site on Skellig Michael, off the Kerry coast. You may recognize the site as where they filmed the famous Star Wars scene in the "Force Awakens." The island is accessible only by boat, and weather conditions can affect crossings. Booking a spot on a guided tour not only ensures safe passage but also enriches the experience with local knowledge.

Web:

- theringofkerry.com/skellig-michael#

Preservation Efforts

The preservation of these ancient sites is a delicate balance, allowing access while protecting them for future generations. As visitors, embracing a mindful approach ensures these historical treasures continue to tell their stories. Simple acts, like sticking to marked paths, not moving any stones, and avoiding leaving any litter, contribute significantly to preservation efforts. Many of these sites, such as the **beehive huts on the Dingle Peninsula**, are part of Ireland's national heritage, and local organizations work tirelessly to maintain them. Supporting these efforts, whether through donations or volunteering, helps ensure these sites remain part of Ireland's cultural landscape.

Web:

- discoverireland.ie/kerry/fahan-beehive-huts

Guided Tours

Embarking on a guided tour of these less-visited ruins not only brings the site's history to life but also supports local historians and archaeologists. Experts in the field can unravel the site's mysteries, offering insights into its archaeological significance, historical context, and intriguing folklore.

In the Boyne Valley, lesser known than its famous neighbor, Newgrange, sites like the **Dowth passage tomb** offer a more intimate glimpse into Ireland's ancient past. Here, guided tours can illuminate the astronomical alignment of the tombs and the significance of the carvings found within.

Web:

- newgrange.com/dowth.htm

On the Aran Islands, a guided tour of the lesser-visited **Dun Duchathair (the Black Fort)** reveals the ingenuity of its Iron Age builders, set against the dramatic backdrop of the Atlantic.

Web:

- aranislands.ie/inis-mor-inishmore-island/inis-mor-island-churches-celtic-sites/dun-duchathair-the-black-fort

Ireland is steeped in history and boasts numerous ancient sites that are must-see. Here are ten of the top ancient sites across the Emerald Isle:

1. **Newgrange** - A prehistoric monument in County Meath, Newgrange is older than Stonehenge and the Egyptian pyramids. It's famous for the winter solstice illumination of its passage and chamber.
2. **Skellig Michael** - This remote island off the coast of Kerry features a well-preserved monastic outpost of the early Christian period, which is also a UNESCO World Heritage site.
3. **Hill of Tara** - Once the ancient seat of power in Ireland, where the High Kings were inaugurated, the Hill of Tara is in County Meath and is rich with archaeological monuments.
4. **The Rock of Cashel** - Also known as St. Patrick's Rock, it's a historic site in Tipperary that was the seat of the kings of Munster and includes a collection of medieval ecclesiastical buildings.
5. **Brú na Bóinne** —This area is one of the world's most significant archaeological landscapes, and it is a landscape of

prehistoric monuments, including the famous passage tombs of Newgrange, Knowth, and Dowth.

6. **Glendalough** - Founded in the 6th century by St. Kevin, this site in County Wicklow includes an impressive monastic settlement with ancient churches and a round tower.

7. **The Burren** - Known for its unique karst landscape, The Burren in County Clare is also home to ancient megalithic tombs and historical sites like the Poulnabrone dolmen.

8. **Dún Aonghasa** - A dramatic prehistoric fort on the Aran Islands, Dún Aonghasa is perched on a cliff overlooking the Atlantic Ocean, providing breathtaking views.

9. **Clonmacnoise**—An early Christian site founded by St. Ciarán in the mid-6th century on the banks of the River Shannon, Clonmacnoise features a collection of medieval church buildings, high crosses, and round towers.

10. **Loughcrew Cairns** - Near Oldcastle, County Meath, this lesser-known but fascinating group of Neolithic passage tombs is known as "the Hills of the Witch."

These sites are important historically and are set in some of Ireland's most picturesque landscapes. They offer both a glimpse into ancient times and a chance to enjoy the country's natural beauty.

Digital Map: To make finding these historical sites easier, here's an interactive digital map showcasing Ireland's lesser-known ancient sites, complete with links to websites, visitor information, and other useful information for your exploration: **World of Wunder's Map of Ireland's Historic Sites:** https://qrco.de/behFrn.

Here's a list of local heritage organizations and guides offering tours of these hidden historical sites, ensuring visitors can find trusted experts to enhance their journey.

- **Heritage Island:** A network of visitor attractions across Ireland, including historical sites, museums, and cultural experiences. **Web:** heritageisland.com
- **Archaeological Institute of Ireland:** Offers guided tours and lectures on archaeological sites and heritage conservation. **Web:** archaeology.ie
- **National Trust for Ireland:** This organization manages and conserves historic buildings, monuments, and landscapes across Ireland and offers guided tours and events. **Web:** nationaltrust.ie
- **Hidden Ireland Tours:** Specializes in small-group tours to lesser-known historical sites, led by experienced guides. **Web:** hiddenirelandtours.com
- **Ancient East Tours:** Provides guided tours of ancient sites and historical landmarks in Ireland's Ancient East region. **Web:** ancienteasttours.com
- **Boyne Valley Tours:** This company offers guided tours of the Boyne Valley, home to many ancient monuments and historical sites. **Web:** boynevalleytours.com
- **Irish Landmark Trust:** This organization provides accommodation in historic buildings across Ireland, some of which offer guided tours to guests. **Web:** irishlandmark.com
- **Local Tourist Information Offices:** Many towns and regions in Ireland have tourist information offices that can provide maps, guides, and recommendations for exploring hidden historical sites in the area. **Web:** varies by location, search online for specific town or region tourist information.

These organizations and guides offer valuable expertise and insights to enhance visitors' journeys, ensuring they can discover and appreciate Ireland's hidden historical treasures with confidence.

To make your trip even more memorable, here are some other unforgettable spots off the beaten path:

1. **Gleninchaquin Park**, County Kerry—This park is known for its awe-inspiring landscapes and tranquil setting, perfect for hiking and picnicking. Secret Garden Glamping offers great overnight accommodation.

2. **The Burren**, County Clare—This lunar-like landscape features ancient tombs and unique flora among its limestone rocks.

3. **Coumshingaun Lough**, County Waterford - A heart-shaped glacial lake nestled in the Comeragh Mountains, offering stunning views and a serene hiking experience.

4. **Glenevin Waterfall**, County Donegal - A picturesque waterfall that cascades over moss-covered rocks, creating a fairy tale setting.

5. **Murlough Bay**, County Antrim—This quiet bay with golden sands and clear waters is surrounded by storied landscapes.

6. **The Cuilcagh Legnabrocky Trail**, County Fermanagh - Known as the "Stairway to Heaven," this trail offers breathtaking views across a unique boardwalk path.

7. **The Swiss Cottage**, County Tipperary—This early 19th-century cottage is known for its unique architecture and historical significance.

8. **Carrick-A-Rede Rope Bridge**, County Antrim - Offers thrilling walks across a rope bridge with stunning ocean views, popular among adventure seekers.

9. **The Coral Strand**, County Galway—This beach is known for its unique red coralline algae, which provides a different kind of beach experience.

10. **Leap Castle**, County Offaly - Claimed to be Ireland's most haunted castle, it offers a mix of thrilling ghostly tales and historical intrigue.

Carrick-a-Rede Rope Bridge, Northern Ireland

These trips to Ireland's ancient and off-the-beaten-path sites offer more than just a look at historic artifacts and amazing scenery; they're a deep dive into the nation's essence, enriched by the narratives and insights provided by those who know these places best.

For guided tours that explore off-the-beaten-path locations in Ireland, several resources can help you find the perfect experience:

- **Ireland.com** offers a range of tours that bring you to less-touristed areas of Ireland, providing a more intimate and immersive experience. These tours can include visits to ancient sites, scenic drives, and local storytelling.

- **Overland Ireland Tours** specializes in tours that include Ireland's lesser-known attractions. They offer itineraries such as the "Ireland to Island" tour, which features a visit to the Skellig Islands, a UNESCO World Heritage site known for its natural beauty and historical significance . overlandirelandtours.com
- **The Little Family Adventure** site suggests a 7-day itinerary that covers both popular spots and hidden gems, ideal for families looking to explore Ireland's countryside and cultural landmarks. littlefamilyadventure.com/off-the-beaten-path-ireland-7-day-itinerary-family-adventure-seekers/

These sources offer various options that cater to different interests, whether you're looking for rugged landscapes, historical insights, or a family-friendly adventure. Each provides unique ways to discover the rich heritage and natural beauty of Ireland away from the typical tourist paths.

6.3 LOCAL FESTIVALS: CELEBRATING WITH THE COMMUNITY

In the heart of Ireland, local festivals are central to community life. These events, whether large or small, bring the towns and villages to life with laughter, music, and socializing. They're not just gatherings; they embody Ireland's strong sense of community and celebrate the unique character of each place. If you want to experience Ireland like a local, you should check out one of these festivals.

Community Spirit

In Ireland, as we said before many times, festivals are key parts of local life, showcasing traditions and talents in cities and rural areas alike. For example, in a small village, you might find everyone celebrating the "Spud Fest," which honors the potato's significant role in Irish history. In another town, you could experience the

Lisdoonvarna Matchmaking Festival, where locals and visitors alike revel in festivities centered around finding love. These events are more than just fun; they're a celebration of community and heritage, bringing people together to enjoy shared traditions and make new memories.

Participation Guidelines

Diving into these communal festivities is a joy, but doing so with respect and openness elevates the experience. Here's how you can immerse yourself meaningfully:

- **Observe First:** Take your cue from the locals. Some moments might invite participation, while others are best appreciated as a spectator.
- **Respect Traditions:** Each festival is steeped in tradition. Whether it's a quiet ritual or a boisterous parade, showing respect is key.
- **Engage Genuinely:** Conversations with locals can enrich your understanding and enjoyment of the festival. Ask questions, share stories, and you'll find the exchange rewarding.
- **Contribute Positively:** Your positive impact enhances the communal spirit by supporting local vendors, helping with setup, or simply keeping the space clean.

Festival Calendar

Mark your calendars! Ireland's local festival scene is bustling, with hidden gems scattered throughout the year. Here's a glimpse:

- **March: Dingle International Film Festival** – A quaint yet highly acclaimed festival in a town known for its cinematic landscapes. **Web:** dinglefilmfest.com/
- **May: Baltimore Fiddle Fair**, West Cork – An intimate

202 | DISCOVERING IRELAND

gathering celebrating traditional and contemporary fiddle music. **Web:** fiddlefair.com
- **July: Willie Clancy Summer School**, County Clare – A week-long celebration of traditional Irish music and dance. **Web:** scoilsamhraidhwillieclancy.com/
- **September: Galway Oyster Festival**—This world-renowned festival heralds the beginning of the oyster season with great fanfare. **Web**: galwayoysterfestival.com/
- **October: Baboró International Arts Festival for Children**, Galway—a creative explosion of theatre, dance, and visual arts for the young and young at heart. **Web:** baboro.ie/

Look for local posters and community boards for the many more festivals that pop up spontaneously or are too quaint to make it onto the mainstream radar.

Cultural Exchange

Local festivals foster cultural exchange, showcasing heritage and inviting immersion in Irish culture. Participation in céilí dances, learning Gaelic, and sharing stories enriches cultural understanding. These interactions showcase Ireland's community spirit, inviting active participation. As the festival ends, many memories of shared dances and stories linger, reflecting Ireland's timeless spirit.

6.4 THE WILD ATLANTIC WAY: HIDDEN STOPS

Navigating the rugged beauty of the Wild Atlantic Way, a journey that stretches over 2,500 kilometers along Ireland's west coast, is akin to unwrapping an endless gift. It's like hitting the jackpot of scenic beauty. Each bend in the road unveils panoramas that leave you breathless, yet it's the stops less known, those secret spots whispered about in the local lore, that truly capture the essence of this wild, enchanting route.

Scenic Gems

Tucked away from the main traveler's path, these hidden gems invite you for moments of solitude and awe:

- **Mullaghmore Head**, County Sligo, offers a dramatic landscape where the power of the Atlantic meets sheer cliffs. The sea's roar is a constant companion here, and on a stormy day, the waves put on a spectacular display. **Web:** discoverireland.ie/sligo/mullaghmore-head
- **Silver Strand Beach in Malin Beg**, County Donegal, accessible via a winding staircase, is a secluded crescent of white sand embraced by cliffs. The journey down feels like stepping into a secret world, where the only sounds are the waves and the call of seabirds. **Web:** thewildatlanticway.com/sight/malin-beg/

Local Lore

Each hidden stop along the Wild Atlantic Way is steeped in stories, adding layers of mystique to the already captivating scenery:

- **The Poisoned Glen**, nestled at the foot of Mount Errigal in Donegal, carries with it tales of ancient battles between gods and mortals. The name itself is a mistranslation; the original Irish 'Gleann Nemhe' means 'Heavenly Glen', which is far more fitting once you've seen its beauty. **Web:** go-to-ireland.com/what-to-see/the-poisoned-glen/
- **The Vanishing Lake of Loughareema** in County Antrim appears and disappears with the rains, shrouded in legends of a ghostly carriage submerged within its depths. Locals will tell you on misty mornings; you can still hear the horses' hooves. **Web:** discovernorthernireland.com/things-to-do/loughareema-the-vanishing-lake-p710151

Activity Recommendations

Exploring these off-the-beaten-path stops isn't just about what you see; it's about what you do and how you connect with the landscape:

- **Near Keem Bay on Achill Island**, take a short hike up to the old coastguard watchhouse. The view from the top, overlooking one of the most beautiful beaches in Ireland, is unparalleled. **Web:** thewildatlanticway.com/sight/keem-strand/
- After visiting **The Sky Road in Clifden**, County Galway, stop by the town's local artisan shops for a taste of Connemara or a cozy meal in one of the family-run pubs, where the seafood is as fresh as the ocean air. **Web:** thewildatlanticway.-com/sight/sky-road/

Traveler Reflections

Hearing from those who've wandered these paths before adds a personal touch, turning these hidden stops into shared secrets:

- A couple from Australia shared, "At **Gleniff Horseshoe**, we felt like we'd stepped into a Tolkien novel. The sheer scale of the cliffs and the silence, broken only by the wind, was something we'll never forget. It was as if we'd found our piece of Middle Earth."
- A solo traveler recounted, "Finding **Stroove Lighthouse** was unexpected. I was driving without a destination in mind when I saw the sign. Walking up to the lighthouse, with nothing but the sea in front and the sound of the waves, it was a moment of pure peace. I sat there for hours, just taking it all in."

Exploring off-the-beaten-path stops along the **Wild Atlantic Way** offers more than scenic beauty—it's a chance to connect deeply with Ireland. Hidden gems reveal the essence of the Emerald Isle, each with its own story. Engaging with locals enriches your journey, leading to unique discoveries and personal insights that transform views into memorable experiences.

6.5 IRELAND'S ISLANDS: REMOTE BEAUTY

Ireland's offshore islands offer a unique experience, each with its unique character and set against the backdrop of the Atlantic Ocean. These islands are more than just land; they're places steeped in stories and traditions, where life follows the rhythm of the sea. Visiting these islands gives you a chance to escape the modern world, immerse yourself in nature, and experience a way of life that intertwines closely with tradition and the natural environment. Talking with locals can enrich your visit, as their stories and insights provide a deeper connection to the island's history and way of life.

Island Life

On islands like **Inishmore in the Aran Islands** and **Cape Clear off the coast of Cork**, life is deeply connected to tradition. These places are strongholds of the Irish language, spoken daily against a backdrop of striking natural scenery, including cliffs weathered by the Atlantic and calm bays where seals sunbathe. More than just their natural beauty, it's the cultural heritage—ancient forts, local pubs with lively storytelling, and traditions maintained by close-knit communities—that makes these islands special. Each one also features a distinct mix of plants and animals, adding to their unique charm.

Transportation Tips

Reaching these remote beauties is part of the adventure. Ferries are the lifelines, connecting the mainland to the islands' rugged shores. Schedules can be as unpredictable as the weather, with services affected by the whims of the Atlantic:

- Always check the ferry timetable in advance, as times can vary with the seasons. Many services offer online booking, ensuring you've got a spot, especially during the busier summer months.
- Consider the weather forecast. The seas can turn quickly, and ferries may be canceled with short notice. Always have a Plan B for accommodation on the mainland in case you're stranded.
- Travel light, but smart. Space on the ferries can be limited, and you'll want to move easily. However, don't forget waterproof gear and layers—the islands' weather can change in the blink of an eye.

Accommodation Options

Staying on an Irish island is an invitation to slow down and soak in the tranquility. We recommend doing it at least once on your journey. Accommodations range from cozy to rustic, mirroring the islands' embrace of simplicity:

- Guesthouses and B&Bs offer a warm, personal touch to your stay. Many are family-run, providing not just a bed but a hearty breakfast and local insights.
- For a more immersive experience, self-catering cottages allow you to settle into island life at your own pace, making temporary homes in whitewashed cottages with views that stretch to the horizon.
- Camping under the stars brings you even closer to the elemental beauty of these lands. Designated sites ensure harmony with nature while respecting delicate ecosystems.

Conservation Efforts

The preservation of the islands' natural and cultural landscapes is a collective endeavor, embraced by both locals and visitors. The raw beauty of these islands, from the undisturbed habitats of seabird colonies to the wildflower-strewn meadows, is a treasure that demands respect:

Leave No Trace is more than a guideline; it's a philosophy. Stick to marked paths, take all rubbish with you, and refrain from disturbing wildlife.

Many islands have conservation programs that visitors can support, either through donations or, in some cases, volunteering. These initiatives range from protecting native species to maintaining walking trails.

Educate yourself about the islands before you visit. Understanding the sensitivity of these ecosystems and the importance of preserving traditional ways of life will enrich your experience and ensure that your visit contributes positively to the islands' legacy.

Visiting the remote islands off Ireland's coast is like stepping into a world where history, culture, and natural beauty blend. These islands are as captivating as any mainland attraction, with the echoes of the past mingling with the calls of seabirds and the ever-present sound of the Atlantic. They offer more than just a break from the usual; they provide a chance to reconnect with nature and experience a slower pace of life that can rejuvenate the mind and spirit.

6.6 ADVENTURE SPORTS IN UNTOUCHED NATURE

Ireland is much more than just beautiful scenery; it's an invitation to engage with nature actively. You can feel the wind, experience the heights, and enjoy the excitement of discovery through adventure sports. From climbing its rugged mountains to surfing the waves along its coasts, Ireland offers a variety of activities for those eager to challenge themselves and explore the wild. Adrenaline junkies get your fix!

Surfers at Donegal's Famous Surf Beach, Tullan Strand (You may have to squint to see the surfers)

Diverse Offerings

In the embrace of Ireland's untouched landscapes, adventure sports find a natural home. The variety is as vast as the terrain itself:

- **Mountain Biking trails** weave through ancient forests and over rolling hills, offering heart-pounding descents and scenic routes for riders of all levels. **The Ballyhoura Mountain Trails** in County Limerick provide a network that's a favorite among enthusiasts.
- **Paragliding over the Cliffs of Moher** offers a bird's eye view of the land's end, where the island dramatically meets the Atlantic. It's an experience that combines serene gliding with exhilarating heights.
- **Kayaking along the coastline** or through the serene lakes of Connemara puts you at the water's level, close enough to touch the heart of Ireland's natural beauty. The chance to paddle through sea caves or alongside seals adds to the allure.
- **Rock Climbing in the Gap of Dunloe or Dalkey Quarry**

challenges you to conquer Ireland's rugged cliffs, rewarding your efforts with views that stretch to eternity.

- **Surfing** may not be the first sport that comes to mind when thinking of Ireland, but the **waves off the coast of Donegal and Sligo** are a siren call to surfers, offering some of the best breaks in Europe.

A Man Kayaks Along Irish Coast

Safety First

With adventure comes the responsibility of safety. It's essential to approach these sports with respect for the forces of nature they engage with:

- Opting for reputable adventure sports providers is key. These experts know the best spots and the safest routes and techniques.
- The importance of wearing appropriate safety gear cannot be

overstated. Helmets for biking and climbing, life jackets for water sports, and harnesses for climbing are non-negotiable.
- Checking weather conditions before heading out ensures you don't find yourself caught in a sudden storm or high winds, which can be especially dangerous in open waters or on high cliffs.

Environmental Impact

Engaging with nature's untouched beauty means we play a part in preserving it for future adventurers:

- **Stick to marked trails and paths** to avoid disturbing local flora and fauna. Ireland's wilderness is home to ecosystems that are as fragile as they are beautiful.
- **Carry in, carry out applies** to everything from snack wrappers to water bottles. Leaving no trace ensures the landscapes remain pristine.
- **Respect wildlife** by keeping a safe distance. Ireland's natural inhabitants, from the puffins nesting on cliff faces to the deer roaming the forests, are best observed without interference.

Personal Growth

The true beauty of adventure sports lies not in the adrenaline rush but in the transformation, they can inspire within us:

- Stepping out of your comfort zone, whether it's catching your first wave or reaching the top of a climb, builds confidence that translates to all areas of life.
- The resilience required to push through challenges, to get back on the bike after a fall, or to keep paddling against the current, fosters a strength of spirit that's invaluable.
- These activities deepen one's connection to the natural world. Feeling the raw power of the wind or the steady push of a

river current can change one's perception of the planet and one's place within it.

- Facing fears and overcoming obstacles can bring a sense of accomplishment. It reminds us that boundaries are often more mental than physical.

Participating in adventure sports in Ireland's untouched landscapes offers more than excitement; it's a chance to discover the natural world and your capabilities. These experiences provide a unique perspective of Ireland, where its wild landscapes serve as the backdrop for personal stories of challenge, achievement, and change.

6.7 CRAFT WORKSHOPS WITH LOCAL ARTISANS

In Ireland, the vibrant culture and tradition are deeply linked to a variety of crafts, each with historical significance and maintained by local artisans. These crafts are more than hobbies; they represent a living piece of Ireland's heritage, connecting the past with the future. Getting involved with these traditions is not just educational; it's a way to connect deeply with Irish culture and add your own experiences to its ongoing story.

Hands-on Learning

Imagine sitting in a workshop, surrounded by the smell of wood shavings or wet clay. Here, under the guidance of an experienced craftsman, you get to try your hand at creating traditional crafts. This is what hands-on learning looks like across Ireland, where visitors are encouraged to participate, not just observe. From Donegal's rugged coasts to Cork's lush valleys, various workshops welcome you to engage directly with traditional Irish crafts.

In County Galway, you might find yourself at a basket-weaving workshop, manipulating willow rods into intricate designs, feeling a connection to an ancient craft with every bend and weave of the material.

Meanwhile, in a Kerry pottery studio, the steady whir of a pottery wheel accompanies your efforts as you mold clay. Here, guided by a local potter, you shape vessels that not only bear the marks of your personal touch but also reflect the centuries-old tradition of Irish pottery making. These experiences offer a unique insight into

Irish culture, allowing you to create personal memories while engaging with the country's rich artisanal heritage.

Craft Diversity

The palette of crafts available across Ireland is as diverse as its landscapes, offering a spectrum of textures, materials, and techniques to explore:

- **Weaving:** From the delicate threads of linen to the rugged warmth of wool, weaving workshops tell the tale of Ireland's relationship with its looms and textiles, a tradition spun from necessity and elevated to art.
- **Pottery:** Earth meets fire in the creation of Irish pottery, a craft that combines the island's rich clays with the creativity of its people to produce pieces as functional as they are beautiful.
- **Blacksmithing:** In the firelit forge, metal takes on new life, hammered and shaped into tools, art, and jewelry that echo the blacksmith's craft of old, a testament to the strength and resilience of Irish culture.
- **Lace-making:** The intricate patterns of Irish lace, once a cottage industry that supported entire communities, continue to enchant in workshops that teach the delicate art of needle and bobbin.

For those interested in exploring artisan workshops in Ireland, there are several excellent resources and locations where you can engage directly with local crafts and traditions:

- **Irish Fibre Crafters**, located in Co. Galway, offers a wide range of workshops and online courses focused on traditional Irish crafts like spinning, weaving, and felting using sustainable natural fibers such as Irish wool and alpaca. It's a great place to learn from experienced artisans and create unique handmade items. **Web:** irishfibrecrafters.com/
- **ÉCONOMUSÉE** Northern Ireland provides a network of artisan workshops where visitors can experience traditional crafts firsthand. This initiative showcases artisans at work in their natural settings, making it a fantastic opportunity to see traditional techniques in action and even participate in the creation process. **Web:** ccght.org/about-the-area/economusee-northern-ireland-artisans-at-work/
- **ConnollyCove** highlights several artisan shops and workshops in Galway, such as Judy Greene Pottery and Cottage Handcrafts in Connemara, where you can observe and participate in the making of traditional Irish crafts and textiles. **Web:** connollycove.com/visit-artisan-workshops-in-ireland/

These venues offer a blend of hands-on experience and cultural immersion, making them perfect for anyone looking to delve deeper into Ireland's rich heritage of crafts and artisanry. Whether you're interested in fiber arts, pottery, or other traditional crafts, these workshops provide a meaningful way to connect with the local culture and learn new skills.

Cultural Connection

Learning Irish crafts is about more than just picking up a new hobby; it's a way to connect with the culture and history that have nurtured these arts for generations. Each lace stitch or pottery piece carries stories and traditions. Participating in these workshops opens a deeper understanding of Ireland's spirit, showcasing the resilience, creativity, and community that defines the country.

When you engage in traditional embroidery or craft a piece of pottery under the guidance of an expert, you're doing more than creating something beautiful. You're engaging in a historical dialogue, connecting with generations past, and contributing your very own chapter to the ongoing Irish story.

Take-Home Treasures

The items you create in these workshops are more than just keepsakes; they are meaningful links to your experience in Ireland. Each crafted item tells a story and captures a memory, embodying a bit of the island's essence. These handcrafted pieces serve as lasting reminders of your time engaged with Irish culture, reflecting the skills you've acquired and the traditions you've observed.

For instance, a basket you weave yourself is not just a vessel for carrying items but a container for the memories of the landscape and the lessons from the artisans who taught you. Similarly, a piece of pottery you make carries the essence of the Irish earth, the heat of the kiln, and the shared moments of laughter around the wheel, making it a deeply personal and traditional keepsake.

Participating in these hands-on workshops with local artisans offers more than just a craft experience; it opens a gateway to understanding Ireland's cultural heart. Through these activities, you get to interact directly with the country's rich heritage, making your travel experience both profound and enlightening. This direct involvement with traditional crafts is where you truly connect with the ongoing Irish narrative.

6.8 THE ROAD LESS TRAVELED: SCENIC DRIVES

Imagine yourself driving on less-traveled roads that curve along steep cliffs, dip into green valleys, and offer ocean views. These roads take you through some of Ireland's most breathtaking landscapes. While you drive, every turn reveals a new vista, each view telling a story of its own. This guide will help you explore Ireland's scenic drives, turning your road trip into an adventure where the journey itself is as exciting as the destinations you reach.

Map of Uncharted Routes

A map sprawled across the table, dotted with lines that snake through Ireland's landscape, is more than just a tool; it's an invitation. (Spoiler Alert! Our maps are digital) Highlighted routes lead you from the dramatic Sky Road in Connemara, with vistas that stretch into infinity, to the serene Blessington Lakes, where water and sky merge in a dance of blues. This map isn't about the quickest route from point A to B; it's about the journeys that enrich your soul.

- **The Beara Peninsula** offers a drive that rivals any scenic route in Ireland, with rugged coastlines and hidden coves. **Web:** bearatourism.com/
- **The Slieve Bloom Mountains** present an inland route where the beauty of Ireland's ancient east unfolds in rolling hills and dense forests. **Web:** slievebloom.ie/

Driving Tips

Navigating these scenic drives requires more than just a sense of adventure; it calls for mindfulness and respect for the road and those who share it.

- **Stay Left:** Remember, Ireland drives on the left. It's easy to forget on less populated roads, but crucial for safety.

- **Narrow Lanes:** Many of Ireland's most scenic roads are also its narrowest. Be prepared to pull in to let oncoming traffic pass and always be mindful of cyclists and walkers.
- **Road Conditions:** Weather can change quickly, especially in coastal areas. Fog, rain, and even sheep can affect driving conditions. Slow down and enjoy the view safely.

Scenic Drive Along Dingle Peninsula, County Kerry

Stop Recommendations

Every scenic drive is dotted with stops that beckon travelers to pause, breathe, and immerse themselves in the moment.

- **Glengesh Pass in Donegal** is a spot where the world seems to open up. Pull over and look out over valleys that have remained unchanged for centuries. **Web:** thewildatlanticway.com/sight/glengesh-pass/
- **Healy Pass,** straddling Cork and Kerry, provides panoramic views at its summit. A small parking area allows for a pause,

perfect for a picnic with a view. **Web:** discoverireland.ie/cork/the-healy-pass
- **Lough Tay,** nicknamed the Guinness Lake, is nestled in the Wicklow Mountains. A viewpoint off the road offers a stunning perspective on this dark water body, framed by white sand that looks remarkably like a pint of Guinness. **Web:** visitwicklow.ie/listing/lough-tay-guinness-lake/

Narrative Journeys

Each of these drives is more than just a passage through beautiful landscapes; they're narratives woven into the very fabric of Ireland. As you travel here are some suggestions to make your road trip one for the books:

- **Listen to Local Radio:** Tuning into local stations provides a soundtrack to your journey, blending music and news with the landscapes you're passing through.
- **Engage with Locals:** Whether it's a chat at a petrol station or a conversation in a café, locals enrich your journey with stories that you won't find in any guidebook.
- **Capture Memories:** Not just through photographs, but by jotting down thoughts or sketching scenes. These personal mementos capture the essence of your experience in a way that a camera alone cannot.

As you journey on remote roads, Ireland's story unfolds with each turn, blending personal and universal themes. Scenic drives offer immersive narratives, with each stop revealing a new chapter and locals adding depth to your experience. In quiet moments, Ireland's essence is palpable. These less-traveled roads reveal both Ireland's heart and a reflection of your own.

6.9 VOLUNTEER OPPORTUNITIES: GIVING BACK WHILE TRAVELING

In Ireland, every traveler finds something that resonates with them. Whether it's the spontaneous laughter in an old pub, a quiet morning on a cliff, or the warm welcome of a local community, Ireland has a way of making everyone feel at home. For those looking to make a deeper connection, volunteering offers a chance to contribute meaningfully. It's more than just helping; it's a way to engage with the heart of Irish life.

Community Projects

Across the island, from the wind-swept coasts to the bustling cities, community projects thrive, each one a testament to the resilience and spirit of the Irish people. Environmental initiatives beckon those with a love for the outdoors, offering chances to protect delicate ecosystems and preserve natural beauty for generations to come. Educational programs seek patient hands and hearts, ready to guide and inspire Ireland's youth, offering them a window to a world beyond their shores.

- Planting native trees in the rewilding efforts of the Burren National Park.
- Assisting in local schools or community centers, bringing new perspectives and skills to eager minds.

How to Get Involved

Stepping into the world of volunteering in Ireland calls for a blend of enthusiasm and respect, an eagerness to contribute paired with an understanding of the needs and wishes of local communities.

- Start with research. Organizations like Volunteer Ireland provide a portal for a variety of projects, detailing needs, locations, and time commitments.
- Reach out directly. A personal touch can make all the difference. Express your interest and ask how you can best contribute to their efforts.
- Be prepared for a commitment. While some opportunities might be a one-off, others may require a more extended stay. Aligning your travel plans with these commitments ensures a fulfilling experience for both you and the community.

Impactful Experiences

The stories that emerge from these volunteer experiences are as varied as the landscape, each one a testament to the impact a single individual can have.

- A traveler from Canada recalls the joy of teaching music in a small village school, where the language of melody created bonds that crossed cultural divides.
- A couple from the United States found a new perspective on conservation while aiding in the preservation of beach habitats, their efforts helping to safeguard nesting grounds for native birds.

These stories come together to show a journey that is both rewarding and insightful, where volunteering becomes a way to understand Ireland truly.

Responsible Volunteering

As the call to contribute grows, so does the responsibility to ensure that these efforts are both ethical and beneficial.

- Choose projects that align with community needs, ensuring that your work supports rather than supplants local efforts.
- Seek sustainability. Efforts should aim for long-term benefits, leaving a lasting positive impact on the community or environment.
- Be mindful of the cultural exchange. Approach every project with an openness to learn, recognizing that this exchange of knowledge and experience is a two-way street.

In these volunteer efforts, travelers find a connection to Ireland that runs deep, a bond forged in the shared endeavor of making a difference. It's here, amid the laughter of children learning a new game, the gratitude of a community seeing their efforts supported, and the quiet satisfaction of a day's work done for the good of the land, that the true heart of Ireland reveals itself. It's a journey that goes beyond sightseeing, beyond the tourist trails, into the very soul of this beautiful island. It will enrich your discovery of Ireland.

When you volunteer during your travels in Ireland, each act of giving enriches your overall experience. Every project and community you engage with adds depth to your journey, leaving lasting memories of genuine connections. These experiences remind you that the most meaningful travels are those that bring us closer to both the places we visit and their residents.

As you continue your travels, the spirit of generosity and connection you've embraced in Ireland serves as a foundation for future adventures. It encourages you to keep integrating your own story with those of the places you visit, weaving yourself into the broader narrative of each destination.

EMBRACING THE GREAT OUTDOORS

Pulling on a pair of boots and feeling the grip as your feet hit the path, there's something about hiking in Ireland that feels like you're walking through a postcard that's come to life. The mountains here aren't just a backdrop for stunning photos; they're storytellers, keepers of legends, and guardians of breathtaking vistas that have been inspiring awe long before Instagram. Whether you're lacing up for your first hike or your hundredth, Ireland's peaks offer trails that whisper tales of ancient battles, serene beauty, and the kind of challenge that makes reaching the summit feel like a personal victory.

7.1 HIKING IRELAND'S MAJESTIC MOUNTAINS

Trail Recommendations

Finding the right trail can feel a bit like matchmaking — it's all about finding the perfect fit. Here are a few to consider, each with its unique charm:

- **Carrauntoohil in County Kerry** is the tallest peak in Ireland and part of the MacGillycuddy's Reeks range. It's a must-do for the bucket list, offering several routes to the summit, including the Devil's Ladder for those up for a challenge. **Web:** discoverireland.ie/kerry/carrauntoohil
- **The Mourne Mountains in County Down** provide a network of paths, with Slieve Donard standing out. It's the highest peak in Northern Ireland and, on a clear day, offers views of Scotland. **Web:** ireland.com/en-us/destinations/re-gions/mourne-mountains/
- **Connemara National Park** offers a range of trails for all abilities. Diamond Hill is a favorite, with well-marked paths leading to panoramic views of the Twelve Bens and the vast Atlantic Ocean. **Web:** nationalparks.ie/connemara/
- For those seeking something less trodden, **Slieve League in County Donegal** offers trails that meander along some of Europe's highest sea cliffs. The path less taken here means views that are hard to beat. **Web:** https://www.slieveleague.com/

Hiking in the Irish Mountains

Preparation Tips

- **Weather Watch:** Ireland's weather can change on a dime. Always check the forecast and prepare for all possibilities. Layers are your best friend.
- **Gear Up:** Good hiking boots are worth their weight in gold. Also, pack a waterproof jacket, no matter how promising the sky looks.
- **Stay Fueled and Hydrated:** Water and snacks are essential. Think energy bars, fruit, or anything that will keep you going without weighing you down.

Guided Hikes

Sometimes, a local guide can transform a hike. They offer insights into the landscape's history, flora, and fauna that you might miss otherwise. Guided hikes are available across Ireland, from the Wicklow Way to the wilds of Connemara. They can cater to all levels, offering safety in more challenging terrains and enriching the experience with tales and tidbits that breathe life into the landscape.

If you're looking to explore Ireland through guided hikes, here are some excellent resources to consider:

- **Wildland Trekking** offers all-inclusive hiking vacations in Ireland, providing a mix of beautiful accommodations, iconic pubs, Irish fare, and hand-selected hikes across the country. This is a great option if you're looking for a comprehensive hiking experience with everything taken care of. **Web:** wildlandtrekking.com/destination/ireland-guided-hikes/
- **Hilltop Treks** specializes in guided walks and hikes around Ireland, including transport from Dublin for most of their walks. They offer a variety of hikes suitable for different skill levels and preferences, making it easy to find a hike that suits your needs. They also organize day tours and walking holidays that include visits to scenic and historic sites. **Web:** hilltoptreks.com/
- **Discover Ireland** provides an ultimate hiking guide that showcases a variety of trails, from the Ballycotton Cliff Walk to more challenging hikes like the Blackrock Loop in Limerick. This resource is particularly useful for those looking to explore specific regions or types of landscapes in Ireland. **Web:** discoverireland.ie/guides/best-hikes-ireland
- **Wilderness Ireland** has options for less traveled paths like the Burren, Aran Islands, and Connemara, where you can enjoy dramatic landscapes and rich archaeological sites. They also guide hikes to the Cliffs of Moher starting from Doolin,

offering a unique approach to one of Ireland's most famous scenic spots. **Web:** wildernessireland.com/blog/ireland-best-hikes/

Each of these providers offers unique perspectives and access to Ireland's rich landscapes and cultural heritage through well-organized hiking tours. Whether you're looking for a leisurely walk or a challenging trek, these resources can help you plan the perfect hiking adventure in Ireland.

Hikers in Irish Forest

Conservation Awareness

The Leave No Trace principles are more than guidelines; they're a promise to protect the very beauty we come to enjoy. Here's a quick checklist:

- **Pack It In, Pack It Out:** If you brought it, bring it back. Litter has no place in nature.
- **Respect Wildlife:** Keep a safe distance. Remember, you're a guest in their home.
- **Stick to Trails:** Veering off can damage fragile ecosystems. Plus, getting lost is no fun.

- **Leave What You Find:** Rocks, plants, and historical artifacts are part of the landscape's story. Let them remain so for the next adventurers.

If you're undecided about which Irish mountain you should hike, we've created a fun and easy quiz to help you determine which mountain best suits your personality! Don't worry—there are no wrong answers.

Which Irish Mountain Are You?

1. What's your idea of a perfect day?

    A. Exploring new and exotic places.
    B. Enjoying the peace and solitude of nature.
    C. Challenging myself with a tough workout.
    D. Spending time with friends and family in a cozy setting.

2. How do your friends describe you?

    A. Adventurous and always on the go.
    B. Calm, thoughtful, and introspective.
    C. Strong, determined, and a natural leader.
    D. Friendly, sociable, and community-oriented.

3. What's your preferred type of holiday?

    A. A backpacking adventure through unfamiliar terrains.
    B. A secluded cabin away from the hustle and bustle.
    C. A planned itinerary packed with activities and challenges.
    D. A cultural trip with a bit of history and lots of local interaction.

4. Choose a beverage that suits your personality.

    A. Strong black coffee.
    B. Herbal tea.
    C. Energy drink.
    D. A pint of your favorite beer.

5. What's your approach to problem-solving?

    A. Dive in headfirst and learn as you go.
    B. Take your time to think through the options.
    C. Tackle it with all your might.
    D. Ask friends or family for their opinions and advice.

6. Which element do you feel most connected to?

    A. Wind – Always moving and full of energy.
    B. Earth – Grounded and nurturing.
    C. Fire – Intense and passionate.
    D. Water – Adaptable and often calming.

7. What's your activity preference at a party?

    A. Leading the group to try something new or exotic.
    B. Sitting quietly at the side, enjoying deep conversations.
    C. Competing in every party game.
    D. Mixing and mingling with every guest.

Results:

Mostly A's: Carrauntoohil

You are Carrauntoohil, the highest mountain in Ireland! Adventurous and vibrant, you enjoy pushing your limits and are unafraid to take on challenges. Like this towering peak, you stand tall and proud, drawing others with your infectious enthusiasm.

Mostly B's: Lugnaquilla

You embody Lugnaquilla, a mountain known for its tranquil and remote beauty. Thoughtful and introspective, you find strength in solitude and often prefer the road less traveled. Your calm demeanor and deep insights make you a grounding force to those around you.

Mostly C's: Slieve Donard

Strong and impressive, you are Slieve Donard, the highest peak in Northern Ireland. You tackle challenges head-on and aren't deterred by a tough climb. Your determination and leadership inspire others to follow wherever you lead.

Mostly D's: Croagh Patrick

Like Croagh Patrick, known for its religious significance and communal pilgrimages, you are sociable and community-focused. You enjoy being surrounded by people and are at your best when you're helping bring others together.

Now that we figured out which mountain is your best match: it's not going to matter which mountain you're going to climb unless you have the right gear. Here's a curated list of essential hiking gear to ensure you're well-equipped for your adventures in Ireland, complete with recommendations for local Irish suppliers:

Essential Hiking Gear List

Waterproof Hiking Boots—Durable and waterproof boots are a must for the wet and muddy Irish terrain.

- **Supplier: 53 Degrees North** - offers a variety of high-quality hiking boots suited for Irish weather.
- **Web:** https://www.53degreesnorth.ie/

Waterproof Jacket - With Ireland's unpredictable weather, a good waterproof jacket is crucial.

- **Supplier: Great Outdoors Superstore (Dublin)** - stocks a range of waterproof jackets that cater to various hiking needs.
- **Web**: greatoutdoors.ie/

Backpack - A comfortable, durable backpack with good support and enough space for your hiking essentials.

- **Supplier: Basecamp (Dublin)** - provides a wide selection of hiking backpacks with different capacities.
- **Web**: basecamp.ie/

Hiking Pants - Waterproof and breathable pants are essential for comfort and mobility.

- **Supplier: 53 Degrees North** - offers waterproof and breathable pants perfect for the Irish climate.

Thermal and Moisture-Wicking Layers - To manage temperature and moisture on longer hikes.

- **Supplier: Cotswold Outdoor (Dublin)** -has a great selection of thermal and moisture-wicking clothing.
- **Web**: cotswoldoutdoor.com/stores/dublin-city.html

Hiking Socks - Wool or synthetic socks to keep your feet dry and comfortable.

- **Supplier: Great Outdoors Superstore (Dublin)** - offers socks designed specifically for hiking.

Map and Compass/GPS - Essential for navigation, especially in remote areas.

- **Supplier: The Scout Shop (Dublin)** - provides various navigation tools including maps, compasses, and GPS devices.
- **Web**: thescoutshop.ie/

First Aid Kit - A basic first aid kit to handle minor injuries on the trail.

- **Supplier: Basecamp (Dublin)** - stocks compact and comprehensive first aid kits for hikers

Headlamp/Flashlight - For any low-light conditions or emergencies.

- **Supplier: 53 Degrees North** - offers a range of headlamps and flashlights suitable for hiking.

Water Bottle or Hydration System - Staying hydrated is crucial, especially on longer treks.

- **Supplier: Outdoor Adventure Store** (various locations in Ireland) - provides a variety of hydration solutions.
- **Web**: outdooradventurestore.ie/

Tips for Choosing Hiking Gear:

- **Local Weather:** Always consider the local weather conditions. In Ireland, be prepared for rain and windy conditions.
- **Fit and Comfort:** Especially for boots and backpacks, ensure they fit well and are comfortable for long durations.
- **Durability:** Opt for gear that is durable and from reputable brands to withstand the rugged Irish landscapes.

By sourcing your hiking gear from local Irish suppliers, you will not only have access to products well-suited for the local terrain but also support the local economy. Happy hiking!

Walking through Ireland's mountains is more than exercise; it's an interaction with history, nature, and the elements. Each step takes you deeper into the heart of the land, offering views that sweep across valleys and oceans, reminding you of the sheer scale and beauty of the world. Whether it's the challenge of Carrauntoohil, the mystery of the Mourne Mountains, the allure of Connemara, or the dramatic cliffs of Slieve League, Ireland's mountains stand as sentinels, inviting you to explore, discover, and protect their timeless beauty. Prepare to be dazzled!

7.2 CYCLING THE GREENWAYS AND BEYOND

Ireland's Greenway routes are perfect for cyclists looking for adventure. These dedicated paths stretch across the landscape, offering safe, car-free routes that take you through some of Ireland's most stunning scenery. From dramatic coastlines where the Atlantic crashes against the cliffs to quiet trails where you're accompanied only by the sound of birds and your bike tires on the path, these greenways are ideal for any cyclist, whether you're experienced or just looking for a leisurely ride. They give you the freedom to explore Ireland's natural beauty at your own pace, making every journey an adventure.

Bicycling In the Irish Countryside

Greenway Routes

Imagine pedaling along the Great Western Greenway, where the majestic peaks of Nephin and the glittering expanse of Clew Bay accompany you. Stretching 42 kilometers from Westport to Achill, it's Ireland's longest greenway, a testament to the beauty of Mayo's land-scapes. Then there's the Waterford Greenway, a 46-kilometer stretch that takes you from the vibrant city of Waterford through the Comeragh Mountains to the seaside town of Dungarvan. Along these routes, every turn brings a new vista, every incline a fresh perspective. They're not just paths but journeys through the very soul of Ireland.

For exploring Ireland's Greenway cycling routes, several resources provide detailed information, maps, and guides to help plan your cycling adventure across various scenic trails:

- **Cycling Ireland** offers a searchable database of cycling routes including detailed information on greenways across Ireland.

You can filter by location, bike type, skill level, and more to find a route that suits your preferences. **Web:** cyclingireland.ie/

- **Discover Ireland** features comprehensive guides on the best cycling routes, including descriptions of the trails, their scenic points, and practical tips for cyclists. This resource is ideal for discovering popular and lesser-known greenways. **Web:** discoverireland.ie/guides/cycling-ireland
- **Around Ireland** provides insights into specific trails like the Boyne Greenway and the Old Rail Trail. This site offers detailed descriptions of the routes, historical contexts, and what you can expect to see and experience along the way. It also offers great walking tours of cities. **Web:** aroundireland.ie/
- **Active Me** highlights trails such as the Great Western Greenway in Mayo, providing in-depth guides, maps, and useful tips for both walking and cycling. This resource is particularly valuable for planning multi-stage cycling trips along Ireland's scenic west coast. They even have apps! **Web:** activeme.ie/

Each of these resources will help you find the right greenway according to your location and cycling ability, ensuring a memorable and enjoyable experience as you explore Ireland's beautiful landscapes.

Bike Rental Options

You don't need to bring your own personal wheels to explore these paths; bike rental options abound, offering everything from sturdy mountain bikes to sleek road cycles. Many rental shops are conveniently located at the start of the greenways, with options for half-day, full-day, or even week-long rentals. For those looking for a guided experience, numerous tours combine cycling with local history and gastronomy, turning a ride into a rich tapestry of experiences. These services often include shuttle support, so you can venture as far as you like without the worry of a long pedal back.

- **Westport Bike Shop** provides rentals and guided tours along the Great Western Greenway, including electric bikes for those who want a little extra push up the hills. **Web:** westportbikeshop.ie/
- **Waterford Greenway Bike Hire** offers a range of options, with multiple pick-up and drop-off points along the route for flexible exploration. **Web:** waterfordgreenwaybikehire.com/

Mountain Biker on Irish Hillside

Cultural Stops

The beauty of cycling Ireland's greenways is not just in the landscapes but in the stories etched into the land. Along the Waterford Greenway, the haunting ruins of the 13th-century Kilmacthomas Workhouse speak of a darker time in Irish history, offering a moment of reflection. In contrast, the vibrant town of Newport, along the Great Western Greenway, delights with its colorful streets, art galleries, and cafes. Each stop is a chance to step off the bike and step into Ireland's past and present, discovering the array of cultures that make this country so unique.

- **Durrow Viaduct**, an architectural marvel along the Waterford Greenway, offers a perfect picnic spot with panoramic views of the surrounding countryside. **Web:** buildingsofire-land.ie/buildings-search/building/22902401/durrow-railway-viaduct-durrow-waterford
- **Mulranny**, with its stunning coastal views and salt marshes, provides a scenic rest stop along the Great Western Greenway, where you can learn about the unique flora and fauna of the area. **Web:** mulranny.ie/

Local Support

The success of Ireland's greenways is deeply entwined with the support of local communities. From the warm welcomes in bike-friendly cafes to the expertise found in local bike shops, the infrastructure surrounding the greenways makes every ride a pleasure. In towns like Achill and Dungarvan, cyclists are celebrated, with festivals and events throughout the year dedicated to the joys of two-wheeled travel. Repair shops dot the routes, ensuring help is always at hand should you encounter a bump along the way.

- **The Greenway Café in Newport** is a haven for cyclists. It offers hearty, locally sourced meals and a friendly atmosphere where tales of the trail are exchanged over cups of steaming coffee. **Web:** greenwayriversidecafe.com
- **The Old Forge in Waterford** provides not just bike repairs but also invaluable advice on the best routes and hidden gems along the greenway. **Web:** tramore.ie/the-old-forge/

Cycling Ireland's greenways allow you to experience the country at a leisurely pace, where each pedal brings you deeper into its essence. It's a chance to see the landscapes, discover the history, and engage with the culture. These paths offer more than just a ride; they are opportunities for adventure and creating lasting memories.

7.3 SURFING THE WILD ATLANTIC WAVES

You saw that right! Surfing! The Atlantic coast of Ireland is a surfer's paradise, where the ocean's endless energy meets the land's rugged beauty. This coast is more than just a surfing spot; it's an adventure, a playground where every wave offers a new challenge. Whether you're a pro searching for massive swells or a newbie catching your first waves, Ireland's surf breaks deliver memorable experiences, inviting you to a thrilling ride on the wild waves.

Woman Surfing Off the Coast in County Kerry

Surf Spots

The Wild Atlantic Way, a scenic route that traces Ireland's rugged western coastline, is dotted with surf spots that cater to every level of experience. Here are a few standouts:

- **Bundoran in County Donegal**, often dubbed Ireland's surf capital, offers a variety of breaks suitable for both beginners and advanced surfers. The Peak, Bundoran's most famous wave, provides a consistent left-hand break that challenges even the most experienced.

- **Lahinch in County Clare** has earned its stripes as a top surf destination, with its beach break offering ideal conditions for novices, while nearby Crab Island presents a more demanding test for advanced surfers.
- **Easkey in County Sligo** holds a special place in the heart of Irish surfing. With two main reef breaks, Easkey Left and Easkey Right, it caters to those with a good grasp of surfing fundamentals looking to push their limits.

Surf Schools

For those keen to catch their first wave or sharpen their skills, Ireland's surf schools offer a blend of top-notch instruction and warm hospitality. Equipped with a range of boards and wetsuits for rent, these schools are your gateway to the surf culture of the Emerald Isle.

- **Bundoran Surf Co. in Donegal** not only provides lessons for all levels but also offers cozy accommodation, making it a one-stop shop for surf enthusiasts. **Web:** bundoransurfco.com/
- **Lahinch Surf School**, one of the longest-running surf schools in the area, prides itself on its team of passionate instructors who ensure a fun and safe learning environment. **Web:** lahinchsurfschool.com/
- **Strandhill Surf School in Sligo** offers a deep dive into the local surf culture, with experienced guides who share both the mechanics of surfing and the soul of the sport. **Web:** sligosurfexperience.com/

Seasonal Advice

While Ireland's surf season runs year-round, each period offers a different flavor of the surfing experience:

- Spring and Autumn present the best of both worlds, with milder weather and consistent swells. These seasons strike a balance, offering waves that cater to a broad spectrum of surfing abilities.
- Summer brings warmer waters and a more relaxed vibe, ideal for beginners. The swells are generally smaller, making it the perfect time for those looking to ease into the sport.
- Winter, with its powerful swells, is a magnet for the daring. The cold waters demand respect and a quality wetsuit, but for those willing to brave the elements, the rewards are unparalleled.

Surfing Community

The heart of Ireland's surfing isn't just the waves—it's the community. This vibrant group of local surfers and visiting wave chasers thrives on a shared love for surfing. Diving into this network can lead you to secret surf spots, pro tips, and new friendships that last long after you've paddled in from your last wave.

Surf Competitions such as the annual **Intercounty Surf Contest in Bundoran** become gatherings that celebrate the sport and its culture, offering a chance to witness Ireland's top surf talent. **Web:** discover bundoran.com/events/intercounties-surf-event/

Local Pubs and Cafes in surf towns are the unofficial meeting spots where tales of the day's surfing are exchanged over hearty meals and pints.

- **Sammys Restaurant in Inch**, County Kerry - Located right on the edge of the sand at Inch Beach, this spot is known for its tasty burgers and carrot cake. It's a great place to warm up with a coffee while watching the surf. **Web:** sammysinch.com/

- **The Strand Bar in Strandhill**, County Sligo - Known for its perfect coastal pub experience and quality Guinness, The Strand Bar is a popular hangout for both locals and visiting surfers. **Web:** thestrandbar.ie/
- **Maddens Bridge Bar in Bundoran**, Donegal - Overlooking the Peak, one of Europe's premier performance waves, Maddens Bridge Bar offers great food and music in an ideal location for watching the surf and unwinding after a day on the waves. **Web:** maddensbridgebar.ie/
- **The Derrylahan Bar and Restaurant in Louisburgh**, County Mayo - A great local pub with superb seafood, perfect for a meal after surfing at nearby Carrowniskey Beach. **Web:** louisburgh.ie/pubs_in_the_louisbugh_area_co_mayo_ireland_derrylahan.html
- **Shells Café in Strandhill, Sligo** - Located right on the waterfront, Shells Café offers great views and delicious meals, making it a lovely spot to refuel after surfing. **Web**: shellscafe.com/

Online Forums and Social Media Groups like 'Surfing in Ireland' on Facebook facilitate connections even before you hit the shores, allowing you to tap into the local surf scene, find surf buddies, or share rides to the best breaks.

Web: facebook.com/groups/1512924892358077

Out in the Atlantic, every wave spins a tale, each wipeout a lesson, and every ride leaves its mark. Ireland's surf spots are more than mere dots on a map—they're the setting of an epic surf story, pulsing with the ocean's rhythm. Here, amidst Ireland's epic coastline, you're not just catching waves; you're syncing with the heartbeats of the Wild Atlantic Way, where the surf community becomes your tribe.

Surfers Off of Irish Coastline

7.4 KAYAKING AND CANOEING THROUGH HISTORY

Ireland beckons canoeing and kayaking enthusiasts with its intricate network of rivers and lakes nestled within the embrace of the Atlantic. Envision the tranquil waters of a lake at dawn, where the only disturbance is the gentle wake of your kayak cutting through reflections of soaring mountains and timeless woodlands. Picture the excitement as you meander along a river and come upon the ruins of an ancient castle, its aged stones whispering stories of the past. This experience is not just about paddling; it's a journey through time on the water, with each stroke drawing you deeper into Ireland's splendid blend of natural and historical wonders.

Waterway Routes

The Shannon River, a silver thread weaving through Ireland's lush mosaic, offers more than just a waterway; it's a corridor through time. Starting from the Shannon Pot in Cavan, this mighty river takes you on a journey through medieval towns, past castles like Clonmacnoise, and into the heart of Ireland's folk tales. Then there's the **Lough Derg Blueway**, where you can paddle in the shadow of Brian Boru's fort, imagining the ancient king's fleet setting sail.

For those drawn to the tales of the high seas, the **Atlantic Sea Kayaking** routes around West Cork reveal hidden coves once frequented by pirates and smugglers. Each stroke along these coastal waters is a step back into a tumultuous past, where every cave and inlet has a story to tell.

Rental and Guide Services

You don't need to own a kayak or canoe to answer the call of Ireland's waterways. Rental services dot the landscape, offering everything from sleek kayaks for solo adventures to sturdy canoes for family jaunts. Many of these providers also offer guided tours, combining local lore with expert paddling instruction to enrich your journey.

In Killaloe, on the banks of Lough Derg, you'll find outfits ready to equip you for a day's exploration, with guides who know every hidden nook and historical tale of the area.

Along the Wild Atlantic Way, specialized services offer sea kayaking adventures equipped with everything needed to navigate the coastal waters safely, including waterproof maps marked with points of historical interest.

Here are some great resources and rental options for kayakers and canoers all over Ireland, ensuring you have everything you need to explore the country's beautiful waterways:

- **Atlantic Sea Kayaking** - Based in Cork, they offer urban kayaking trips under the city's bridges and are renowned for their nighttime bioluminescent kayaking tours on Lough Hyne. **Web:** atlanticseakayaking.com/

- **Paddle Your Own Canoe** - Offers canoe rentals and organizes multi-day trips down the River Barrow, passing through scenic countryside, towns, and historical sites. No previous canoeing experience is needed. **Web:** paddleyourowncanoe.ie/
- **River Run** provides kayak and canoe rentals and lessons, ideal for exploring Irish waters. It ranks top among destinations for paddling adventures in Ireland. **Web:** riverrun.ie/river-run/
- **Outdoors Ireland**—Located in Killarney, Outdoors Ireland offers kayaking across the famous Lakes of Killarney, exploring hidden inlets and islands with expert guides. **Web:** outdoorsireland.com/
- **Canoeing Ireland** - Offers a variety of canoeing and kayaking experiences across Ireland, including sea kayaking in diverse locations. **Web:** canoe.ie/
- **Go with the Flow River Adventures** - Specializes in canoeing trips along the Barrow River, providing a serene paddling experience through one of Ireland's most scenic waterways. **Web:** gowiththeflow.ie/

These providers offer a range of services from rentals and guided tours to multi-day kayaking and canoeing adventures, perfect for both beginners and experienced paddlers looking to explore Ireland's rivers and lakes. They'll ensure you experience Ireland's lakes and rivers safely and excitingly!

Safety Guidelines

The tranquility of Ireland's lakes and the gentle flow of its rivers might lull you into a sense of security, but safety is paramount. Even the most serene water can surprise you, and the Atlantic's moods change like the wind.

- **Always wear a life jacket**, no matter your level of experience. The waters respect no one.

- **Check the weather before setting out.** Ireland's weather is as changeable as a melody on an old fiddle.
- **Know your route.** Whether you're making a loop around a calm lake or a stretch of river between two historic towns, understanding the waterway's nuances can make a good day on the water unforgettable.
- **Understanding tides and currents is crucial for sea kayaking.** The coast has its rhythm, and dancing in tune with it makes for a harmonious experience.

Wildlife Watching

As you paddle Ireland's waterways, you're never alone. Otters might escort you along a river bend, their curious eyes peeking above the waterline. In the coastal areas, seals often bob alongside, as if guiding you to the next point of interest. And above, the cries of seabirds provide a soundtrack to your adventure.

On **Lough Leane in Killarney National Park**, keep an eye out for the white-tailed eagles, a conservation success story that soars once again in Ireland's skies. **Web:** national-parks.org/ireland/killarney

In the sheltered bays along the **Wild Atlantic Way**, you might spot dolphins curiously approaching, a reminder of the wildness and wonder that lies just beyond the shore. **Web:** thewildat-lanticway.com/

Paddling through Ireland's waterways is more than just exercise; it's a trip through the country's history. Each river and lake reflect stories from both the past and present, showing you a side of Ireland that's deeply connected to its people and their tales. As you travel these waters, you're following the same paths taken by ancient settlers (think Vikings), medieval traders, and legendary figures whose lives helped shape this land. It's a unique way to see Ireland, where history meets nature and offers insights that are as meaningful as they are picturesque.

7.5 FISHING IN SERENE LAKES AND RIVERS

Right smack in the middle of Ireland, where the water's as reflective as the sky and the rivers murmur old land secrets, fishing becomes a real tango with nature. It's not just about snagging a big one; it's about those chill moments surrounded by the stunning views of Ireland's lakes and rivers. These waters are bursting with stories and brimming with life, giving anglers a golden shot to bond with the great outdoors on a personal level.

Fishing Spots

Across the island, waters await with promises of quietude and the thrill of the catch. **Lough Corrib**, sprawling beneath Galway's skies, is renowned for its trout and pike, a favorite among fly fishermen for its vast expanse and abundant waters. Here, the early morning mist unveils a scene so tranquil it demands reverence. Moving east, **the River Moy** in Mayo beckons with the promise of salmon. Its banks, lined with greenery, have witnessed countless anglers in their quest for the elusive Atlantic salmon, making it one of Ireland's most celebrated fishing destinations.

For those seeking a blend of historical allure and fishing adventure, **the lakes of Killarney** offer an unparalleled experience. With the ancient Ross Castle looming in the distance, these waters not only provide trout and salmon but also a sense of connection to Ireland's rich past.

Licenses and Regulations

Navigating the legal waters is as crucial as fishing itself to ensure the sustainability of these natural treasures. In Ireland, the requirements for fishing licenses vary depending on the water body and the type of fish sought. Freshwater fishing, particularly for salmon and sea trout, generally requires a license issued by the relevant regional fisheries board. **Web:** gov.ie/en/service/buy-a-salmon-fishing-licence/

For trout, pike, and coarse fishing in many areas, licenses are not needed, but permission from landowners may be required for access. **Web:** store.fishinginireland.info/

Always check the local regulations before planning your fishing trip, as rules can differ significantly from one area to another.

Conservation laws aim not only to preserve fish populations but also to maintain the health of Ireland's aquatic ecosystems. Adherence to these rules ensures that the joys of fishing can be experienced by generations to come.

Fishing Boats in Cobh, Near Cork with St. Colman's Cathedral in Background

Guided Fishing Trips

For those less familiar with Ireland's waters or keen on maximizing their chances of a successful catch, guided fishing trips offer a wealth of local knowledge. Guides not only know the best spots and the right times to visit but also provide insights into the habits of local fish species, enhancing your fishing experience.

Guides can tailor trips to your skill level, whether you're a seasoned angler or holding a rod for the first time. They also offer an opportunity to learn more about catch and release practices, ensuring you contribute to the conservation of Ireland's aquatic life.

Here are some of the best-guided fishing trips in Ireland, catering to both beginners and seasoned anglers looking for a memorable experience. With all of them, you must plan and book early:

- **Atlantic Salmon and sea Trout fishing, Connemara**— Offering guided trips with English/French-speaking Ghillies in the wild waters of the West of Ireland. Prices vary per group size and date. **Web**: connemarawildescapes.ie/atlantic-salmon-sea-trout-fishing-erriff-river-connemara-county-galway-french-speaking-ghillie-guide-full-day
- **Pike shore fishing, Lough Corrib, Connemara**—Highly rated by international anglers, this guided fishing trip chases trophy pike on Lough Corrib. It starts in mid-July and runs until mid-December, and it's a favorite for pike enthusiasts. **Web**: tourhq.com/tours_bkn/viewtour/173443/pike-shore-fishing-on-lough-corrib-galway-private-guided-frencheng
- **Aran Sea Tours & Fishing, Lower Kilronan** - This service provides a stylish way to experience local fisheries with trips starting at $400. It's a great choice for those looking to explore the sea around Lower Kilronan. **Web**: fishingbooker.com/charters/view/29510
- **Irish Fishing Tours, Lough Derg** - Located in County Tipperary, this tour operates on the largest lake along Ireland's River Shannon, combining great fishing with a unique holiday experience. **Web**: discoverloughderg.ie/irish-fishing-tours/
- **Yellow Dog Flyfishing, Ireland** - Specializes in fly fishing trips that offer a blend of amazing history, wonderful

hospitality, and plentiful fishing opportunities. **Web**: yellowdogflyfishing.com/collections/fly-fishing-ireland

- **Angling Services Ireland** - Provides high-quality angling experiences ranging from day trips to inclusive holiday itineraries. **Web**: anglingservicesireland.com/
- **Predator Guiding** - With over 15 years of experience, they offer guided pike fishing tours on Lough Derg. Their lodge provides direct access to the water, making it a great base for a fishing holiday. **Web**: predatorguiding.com/
- **Galway Bay Fishing**—Offers daily fishing trips around Galway Bay, the Aran Islands, and the West Coast of Ireland. It is perfect for those wanting a comprehensive coastal fishing experience. **Web**: galwaybayfishing.com/

These tours offer a variety of fishing adventures across Ireland's rich and diverse aquatic landscapes, providing expert guidance and local knowledge to enhance your fishing experience.

Catch and Release

The practice of catch and release plays a pivotal role in conserving fish populations and supporting sustainable fishing practices. It allows anglers to enjoy the thrill of the catch while ensuring the fish's survival and health upon release. When practicing catch and release, it's crucial to handle fish with care, using barbless hooks to minimize injury and keeping the fish in the water as much as possible to reduce stress. Understanding the proper technique for releasing fish back into the water significantly increases their chances of survival, contributing to the conservation of Ireland's rich aquatic biodiversity.

In the secluded spots of Ireland, where rivers slice through the land, and lakes mirror the shifting skies, fishing turns into more than just a hobby. It's a chance to connect with nature, a break from the daily hustle where time is only marked by a pull on your fishing line. In these calm Irish waters, every angler finds a bit of peace, a place to relax and unwind. Find your Zen and book a fishing excursion!

7.6 GOLFING ON WORLD-CLASS LINKS

The allure of Ireland's golf courses is undeniable, with their challenging links set against the backdrop of some of the most stunning scenery you're likely to find anywhere on the globe. These courses aren't just about the game; they're about experiencing Ireland in a way that combines sport with unparalleled natural beauty. The wind whispering through ancient dunes, the feel of the sea spray as you tee off, and the lush green fairways that seem to roll on forever make each round a memorable adventure. And remember, what happens on the course stays on the course! Ha!

Golf Course in Adare, County Limerick

Iconic Courses

Ireland is home to numerous iconic golf courses, each offering its unique challenges and breathtaking views.

- **Royal County Down Golf Club:** Nestled at the foot of the Mourne Mountains in Northern Ireland, this course is a masterpiece of golfing design, regularly ranked among the top courses in the world. Its natural beauty is matched only by the complexity of its layout, which demands precision and strategy from every golfer. **Web:** royalcountydown.org/
- **Ballybunion Golf Club:** Situated on the northwest coast of County Kerry, the Old Course at Ballybunion is a jewel in the crown of Irish golf. With its dramatic cliff-top setting, this course offers a mix of rugged terrain and classic links play that has been challenging golfers since the 19th century. **Web:** ballybuniongolfclub.com/
- **Portmarnock Golf Club:** Located on a small peninsula just north of Dublin City, Portmarnock's links course offers a pure golfing experience. It has a rich history and a layout that requires a keen tactical approach. The sea breeze adds an extra layer of challenge, changing the course's character from day to day. **Web:** portmarnockgolfclub.ie/

Golfing Packages

For those looking to immerse themselves in Ireland's golfing experience, several packages offer access to multiple courses along with accommodations that range from cozy bed and breakfasts to luxurious castle hotels. These packages often include:

- Customized itineraries that cater to your skill level and interests, ensuring you hit the courses that are right for you.
- Transportation options, from car rentals to private drivers, so you can focus on your game rather than the logistics of getting from one course to another.
- Caddie services and club rentals, allowing you to experience the course as intended without the hassle of bringing your personal clubs.

- Exploring different courses across Ireland with these packages enhances your golfing experience and offers a glimpse into the island's varied landscapes and cultures.

Golf Etiquette

Understanding and adhering to golf etiquette in Ireland is crucial for ensuring a respectful and enjoyable experience for all players. This includes:

- Dress code: While specific requirements may vary by club, smart-casual attire is generally expected. It's always best to check with the course ahead of time.
- Pace of play: Keeping up with the group ahead of you and being ready to play when it's your turn helps maintain the flow of the game and ensures everyone's enjoyment.
- Care for the course: Repairing divots, raking bunkers, and being mindful not to damage the greens are all ways to preserve the course's quality for fellow golfers.

Here are three websites that offer golf packages in Ireland:

- **Golf Escapes** - They provide a variety of golf holiday packages in Ireland, offering unforgettable golf trips with stunning packages for this year. You can check their offerings at: **Web**: golf-escapes.com/
- **Hidden Links Golf** - Specializes in Ireland golf packages and vacations that deliver the ultimate Ireland golfing experience, covering famous links like Ballybunion and Lahinch. More information is available at: **Web**: hiddenlinksgolf.com/
- **Golfbreaks** - Offers comprehensive golf tours across Ireland, including the Southwest Ireland Golf Tour, featuring some of the best links' courses in the world. Detailed packages can be found at: **Web**: golfbreaks.com/en-us/

Golfing Community

The heart of Ireland's golfing experience is its vibrant community. From local clubs where members share tips and tales over a pint to international tournaments that draw players from around the globe, the sense of camaraderie is palpable.

Joining a local club for the duration of your stay can offer a deeper dive into Ireland's golf culture. It provides opportunities to play with locals and learn from their knowledge of the course.

Participating in open competitions is another way to engage with the community. These events are welcoming to visitors and offer a chance to test your skills against a broader field.

Social media and online forums dedicated to Irish golfing can help you connect with fellow golf enthusiasts, plan outings, and even arrange friendly matches.

The golf courses in Ireland are more than just places to hit a few balls; they're steeped in tradition and surrounded by stunning scenery. Each round is a new adventure, each shot an opportunity to enjoy, and each course has its unique appeal. Whether you're here for the challenging links or the scenic views, golfing in Ireland leaves a lasting impression well beyond the last putt.

7.7 HORSEBACK RIDING IN THE COUNTRYSIDE

The Irish countryside is a mix of green fields, rugged hills, and old trails, all beneath skies that change from the muted grays of morning to bright sunset colors. Horseback riding here goes beyond a simple activity; it's a way to truly experience Ireland's core, syncing with the land's rhythm and the consistent clop of hooves on the ground. It's a chance for every rider to connect deeply, not just with their horse, but with the spirit of Ireland itself.

Woman Riding Horse On Beach at Sunset

Riding Trails

Across the island, trails ribbon through landscapes that look as though they've been lifted from the pages of a storybook. Here are some highlights:

- **The Wicklow Way** offers riders a chance to meander through the "Garden of Ireland," with trails that lead through dense woodlands and open moorlands, offering views that stretch to the horizon. **Web:** wicklowequitours.com/
- **The Dingle Peninsula in Kerry** is another gem. Trails wind around the rugged coastline, offering glimpses of ancient

beehive huts and early Christian chapels against the backdrop of the wild Atlantic. **Web:** dinglehorseriding.com/

- **The Burren in Clare**, with its lunar-like landscape, presents a stark beauty. Riding here, among the limestone pavements dotted with rare flora, feels like traversing another world. **Web:** mountainviewtrekking.com/trails.php

Equestrian Centers

For those looking to saddle up, Ireland is dotted with equestrian centers that cater to every age and skill level. These centers not only offer lessons and tours but also share a deep love for horses and riding.

- **Castle Leslie Equestrian Center** in Monaghan boasts top-class facilities and offers rides on its 1,000-acre estate. Trails lead riders through ancient woodlands and serene lakes. **Web:** castleleslie.com/equestrian/
- **Cleggan Beach Riding Center** in Connemara specializes in beach rides. It offers an unforgettable experience of galloping along the Atlantic's edge, with the sea breeze as your companion. **Web:** galwaytourism.ie/things-to-do/horse-riding/cleggan-beach-riding-centre/
- **Clonshire Equestrian Centre** in Adare provides comprehensive riding experience, with well-trained horses and a range of activities from cross-country to show jumping. **Web:** clonshire.com/

Woman Learning How to Ride

Cultural Connection

In Ireland, horses and history are intertwined. The horse holds a place of honor in Irish culture, symbolizing strength, loyalty, and freedom. This connection deepens the riding experience, adding layers of meaning to every ride.

- **Festivals:** Events like the **Dublin Horse Show** in August, draw visitors from across the globe, showcasing Ireland's equestrian heritage through competitions, exhibitions, and shows. **Web:** dublinhorseshow.com/
- **Literature and Folklore:** The horse features prominently in Irish mythology, from the mighty Morrigan transforming into

a horse at Samhain to the magical Echraidhe that could traverse land and sea.

- Riding through areas steeped in history, such as the **Boyne Valley**, you're tracing the hoofprints of history, where battles were fought, and legends were born. **Web:** ireland.com/en-us/destinations/county/meath/boyne-valley/

Safety and Welfare

Prioritizing safety ensures that horseback riding is enjoyable and respectful towards the animals that make the experience possible.

- **Helmet and Gear:** Wearing appropriate safety gear, including a helmet, is non-negotiable. Many centers provide these essentials, ensuring you're well-equipped for the ride.
- **Welfare-Focused Centers:** It is crucial to choose centers that prioritize horse welfare. Look for places that maintain small group sizes, offer horses rest days, and match horses to riders based on experience and compatibility.
- **Riding Etiquette:** Understanding basic riding etiquette, such as how to approach and handle horses, maintaining a calm demeanor, and following the guide's instructions, enhances safety for everyone.

Trekking through Ireland's countryside on horseback is the ultimate way to soak in the scenery—it's both up-close and far-reaching. It's your chance to dial it back a notch and catch the fine details: how the light dances across the fields, the sweet smell of wildflowers you trot past, and the rhythmic stride of your horse. Sitting in the saddle, you blend right into the canvas of Ireland, living out the beauty of the landscape step by step. For any horse enthusiast, riding through Ireland is an absolute must-do.

Riders On a Beach in Ireland

7.8 ROCK CLIMBING AND CAVING ADVENTURES

Ireland, with its rugged landscapes and hidden underground worlds, offers climbers and spelunkers a playground of natural wonders. The thrill of scaling a cliff face or delving into the earth's depths connects you to the raw, untamed spirit of this land in a way few other activities can. It's in these vertical and subterranean adventures where you truly feel the pulse of Ireland's ancient bedrock under your fingertips or see the history of millennia etched into the walls of vast caverns. That's if you're not too afraid to notice while hanging from a ledge.

Climbing Locations

The island's geological diversity presents a variety of climbing challenges, from coastal crags kissed by sea spray to inland cliffs that pierce the sky.

- **Fair Head in County Antrim** is a climber's paradise, offering over 400 routes on dolerite cliffs. Here, you can chase the sun until it dips below the horizon, bathing the rock in golden hues. **Web:** explorefairhead.com/climbing/

- **Dalkey Quarry,** just a stone's throw from Dublin, provides a more accessible but equally thrilling climb, with granite walls that cater to both the novice seeking to learn and the expert honing their craft. **Web:** hikeandclimb.ie/rock-climbing-dublin/
- **Ailladie,** also known as the Cliffs of Moher's lesser-known cousin in County Clare, is a limestone sea cliff that demands respect. Here, climbers battle not just gravity but the Atlantic wind, adding an extra layer of challenge. **Web:** mountainproject.com/area/108990482/ailladie

Caving Exploration

Below the surface, Ireland's limestone regions harbor a hidden world of caves, each a labyrinth waiting to be explored.

- **Marble Arch Caves in County Fermanagh** invite you into an underworld of rivers, waterfalls, and fossil-studded passageways. The guided tours here offer a gentle introduction to caving, suitable for families and those looking to dip their toes into spelunking. **Web:** marblearchcaves. co.uk/
- For the more adventurous, **Pollnagollum Cave in the Burren** beckons. Part of the extensive Burren cave system, it's a place where water has sculpted beauty from the rock, creating a playground for experienced cavers. **Web:** burrenoec.com/activities-in-the-burren/caving-in-the-burren/

Equipment and Guides

Whether you're reaching for the sky or exploring the depths, having the right gear and guidance is key. Climbing essentials include harnesses, helmets, and climbing shoes, all of which can be rented from local outdoor centers. For caving, add a headlamp, waterproof clothing, and sturdy boots to the list.

Local guides can transform these adventures, offering not just safety expertise but insights into the geology, history, and tales of the areas you're exploring. Many outdoor centers provide courses and guided excursions, ensuring you get the most out of your adventure, whether it's your first climb or you're an experienced caver.

Environmental Considerations

The very landscapes that call to climbers and cavers are delicate ecosystems, home to unique flora and fauna and vulnerable to human impact.

- **Stick to established routes** to minimize erosion and disturbance. In caving, this also means avoiding sensitive formations that have taken thousands of years to form.
- **Pack out what you pack in**, ensuring that these natural playgrounds remain pristine for future adventurers and the wildlife that calls them home.
- **Respect closures**, especially during nesting or breeding seasons. Many climbing areas are home to rare bird species, and access might be restricted at certain times of the year to protect them.

Climbing Ireland's cliffs or exploring its caves offers more than just a physical challenge; it's about connecting with the terrain. It's a relationship based on mutual respect, curiosity, and the excitement of discoveries. Whether you're gripping a rugged cliff face or stepping deeper into a cave, each move is part of Ireland's unique adventure landscape, blending the adrenaline of the climb with the intrigue of what lies below. This is where every climber and explorer can engage with Ireland's wild side. Will you dare to be wild?

Wild Goats in Northern Ireland

7.9 ECO-TOURS: WITNESSING IRELAND'S WILDLIFE

Nature has always had a way of crafting scenes that no painter could hope to replicate, and Ireland's wildlife is like a live gallery, constantly changing with the seasons. The opportunity to observe these creatures in their natural habitats is not just a privilege; it feels like being let in on a secret, one that unfolds in the rustling of leaves, the shadowy figures in the twilight, and the silent ripples on a lake's surface. If you want to experience what only Ireland can offer, then go on an Eco-tour.

Wildlife Tours

Ireland is home to an array of eco-tours that bring you face-to-face with the country's wildlife, not through glass or fences, but in the open air where it belongs.

- **Birdwatching in the Wexford Slobs** offers a chance to see migrating birds from the Arctic, turning the sky into a

fluttering tapestry each winter. **Web:**
wexfordwildfowlreserve.ie/
- **Seal watching off the coast of Kerry** lets you glide in kayaks
  alongside these playful creatures and observe their antics up
  close. **Web:** seafariireland.com/index.php/seafari-cruises-
  kenmare-bay/
- **Deer spotting in Killarney National Park** during the rutting
  season is a powerful display of nature's drama, best
  experienced from a respectful distance. **Web:** killarneyguide.
  ie/view-red-deer/

Here are three Ireland-based eco-tour companies that offer tours in
Ireland, each providing unique opportunities to explore the natural
beauty and wildlife of the region:

- **Wild N Happy Travel** specializes in eco-tours that take
  travelers off the beaten path in Ireland. It emphasizes
  sustainable travel and local experiences. Its tours range from
  day trips to multi-day adventures across various Irish
  landscapes. **Web:** wildnhappytravel.com/
- **Blasket Island Eco Tour**—Operated by Dingle Boat Tours,
  this eco-tour focuses on the wildlife and natural scenery
  around Blasket Island in County Kerry. It offers a chance to
  see marine life and learn about the local history and folklore.
  Web: dingleboattours.com/tours/blasket-island/wildlife-eco-
  tour/
- **HilltopTreks** offers walking, hiking, and adventure tours
  throughout Ireland, including eco-friendly options that
  explore the country's rich landscapes and cultural heritage.
  Their tours are designed to provide an immersive natural
  experience. **Web:** hilltoptreks.com/

Each company provides a distinct approach to eco-tourism, catering
to different interests and ways of exploring Ireland's ecological

wonders. Each experience is guided by experts who know the land and its inhabitants like the back of their hand, ensuring you get the most out of the trip without stepping too heavily on nature's toes.

Conservation Efforts

The beauty of these tours lies in their commitment to conservation, offering insights into Ireland's efforts to protect its natural heritage.

Eco-tours contribute to local conservation projects, turning each trip into a step towards preserving Ireland's biodiversity. Guides share stories of habitat restoration and species protection, highlighting the importance of every creature, from the smallest insect to the largest mammal. This approach turns each excursion into a lesson in environmental stewardship, reminding us that we're all part of a larger ecosystem.

Ethical Guidelines

- **Respect** is the watchword when it comes to wildlife observation. Here are a few guidelines that ensure our curiosity doesn't become an intrusion.
- **Keep noise to a minimum** to avoid startling animals; often, silence rewards you with the most intimate encounters.
- **Use binoculars or zoom lenses** for a closer look, keeping a safe distance that respects the animals' need for space.
- **Follow the guide's lead**, as they know how to navigate the area without causing harm or stress to wildlife.

By adhering to these simple principles, we ensure our presence is as unobtrusive as possible, allowing nature to continue its rhythm undisturbed.

Sheep On the Side of Road, County Mayo

Unique Species

Ireland's fauna might not feature the large predators of other conti-nents, but its unique species are no less fascinating.

- The Irish hare, distinct from its European cousin, is a sight to behold in the early dawn across the peatlands.
- Puffins, with their colorful beaks and clownish walk, bring a burst of color to the cliffs they inhabit during the breeding season.
- The red deer of Killarney, the largest and oldest of its kind in Ireland, roams the national park with a majesty that harks back to ancient times.

Spotting these creatures in their element is a reminder of the diversity and resilience of wildlife, even on a relatively small island like Ireland.

As this chapter comes to an end, remember that Ireland's natural beauty is more than just visually striking; it's a fragile ecosystem that we're lucky to experience. From the birds in the sky to the seals along the coast, each animal contributes to the overall vitality of this environment. Our eco-tours and conservation efforts are crucial for preserving this balance, ensuring that future generations can also enjoy Ireland's wildlife. Let's remember what we've learned from observing nature and its inhabitants.

NAVIGATING IRELAND'S LGBTQ+ LANDSCAPE

Welcome to Gay Ireland, a land of breathtaking landscapes, rich history, profound social progress, and vibrant LGBTQ+ culture. I know Ireland isn't known as a gay mecca for travelers, but perhaps it should be. This chapter offers a comprehensive guide for LGBTQ+ travelers seeking to explore Ireland's welcoming community.

8.1 EXPANDED HISTORY OF THE LGBTQ+ EXPERIENCE IN IRELAND

Ireland's journey towards LGBTQ+ acceptance and rights has been transformative, marking significant progress from a historically conservative stance to becoming a leader in LGBTQ+ equality on the global stage.

Decriminalization of Homosexuality

Homosexuality was decriminalized in Ireland in 1993, a landmark decision that came after years of activism and legal challenges. This pivotal moment was largely influenced by the European Court of

Human Rights ruling in the case of David Norris, a gay rights activist who challenged the Irish state over the criminalization of homosexual acts. The decriminalization marked the beginning of a new era for LGBTQ+ rights in Ireland, setting the stage for further reforms and the promotion of equality.

Legalization of Same-Sex Marriage

In 2015, Ireland made history by becoming the first country in the world to legalize same-sex marriage through a popular vote. The referendum saw a significant turnout, with over 60% of voters supporting the amendment to the constitution. This event was not only a triumph for the LGBTQ+ community in Ireland but also a powerful message to the world about the importance of democracy and equality. The successful referendum reflected a profound shift in societal attitudes and showcased the Irish public's commitment to inclusivity and human rights.

Additional Legal Protections and Social Changes

Following these key milestones, Ireland has implemented a range of legal protections to safeguard LGBTQ+ individuals from discrimination and hate crimes. The Employment Equality Act and the Equal Status Act, both amended to strengthen community protections, prohibit discrimination based on sexual orientation in employment, vocational training, advertising, collective agreements, and the provision of goods and services.

In addition to legal reforms, Ireland has seen an increase in the visibility and representation of LGBTQ+ individuals in media, politics, and public life, which has helped normalize LGBTQ+ identities and relationships in the broader cultural consciousness. Public figures, including Leo Varadkar, who became the first openly gay Taoiseach (Prime Minister) in 2017, have also played significant roles in promoting LGBTQ+ rights and visibility.

Current Atmosphere and Continued Advocacy

Today, Ireland boasts a vibrant and active LGBTQ+ community with numerous organizations dedicated to supporting various segments of the community, including youth, elderly, and transgender individuals. Annual pride events, cultural festivals, and advocacy campaigns continue to promote and celebrate LGBTQ+ life across the country.

Despite these advances, the journey is not complete. Challenges remain, particularly in rural areas where conservative views may still prevail, and among certain demographics facing higher rates of discrimination and mental health issues. Ongoing efforts by activists and community organizations strive to address these issues, ensuring that Ireland's progress continues and that the rights and well-being of LGBTQ+ individuals are universally respected and upheld.

This historical and ongoing narrative of progress and advocacy highlights Ireland as not only a travel destination rich in culture and beauty but also as a beacon of LGBTQ+ rights and acceptance. Whether visiting to participate in the bustling pride festivities, engaging with the community, or exploring Ireland's beautiful landscapes, LGBTQ+ travelers can witness and partake in a society that celebrates diversity and champions equality.

8.2 FESTIVALS AND EVENTS

Dublin Pride

- **What is it?** It is the largest pride festival in Ireland.
- **Where is it?** Dublin
- **When is it?** Late June
- **How much is it?** Mostly free; some events are ticketed for around €10-€30.
- **Web:** dublinpride.ie/
- **Instagram:** @dublinpride

Participants During the Dublin Pride Festival

Outburst Queer Arts Festival

- **What is it?** A festival showcasing queer arts including film, literature, and visual arts.
- **Where is it?** Belfast, Northern Ireland
- **When is it?** November
- **How much is it?** Events range from free to £15.
- **Web:** outburstarts.com/
- **Instagram:** @outburstarts

Cork Pride

- **What is it?** A week-long celebration of LGBTQ+ culture and community.
- **Where is it?** Cork
- **When is it?** Early August
- **How much is it?** Mostly free; some ticketed events.
- **Web:** corkpride.com/
- **Instagram:** @corkpride

GAZE LGBT Film Festival

- **What is it?** Film festival celebrating LGBTQ+ cinema.
- **Where is it?** Dublin
- **When is it?** Late July to early August
- **How much is it?** Around €10 per screening.
- **Web**: gaze.ie/
- **Instagram:** @gazefilmfest

Limerick Pride

- **What is it?** Festival with a parade, music, and community events.
- **Where is it?** Limerick
- **When is it?** July
- **How much is it?** Free to €10 for certain events.
- **Web:** limerickpride.ie/
- **Instagram:** @limerickpride

International Dublin Gay Theatre Festival

- **What is it?** Celebrates the contributions of gay individuals to theater.
- **Where is it?** Dublin
- **When is it?** Early May
- **How much is it?** €10-€15 per show.
- **Web:** gaytheatre.ie/
- **Instagram:** @dublingaytheatre

Galway Community Pride

- **What is it?** Community-focused pride celebrations.
- **Where is it?** Galway
- **When is it?** Mid-August
- **How much is it?** Mostly free.

- **Web:** galwaypride.ie/
- **Instagram:** @galwaypride

Waterford Pride

- **What is it?** Pride festival with events centered around LGBTQ+ rights and celebration.
- **Where is it?** Waterford
- **When is it?** Late August
- **How much is it?** Free and ticketed events.
- **Web:** prideofthedeise.com/
- **Instagram:** @waterfordpride

Belfast Pride

- **What is it?** The largest pride event in Northern Ireland.
- **Where is it?** Belfast, Northern Ireland
- **When is it?** Late July to early August
- **How much is it?** Mostly free.
- **Web:** belfastpride.com/
- **Instagram:** @belfastpride

Mayo Pride

- **What is it?** Smaller, community-oriented pride festival.
- **Where is it?** County Mayo
- **When is it?** Early July
- **How much is it?** Free to minimal charge for certain events.
- **Website:** mayopride.com/
- **Instagram:** @mayopride

8.3 RESTAURANTS AND PUBS

Pantibar

- **What is it?** Popular bar and restaurant owned by Panti Bliss, a renowned drag performer.
- **Where is it?** Dublin, Capel Street
- **How much is it?** €15-€20 per person.
- **Web:** pantibar.com/
- **Instagram:** @pantibardublin

Pantibar in Dublin City Centre

Oscar's Bar and Kitchen

- **What is it?** Bar and restaurant with a friendly vibe and a menu that includes comfort food.
- **Where is it?** Dublin, Smithfield
- **How much is it?** €15-€30 per person.
- **Website:** oscarscafebar.com/

- **Instagram:** @oscarscafebar

Brasserie Sixty6

- **What is it?** Upscale restaurant offering a wide range of dishes prepared with fresh ingredients.
- **Where is it?** Dublin, George's Street
- **How much is it?** €20-€40 per person.
- **Web:** brasseriesixty6.com/
- **Instagram:** @brasseriesixty6

Cafe Bliss

- **What is it?** A cozy cafe offering a diverse, vegetarian-friendly menu.
- **Where is it?** Dublin, Montague Street
- **How much is it?** €10-€15 per person.
- **Web:** blisscafe.ie/
- **Instagram:** @cafeblissdublin

Mykonos Taverna

- **What is it?** Authentic Greek restaurant known for its lively atmosphere and delicious Mediterranean cuisine.
- **Where is it?** Dublin, Dame Street
- **How much is it?** €15-€30 per person.
- **Web:** mykonosdublin.com/
- **Instagram:** @mykonostavernadublin

Pho Viet

- **What is it?** A Vietnamese restaurant that offers traditional Pho and other Vietnamese specialties.
- **Where is it?** Dublin, Parnell Street
- **How much is it?** €10-€20 per person.

- **Web:** phokim.ie/menu
- **Instagram:** @phovietdublin

Brother Hubbard North

- **What is it?** Cafe and restaurant serving Middle Eastern-inspired dishes, popular for brunch and coffee.
- **Where is it?** Dublin, Capel Street
- **How much is it?** €10-€25 per person.
- **Web:** brotherhubbard.ie/
- **Instagram:** @brother_hubbard_north

The Chili Shack

- **What is it?** American-style diner known for its chili, burgers, and relaxed vibe.
- **Where is it?** Galway, Quay Street and Dublin, Prussia Street
- **How much is it?** €10-€20 per person.
- **Web:** facebook.com/TheChiliShackGalway/
- **Instagram:** @thechilishack

8.4 DANCE CLUBS AND DISCOTHEQUES

The George

- **What is it?** Iconic LGBTQ+ nightclub known for its vibrant drag performances and dance parties.
- **Where is it?** Dublin, South Great George's Street
- **How much is it?** €5-€10 entry.
- **Website:** thegeorge.ie/
- **Instagram:** @thegeorgedublin

Mother Club

- **What is it?** It is a trendy nightclub and a hotspot for the LGBTQ+ community, known for its electronic music and lively dance floor.
- **Where is it?** Dublin, Eustace Street
- **How much is it?** €10 entry.
- **Website:** motherclub.ie/
- **Instagram:** @motherdublin

Boombox

- **What is it?** Belfast's popular gay club, featuring regular drag shows and themed nights.
- **Where is it?** Belfast, Donegall Street
- **How much is it?** £5-£10 entry.
- **Website:** facebook.com/boomboxbelfast
- **Instagram:** @boomboxbelfast

Kremlin

- **What is it?** Northern Ireland's first gay-owned and managed club, offering a Soviet-themed setting with a large dance floor.
- **Where is it?** Belfast, Donegall Street
- **How much is it?** £5-£10 entry.
- **Website:** facebook.com/Kremlin.Belfast
- **Instagram:** @kremlinbelfast

Pantibar

- **What is it?** Not just a bar but a lively spot for dancing and drag shows, especially popular early in the evening.
- **Where is it?** Dublin, Capel Street
- **How much is it?** Free entry: drinks are priced separately.
- **Website:** facebook.com/PantiBarDublin/

- **Instagram:** @pantibardublin

Euphoria

- **What is it?** Occasional large-scale gay dance parties featuring international DJs and performers.
- **Where is it?** Dublin, various large venues
- **How much is it?** €20-€30 entry.
- **Website:** facebook.com/euphoriadublin/
- **Instagram:** @euphoriaireland

PrHomo

- **What is it?** A weekly LGBTQ+ nightclub event known for its energetic vibe and themed nights.
- **Where is it?** Dublin, Liffey Street Lower
- **How much is it?** €5-€10 entry.
- **Website:** facebook.com/DiscoBabyDublin/
- **Instagram:** @prhomodublin

8.5 GAY-FRIENDLY ACCOMMODATIONS

The Dean Dublin

- **What is it?** Stylish, modern hotel in the city center, known for its artsy vibe and excellent service.
- **Where is it?** Dublin, Harcourt Street
- **How much is it?** Starts at €120 per night.
- **Website:** thedean.ie/dublin/
- **Instagram:** @thedean.dublin

The Merchant Hotel

- **What is it?** Luxury hotel offering opulent decor and top-notch amenities in a historic building.

- **Where is it?** Belfast, Skipper Street
- **How much is it?** Starts at £200 per night.
- **Website:** themerchanthotel.com/
- **Instagram:** @merchantbelfast

Brooks Hotel

- **What is it?** Boutique hotel with a warm atmosphere, centrally located and offering a personalized experience.
- **Where is it?** Dublin, Drury Street
- **How much is it?** Starts at €150 per night.
- **Website:** brookshotel.ie/
- **Instagram:** @brookshoteldublin

The G Hotel

- **What is it?** A uniquely designed luxury hotel by famous milliner Philip Treacy, known for its bold aesthetics.
- **Where is it?** Galway, Wellpark
- **How much is it?** Starts at €140 per night.
- **Website:** theghotel.ie/
- **Instagram:** @theghotelgalway

The Clarence

- **What is it?** Upscale boutique hotel, co-owned by Bono and The Edge of U2, located in Dublin's Temple Bar district.
- **Where is it?** Dublin, Wellington Quay
- **How much is it?** Starts at €150 per night.
- **Website:** theclarence.ie/
- **Instagram:** @theclarencehotel

The Fitzwilliam Hotel

- **What is it?** Five-star hotel offering contemporary elegance and superb service, right next to St. Stephen's Green.
- **Where is it?** Dublin, St. Stephen's Green
- **How much is it?** Starts at €200 per night.
- **Website:** fitzwilliamhoteldublin.com/
- **Instagram:** @fitzwilliamhotel

Culloden Estate and Spa

- **What is it?** Luxury estate providing serene accommodations with a spa located just outside Belfast.
- **Where is it?** Belfast, Bangor Road
- **How much is it?** Starts at £180 per night.
- **Website:** cullodenestateandspa.com/
- **Instagram:** @cullodenestate

Generator Hostel

- **What is it?** A trendy, budget-friendly hostel known for its vibrant social atmosphere and modern design.
- **Where is it?** Dublin, Smithfield Square
- **How much is it?** Dorm beds from €30, private rooms from €90.
- **Website:** staygenerator.com/hostels/dublin
- **Instagram:** @generatorhostels

The Shelbourne

- **What is it?** It is an iconic five-star hotel known for its historic significance and luxurious accommodations.
- **Where is it?** Dublin, St. Stephen's Green
- **How much is it?** Starts at €250 per night.
- **Website:** theshelbourne.com/

- **Instagram:** @theshelbournedublin

Hotel Isaacs Cork

- **What is it?** Charming hotel with a rustic feel, offering comfortable rooms and a popular restaurant.
- **Where is it?** Cork, MacCurtain Street
- **How much is it?** Starts at €100 per night.
- **Website:** hotelisaacscork.com/
- **Instagram:** @hotelisaacscork

8.6 HISTORICAL PLACES OR SITES RELATED TO THE LGBTQ+ COMMUNITY IN IRELAND.

Ireland's landscape is painted not just with its lush hills and timeless ruins but also with landmarks that tell the tale of the LGBTQ+ community's path to acceptance and equality. This commitment to honoring such a crucial part of its history shines through at various significant sites across the country. These spots provide a unique glimpse into the critical moments, cultural shifts, and courageous individuals who have been pivotal in advancing LGBTQ+ rights and visibility in Ireland.

From statues and museums dedicated to trailblazing figures to lively venues and community centers that have acted as both sanctuaries and platforms for advocacy, each location contributes to the broader narrative of the community's challenges and victories. These places are more than educational; they're a celebration of the LGBTQ+ community's enduring impact on Ireland's societal tapestry.

Oscar Wilde Statue

- **Where is it?** Merrion Square, Dublin
- **What is it?** A statue commemorating the famous Irish writer, Oscar Wilde.
- **How much is it?** Free

- **Website:** No official website
- **Instagram:** N/A

The George, Dublin

The George

- **Where is it?** South Great George's Street, Dublin
- **What is it?** One of Dublin's oldest and most famous gay bars and clubs.
- **How much is it?** Entry fees vary depending on the event.
- **Website:** thegeorge.ie/
- **Instagram:** @thegeorgedublin

Pantibar

- **Where is it?** Capel Street, Dublin
- **What is it?** It is a popular gay bar owned by Panti Bliss, an

iconic drag queen and gay rights activist in Ireland. She's iconic, so we include it in our historical places.

- **How much is it?** Free entry: drinks and food are priced separately.
- **Website:** facebook.com/PantiBarDublin/
- **Instagram:** @pantibardublin

Gay Community News (GCN)

- **Where is it?** Digital and print in various locations, headquartered in Dublin.
- **What is it?** Ireland's national monthly free gay magazine.
- **How much is it?** Free
- **Website:** gcn.ie/
- **Instagram:** @gcnmag

Cork Gay Project

- **Where is it?** Cork City, Cork
- **What is it?** An organization and community space offering support and resources for gay and bisexual men.
- **How much is it?** Access to the space and many events are free.
- **Website:** gayproject.ie/
- **Instagram:** @corkgayproject

Irish Queer Archive

- **Where is it?** National Library of Ireland, Dublin
- **What is it?** One of the largest collections of material relating to LGBTQ+ life in Ireland.
- **How much is it?** Free
- **Website:** nli.ie/
- **Instagram:** @national_library_of_ireland

Belong To Youth Services

- **Where is it?** Parliament Street, Dublin
- **What is it?** An organization focused on supporting lesbian, gay, bisexual, transgender, and queer young people in Ireland.
- **How much is it?** Free; donations are welcome.
- **Website:** belongto.org/
- **Instagram:** @belongtoyouthservices

The Outing Festival

- **Where is it?** Various locations, including Lisdoonvarna
- **What is it?** It is an LGBTQ+ music, arts, and matchmaking festival, originally part of the traditional Lisdoonvarna Matchmaking Festival.
- **How much is it?** Ticket prices vary based on events.
- **Website:** theouting.ie/
- **Instagram:** @theoutingfestival

Kilmainham Gaol

- **Where is it?** Inchicore Road, Kilmainham, Dublin
- **What is it?** It is a former prison-turned-museum with exhibitions that touch on historical figures believed to be part of the LGBTQ+ community.
- **How much is it?** Admission is approximately €9 for adults.
- **Website:** kilmainhamgaolmuseum.ie/
- **Instagram:** @kilmainhamgaol

Ireland's landscape is dotted with sites that weave together historical and modern LGBTQ+ stories, spotlighting both achievements and challenges. Iconic landmarks like the Oscar Wilde Statue pay tribute to LGBTQ+ figures and the adversities they've overcome. Hotspots like The George and Pantibar pulse with community life and activism, offering a peek into the vibrant day-to-day. Meanwhile, treasures like the Irish Queer Archive give a deep dive into the historical backdrop, linking past battles with today's push for equality. These sites do more than educate—they're living memories and beacons for ongoing advocacy. Delving into these locations not only enriches your understanding of Ireland's cultural fabric and shifting social policies but also stirs a sense of advocacy and connection, both within the LGBTQ+ community and beyond.

Cautions and Tips

While Ireland is widely recognized for its friendly and open attitude towards LGBTQ+ visitors, it's important to remain aware of local norms and cultural sensitivities, especially in rural areas. Here are some tips for a safe and enjoyable trip:

- **Research Local Laws and Customs:** While LGBTQ+ rights in Ireland are progressive, it's always good to be aware of local laws and cultural attitudes, especially when displaying affection publicly.
- **Stay Informed About Events:** Some events might be more popular and can get crowded. It's a good idea to book tickets any accommodations well in advance.
- **Use Respectful Communication:** Always be respectful when interacting with locals and other tourists, regardless of the setting.
- **Safety First:** Keep your belongings secure and stay aware of your environment, especially at night and in less familiar areas.

Exploring Ireland's LGBTQ+ scene with an understanding of these elements will help ensure that your visit is as enjoyable and fulfilling as possible. Whether you're attending a spirited festival, dining in a cozy restaurant, dancing the night away, or relaxing in a luxurious hotel, Ireland offers a rich array of experiences that welcome and celebrate the LGBTQ+ community.

NAVIGATING THE EMERALD ISLE

A LOCAL'S GUIDE TO GETTING AROUND

P icture this: You've just landed, buzzing with excitement, ready to soak up every inch of Ireland's lush landscapes and vibrant cities. But there's a catch – getting from A to B isn't always a straight line, especially when you're aiming to wander off the beaten path. Fear not! This chapter isn't about taking the usual points A to B; it's about zigzagging through Ireland with the savvy of someone who's done it all before.

County Map of Ireland with Major Cities

NAVIGATING PUBLIC TRANSPORT LIKE A LOCAL

Navigating Ireland's public transport system is a lot like making a good Irish stew. It requires a bit of knowledge, the right ingredients, and a touch of patience. Whether it's hopping on a bus in a bustling city or catching a train through rolling countryside, understanding how the system ticks can turn potential travel headaches into smooth sailing.

Man at Dublin Train Station

Understanding the System

The backbone of Ireland's public transport includes buses, trains, and trams, each serving different slices of the country. Buses reach wide, trains offer comfort and scenic views, and trams glide through city streets. While cities like Dublin boast a more intricate web of options, including the Luas tram system, rural areas lean heavily on buses for public transport. For cross-country jaunts, trains are your best bet, connecting major hubs with speed and comfort.

Transport Apps and Cards

Apps like Transport for Ireland (TFI) and Leap Card streamline the process, putting schedules and ticketing right at your fingertips. The Leap Card, a pay-as-you-go smart card, works across buses, trains, and trams in major cities, offering discounts and capping daily expenses so you never overspend. For planning routes, Google Maps is surprisingly reliable, offering real-time public transport info. Google Maps is also great for downloading maps to use offline.

Web: transportforireland.ie/ and leapcard.ie/Home/index.html

Schedule Insights

City transport runs like clockwork, offering frequent services. Once you venture into the countryside, however, timetables become more like guidelines. Buses might run less often, making missing one a real hiccup in your plans. Always have a plan B, like a cozy café or a nearby attraction to explore while you wait.

Cultural Nuances

Riding public transport in Ireland is more than just getting from one place to another; it's an opportunity to dip into the local culture. Don't be surprised if a bus driver goes off-route to drop someone closer to their home or if chatting with a fellow passenger turns into a mini-history lesson. These interactions add flavor to your journey, making each trip memorable. In this instance, talking to strangers is good.

Quick Tips for Using Public Transport:

- **Use Transport Apps:** Download apps like "Transport for Ireland" for real-time schedules and route planning.
- **Get a Transport Card:** Invest in a Leap Card for convenient and discounted travel on buses, trains, and trams.
- **Plan Your Route:** Check routes and schedules in advance to avoid delays and missed connections. The websites for your mode of transport have excellent maps to reference.
- **Arrive Early:** Allow extra time for unexpected delays, especially during peak hours.
- **Stay Informed:** Follow public transport updates on social media for news and alerts on service disruptions.

Tour Bus on The Ring of Kerry

It's Quiz Time again! No grumbling. Take this quiz to see what mode of transport is best for you.

What's Your Irish Transport Match?

1. What's your priority when traveling?

A. Efficiency – I want to get to my destination quickly.
B. Comfort – I prefer relaxed and comfortable journeys.
C. Cost – I'm looking for the most budget-friendly option.

2. How do you describe your traveling style?

A. Adventurous – I like to explore and don't mind transfers.
B. Scheduled – I prefer planned routes and timetables.
C. Spontaneous – I go wherever the road takes me, with flexibility.

3. What kind of areas do you plan to visit?

A. Mostly urban areas, staying within city limits.
B. A mix of cities and some rural or scenic areas outside the cities.
C. Primarily rural areas and off the beaten paths.

4. What do you usually carry with you on day trips?

A. Just a small bag with essentials.
B. A backpack with everything I might need for the day.
C. Several items, so I usually carry quite a bit of luggage.

5. What's your ideal travel time for daily excursions?

A. Less than 30 minutes.
B. About an hour or so.
C. I don't mind long journeys if the views are worth it.

6. How important is having direct routes to your destinations?

A. Very important—I prefer going straight to my destination.
B. Somewhat important—I don't mind a few stops if it's efficient.
C. Not important—I like to see as many places as possible.

Yellow Bus on Dublin Street

Results:

Mostly A's: Trams

You're best suited for trams, especially if you stay within cities like Dublin where trams are efficient for short, quick hops around town.

Mostly B's: Trains

Trains are your go-to mode of transport. Ideal for enjoying comfortable rides between major cities and scenic rural areas, Irish Rail offers extensive connectivity with reliable schedules.

Mostly C's: Buses

Buses will serve you well, providing the flexibility to explore a wide range of destinations, including those off the beaten path. Bus Éireann and other local services offer comprehensive routes covering both urban and rural Ireland.

This quiz can guide you in choosing the best mode of public transportation in Ireland according to your travel preferences and the nature of your trip. Enjoy your travels!

Now that you've decided which mode of transportation here's a checklist of **"Must-Have Apps for Navigating Ireland Like a Local,"** designed to enhance your travel experience through convenient scheduling, route planning, and ticket purchasing:

TFI Live App

- It is perfect for planning routes and accessing real-time departure information for public transportation across Ireland, including Bus Éireann, Dublin Bus, and more.
- Download: Available for both iOS and Android devices. transportforireland.ie/available-apps/tfi-live/

TFI Leap Card Top-Up App

- Manage your TFI Leap Card on the go. Top up your balance, check your transaction history, and more, using NFC technology.
- Download: Android (NFC-enabled devices only). leapcard.ie/leap-top-up-app

TFI Go App

- Purchase and store tickets directly on your phone, helping you go paperless and ensuring easy ticket access for buses and trams.
- Download: Available for both iOS and Android devices. transportforireland.ie/tfi-go-app/

Luas

- Ideal for tram riders in Dublin, providing route maps and real-time schedule updates.
- Download: iOS, Android luas.ie/

Irish Rail

- Get train times and book tickets across all Irish Rail services.
- Download: iOS, Android irishrail.ie/en-ie/travel-information/mobile-and-apps

FreeNow

- Book and pay for taxis throughout Ireland. Great for areas where other rideshare apps might not be available.
- Download: iOS, Android free-now.com/ie/

Moovit App

- The Most Popular Urban Mobility App in Ireland. All local mobility options in one app
- Download: iOS, Android moovitapp.com/index/en/ public_transit-Ireland-502

Taxis

- Taxis are another great way to get around the cities and sometimes can be hired for tours. You can get more information here about using taxis, including a fare estimator and taxi company links in various cities: ireland.com/en-gb/plan-your-trip/travel/taxis-in-ireland/

XE Currency

- An essential tool for international travelers to convert currency easily, even offline.
- Download: iOS, Android xe.com/apps/

Each of these apps offers unique features that can help streamline your travel experiences in Ireland, from quick ticket purchases to navigating complex transport networks with real-time data. Whether you're a frequent commuter or a tourist exploring the Emerald Isle, these apps will help you navigate Ireland like a local.

For more detailed information, you can visit the websites of Transport for Ireland, which provides comprehensive details about these apps and other useful travel tools.

In weaving through Ireland's cities and countryside, armed with a bit of know-how and the right tools, you'll find yourself slipping into the rhythm of local life. Whether it's striking up a conversation on a tram in Dublin or watching the world go by from a train window, each journey contributes to the patchwork of your Irish adventure.

Of course, rent a car for those of you who are daring and adventurous. It will allow you the freedom to come and go as you please and be on your own schedule. Just make sure to check with your insurance company about coverage in a foreign country. Most importantly, don't forget to drive on the left side and wear your seatbelt! Apps such as Google Maps or Waze make navigating Ireland a breeze.

9.2 ESSENTIAL IRISH PHRASES FOR TRAVELERS

Strolling through the cobbled streets of Dublin or finding your way around the wild, windswept landscapes of Connemara requires more than just a sense of adventure. A few Irish phrases in your pocket can bridge worlds, turning brief encounters into meaningful exchanges. Here's how you can sprinkle a bit of linguistic magic into your travels across Ireland.

Greetings and Politeness

A smile accompanied by a heartfelt **"Dia dhuit"** (Hello) can open doors to Ireland's soul. This greeting, literally meaning "God to you," reflects the deep-rooted warmth of the Irish spirit. Responses vary from a simple **"Dia is Muire dhuit" (Hello to you too)** to a nod of acknowledgment. Remember, a **"Please"** (Le do thoil) and "Thank you" (Go raibh maith agat) never go amiss, weaving respect and appreciation into everyday interactions.

- **Good morning: "Maidin mhaith"**
- **Good evening: "Tráthnóna maith"**
- **Excuse me: "Gabh mo leithscéal"**

Incorporating these phrases into your daily interactions not only demonstrates respect but also invites warmer, more engaging conversations with locals.

Directions and Assistance

Finding your way around might lead you down paths less traveled, and knowing how to ask for directions makes the journey smoother. **"An bhfuil tú in ann cabhrú liom, le do thoil?" (Can you help me, please?)** is your key to unlocking assistance and advice. When looking for specific places, **"Cá bhfuil an..."** followed by your destination, such as **"leithreas" (toilet), "stáisiún traenach" (train station), or "óstán" (hotel),** guides you to your next stop.

- **How do I get to...?: "Conas a fhaighim go dtí...?"**
- **Is this the right way to...?: "An é seo an bealach ceart go dtí...?"**
- **Can you show me on the map?: "An féidir leat taispeáint dom ar an léarscáil?"**

Armed with these phrases, navigating the winding roads and quaint lanes of Ireland will become part of the adventure.

Dining and Allergies

Ireland's culinary landscape is a feast for the senses, and diving into it requires a bit of linguistic prep, especially for those with dietary preferences or allergies. **"An bhfuil biachlár agaibh?" (Do you have a menu?)** to start your culinary journey. If you have dietary restrictions, **"Tá ailléirge agam le..." (I am allergic to...)** followed by **"cnónna" (nuts),** "glútan" (gluten), or "bainne" (dairy) ensures your needs are met.

- **I'm vegetarian: "Táim veigeatóir"**
- **Is this dish spicy?: "An bhfuil an mhias seo spíosrach?"**
- **Can I have...?: "An féidir liom... a bheith agam?"**

These phrases not only help you navigate menus but also enrich your dining experience, allowing you to savor Ireland's flavors worry-free.

Cultural Connection

Language is more than words; it's a gateway to understanding a culture. Sprinkling your conversations with Irish phrases does more than just break the ice; it will help you feel more a part of the fabric of daily life, turning fleeting moments into lasting memories.

- **Cheers:** "**Sláinte**" is more than a toast; it's a celebration of health, happiness, and good company.
- **How are you?:** "**Conas atá tú?**" shows genuine interest in the well-being of those you meet, often leading to heartfelt exchanges.
- **I love Ireland:** "**Is breá liom Éire**" expresses your appreciation for the country's beauty and warmth, resonating deeply with locals.

Using these phrases, you're not just a visitor; you're an active participant in the vivid mosaic of Irish life, building bridges of understanding and shared experiences.

Using apps like Duolingo duolingo.com/ or Google Translate translate.google.com/about/, can make your Irish speaking even better!

Up for a challenge? Here's a fun "Test Your Irish" game designed to challenge your knowledge of Irish phrases and their meanings. This game is perfect for honing your Irish language skills during a train ride or while waiting for your pint to settle.

How to Play:

- Read each Irish phrase listed below.
- Choose the correct English translation from the options provided.
- Check your answers at the end to see how well you know your Irish! No cheating! 😊

IRISH PHRASES GAME:

1. Phrase: "Cén chaoi a bhfuil tú?"

    A. What is your name?
    B. How are you?
    C. Where are you from?

2. Phrase: "Go raibh maith agat"

    A. Good night
    B. Please
    C. Thank you

3. Phrase: "Slán leat"

    A. Goodbye
    B. Good luck
    C. See you later

4. Phrase: "Cad is ainm duit?"

    A. What is your name?
    B. What is this?
    C. Where are you going?

5. Phrase: "Oíche mhaith"

    A. Good evening
    B. Good night
    C. Good morning

6. Phrase: "Tá sé go hálainn"

  A. It is beautiful
  B. It is raining
  C. It is cold

7. Phrase: "An bhfuil tú réidh?"

  A. Are you ready?
  B. Are you alone?
  C. Are you serious?

8. Phrase: "Cá bhfuil an leithreas?"

  A. Where is the restaurant?
  B. Where is the bathroom?
  C. Where is the exit?

9. Phrase: "Ní thuigim"

  A. I don't understand
  B. I don't know
  C. I don't think so

10. Phrase: "Ádh mór ort"

  A. Welcome
  B. Good luck
  C. Great job

ANSWERS:

1. B) How are you?
2. C) Thank you
3. A) Goodbye

4. A) What is your name?
5. B) Good night
6. A) It is beautiful
7. A) Are you ready?
8. B) Where is the bathroom?
9. A) I don't understand
10. B) Good luck

Test your skills and see how many you got right! This is a great way to immerse yourself in the Irish language and culture, especially useful if you're planning a visit or just want to broaden your linguistic horizons. Enjoy playing and learning!

Here are some personal stories from travelers to Ireland, each sharing how a simple interaction through language helped bridge cultures and create meaningful connections:

Sarah from Canada: During her visit to a traditional pub in Dublin, Sarah attempted to order in Irish, using the phrase "Pionta Guinness, le do thoil" (a pint of Guinness, please). The bartender, delighted with her effort, responded warmly, leading to an impromptu Irish language lesson from the locals at the bar. This interaction opened conversations about Irish culture and history and even led to some lifelong friendships.

Mark from the United States: While hiking along the cliffs of Moher, Mark greeted a passing local with "Dia dhuit" (Hello in Irish). The locals, surprised and pleased, stopped to chat. They ended up sharing a half-hour conversation about the best local trails and the history of the area, giving Mark insights no travel guide could offer.

Anya from Russia: In a cozy café in Cork, Anya complimented the server on the "blasta" (tasty) scones using the local dialect. This sparked a conversation about Irish baking traditions and the server ended up sharing not only the café's recipe but also recommending other local foods to try. Anya felt a deeper connection to the culture through these culinary secrets.

Javier from Spain: Javier, attending a Gaelic football match, shouted "Ádh mór!" (good luck) to the players. Fans around him appreciated his use of the Irish phrase and began explaining the rules of the game, embracing him as part of their community for the day. This experience gave him a profound sense of belonging far away from home.

Emma from Australia: Lost in Galway, Emma asked for directions to the "leithreas" (toilet), a word she had picked up from a travel app. Her correct pronunciation impressed a local old lady, who not only directed her but also shared stories about the city's landmarks as they walked to Emma's destination together.

These tales show just how mighty language is as a bridge to culture, turning plain old trips into deeply rich, all-in experiences. Just by dropping a couple of Irish phrases, travelers find doors swinging wide open to heartwarming interactions with locals, diving deeper into Ireland's traditions. This not only spices up their travels but often leads to unexpected friendships and a more vibrant understanding of Ireland's lively culture.

As you roam Ireland's emerald fields, lively towns, and rugged coasts, arm yourself with a few local phrases. They're more than simple tools for chatting; they're the keys to unlocking the true spirit of Ireland, opening gates to deeper understanding, lasting friendships, and a real connection with this magical place. And who knows? If you play your cards right, you might even snag a free pint of Guinness! Cheers to that, eh? Or should I say Sláinte? Ha!

9.3 STAYING CONNECTED: SIM CARDS AND WI-FI

Ah, the modern traveler's conundrum – to truly immerse in the beauty of a new place while still staying connected to the wider world. Ireland, with its blend of ancient landscapes and modern living, offers you the best of both. Here's how to keep those Instagram stories flowing and Google Maps guiding without missing a beat.

SIM Card Advice

First things first, let's talk about staying connected on the go. Picking up a local SIM card upon arrival not only keeps you connected but can also be kinder to your wallet compared to those pesky roaming charges. Here's how you can go about it:

- **Where to Buy:** Kiosks at airports and convenience stores across cities like Dublin and Cork are good starting points. They're hard to miss.
- **Choosing a Provider:** Ireland has a handful of key players – think Vodafone, Three, and Eir. A quick chat with the staff can help you decide which one fits your travel plans best, focusing on coverage and data packages.
- **Prepaid Plans:** These are generally the way to go. You can grab a plan that lasts you the duration of your trip, offering a mix of calls, texts, and all-important data for navigating and social media updates.
- **Activation:** It's usually a breeze. Pop the SIM into your unlocked phone (yes, do check it's unlocked before you leave home), follow a couple of simple activation steps, and you're all set.
- **Use your own:** Check with your cell phone provider about international plans. Sometimes, these can be worth it. I have used my cell phone provider in multiple countries with no issues. Once you land, it automatically picks up the local carrier.

Remember, the goal here is seamless connectivity, letting you share those breathtaking cliffside selfies without a hitch. Please watch your step!

Wi-Fi Availability

Now, for those moments when you're settled in a cozy café or back at your accommodation, Wi-Fi becomes your best friend. Here's the lowdown:

- **Urban vs. Rural:** As you might expect, Wi-Fi is more widely available and robust in city centers. That said, many rural retreats also offer Wi-Fi, though the speed might take you back in time a little.
- **Public Hotspots:** Cities offer a variety of public Wi-Fi spots – libraries, cafes, and even some buses and trains let you hop on the internet for free. Just look for the Wi-Fi symbol or ask around.
- **Accommodations:** From chic city hotels to quaint countryside B&Bs, most places understand the traveler's need to connect. Wi-Fi is often included, but it's worth checking when you book.

Just a heads up, while sipping on that perfectly brewed Irish coffee (or whiskey for you drinkers) and uploading your day's adventure, remember public Wi-Fi isn't always the fastest. Patience is key.

Data Safety Tips

With great connectivity comes great responsibility, especially when it comes to safeguarding your data. Here are a few pointers to keep your digital safe while using public Wi-Fi:

- **Avoid Sensitive Transactions:** Save those bank logins and online shopping sprees for when you're on a secure network. Public Wi-Fi and sensitive data don't mix well.
- **Use a VPN:** A **Virtual Private Network (VPN)** is like a cloak for your online activity. It keeps your data encrypted, away from prying eyes. There are plenty of reputable VPN services

out there, so consider subscribing to one for the duration of
your travels.

- **Stay Updated:** Keep your device's software up to date. Those
  updates often include security patches that protect against the
  latest cyber threats.

A little vigilance goes a long way in keeping your digital life secure as
you roam.

Staying in Touch

Today, staying connected is more than just posting updates; it's about
ensuring safety, convenience, and peace of mind during your travels.
Here's why:

- **Travel Logistics:** From booking tickets to finding that hidden
  gem of a restaurant, a connected device makes travel
  smoother. Not to mention, digital boarding passes and
  reservation confirmations are becoming the norm.
- **Emergency Contact:** Let's hope it's never needed, but having
  a way to reach out in emergencies is crucial. Whether it's
  contacting local services or reaching out to family back home,
  a connected phone is your lifeline.
- **Sharing the Journey:** Then there's the joy of sharing. Live
  videos, instant updates, and real-time chats let you bring your
  loved ones along for the ride, making those moments even
  more special.

Digital Journal Prompt: Crafting Your Connected Time in Ireland

Reflect & Plan: Your Digital Adventure in the Emerald Isle

As you prepare for your journey to Ireland, take a moment to think
about how you'll use your connected time to enhance your travel
experience. Ireland, with its rich history, stunning landscapes, and

vibrant culture, offers countless opportunities to create memorable experiences. This journal prompt encourages you to reflect on your interests and plan your activities, ensuring you make the most of your time connected digitally while in Ireland.

1. Local Lore and Legends:

- Ireland's history is steeped in myths and folklore. How can you use your connected time to delve deeper into these stories? Consider researching local legends specific to the areas you'll be visiting. Could you plan a visit to the legendary Giant's Causeway and learn about the tales of Finn McCool? Reflect on how understanding these stories could enrich your visits to historical sites.

2. Scouting Unique Locations:

- Ireland is known for its breathtaking vistas. How will you use digital tools to discover the best spots for unforgettable views? Think about using apps or websites to find the top vantage points for sunrise or sunset. Could you plan an evening at Killiney Hill to watch the sunset over Dublin Bay? List the tools and resources you'll use to find these spots.

3. Culinary Explorations:

- Reflect on how you might use your online connectivity to discover and plan visits to renowned eateries or hidden gems. Are there specific types of Irish cuisine you're eager to try? Use your connected time to look up reviews, menus, and the best times to visit popular cafes or restaurants. Perhaps there's a quaint café in Galway where you could draft your next blog post?

4. Cultural Events and Local Experiences:

- Ireland's cultural scene is vibrant with music, dance, and public gatherings. How can you use the internet to find out about local events or festivals happening during your stay? Think about experiencing traditional Irish music live at a pub or attending a hurling match. Note the websites or social media pages that could keep you updated.

5. Planning and Documenting Your Travel:

- How will you keep track of your travels and share them with others? Consider whether you'll keep a digital travel journal or blog. What platforms will you use, and how can you ensure regular updates? Plan how you might schedule time each day to document your experiences.

Reflection:

After considering the above areas, reflect on how integrating these digital plans could enhance your travel experience in Ireland. How does each activity align with your interests and travel goals? How can you balance your screen time with immersive experiences to ensure a fulfilling trip?

Take a few moments to jot down your thoughts, ideas, and plans. This reflection will not only prepare you for your journey but also ensure that you use your connected time wisely to enrich your exploration of Ireland. Safe travels and happy journaling! In the end, whether it's sharing a sunset over Galway Bay with the world or finding the way back to your lodge nestled in the Wicklow Mountains, staying connected lets you navigate Ireland with ease and share those magical moments as they unfold.

9.4 MONEY MATTERS: CURRENCY AND TIPPING

Ah, the green pastures of Ireland, where the landscapes are as rich as the culture. But let's talk green of another sort – the kind that'll ensure you're sipping that pint without worry or dining by the quayside as seamlessly as a local. Understanding the currency landscape and the nuances of financial etiquette in Ireland isn't just practical; it's your ticket to a hassle-free adventure.

Currency Overview

In this land of myth and melody, two currencies sing in harmony. The Euro dances through the Republic, while the Pound Sterling keeps the rhythm in Northern Ireland. Navigating this dual currency system is much like learning a traditional Irish jig – a bit tricky at first, but follow the steps, and you'll be in the flow in no time.

For the best exchange rates, avoid the airport dance and seek out local banks or ATMs (known as 'cash machines' around here). They usually offer more favorable rates and lower fees.

Keep an eye on the exchange rates before your trip. Apps like XE Currency offer real-time updates so you know exactly when to make your move.

Remember, while the dance floors may be shared, the tunes are different. Always double-check your currency before making transactions in border areas to avoid a mix-up.

Tipping Etiquette

Tipping in Ireland doesn't follow a strict script, but there are a few steps you can follow to ensure you're in tune with local customs.

- **Restaurants:** If service isn't included, a tip of 10-15% of the bill shows your appreciation for good service. Some places

might add a service charge directly to the bill, especially for
larger groups, so keep an eye out.

- **Pubs:** Tipping at the bar is not common practice, but if you
  find yourself settling in for a meal, the same 10-15% rule
  applies as in restaurants.
- **Taxis:** Rounding up to the nearest Euro is a kind gesture for a
  smooth ride or up to 10% for exceptional service on longer
  journeys.
- **Hospitality:** For the porter, housekeeping, or the friendly
  local guide, a small token of appreciation is always welcomed.

Think of tipping as the encore to a performance – not mandatory, but
a wonderful way to show your applause.

Budgeting Tips

Keeping a keen eye on your spending allows you to enjoy Ireland's
riches without the worry of a dwindling purse.

- **Daily Budget:** Set a daily limit and stick to it. Divide your
  expenses into categories like meals, attractions, transport, and
  the occasional treat.
- **Savings on Sightseeing:** Investigate tourist passes like the
  Dublin Pass, which offers free entry and discounts to
  numerous attractions. It's like having a backstage pass to the
  city's best shows. This guide also has many examples of free
  events or attractions to see and attend. **Web:** gocity.com/en/
  dublin
- **Eat Like a Local:** Venture into local markets or grab a bite at
  pubs during lunch. The food is hearty, the experience
  authentic, and the price tag often friendlier than dinner
  menus.
- **Accommodation:** Mix it up. Balance nights in budget-
  friendly hostels or B&Bs with the occasional splurge. Many

places offer a traditional Irish breakfast, saving you the cost of one meal.

Cash vs. Card

In Ireland's melody of modernity and tradition, both cash and cards play their part.

- **Card Friendly:** Most places in cities and towns sing along fine with debit and credit cards. Contactless payments make the chorus even smoother, perfect for those quick transactions.
- **Carry Cash:** In rural areas, where the internet might not reach every corner, or at local markets and smaller establishments, cash is king. Keeping a small stash ensures you're never caught off-beat.
- **ATM Tips:** When withdrawing cash, choose to be charged in the local currency for a better rate. Also, inform your bank of your travel plans to avoid any frozen funds mid-jig.

As you navigate Ireland's financial landscape, remember, it's all part of the journey. Whether you're counting your Euros in a bustling Dublin café or your Pounds in a quaint Belfast bookshop, managing your money smartly means you can focus on the rhythm of Irish life—from its breathtaking landscapes to its warm-hearted people.

9.5 PACKING ESSENTIALS FOR THE IRISH WEATHER

Ah, Ireland! A land where four seasons can parade through in one day, asking its visitors to be as adaptable and spirited as the weather itself. So, when it comes to packing, imagine you're preparing for a performance where costume changes are not only expected but essential. Move over Madonna!

Person Packing for Trip

Weather Preparedness

The Irish climate, with its penchant for surprise performances, demands a versatile wardrobe. It's all about layers – think of them as your ensemble cast. Starting with a breathable base layer, add a warm middle layer, and top it all off with a waterproof shell. This trio allows you to adapt your outfit, ensuring comfort whether the day brings a sunlit sonnet or a windy drama. Don't forget a lightweight, waterproof jacket. It's your trusty understudy, ready to shine when showers steal the scene.

No joke! In October, I stayed in a little town outside Galway, where peet was used to heat the cottage. I have never been so cold in my life, and I'm from Minnesota. I wore every layer I had available. Brrr!

A foldable, waterproof poncho can be a lifesaver, too, easily stashed in your daypack for when the weather turns. For those sunnier interludes, a hat and sunglasses will keep you protected and ready to bask in the glow of your surroundings.

Footwear Recommendations

A pair of waterproof, breathable walking shoes is the star of the show for city explorers and countryside adventurers alike. They're ready to tackle cobbled streets or embrace the rugged beauty of the countryside without missing a beat. For those drawn to Ireland's wilder acts, hiking boots are a must. Look for options with good ankle support and grip, ensuring you're steady on your feet, whether you're scaling cliffs or traversing lush, rolling hills. For a casual stroll through Ireland's charming towns, pack a comfortable pair of sneakers or walking sandals – they'll keep your feet happy as you discover local cafes, museums, and hidden gems.

Travel Gadgets

In Ireland, where the elements play a pivotal role, a few tech companions can make your experience smoother. A portable umbrella, compact yet sturdy, ensures you're ready for impromptu rain scenes. A waterproof phone case protects your digital lifeline from unexpected splashes or downpours, keeping your ability to capture moments or navigate landscapes intact.

Don't forget a power bank. It's the unsung hero, ensuring your devices stay charged as you roam through Ireland's spellbinding settings. For those magical dusks and dawns, a lightweight, portable tripod can help you capture the natural beauty in all its glory, turning fleeting moments into lasting memories.

Packing Light and Smart

- The trick to mastering Ireland's variable climate without overpacking is **selecting items that play well together**. Opt for a casual wardrobe – a collection of versatile pieces that can be mixed, matched, and layered to suit any weather the day may bring. Think neutral colors for easy pairing, favoring items that can transition from a day of adventure to a casual evening out.

- **Compression bags can be real space savers**, allowing you to pack more into your luggage by squeezing out the air. They also double as excellent organizers, keeping your ensemble pieces ready for their cue. Remember, every item you pack should earn its place, serving multiple purposes or being essential to your comfort and enjoyment.
- For those tech essentials, **consider a multi-purpose travel adapter that includes USB ports**. This ensures you can charge multiple devices with a single outlet. It's a small but mighty addition to your travel kit, keeping you connected and powered up, ready to embrace whatever adventures lie ahead.

As you prepare for your journey to Ireland, let your packing list be guided not just by the weather but by the promise of adventure, the joy of discovery, and the warmth of the encounters that await. With each item you choose, you're setting the stage for an unforgettable experience. You don't want to skimp on the planning part of your trip!

9.6 HEALTH AND SAFETY: WHAT YOU NEED TO KNOW

When you visit Ireland, you'll find more than just its green scenery and rich history. It's a place full of adventure, ready for you to create your own stories. However, it's wise to be cautious as you explore, to ensure your trip goes as smoothly as the country's famous hills.

Travel Insurance

Before you set foot on Irish soil, wrapping your journey in a cloak of travel insurance ensures peace of mind. It's not just about safe-guarding against the unexpected; it's about crafting a safety net that spans from health mishaps to accidental adventures with mischievous leprechauns (or, more likely, lost luggage and flight delays). Opt for a policy that covers:

- Medical expenses because even a sprained ankle on a cobbled Dublin Street can become a costly affair without coverage.
- Trip cancellations or interruptions, ensuring that a sudden turn of events doesn't leave you out of pocket.
- Theft or loss of belongings, providing a buffer against the bumps that might occur along the way.

Selecting comprehensive coverage turns potential pitfalls into mere stepping stones, allowing you to traverse Ireland's beauty with assurance.

Emergency Services

In the rare event that the road less traveled leads to an unforeseen juncture, knowing how to summon help is paramount. Ireland's emergency services are a beacon in any storm, **reachable by dialing 112 or 999**. These numbers are your lifeline, connecting you to:

- Medical assistance, whether it's a need for an ambulance or directions to the nearest clinic.
- The Gardaí (police), should you find yourself in a pickle or facing a situation that requires immediate attention.
- Fire services, because sometimes, the warmth of Irish hospitality is surpassed only by an actual need for the fire brigade.

Keeping these numbers handy ensures that help is but a call away, casting a safety spell over your Irish escapade.

312 | DISCOVERING IRELAND

Common Concerns

While Ireland unfurls its landscapes and lore with welcoming arms, staying vigilant on the road ensures the story remains a merry one. Road safety is a chapter worth noting, especially for:

- **Travelers taking the wheel**, adapting to driving on the left side of the road, where rural lanes whisper tales of narrow bends and stone walls.
- **Pedestrians,** be alert at crossings and remember to look both ways—the opposite direction than you might be used to.
- **Cyclists,** wearing your armor (helmets and reflective gear) and staying knightly vigilant on shared roads.

Heeding these tales of the road weaves a journey free from unwelcome twists, ensuring the path unfolds with pleasant surprises.

Local Healthcare Services

Even in the heart of a Celtic dream, practical needs may call for attention. Navigating Ireland's healthcare services is akin to finding your way through a labyrinth with a helpful guide at your side. Should you need medical attention, here's how to proceed:

- **Pharmacies,** marked by the green cross, are your first port of call for minor ailments. Pharmacists offer advice and remedies, acting as gatekeepers to the realm of wellness.
- **General Practitioners (GPs)** stand ready for when a pharmacy's potions aren't quite enough. For non-emergency care, a visit to a GP ensures you're in capable hands. Note that fees apply for visitors, so having your travel insurance details at the ready is wise.
- **Hospitals** are well-equipped to handle more serious concerns. In emergencies, public hospital services are available to all,

though your travel insurance will likely cover private care options, offering a different level of comfort and speed.

Understanding these pillars of healthcare support paints your journey with strokes of confidence, ensuring well-being as you explore the nooks and crannies of this enchanting land.

With the right knowledge and preparation, your trip to Ireland becomes more than just sightseeing—it's a deep dive into the country's culture and charm. Make sure you're prepared for anything by having insurance, emergency contact numbers, road tips, and health information handy. This way, you can explore Ireland safely and freely, fully enjoying the adventure.

9.7 SUSTAINABLE TRAVEL: LEAVING NO TRACE

I know, I know! You're thinking, not this again. But, in Ireland, the landscapes are rich with history, and the air is remarkably fresh. As visitors, we need to respect this environment. The green fields, cliffs, and historical sites rely on everyone to minimize their impact. This way, Ireland can remain beautiful and historic for future generations.

Environmental Impact

Traveling through Ireland awakens a sense of connection to the earth beneath our feet. Yet, this connection comes with a responsibility to minimize our environmental footprint. Each choice, from the paths we walk to the places we rest, echoes across the landscape, affecting wildlife, plant life, and the natural heritage that makes Ireland uniquely captivating. Recognizing our impact is the first step towards transforming our travel ethos from mere visitors to guardians of the land.

Leave No Trace Principles

Yes, I know, this again! But it's important. Adopting the Leave No Trace principles while exploring Ireland's natural and heritage sites isn't just a practice; it's a pledge to the future. These guidelines serve as a compass, directing our actions toward sustainability:

- **Plan and Prepare:** Understand the environment you're entering. Knowledge of local regulations and weather conditions ensures both your safety and the preservation of natural habitats.
- **Travel and Camp on Durable Surfaces:** Stick to marked trails and established campsites. The beauty of untouched landscapes lies in their continuity; let's keep it that way.
- **Dispose of Waste Properly:** Whether it's a snack wrapper or an apple core, leave nothing behind but your footprints. Biodegradable doesn't mean instantly dissolvable.
- **Leave What You Find:** From wildflowers to historical artifacts, each element is a thread in the tapestry of Ireland's story. Admire, but don't alter or remove.
- **Minimize Campfire Impacts:** Where fires are permitted, use established fire rings, and keep flames small. The warmth of a fire should leave no scars on the land.
- **Respect Wildlife:** Observe from a distance. Feeding or approaching wildlife disrupts their natural behaviors and diet, altering the ecosystem's balance.
- **Be Considerate of Other Visitors:** Share the trails and sites with respect and kindness. Our collective enjoyment of these spaces depends on our mutual consideration.

Supporting Local

The heart of sustainable travel beats strongest when we support local communities, infusing vitality into the places we visit. Opting for locally owned accommodations, dining in family-run eateries, and choosing experiences crafted by local hands does more than enrich your journey; it circulates your investment directly into the community. This support helps preserve cultural traditions, promotes local craftsmanship, and fosters a tourism model that benefits both travelers and residents. It also makes for the best memories!

- **Shop Local:** From farmers' markets to artisan boutiques, purchasing local products not only gives you a genuine piece of Ireland but also contributes to the local economy.
- **Eat Local:** Savoring dishes prepared with locally sourced ingredients offers a taste of the region's soul while supporting sustainable agriculture.
- **Experience Local:** Engage with experiences that highlight Ireland's culture and natural beauty, from guided walks by local historians to workshops with artisan craftspeople.

Eco-Friendly Practices

As we wander through Ireland's mystic landscapes and vibrant cities, adopting eco-friendly practices ensures our journey enriches rather than exhausts. Small adjustments to our travel habits can have profound effects:

- **Reduce Single-Use Plastics:** Carry a reusable water bottle, coffee cup, and shopping bag. Many places now offer refilling stations, welcoming the effort towards sustainability.
- **Conserve Resources:** Be mindful of water and energy use in your accommodations. Simple acts like turning off lights and taking shorter showers contribute to conservation efforts.
- **Choose Public Transport and Walking:** Whenever possible, opt for public transport, cycling, or walking. It reduces emissions and offers a more immersive experience of Ireland's charm.
- **Offset Carbon Footprint:** Consider offsetting your travel

carbon footprint through reputable programs that fund renewable energy and conservation projects.

In Ireland, the weather itself—from each raindrop to every sunbeam —adds to the country's dynamic natural scenery. As visitors, we're more than just observers; we're active contributors to its ongoing story. By making thoughtful decisions, respecting the land and its people, and committing to sustainable practices, we help maintain the beauty and vitality of this enchanting island for future visitors.

9.8 CULTURAL ETIQUETTE: RESPECT AND UNDERSTANDING

In Ireland, where history, tradition, and modern life blend seamlessly, understanding the local customs greatly enhances your visit. This isn't about following strict rules. Instead, it's about enjoying the warmth of Irish hospitality, appreciating the longstanding traditions, and exploring the country with respect and openness. This approach not only makes your trip more enjoyable but also helps you connect more deeply with the places and people you encounter.

Respecting Traditions

Ireland's traditions are as varied as its landscapes, each carrying its significance and story. From the communal spirit of a ceilidh to the solemnity of historical commemorations, participating with sensitivity and interest shows your respect for the culture.

At traditional music sessions, often held in pubs, listening is as important as the music itself. Clapping along or tapping your foot is welcome, but saving conversations for the breaks between tunes allows everyone to savor the experience.

Historical sites, from ancient stone circles to battlefields, are not just tourist spots but sacred grounds that hold the collective memory of the nation. Walking through these places with mindfulness pays homage to those who walked these lands before us.

Acknowledging the importance of these traditions and sites goes beyond mere observation; it's an active appreciation of Ireland's cultural heritage.

Social Etiquette

The social dance of Ireland, with its casual banter and deep-rooted courtesy, invites you to step in with grace and goodwill. Here are a few steps to help you glide through social interactions:

Greetings in Ireland are warm and often accompanied by a handshake or, among friends, a hug. A simple "Hello" or "How are you?" opens doors to conversations, with the understanding that these inquiries often genuinely invite you to share a bit about yourself.

The pub culture is at the heart of Irish social life. Joining a group at a table is common, but waiting for an invitation or a nod of acknowledgment ensures you're stepping in at the right moment. Buying a round, if you've been welcomed into a group, is a gesture of camaraderie deeply appreciated.

Chatting is an art form here, where stories are shared, and laughter is abundant. While engaging, being mindful not to dominate the conversation allows for a richer exchange of tales and insights.

Navigating these social nuances with attentiveness and participation fosters connections that often last far beyond your stay.

Cultural Sensitivity

Ireland's landscape is dotted with sites of profound historical and religious importance, each deserving of reverence and thoughtful consideration.

When visiting religious sites, such as the many cathedrals, abbeys, and shrines, dress modestly and speak softly. These are places of worship and reflection for many, and your mindfulness ensures a harmonious atmosphere for all.

Historical sites, especially those connected to the more turbulent chapters of Ireland's past, are best approached with a sense of solemnity. Many families have personal connections to these events, and a respectful demeanor acknowledges the depth of their significance.

This sensitivity not only deepens your understanding of Ireland's complex history but also reflects a respect that is warmly received by those who call this land home.

Interaction with Locals

The real magic of Ireland often unfolds in the moments shared with locals, where stories, laughter, and sometimes even a song, (or a pint of Guinness) bridge the gap between visitor and resident.

Showing interest in local customs, asking questions with genuine curiosity, and embracing the opportunity to learn transforms simple interactions into meaningful exchanges. Complimenting the beauty of the area, the local cuisine, or the warmth of the welcome you've received is more than just polite; it's a recognition of the pride many Irish people feel for their country.

Remember, humor is a cornerstone of Irish communication. Joining in the banter with a light heart and not taking yourself too seriously invites a level of interaction that's uniquely Irish. These moments of connection are where the heart of Ireland truly beats. It's in the shared stories at a village pub, the laughter at a local market, and the shared awe at a scenic overlook where the spirit of Ireland is most vibrant.

Exploring Ireland's culture respectfully and with an open mind leads to a richer experience. This includes being quiet at historical sites, joining in the fun at lively pubs, and having warm chats with locals.

It's through these interactions that you will get to know Ireland more profoundly. As you travel through its green hills, ancient sites, and bustling streets, you'll not only see the beauty of the country but also connect with the spirit of its people.

9.9 USEFUL APPS AND DIGITAL TOOLS FOR YOUR TRIP

Navigating Ireland's winding roads and vibrant cultural landscape can be as thrilling as it is daunting. But fear not, for the digital age brings a trove of tools at your fingertips, ensuring your sojourn across this Emerald Isle is as seamless as the flow of an Irish folk song. From plotting your course across the rolling hills to uncovering the rich tapestry of Ireland's heritage, these apps are your faithful companions on this adventure.

Navigation Apps

Gone are the days of cumbersome maps and perplexing directions. The modern traveler has access to a suite of navigation apps, that tailor your journey to your specific whims and fancies.

- **Google Maps:** A reliable guide through both city streets and rustic lanes, offering real-time traffic updates, route options, and even walking paths. Did you know that you can download a map on Google Maps of the area that you're looking to explore, and use it offline? Yep! Google it! Ha!
- **Maps.me:** This app is perfect for the off-the-grid explorer. Like Google Maps, it allows for detailed offline maps, ensuring you're never truly lost, even when Wi-Fi is but a distant memory.
- **Waze:** Community-driven and perfect for real-time updates on traffic, hazards, and even speed checks, Waze turns every journey into a communal voyage.

Cultural Guides

Ireland's culture is deeply connected to its music, art, and historic sites. Explore these aspects more fully with apps that provide valuable insights and enhance your experience.

- **Rick Steves Audio Europe:** Offering insightful walking tours of Ireland's historic sites, this app brings the rich narrative of Ireland's past into the present. (Yes, we know he's the competition. But he's the King of Guides! We respect that.) **Web:** ricksteves.com/europe/ireland
- **Culture Trip:** Explore Ireland's culture, from hidden gems to celebrated landmarks, with tips, articles, and guides curated by locals and travel experts. **Web:** theculturetrip.com/europe/ireland
- **Duolingo:** While not a guide per se, picking up a few phrases in Irish Gaelic adds a layer of richness to your interactions. This friendly app makes language learning a breeze. **Web:** duolingo.com

Travel Planning

A selection of planning apps makes crafting your Irish escapade with precision and imagination effortless, ensuring your adventure unfolds like a well-told tale.

- **TripIt:** Consolidate your travel plans into one sleek itinerary, from flights to ferries, and accommodations to attractions. The app is available for download. **Web:** tripit.com/web
- **Roadtrippers:** If the call of the open road is irresistible, this app helps plot scenic routes, pinpointing must-visit stops along the way. **Web:** roadtrippers.com/
- **Booking.com:** Accommodations, experiences, and everything in between, this app offers a wealth of options to suit every taste and budget. **Web:** booking.com

Emergency Apps

While the hope is for smooth sailing, being prepared for any eventuality ensures your peace of mind as you traverse the Irish landscape.

Emergency Plus: Instant access to local emergency numbers and GPS pinpointing, this app is a vital safety net, connecting you to help whenever needed.

Web:

- Android: play.google.com/store/apps/details?id=com. threesixtyentertainment.nesn&hl=en_AU
- iOS: apps.apple.com/au/app/emergency-plus/id691814685

what3words: Revolutionizing location sharing, this app breaks down the world into 3m x 3m squares, each with a unique three-word identifier, making even the most remote locations easily sharable in an emergency.

Web:

- what3words.com/products/what3words-app

With helpful apps, your trip to Ireland becomes more engaging. You're not just a tourist; you turn into a storyteller, historian, and explorer, using your smartphone instead of traditional tools. These apps help you discover hidden spots like secluded beaches, learn about ancient ruins, and travel safely.

As you explore Ireland, think of it as a collection of experiences ready for you to discover. With digital tools to help guide your way, you're well-equipped to explore the country's highlights and make memorable moments along the journey. So, let's embrace the adventure, enjoy discoveries, and remember that with these tools, you're never truly traveling alone.

IDEAS FOR ITINERARIES

I know some of you are planners! And that's great! These sample itineraries provide a structured yet flexible framework for experiencing Ireland tailored to different interests, ensuring visitors can maximize their enjoyment and engagement with what Ireland has to offer. Adjusting the number of days and specific activities can further customize the experience for any duration or specific interest. Note that we don't have activities for the entire day. My rule for successful travel is to have one or two big things per day. Other than that, see where the road takes you. Get lost in the city for a while, have lunch at a local pub, or enjoy the lush countryside. You won't regret it.

Expanding the itineraries for 14-day and 21-day stays in Ireland will provide more depth and opportunity to explore additional areas and activities, so we've extended each itinerary for the various travel interests. Play around with these. Mix and match if you need to. This is meant just to be a roadmap for those who desire some extra guidance. Don't be afraid to take the road less traveled. In Ireland, you'll be amazed at what you find.

THRILL SEEKERS ITINERARY

7-Day Itinerary

Day 1: Dublin

- **Morning:** Indoor skydiving at iFLY Dublin. Duration: 2 hours. Cost: €50.
- **Afternoon/Evening:** Wakeboarding at Wakedock. Duration: 2 hours. Cost: €40.

Day 2: Wexford

- **Morning:** Sea kayaking with The Irish Experience. Duration: 3 hours. Cost: €55.
- **Afternoon/Evening:** Coasteering along the Wexford coastline. Duration: 3 hours. Cost: €45.

Day 3: Waterford

- **Morning:** Mountain biking on the Waterford Greenway. Duration: 4 hours. Cost: Bike rental €25.
- **Afternoon/Evening:** Surfing lessons at Tramore Beach. Duration: 2 hours. Cost: €35.

Day 4: Cork

- **Morning:** Sailing in Cork Harbour. Duration: 3 hours. Cost: €60.
- **Afternoon/Evening:** Rock climbing at Awesome Walls Cork. Duration: 2 hours. Cost: €16.

Day 5: Kerry

- **Morning:** Kite surfing in Castlegregory. Duration: 3 hours. Cost: €70.
- **Afternoon/Evening:** Horseback riding on Dingle Peninsula. Duration: 2 hours. Cost: €45.

Day 6: Clare

- **Morning:** Caving in the Burren. Duration: 4 hours. Cost: €50.
- **Afternoon/Evening:** Cliff walking at Cliffs of Moher. Duration: 2 hours. Cost: €6 (parking).

Day 7: Galway

- **Morning:** Windsurfing at Rusheen Bay. Duration: 2 hours. Cost: €50.
- **Afternoon/Evening:** Return to Dublin.

14-Day Extension

Day 8-9: Mayo

- **Two-Day Adventure:** Great Western Greenway cycling and overnight camping at Wild Nephin Ballycroy National Park. Bike rental €25/day, camping free.

Day 10: Sligo

- **Morning:** Stand-up paddleboarding on Lough Gill. Duration: 3 hours. Cost: €40.
- **Afternoon/Evening:** Zip-lining at Union Wood. Duration: 2 hours. Cost: €30.

Day 11: Donegal

- **Morning:** Sea stack climbing near Bundoran. Duration: 4 hours. Cost: €85.
- **Afternoon/Evening:** Surfing at Tullan Strand. Duration: 2 hours. Cost: €35.

Day 12: Northern Ireland

- **Morning:** Giant's Causeway and Carrick-a-Rede rope bridge visit. Duration: Full day. Cost: Carrick-a-Rede €9.

Day 13: Derry

- **Morning:** Bog snorkeling in Derry. Duration: 2 hours. Cost: €25.
- **Afternoon/Evening:** Derry city walls historical walk. Duration: 2 hours. Cost: Free.

Day 14: Return to Dublin

21-Day Extension

Day 15-16: Louth

- **Two-Day Hiking Trip:** Trek through the Cooley Peninsula with an overnight stay in Carlingford. Duration: 2 days. Cost: Accommodation approx. €100.

Day 17: Meath

- **Morning:** Hot air balloon ride over the Boyne Valley. Duration: 3 hours. Cost: €195.
- **Afternoon/Evening:** Falconry experience at Slane Castle. Duration: 2 hours. Cost: €50.

Day 18: Wicklow

- **Morning:** Paragliding off the Wicklow Mountains. Duration: 2 hours. Cost: €95.
- **Afternoon/Evening:** Exploring Glendalough's historic sites. Duration: 3 hours. Cost: Free.

Day 19-20: Kildare

- **Two-Day Motor Racing Course** at Mondello Park. Duration: 2 days. Cost: €350.

Day 21: Return to Dublin

These expanded itineraries offer a richer, more diverse experience, allowing for deeper exploration and a broader array of activities that showcase the best of Ireland. Each plan caters specifically to the interests of different types of travelers, ensuring that whether they seek adventure, history, nature, partying, or a mix of everything, they will have a fulfilling and memorable trip.

HISTORY BUFFS ITINERARY

7-Day Itinerary

Day 1: Dublin

- **Morning:** Visit Dublin Castle and the Chester Beatty Library. Duration: 3 hours. Cost: €10.
- **Afternoon/Evening:** Tour of Christ Church Cathedral and Dublinia Museum. Duration: 2 hours each. Cost: €14.

Day 2: Meath

- **Morning:** Explore the ancient passage tombs at Newgrange and Knowth. Duration: 4 hours. Cost: €13.
- **Afternoon/Evening:** Visit the Hill of Tara, the ancient seat of the High Kings of Ireland. Duration: 2 hours. Cost: Free.

Day 3: Louth

- **Morning:** Tour of Monasterboice, home to some of Ireland's best-preserved Celtic crosses. Duration: 1.5 hours. Cost: Free.
- **Afternoon/Evening:** Visit the Battle of the Boyne site and museum. It will take 2 hours and cost €5.

Day 4: Armagh (Northern Ireland)

- **Morning:** Visit Saint Patrick's Cathedral and the Armagh Public Library. Duration: 2 hours. Cost: Free.
- **Afternoon/Evening:** Explore Navan Fort, an ancient ceremonial monument. Duration: 2 hours. Cost: £7.

Day 5: Down (Northern Ireland)

- **Morning:** Tour the Downpatrick & County Down Railway and visit the grave of St. Patrick. Duration: 3 hours. Cost: £8.
- **Afternoon/Evening:** Visit the Ulster Folk and Transport Museum. Duration: 3 hours. Cost: £11.

Day 6: Belfast (Northern Ireland)

- **Morning:** Explore Titanic Belfast. Duration: 3 hours. Cost: £19.
- **Afternoon/Evening:** Visit Belfast City Hall and take a political taxi tour. Duration: 3 hours. Cost: £35 (taxi tour).

Day 7: Return to Dublin

- **Morning:** Visit the National Museum of Ireland - Archaeology. Duration: 3 hours. Cost: Free.
- **Afternoon/Evening:** Depart from Dublin.

14-Day Extension

Day 8: Kildare

- **Morning:** Visit the Irish National Stud and Japanese Gardens. Duration: 3 hours. Cost: €13.
- **Afternoon/Evening:** Tour of Castletown House, a Palladian country house. Duration: 2 hours. Cost: €10.

Day 9-10: Cork

- **Two-Day Trip:** Explore the historic city of Cork, including the Cork City Gaol, St. Fin Barre's Cathedral, and the Butter Museum. Accommodation approx. €100/night.

Day 11: Kerry

- **Morning:** Visit the Derrynane House and National Historic Park. Duration: 3 hours. Cost: €5.
- **Afternoon/Evening:** Explore the Skellig Michael (if accessible, weather permitting). Duration: Full day. Cost: Boat trip €100.

Day 12: Clare

- **Morning/Evening:** Tour of Bunratty Castle and Folk Park. Duration: 3 hours. Cost: €15.
- **Afternoon/Evening:** Visit the Craggaunowen – The Living Past Experience. Duration: 2 hours. Cost: €9.

Day 13: Galway

- **Morning/Evening:** Explore the medieval streets of Galway and visit the Galway City Museum. The tour lasts 3 hours and is Free.
- **Afternoon/Evening:** Visit the ancient Clonmacnoise monastery by the River Shannon. Duration: 2 hours. Cost: €8.

Day 14: Return to Dublin

21-Day Extension

Day 15: Roscommon

- **Morning:** Visit Rathcroghan, a complex of ancient ring forts. Duration: 3 hours. Cost: €5.
- **Afternoon/Evening:** Explore the King House in Boyle. Duration: 2 hours. Cost: €5.

Day 16-17: Sligo

- **Two-Day Trip:** Tour Yeats' country, visit his grave at Drumcliffe, and explore the Sligo Abbey and the Museum of Country Life. Accommodation approx. €100/night.

Day 18: Mayo

- **Morning:** Visit the Ceide Fields, the oldest known field systems in the world. Duration: 3 hours. Cost: €5.
- **Afternoon/Evening:** Explore the National Museum of Ireland - Country Life. Duration: 2 hours. Cost: Free.

Day 19: Leitrim

- **Morning:** Visit Parke's Castle on the shores of Lough Gill.
  Duration: 2 hours. Cost: €5.
- **Afternoon/Evening:** Explore the Arigna Mining Experience.
  Duration: 2 hours. Cost: €10.

Day 20: Longford

- **Morning:** Visit Corlea Trackway Visitor Centre, an Iron Age
  bog road. Duration: 2 hours. Cost: Free.
- **Afternoon/Evening:** Explore the ruins of Abbeyshrule
  Cistercian Abbey. Duration: 1 hour. Cost: Free.

Day 21: Return to Dublin

- **Morning:** Last-minute shopping or museum visits.
- **Afternoon/Evening:** Depart.

This history-focused itinerary ensures a comprehensive exploration
of Ireland's rich past, from ancient times through to modern history,
covering both well-known and off-the-beaten-path historic sites.

NATURE ENTHUSIASTS ITINERARY

7-Day Itinerary

Day 1: Dublin

- **Morning:** Walk in Phoenix Park, one of the largest enclosed
  public parks in any European capital city. Duration: 2 hours.
  Cost: Free.
- **Afternoon/Evening:** Visit the National Botanic Gardens.
  Duration: 2 hours. Cost: Free.

Day 2: Wicklow

- **Morning:** Hiking in Glendalough, Wicklow Mountains National Park. Duration: 4 hours. Cost: Free.
- **Afternoon/Evening:** Visit Powerscourt Waterfall and Gardens. Duration: 3 hours. Cost: €11.

Day 3: Kilkenny

- **Morning:** Explore Woodstock Gardens and Arboretum in Inistioge. Duration: 3 hours. Cost: €5.
- **Afternoon/Evening:** Walk along the River Nore through Kilkenny city. Duration: 2 hours. Cost: Free.

Day 4: Cork

- **Morning:** Visit Fota Wildlife Park. Duration: 4 hours. Cost: €16.
- **Afternoon/Evening:** Explore the gardens and greenhouse at Blarney Castle. Duration: 3 hours. Cost: €18.

Day 5: Kerry

- **Morning:** Hike in Killarney National Park, visiting Muckross House and Gardens. Duration: 4 hours. Cost: €9 for Muckross House.
- **Afternoon/Evening:** Scenic drive through the Ring of Kerry. Duration: Remainder of the day. Cost: Free.

Day 6: Clare

- **Morning:** Visit the Cliffs of Moher and hike along the coastal Burren Way. Duration: 4 hours. Cost: €8 (parking).
- **Afternoon/Evening:** Explore Burren National Park. Duration: 3 hours. Cost: Free.

Day 7: Galway

- **Morning:** Stroll through Connemara National Park. Duration: 4 hours. Cost: Free.
- **Afternoon/Evening:** Return to Dublin to depart.

14-Day Extension

Day 8: Mayo

- **Full Day:** Visit Achill Island, cycle or walk along the Great Western Greenway. Duration: Full day. Cost: Bike rental €20.

Day 9: Sligo

- **Morning:** Hike up Benbulbin and visit the Glencar Waterfall. Duration: 4 hours. Cost: Free.
- **Afternoon/Evening:** Travel to Donegal.

Day 10: Donegal

- **Morning:** Explore Glenveagh National Park and Castle. Duration: 4 hours. Cost: Castle tour €7.
- **Afternoon:** Walk along the beaches of the Wild Atlantic Way near Ardara. Duration: 3 hours. Cost: Free.

Day 11: Northern Ireland

- **Morning:** Visit the Giant's Causeway. Duration: 3 hours. Cost: £12.50.
- **Afternoon/Evening:** Explore the Carrick-a-Rede Rope Bridge. Duration: 2 hours. Cost: £9.

Day 12: Northern Ireland

- **Morning:** Walk in the Mourne Mountains. Duration: 4 hours. Cost: Free.
- **Afternoon/Evening:** Visit Tollymore Forest Park. Duration: 2 hours. Cost: £5 (car parking).

Day 13: Howth

- **Morning:** Visit Howth Head for a coastal walk. Duration: 3 hours. Cost: Free.
- **Afternoon/Evening:** Explore the seaside town of Howth. Duration: 2 hours. Cost: Free.

Day 14: Return to Dublin to depart.

21-Day Extension

Day 15: Laois

- **Morning:** Explore the Slieve Bloom Mountains on a guided nature walk. Duration: 4 hours. Cost: Guided walk €25.
- **Afternoon/Evening:** Visit the Rock of Dunamase. Duration: 2 hours. Cost: Free.

Day 16: Tipperary

- **Morning:** Hike in the Galtee Mountains. Duration: 4 hours. Cost: Free.
- **Afternoon/Evening:** Visit Cahir Castle and the Swiss Cottage. Duration: 3 hours. Cost: €9.

Day 17-18: Cork

- **Two-Day Trip:** Stay on Cape Clear Island, explore its wildlife, and enjoy birdwatching. Duration: 2 days. Cost: Ferry €16, accommodation varies.

Day 19: Kerry

- **Morning:** Whale watching in Dingle Bay. Duration: 3 hours. Cost: €50.
- **Afternoon/Evening:** Visit the Dingle Oceanworld Aquarium. Duration: 2 hours. Cost: €15.

Day 20: Limerick

- **Morning:** Visit Curraghchase Forest Park. Duration: 3 hours. Cost: Free.
- **Afternoon/Evening:** Explore the historic town of Adare. Duration: 2 hours. Cost: Free.

Day 21: Return to Dublin to depart.

This itinerary offers a comprehensive exploration of Ireland's natural beauty and landscapes, allowing nature lovers to immerse themselves in the country's most scenic and tranquil spots. Each segment introduces new regions and unique natural attractions, ensuring a memorable and enriching travel experience.

CITY LOVERS ITINERARY

7-Day Itinerary

Day 1: Dublin

- **Morning:** Start with a visit to the Guinness Storehouse to learn about Dublin's famous brew and enjoy panoramic city views. The tour lasts 2 hours and costs €25.
- **Afternoon/Evening:** Explore the historic Trinity College and see the Book of Kells. Duration: 2 hours. Cost: €14.

Day 2: Dublin

- **Morning:** Visit the National Gallery of Ireland and enjoy some of Europe's finest art. Duration: 2 hours. Cost: Free.
- **Afternoon/Evening:** Walk through Grafton Street for shopping and street performances. Duration: 3 hours. Cost: Free (shopping costs vary).

Day 3: Cork

- **Morning:** Explore the Cork City Gaol and get a glimpse of 19th-century prison life. Duration: 2 hours. Cost: €10.
- **Afternoon/Evening:** Visit the English Market, a roofed food market known since 1788. Duration: 2 hours. Cost: Free (shopping costs vary).

Day 4: Cork

- **Morning:** Visit St. Fin Barre's Cathedral and appreciate its stunning architecture. Duration: 1.5 hours. Cost: €6.
- **Afternoon/Evening:** Take a walking tour of Cork's historic center. Duration: 2 hours. Cost: €15.

Day 5: Galway

- **Morning:** Wander through the vibrant streets of Galway and visit the Galway Cathedral. Duration: 2 hours. Cost: Free.
- **Afternoon/Evening:** Explore the Galway City Museum to learn about the local history. Duration: 2 hours. Cost: Free.

Day 6: Limerick

- **Morning:** Tour the iconic King John's Castle overlooking the River Shannon. Duration: 2 hours. Cost: €12.
- **Afternoon/Evening:** Visit the Hunt Museum with its remarkable collection of antiquities. Duration: 2 hours. Cost: €7.

Day 7: Return to Dublin

- **Morning:** Stroll through Dublin's Docklands, the modern part of the city. Duration: 2 hours. Cost: Free.
- **Afternoon/Evening:** Finish with some leisure time at St Stephen's Green. Duration: 2 hours. Cost: Free.

14-Day Extension

Day 8: Belfast

- **Morning:** Visit the Titanic Belfast exhibition to learn about the city's shipbuilding history. It will take 3 hours and cost £19.
- **Afternoon/Evening:** Take a Black Taxi Tour to understand historical political conflicts. The tour lasts 1.5 hours and costs £35.

Day 9: Belfast

- **Morning:** Visit the Ulster Museum and Botanic Gardens. Duration: 3 hours. Cost: Free.
- **Afternoon/Evening:** Explore the Cathedral Quarter, known for its vibrant nightlife and street art. Duration: 2 hours. Cost: Free.

Day 10: Derry

- **Morning:** Walk along the Derry Walls and visit the Tower Museum. Duration: 3 hours. Cost: £5.
- **Afternoon/Evening:** Visit the Museum of Free Derry. Duration: 2 hours. Cost: £4.

Day 11: Donegal

- **Morning:** Explore the historic Donegal Town and its castle. Duration: 2 hours. Cost: €8.
- **Afternoon/Evening:** Visit the Slieve League Cliffs for some of the best views in Ireland. Duration: 3 hours. Cost: Free.

Day 12: Return to Dublin

- **Morning:** Visit the Irish Museum of Modern Art (IMMA). Duration: 2 hours. Cost: Free.
- **Afternoon/Evening:** Spend some leisure time in Temple Bar, Dublin's cultural quarter. Duration: 3 hours. Cost: Free (drinks and dining costs vary).

Day 13: Waterford

- **Morning:** Visit the Waterford Crystal Factory for a tour and glass-making demonstration. Duration: 2 hours. Cost: €14.

- **Afternoon/Evening:** Explore the historic Reginald's Tower and the Viking Triangle. Duration: 2 hours. Cost: €5.

Day 14: Kilkenny

- **Morning:** Tour medieval Kilkenny Castle and its beautiful gardens. Duration: 2 hours. Cost: €8.
- **Afternoon/Evening:** Wander through the artisan stores and craft galleries in Kilkenny. Duration: 2 hours. Cost: Free (shopping costs vary).

21-Day Extension

Day 15: Carlow

- **Morning:** Visit the Carlow County Museum and Carlow Castle ruins. Duration: 2 hours. Cost: Free.
- **Afternoon/Evening:** Explore the Altamont Gardens, known for their beauty and tranquility. Duration: 2 hours. Cost: Free.

Day 16: Wexford

- **Morning:** Visit the Irish National Heritage Park, an open-air museum. Duration: 3 hours. Cost: €10.
- **Afternoon/Evening:** Explore the historic Wexford Town with its narrow streets and vibrant waterfront. Duration: 2 hours. Cost: Free.

Day 17-18: Wicklow

- **Two-Day Trip:** Stay in Wicklow, visit the Wicklow Mountains National Park, and explore the historical Powerscourt Estate with its world-renowned gardens. Accommodation and meals: Approx. €150/day.

Day 19: Meath

- **Morning:** Explore the ancient Hill of Tara, the traditional seat of the High Kings of Ireland. Duration: 2 hours. Cost: Free.
- **Afternoon/Evening:** Visit Trim Castle, the largest Norman castle in Ireland. Duration: 2 hours. Cost: €5.

Day 20: Louth

- **Morning:** Visit Monasterboice, an early Christian settlement with high crosses and a round tower. Duration: 1.5 hours. Cost: Free.
- **Afternoon/Evening:** Explore Mellifont Abbey, the first Cistercian abbey in Ireland. Duration: 1.5 hours. Cost: €5.

Day 21: Return to Dublin

- **Morning:** Last-minute shopping or visiting any missed sights in Dublin.
- **Afternoon/Evening:** Departure.

This itinerary offers City Lovers a deep dive into Ireland's urban environments, combining history, culture, and modern attractions seamlessly.

LGBTQ+ ITINERARY

7-Day Itinerary

Day 1: Dublin

- **Morning:** Start with a visit to the Oscar Wilde Statue at Merrion Square to honor one of Dublin's most famous LGBTQ+ historical figures. Duration: 1 hour. Cost: Free.

- **Afternoon/Evening:** Explore the Dublin LGBTQ+ Pride Archive at the National Library of Ireland. It will take 2 hours and is Free.

Day 2: Dublin

- **Morning:** Visit the Irish Museum of Modern Art (IMMA), which often features exhibitions by LGBTQ+ artists. Duration: 2 hours. Cost: Free.
- **Afternoon/Evening:** Relax in the iconic The George, Dublin's oldest gay bar and nightclub, for some afternoon fun or a drag show if available. Duration: 3 hours. Cost: Depends on drinks/events.

Day 3: Cork

- **Morning:** Check out Cork's local LGBTQ+ center, LINC (Lesbians in Cork), which offers community activities and resources. Duration: 1 hour. Cost: Free.
- **Afternoon/Evening:** Visit Chambers Bar, Cork's lively gay bar known for its friendly atmosphere and nightly entertainment. The visit lasts 2 hours and costs depending on the drinks.

Day 4: Cork

- **Morning:** Explore the Cork City Gaol, which provides a unique historical perspective and often hosts exhibitions. Duration: 2 hours. Cost: €10.
- **Afternoon/Evening:** Wander around Fitzgerald Park and visit the Cork Public Museum. It will take 2 hours and is Free.

Day 5: Galway

- **Morning:** Visit Teach Solais, the LGBTQ+ resource center in Galway, and participate in any community activities available. The activity will last 2 hours and is Free.
- **Afternoon/Evening:** Enjoy some leisure time at the trendy cafes or shops in Galway's Latin Quarter. Duration: 3 hours. Cost: Depends on shopping.

Day 6: Limerick

- **Morning:** Explore King John's Castle or take a historical walking tour of Limerick. Duration: 2 hours. Cost: €12 for the castle.
- **Afternoon/Evening:** Visit Strokers Gay Bar, one of the local favorites, for a relaxed evening. It lasts 3 hours and costs depending on the drinks.

Day 7: Return to Dublin

- **Morning:** If available, attend a workshop or a talk at The Outhouse, an LGBTQ+ community and resource center on Capel Street. The workshop or talk will last two hours and usually will be Free.
- **Afternoon/Evening:** Spend your last afternoon shopping or revisiting any spots in Dublin you loved. Duration: 3 hours. Cost: Depends on shopping.

14-Day Extension

Day 8: Belfast

- **Morning:** Visit the MAC (Metropolitan Arts Centre) which often hosts LGBTQ+-themed exhibitions. Duration: 2 hours. Cost: Free.

IDEAS FOR ITINERARIES | 343

- **Afternoon/Evening:** Explore Belfast's gay nightlife, starting early at Kremlin, Northern Ireland's best-known gay venue. Duration: 3 hours. Cost: £5 entry fee.

Day 9: Belfast

- **Morning:** Explore the Titanic Belfast. Though not LGBTQ+ specific, it's a not-to-miss attraction. Duration: 3 hours. Cost: £19.
- **Afternoon/Evening:** Chill at Maverick Bar, known for its friendly LGBTQ+ atmosphere and regular drag performances. Duration: 3 hours. Cost: Depends on drinks.

Day 10: Derry

- **Morning:** Visit The Rainbow Project in Derry, an LGBTQ+ advocacy organization, to learn about its work and the local community. The visit will last 2 hours and is Free.
- **Afternoon/Evening:** Walk on the historic Derry Walls and visit the Peace Bridge. Duration: 2 hours. Cost: Free.

Day 11: Donegal

- **Day Trip:** Explore the stunning landscapes of Donegal, a welcoming county with breathtaking scenery, perfect for a relaxing day. Duration: Full day. Cost: Free, aside from travel expenses.

Day 12: Return to Dublin

- **Morning:** A second visit to The George for any events or brunch. Duration: 3 hours. Cost: Depends on the event.
- **Afternoon/Evening:** Attend a performance or film at the Irish Film Institute, which often features LGBTQ+ themes. Duration: 2 hours. Cost: €10.

Day 13: Wicklow

- **Day Trip:** Visit the romantic Powerscourt Estate and Gardens and enjoy the scenic beauty of Wicklow Mountains National Park. Duration: Full day. Cost: Garden entry €11.

Day 14: Return to Dublin

- **Morning:** Last-minute shopping in Dublin's creative quarter. Duration: 2 hours. Cost: Depends on shopping.
- **Afternoon/Evening:** Departure.

21-Day Extension

Day 15: Carlow

- **Morning:** Visit Duckett's Grove, a ruined 19th-century great house once owned by a prominent LGBTQ+ Irish figure. Duration: 2 hours. Cost: Free.
- **Afternoon/Evening:** Explore the surrounding Carlow countryside. Duration: 3 hours. Cost: Free.

Day 16-17: Kilkenny

- **Two-Day Stay:** Explore Kilkenny Castle, and local art galleries, and enjoy the vibrant small-town atmosphere. Duration: 2 days. Cost: Castle entry €8, accommodation varies.

Day 18: Waterford

- **Morning:** Visit Waterford Treasures – Three Museums in the Viking Triangle. Duration: 3 hours. Cost: €10.
- **Afternoon/Evening:** Explore local craft stores and the historic parts of Waterford. Duration: 2 hours. Cost: Free.

Day 19: Wexford

- **Morning:** Attend any LGBTQ+ events or explore the local beaches. Duration: 4 hours. Cost: Free.
- **Afternoon/Evening:** Visit Johnstown Castle and gardens. Duration: 2 hours. Cost: €10.

Day 20: Wicklow

- **Morning:** Return to Wicklow for any missed sights or a relaxing day in nature. Duration: Full day. Cost: Free.

Day 21: Return to Dublin

- **Morning:** Last chances for souvenirs and revisiting favorite spots. Duration: 3 hours. Cost: Depends on shopping.
- **Afternoon/Evening:** Departure.

This itinerary ensures LGBTQ+ travelers can experience a welcoming and diverse range of activities, with plenty of opportunities to explore Ireland's rich cultural scene and vibrant nightlife.

BEST OF ALL WORLDS ITINERARY

7-Day Itinerary

Day 1: Dublin

- **Morning:** Tour of Dublin Castle and the Chester Beatty Library, exploring Ireland's history and culture. Duration: 3 hours. Cost: €10.
- **Afternoon/Evening:** Relax in St. Stephen's Green and then explore the nearby shopping on Grafton Street. Duration: 3 hours. Cost: Free.

Day 2: Wicklow

- **Morning:** Hiking in the Wicklow Mountains National Park, visiting sites like the Glendalough Valley. Duration: 4 hours. Cost: Free.
- **Afternoon/Evening:** Visit Powerscourt Estate and Gardens for a stroll in one of Ireland's most beautiful landscapes. Duration: 3 hours. Cost: €11.

Day 3: Cork

- **Morning:** Explore the historic Cork City Gaol and gain insights into Irish penal history. Duration: 2 hours. Cost: €10.
- **Afternoon/Evening:** Check out local art at the Crawford Art Gallery and enjoy a coffee in the vibrant city center. Duration: 2 hours. Cost: Free.

Day 4: Killarney

- **Morning:** Kayaking on the Lakes of Killarney, an exhilarating experience surrounded by stunning scenery. Duration: 3 hours. Cost: €35.
- **Afternoon/Evening:** Visit Muckross House and Traditional Farms for a taste of 19th-century Irish life. Duration: 3 hours. Cost: €9.

Day 5: Clare

- **Morning:** Visit the Cliffs of Moher, one of Ireland's most famous natural attractions. Duration: 2 hours. Cost: €8.
- **Afternoon/Evening:** Explore the unique lunar landscape of Burren National Park. Duration: 3 hours. Cost: Free.

Day 6: Galway

- **Morning:** Stroll through Galway City, visiting the bustling market and the medieval city walls. Duration: 3 hours. Cost: Free.
- **Afternoon/Evening:** Enjoy some local seafood and explore more of the vibrant arts scene in the city. Duration: 3 hours. Cost: Varies.

Day 7: Return to Dublin

- **Morning:** Return to Dublin and visit the Guinness Storehouse, where you will learn about the brewing process and taste a pint. The tour lasts 2 hours and costs €25.
- **Afternoon/Evening:** Explore Dublin's Temple Bar area, known for its lively atmosphere and cultural events. Duration: 3 hours. Cost: Free (unless dining or drinking).

14-Day Extension

Day 8: Belfast

- **Morning:** Tour the Titanic Belfast and learn about the ship's history. Duration: 3 hours. Cost: £19.
- **Afternoon/Evening:** Explore the Botanic Gardens and Ulster Museum in Belfast. Duration: 3 hours. Cost: Free.

Day 9: Derry

- **Morning:** Walk on the historic walls of Derry and learn about its turbulent history. Duration: 2 hours. Cost: Free.
- **Afternoon/Evening:** Visit the Museum of Free Derry to understand the city's civil rights movement. Duration: 2 hours. Cost: £4.

Day 10: Donegal

- **Morning:** Surfing in Bundoran, Ireland's surfing capital. Duration: 3 hours. Cost: €40.
- **Afternoon/Evening:** Visit Donegal Castle in the heart of the county town. Duration: 2 hours. Cost: €8.

Day 11: Sligo

- **Morning:** Hike up Benbulbin, known for its distinctive shape and panoramic views. Duration: 4 hours. Cost: Free.
- **Afternoon/Evening:** Explore the Yeats Building and learn about the poet's connection to Sligo. Duration: 2 hours. Cost: €5.

Day 12: Mayo

- **Morning:** Visit the National Museum of Ireland – Country Life to see how people lived in rural Ireland. Duration: 3 hours. Cost: Free.
- **Afternoon/Evening:** Take a boat trip to Clew Bay, known for its stunning views and history. The trip lasts 3 hours and costs €30.

Day 13: Roscommon

- **Morning:** Explore Rathcroghan, a complex of ancient royal sites and ritual landscapes. Duration: 3 hours. Cost: €7.
- **Afternoon/Evening:** Visit Boyle Abbey, an impressive example of Ireland's Cistercian heritage. Duration: 2 hours. Cost: €5.

Day 14: Return to Dublin

- **Morning:** Last-minute shopping.
- **Afternoon/Evening:** Departure.

21-Day Extension

Day 15: Kildare

- **Morning:** Visit the Irish National Stud and Japanese Gardens, exploring beautiful landscapes and thoroughbred horses. The tour lasts 3 hours and costs €13.
- **Afternoon/Evening:** Tour Castletown House, a splendid Palladian-style country house. It will take 2 hours and cost €10.

Day 16: Carlow

- **Morning:** Explore the Delta Sensory Gardens, a peaceful retreat. Duration: 2 hours. Cost: €5.
- **Afternoon/Evening:** Visit Huntington Castle and its gardens. Duration: 2 hours. Cost: €7.

Day 17-18: Wexford

- **Two-Day Trip:** Visit the Wexford Wildfowl Reserve and explore the ancient ruins at the Irish National Heritage Park. Duration: 2 days. Cost: €8 for Heritage Park.

Day 19: Waterford

- **Morning:** Tour the Waterford Crystal Factory and witness glass blowing. Duration: 2 hours. Cost: €17.
- **Afternoon/Evening:** Walk through the historic Viking

Triangle and visit Reginald's Tower. Duration: 2 hours. Cost: €6.

Day 20: Wicklow

- **Morning:** Hike in the Wicklow Mountains, visiting locations like Lough Tay and Lough Dan. Duration: 4 hours. Cost: Free.
- **Afternoon/Evening:** Relax in the therapeutic seaweed baths at Brittas Bay. The session lasts one hour and costs €25.

Day 21: Return to Dublin

- **Morning:** Last-minute shopping or cultural visits in Dublin. Duration: 3 hours. Cost: Free.
- **Afternoon/Evening:** Departure.

These itineraries blend various experiences across Ireland, ensuring a full spectrum of activities, from urban exploration and historical insights to thrilling adventures and serene nature escapes. They are perfect for the traveler wanting to experience it all.

PARTY ANIMALS ITINERARY

7-Day Itinerary

Day 1: Dublin

- **Morning:** Start with a relaxed brunch at The Church, a bar and restaurant located in a converted church with a vibrant atmosphere. The brunch lasts 2 hours and costs €15-€25.
- **Afternoon/Evening:** Explore the Temple Bar area, known for its busy pubs and street performers. Duration: 3 hours. Cost: Free (drinks and snacks cost extra).

Day 2: Dublin

- **Morning:** Recover from the night before with a late start and a visit to the Guinness Storehouse to learn about Dublin's most famous export and enjoy a pint at the Gravity Bar. Duration: 2 hours. Cost: €25.
- **Afternoon/Evening:** Attend a live music session at Whelan's, a legendary venue for up-and-coming bands. The session lasts 3 hours and costs €10-€20 (depending on the event).

Day 3: Cork

- **Morning:** Travel to Cork. Check into your hotel and explore the local scene.
- **Afternoon/Evening:** Start the evening early at The Franciscan Well Brewery, enjoying craft beers in their beer garden. Duration: 3 hours. Cost: €5-€10 per pint.

Day 4: Cork

- **Morning:** Visit the English Market for some local flavor and a light lunch. Duration: 2 hours. Cost: €10-€20.
- **Afternoon/Evening:** Experience Cork's nightlife starting at Cyprus Avenue, another excellent live music venue known for rock and indie performances. Duration: 4 hours. Cost: €15-€30.

Day 5: Galway

- **Morning:** Travel to Galway. Spend your day relaxing by the seaside or exploring the city.
- **Afternoon/Evening:** Dive into Galway's nightlife with a visit to Roisin Dubh, a cornerstone of Galway's social life, known for great gigs and vibrant crowds. Duration: 4 hours. Cost: €10-€20.

Day 6: Galway

- **Morning:** Take a leisurely walk along Salthill Promenade to recover from the night before.
- **Afternoon/Evening:** Spend another night experiencing the best of Galway's pubs, starting with The Quays, famous for its lively atmosphere and good music. Duration: All night. Cost: Drinks cost.

Quays Irish Pub & Restaurant, Galway

Day 7: Return to Dublin

- **Morning:** Return to Dublin.
- **Afternoon/Evening:** For your last evening, check out The Grand Social for their famous flea market and stay for the night with DJs spinning a variety of tunes. Duration: All night. Cost: €5-€10.

14-Day Extension

Day 8: Belfast

- **Morning:** Travel to Belfast.
- **Afternoon/Evening:** Explore the Cathedral Quarter with its array of bars and pubs; start at The Dirty Onion, a rustic bar with live traditional music. Duration: All night. Cost: Drinks cost.

Day 9: Belfast

- **Morning:** Visit St. George's Market for breakfast and some local shopping. Duration: 2 hours. Cost: Free (shopping costs vary).
- **Afternoon/Evening:** Experience a pub crawl through Belfast's best bars, including The Crown Liquor Saloon, a Victorian gin palace. Duration: All night. Cost: Drinks cost.

Day 10: Derry

- **Morning:** Travel to Derry.
- **Afternoon/Evening:** Check out some of Derry's traditional pubs, like Peadar O'Donnell's, for live music and a great crowd. Duration: All night. Cost: Drinks cost.

Day 11: Donegal

- **Morning:** Head to Donegal, famous for its rugged landscapes and traditional Irish pubs.
- **Afternoon/Evening:** Enjoy the local scene with a visit to The Reel Inn, Donegal Town, for authentic Irish music. Duration: All night. Cost: Drinks cost.

Day 12: Sligo

- **Morning:** Travel to Sligo.
- **Afternoon/Evening:** Visit Thomas Connolly Sligo, a historic pub known for craft beers and lively music sessions. Duration: All night. Cost: Drinks cost.

Day 13: Return to Dublin

- **Morning:** Return to Dublin for one last hurrah.
- **Afternoon/Evening:** Spend your final evening in Dublin at The Cobblestone, a snug pub in Smithfield with traditional music and a great atmosphere. Duration: All night. Cost: Drinks cost.

Day 14: Last-Minute Shopping and Sightseeing/Departure

21-Day Extension

Day 15: Kilkenny

- **Morning:** Head to Kilkenny, a medieval city with a vibrant nightlife.
- **Afternoon/Evening:** Experience Kilkenny's local pubs and music scenes, starting at The Field Bar and Restaurant for good food and live music. Duration: All night. Cost: Drinks cost.

Day 16: Waterford

- **Morning:** Travel to Waterford.
- **Afternoon/Evening:** Visit Tully's Bar for a quintessential Irish pub experience known for its traditional music and vibrant local crowd. Duration: All night. Cost: Drinks cost.

Day 17: Wexford

- **Morning:** Head to Wexford.
- **Afternoon/Evening:** Check out The Sky and the Ground, a popular local pub with a back garden and a selection of craft beers and live music. Duration: All night. Cost: Drinks cost.

Day 18-19: Wicklow

- **Two-Day Stay:** Explore the town and enjoy the nightlife. Visit The Harbour Bar in Bray, voted the Best Bar in the World by Lonely Planet in 2010. Duration: 2 days. Cost: Accommodation and drinks.

Day 20: Limerick

- **Morning:** Travel to Limerick.
- **Afternoon/Evening:** Spend the evening at Dolan's Pub, known for its live music sessions and great atmosphere. Duration: All night. Cost: Drinks cost.

Day 21: Return to Dublin

- **Morning:** Travel back to Dublin.
- **Afternoon/Evening:** If time permits, one last stroll through Dublin's streets before departure.

This itinerary ensures that Party Animals will experience a diverse range of Ireland's best nightlife, music scenes, and lively cultural atmospheres, making every night one to remember. Well, at least we hope you remember. Ha!

A Word of Advice

Most of the activities and events on all the itineraries require booking ahead (even those that are free), so don't forget to take your chosen itinerary, tweak it, and get booked (in some cases, you will save money, too!).

As you venture through the carefully curated paths laid out in these itineraries, remember that the true spirit of travel lies in the unexpected joys and serendipitous moments that arise along the way. While these guides offer a wide variety of activities designed to showcase the best of Ireland, they are merely starting points. Each day promises new opportunities to delve deeper into the local culture, meet new friends, or uncover hidden gems. Whether you choose to wander through the cobblestone streets of a quaint village, engage with locals over a pint, or simply take in the breathtaking landscapes, Ireland offers a unique experience at every turn. Let your curiosity guide you, and be open to the adventures that await beyond the planned routes. Happy travels!

CONCLUSION

Ah, what a jaunt we've had together, eh? From the mist-kissed cliffs that have whispered ancient secrets to us, to the cobbled streets echoing with laughter and music, and into the warm embraces of locals sharing their tales over a pint – we've traversed the heart and soul of Ireland, one page at a time. It's been a ride, or should I say, a hearty stroll filled with the rugged beauty of landscapes and the undeniable warmth of its people.

We've meandered off the well-trodden paths to uncover Ireland's hidden gems, indulged in a culinary scene as rich as a thick Irish stew, and danced through the vibrant nightlife like there was no tomorrow —all while getting our boots muddy in the thrill of outdoor adventures. And let's not forget those practical tips sprinkled throughout, ensuring your travel experience is as smooth as a creamy Guinness.

Central to our journey has been the mantra of cultural immersion. Because, let's face it, to truly know Ireland is to live its music, to breathe its stories, and to laugh and cry with its people. It's been my vision to guide you not just to see Ireland but to feel it, to experience activities that resonate with the authentic Irish lifestyle far beyond the usual tourist tick-boxes.

As we tread softly on this Emerald Isle, let's remember the importance of traveling sustainably. We've talked about respecting the natural environment and supporting local communities—it's about leaving Ireland as lush and vibrant as we found it, ready to embrace the next wunderer with open arms.

Young Wunderer with Irish Church in Background

Now, don't just sit there dreaming of emerald hills and fairy forts! I wrote this book to light a fire under your wunderlust, to get you to step out of your comfort zone and discover the wonders of Ireland for yourself. There's an adventure out there with your name on it, and it's high time you claimed it. Use this guide, plan your journey, and dive headfirst into creating your unforgettable memories and stories to share.

This is your call to adventure—a summons to embark on your journey of discovery, armed with insights and knowledge you've gleaned from our shared escapades. Ireland doesn't just wait; it calls, beckons, and serenades you to explore its depths and heights, its laughter, and its silence.

Thank you, truly, for joining me on this written journey through Ireland. I hope this book finds a special place in your backpack, serving as a trusty companion as you navigate the winding roads and hidden pathways of the Emerald Isle. May it inspire in you a deep love for Ireland, a yearning to explore further, and a desire to return, time and time again. Much like I fell in love with Ireland the first time I explored it.

Sláinte, my fellow adventurer. May the road rise to meet you, and your heart always be light. Off you go now, the World of Wunder awaits.

BONUS

We want your journey to Ireland to be as easy and enjoyable as possible. For effortless navigation through the heart of Ireland, simply scan the QR code to access the eBook version. That's right! You're getting two books for the price of one! Say goodbye to cumbersome folding maps—our digital portal puts Ireland's best attractions right at your fingertips. Scan, click, and explore—the country's iconic landmarks, hidden gems, and local favorites are just a tap away!

Scan the QR code for your bonus ebook!

https://qrco.de/bfA8w3

Connect with us online and become part of the World of Wunder community.

We love seeing our guidebooks in action; share your travel photos with the community on social media with #worldofwunderers.

ABOUT THE AUTHOR

Meet the intrepid minds behind World of Wunder, where exploration meets expertise in the world of travel. Our guidebook series isn't just about mapping out destinations; it's a passionate ode to wanderlust— a testament to the insatiable curiosity to explore the world. Each author is a local luminary, a beacon illuminating the lesser-known marvels, hidden gems, and off-the-beaten-path wonders of their home.

But what exactly is 'Wunder'? It's more than just a word— it's a celebration of wanderlust, encapsulating the enthusiasm and thrill of discovery. Our authors embody this spirit, infusing their narratives with a blend of cultural insight, historical anecdotes, and personal tales that paint a vivid portrait of their locale.

In our guides, expect to traverse uncharted territories, unraveling the secrets tucked away from the mainstream tourist trail. From secluded villages with centuries-old traditions to breathtaking natural vistas that defy description, our authors invite you to delve deeper, urging you to savor the untamed essence of a destination.

We take pride in uncovering the pulse of local life— sharing the locals' favorite haunts for gastronomic delights, the tucked-away eateries serving authentic cuisine, and the hidden bars pouring concoctions known only to the savviest of residents. Food and drink aren't just sustenance; they're gateways to cultural understanding, and our guides ensure you savor every nuance.

World of Wunder isn't for the casual traveler—it's crafted for the enterprising adventurer, the seeker of authenticity, the one who craves experiences beyond the ordinary. Whether you're an avid backpacker, a cultural enthusiast, or simply someone hungry for the extraordinary, our guides are your passport to the uncharted realms of discovery. Let the journey begin!

We hope you loved exploring Ireland with our guide! Your experiences and stories are invaluable to us. Please take a moment to leave a review and share your joy of Ireland with others. Your insights can inspire fellow adventurers to discover the magic of the Emerald Isle!

https://qrco.de/bfA91V

REFERENCES

Celtic Ireland in the Iron Age: the Celts https://www.wesleyjohnston.com/users/ireland/past/pre_norman_history/iron_age.html

The Vikings in Ireland - Vikingeskibsmuseet https://www.vikingeskibsmuseet.dk/en/professions/education/the-viking-age-geography/the-vikings-in-the-west/ireland

The Mythical High Kings of Ireland: Legends, Tales, and Historical Facts https://www.irishhistory.com/ancient-ireland/high-kings-of-ireland/the-mythical-high-kings-of-ireland-legends-tales-and-historical-facts

Great Famine (Ireland) - Wikipedia https://en.wikipedia.org/wiki/Great_Famine_(Ireland)

Ireland climate: average weather, temperature, rain https://www.climatestotravel.com/climate/ireland

Upcoming Holidays and Festivals in Ireland https://www.ricksteves.com/europe/ireland/festivals

Ireland Off the Beaten Path: 17 Secret Spots + Hidden Gems https://www.ourescapeclause.com/ireland-off-the-beaten-path/

The Cost of Travel in Ireland (2023): A Detailed Budget ... https://www.neverendingfootsteps.com/cost-of-travel-ireland-budget/

Castle hotel stays in Ireland https://www.ireland.com/en-us/plan-your-trip/accommodation/castles-in-ireland/

Sustainable stays https://www.ireland.com/en-us/plan-your-trip/accommodation/sustainable-stays-in-ireland/

The 18 Best Boutique Hotels in Ireland https://www.thehotelguru.com/en-us/best-hotels/ireland/boutique-hotels

THE 15 BEST Farm Stays in Ireland (2024) https://www.farmstayplanet.com/farm-stay-rural-travel-guides/ireland/

Farm to fork: Ireland's restaurants with kitchen gardens https://www.ireland.com/en-us/magazine/food-and-drink/restaurants-with-kitchen-gardens/

The 10 best whiskey distillery tours in Ireland https://www.irelandbeforeyoudie.com/the-10-best-whiskey-distillery-tours-in-ireland/

Top 5 Irish Seafood Towns: Prepare to Get Hooked! https://www.irelandbeforeyoudie.com/top-5-irish-seafood-towns/

Delicious Irish Food Festivals Happening In 2024 https://vagabondtoursofireland.com/blog/delicious-irish-food-festivals

Top 10 pubs for Irish traditional music - Visit Dublin https://www.visitdublin.com/guides/best-trad-music-dublin

Dublin Literary Pub Crawl https://www.dublinpubcrawl.com/

8 Day Haunted Ireland Tour – Private Chauffeured https://irishtoursforyou.com/product/11-day-haunted-ireland-tour-private-chauffeured/

Ireland Off the Beaten Path: 17 Secret Spots + Hidden Gems https://www. ourescapeclause.com/ireland-off-the-beaten-path/

Hidden gems along the Wild Atlantic Way https://www.ireland.com/en-us/magazine/ touring-holidays/hidden-gems-along-the-wild-atlantic-way/

Adventure Sports in Ireland https://www.askaboutireland.ie/reading-room/sports- recreation/sport/adventure-sports-in-irela/

Ireland Off the Beaten Path: 17 Secret Spots + Hidden Gems https://www. ourescapeclause.com/ireland-off-the-beaten-path/

Greenways Ireland, your 2023 Guide to Greenways in Ireland https://greenwaysire land.org/

Best surf school on the Wild Atlantic Way - Surf Mayo ... https://www.tripadvisor. co.uk/ShowUserReviews-g1204677-d2277581-r908723937-Surf_Mayo-Louis burgh_County_Mayo_Western_Ireland.html

Ireland Eco Tours https://wildnhappytravel.com/eco-tours-in-ireland/

6 Useful Apps for Ireland | Irish Travel Tips https://olliestours.com/blog/6-useful- apps-for-ireland-ollies-tours/

Ireland - Language, Culture, Customs and Etiquette https://www.commisceo-global. com/resources/country-guides/ireland-guide

Visitor Travel Info for Tourists - Dublin - Transport for Ireland https://www.transport forireland.ie/getting-around/visitor-travel-information/#:

How to travel sustainably in Ireland https://www.ireland.com/en-us/magazine/adven ture-activities/how-to-travel-sustainably/

Adventure Sports in Ireland: https://www.askaboutireland.ie/reading-room/sports- recreation/sport/adventure-sports-in-irela/

Allen, Darina. "Ballymaloe Farm." Ballymaloe House, Shanagarry, County Cork, Ireland. Available at: ballymaloe.com/

Aran Islands: https://www.aranislands.ie/inis-mor-inishmore-island/inis-mor-island- churches-celtic-sites/dun-duchathair-the-black-fort

Ardlenagh View. (n.d.). Retrieved from http://ardlenaghview.com/

Ashford Castle. (n.d.). Retrieved from http://ashfordcastle.com

Baboró International Arts Festival for Children. (n.d.). Retrieved from https://www. baboro.ie/

Ballygally Castle Hotel. (n.d.). Retrieved from https://www.hastingshotels.com/bally gally-castle/

Bantry House. (n.d.). Retrieved from http://bantryhouse.com/

B&B Ireland. (n.d.). Retrieved from http://bandbireland.com

Beara Tourism. (n.d.). Retrieved from https://bearatourism.com/

Visit Belfast. (n.d.). Belfast's Christmas Market. Retrieved from https://visitbelfast.com/

TripAdvisor. (n.d.). Best surf school on the Wild Atlantic Way - Surf Mayo. Retrieved from https://www.tripadvisor.co.uk/ShowUserReviews-g1204677-d2277581- r908723937-Surf_Mayo-Louisburgh_County_Mayo_Western_Ireland.html

Blarney Castle. (n.d.). Retrieved from http://blarneycastle.ie/

Boutique Hotel Directory. (n.d.). Retrieved from http://boutiquehotel.me

Boyne Valley Tours. (n.d.). Retrieved from https://www.boynevalleytours.com/

Burren Slow Food Festival. (n.d.). Retrieved from http://slowfood.com/festival

Bushmills Distillery. (n.d.). Retrieved from https://bushmills.com/distillery/

Castle Leslie Equestrian Center. (n.d.). Retrieved from http://castleleslie.com

Cleggan Beach Riding Center. (n.d.). Retrieved from http://galwaytourism.ie

ClimatestoTravel. (n.d.). Climate of Ireland. Retrieved from https://www.climatesto
travel.com/climate/ireland

Cork International Choral Festival. (n.d.). Retrieved from https://corkchoral.ie/

Cork Jazz Festival. (n.d.). Retrieved from https://guinnesscorkjazz.com/

Cork Vegfest. (n.d.). Retrieved from https://www.facebook.com/corkvegfest/

Cornucopia, Dublin. (n.d.). Retrieved from https://www.cornucopia.ie/

Cotswold Outdoor. (n.d.). Dublin City Store. Retrieved from https://cotswoldoutdoor.
com/stores/dublin-city.html

Discover Northern Ireland. (n.d.). C.S. Lewis Tour in Belfast. Retrieved from https://
discovernorthernireland.com/things-to-do/c-s-lewis-trail-p709901

Cycling Ireland. (n.d.). Retrieved from http://cyclingireland.ie

Cyprus Avenue. (n.d.). Retrieved from https://cyprusavenue.ie/

De Barra's Folk Club. (n.d.). Retrieved from https://debarra.ie/

District 8. (n.d.). Retrieved from https://district8dublin.com/

Dromoland Castle. (n.d.). Retrieved from http://dromoland.ie

Dublin Events. (n.d.). Ring Forts. Retrieved from https://dublinevents.com/ring-forts/

Dublin Ghost Bus Tour. (n.d.). Retrieved from https://www.ghostbus.ie/

Dublin Literary Pub Crawl. (n.d.). Retrieved from https://dublinpubcrawl.com/

Dublin Theatre Festival. (n.d.). Retrieved from http://dublintheatrefestival.ie/

Eddie Rocket's. (n.d.). Retrieved from https://www.eddierockets.ie/

Elbow Lane Brew & Smokehouse. (n.d.). Retrieved from https://elbowlane.ie/

Fáilte Ireland. (n.d.). Retrieved from https://www.failteireland.ie/

Fairyhouse Easter Festival. (n.d.). Retrieved from https://fairyhouse.ie/

Fishy Fishy Café. (n.d.). Retrieved from https://fishyfishy.ie/

Galway Bay Brewery. (n.d.). Retrieved from https://galwaybaybrewery.com/

Galway International Arts Festival. (n.d.). Retrieved from https://www.giaf.ie/

Galway Oyster Festival. (n.d.). Retrieved from https://www.galwayoysterfestival.com/

Galway Tourism. (n.d.). Galway's Christmas Market. Retrieved from https://galway
tourism.ie/

Gandon Inn. (n.d.). Retrieved from http://gandoninn.ie/

Ghost Bus Tour, Dublin. (n.d.). Retrieved from https://www.ghostbus.ie/

Glengarriff Bamboo Park. (n.d.). Retrieved from http://www.bamboopark.com/

Guinness Storehouse. (n.d.). Retrieved from https://guinness-storehouse.com

Go Visit Donegal. (n.d.). Gweedore, Donegal. Retrieved from https://www.govisitdone
gal.com/

Holiday Homes Direct. (n.d.). Holiday Home in Sneem. Retrieved from https://www.
holidayhomesdirect.ie/

House Dublin. (n.d.). Retrieved from http://housedublin.ie/

Ice House Hotel. (n.d.). Retrieved from http://icehousehotel.ie

Aran Islands. (n.d.). Inishmore Island. Retrieved from https://www.aranislands.ie/inis-mor-inishmore-island/inis-mor-island-churches-celtic-sites/dun-duchathair-the-black-fort

Jameson Distillery, Cork. (n.d.). Retrieved from https://www.jamesonwhiskey.com/en-IE/visit-us/jameson-distillery-midleton

Jameson Distillery, Dublin. (n.d.). Retrieved from https://www.jamesonwhiskey.com/en-IE/visit-us/jameson-distillery-bow-st

Johnnie Fox's. (n.d.). Retrieved from https://www.jfp.ie/

Kinsale Adventure Center. (n.d.). Retrieved from http://kinsaleoutdoors.com

Kinsale Outdoor Education Center. (n.d.). Retrieved from http://kinsaleoutdoors.com

Knockranny House Hotel & Spa. (n.d.). Retrieved from http://knockrannyhousehotel.ie/

Kylemore Abbey. (n.d.). Retrieved from http://kylemoreabbey.com/

Lahinch Surf School. (n.d.). Retrieved from https://www.lahinchsurfschool.com/

Leahy's Open Farm. (n.d.). Retrieved from http://leahysopenfarm.ie/

Light House Cinema, Dublin. (n.d.). Retrieved from https://lighthousecinema.ie/

Lindisfarne Guest House, Dingle. (n.d.). Retrieved from https://lindisfarne.ie/

Listowel Writers' Week. (n.d.). Retrieved from https://writersweek.ie/

Loop Head Lighthouse. (n.d.). Retrieved from https://www.loophead.ie/

Loughcrew Megalithic Centre. (n.d.). Retrieved from https://www.loughcrewmegalithiccentre.com/

Lyric Theatre, Belfast. (n.d.). Retrieved from https://lyrictheatre.co.uk/

Mallow Castle. (n.d.). Retrieved from https://www.visitmallow.ie/

Marble Arch Caves. (n.d.). Retrieved from https://marblearchcaves.co.uk/

Midleton Distillery. (n.d.). Retrieved from https://www.jamesonwhiskey.com/en-IE/visit-us/jameson-distillery-midleton

Mill Park Hotel, Donegal. (n.d.). Retrieved from https://www.millparkhotel.com/

Moher Hill Open Farm. (n.d.). Retrieved from http://moherfarm.ie/

Visit Mourne Mountains. (n.d.). Mourne Mountains. Retrieved from https://www.visitmournemountains.co.uk/

Muckross House, Gardens & Traditional Farms. (n.d.). Retrieved from https://www.muckross-house.ie/

Museum of Literature Ireland. (n.d.). Retrieved from https://www.moli.ie/

National Gallery of Ireland. (n.d.). Retrieved from https://www.nationalgallery.ie/

National Leprechaun Museum. (n.d.). Retrieved from https://www.leprechaunmuseum.ie/

Newgrange. (n.d.). Retrieved from https://www.newgrange.com/

Newgrange Farm. (n.d.). Retrieved from https://www.newgrangefarm.com/

Noël Carroll, Landscape Gardener. (n.d.). Retrieved from https://www.carrolllandscape.ie/

Old Head Golf Links. (n.d.). Retrieved from http://oldhead.com

Old Jameson Distillery, Dublin. (n.d.). Retrieved from https://www.jamesonwhiskey.com/en-IE/visit-us/jameson-distillery-bow-st

Paddywagon Tours. (n.d.). Retrieved from http://paddywagontours.com

Parknasilla Resort & Spa. (n.d.). Retrieved from http://parknasillaresort.com/

Pauline Bewick Art Gallery. (n.d.). Retrieved from http://paulinebewick.ie

Cork Bird News. (n.d.). Peregrine Falcon Watching. Retrieved from https://www.cork
birdnews.com/birdwatchingtrips

Pico de Loro, Cork. (n.d.). Retrieved from https://www.picodelorocork.com/

Puffin Dive Center. (n.d.). Retrieved from http://puffin.ie/

Rathlin Community. (n.d.). Rathlin Island. Retrieved from https://www.rathlincommu
nity.org/

Seafari Cruises, Kenmare. (n.d.). Retrieved from https://www.seafariireland.com/

Sean's Bar, Athlone. (n.d.). Retrieved from https://seansbar.ie/

Living the Sheep's Head Way. (n.d.). Sheep's Head Peninsula. Retrieved from https://
livingthesheepsheadway.com/

Living the Sheep's Head Way. (n.d.). Sheep's Head Way. Retrieved from https://
livingthesheepsheadway.com/

Skelligs Chocolate. (n.d.). Retrieved from https://skelligschocolate.com/

Slieve League. (n.d.). Retrieved from http://slieveleague.ie/

St. Patrick's Day Festival. (n.d.). Retrieved from https://www.stpatricksfestival.ie/

St. Stephen's Green. (n.d.). Retrieved from http://stephensgreen.com/

St. Stephen's Green Shopping Centre. (n.d.). Retrieved from http://stephensgreen.com/

St. Stephen's Green Park. (n.d.). Retrieved from http://stephensgreen.com/

TripAdvisor. (n.d.). Surf Mayo. Retrieved from https://www.tripadvisor.
co.uk/ShowUserReviews-g1204677-d2277581-r908723937-Surf_Mayo-Louis
burgh_County_Mayo_Western_Ireland.html

The English Market, Cork. (n.d.). Retrieved from https://www.englishmarket.ie/

The Gobbins Cliff Path, County Antrim. (n.d.). Retrieved from https://www.thegobbin
scliffpath.com/

The King Sitric. (n.d.). Retrieved from https://www.kingsitric.ie/

The Merry Ploughboy. (n.d.). Retrieved from https://www.merryploughboys.com/

The Old Bank, Kinsale. (n.d.). Retrieved from https://theoldbanktownhouse.com/

The Port House, Dublin. (n.d.). Retrieved from https://porthouse.ie/

The Quays, Galway. (n.d.). Retrieved from https://quaysbar.com/

The Viking Triangle, Waterford. (n.d.). Retrieved from https://waterfordvikingtriangle.
com/

Titanic Experience, Cobh. (n.d.). Retrieved from https://titanicexperiencecobh.ie/

Titanic Experience, Belfast. (n.d.). Retrieved from https://www.titanicbelfast.com/

Titanic Experience, Cork. (n.d.). Retrieved from https://www.titanicexperiencecobh.ie/

Titanic Experience, Donegal. (n.d.). Retrieved from https://www.done
gal.ie/EnjoyDonegal/DonegalAttractions/TitanicExhibitionDonegal/

Titanic Trail Walking Tour, Cobh. (n.d.). Retrieved from https://titaniccobh.com/

Titanic Walking Tour, Belfast. (n.d.). Retrieved from https://titanicbelfast.com/

Discover Northern Ireland. (n.d.). Tollymore Forest Park. Retrieved from https://www.
discovernorthernireland.com/

Discover Ireland. (n.d.). Tom Crean's House, Kerry. Retrieved from https://www.discov
erireland.ie/

Heritage Ireland. (n.d.). Trim Castle. Retrieved from https://www.heritageireland. ie/en/

Trinity City Hotel, Dublin. (n.d.). Retrieved from https://www.trinitycityhotel.com/

Turoe Pet Farm. (n.d.). Retrieved from http://turoepetfarm.com/

Underwater Ireland. (n.d.). Retrieved from http://underwater.ie/

Vagabond Tours. (n.d.). Retrieved from http://vagabond.ie

Valentia Island. (n.d.). Retrieved from https://www.valentiaisland.ie/

Waterford & Suir Valley Railway. (n.d.). Retrieved from https://www.wsvrailway.ie/

Westport House. (n.d.). Retrieved from https://www.westporthouse.ie/

Visit Wicklow. (n.d.). Wicklow Way. Retrieved from https://visitwicklow.ie/listing/ wicklow-way/

Wild Nephin Ballycroy National Park. (n.d.). Retrieved from https://www.wildnephin nationalpark.ie/

Wild Rover Tours. (n.d.). Retrieved from http://wildrovertours.com/

Wilmot's Bistro, Greystones. (n.d.). Retrieved from https://www.wilmots.ie/

Youghal Clock Gate Tower. (n.d.). Retrieved from https://youghalclockgate.ie/

IMAGE CREDITS:

AnnetteJO. (2014, January 20). Ireland landscape. Retrieved from https://pixabay.com/ photos/ireland-landscape-irish-heaven-sea-248732/

Balabaud, Thomas. (n.d.). Retrieved from https://pexels.com/pexels-thomas-balabaud-735585

Crane, Pam. (n.d.). Retrieved from https://pexels.com/pexels-pam-crane-3712506

Darndale. (n.d.). Boats, Dingle, Ireland. Retrieved from https://pixabay.com/photos/ boats-dingle-ireland-kerry-water-432455/

Dimkidama. (n.d.). Retrieved from https://pexels.com/dimkidama-6436204

DALL·E (2024, May 1). A traditional Irish dish, Boxty, served on a rustic plate.

DALL·E (2024, May 1). A traditional Irish dish, Guinness Pie, served in a rustic setting with a pint of Guinness.

DALL·E (2024, May 6). A realistic depiction of a traditional Irish teatime in a cozy, vintage-style room.

DALL·E 2024-05-20 09.37.55 - A picturesque scene of Ireland featuring lush green hills, a charming stone cottage with a thatched roof, and a vibrant rainbow.

Farren, Benjamin. (n.d.). Retrieved from https://pexels.com/pexels-benjaminfarren-21790502

Geib, David. (n.d.). Retrieved from https://pexels.com/pexels-david-geib-1265112

Getty Images. November 16, 2022. Beach BBQ Festival in Bray, Ireland. https://www. istockphoto.com/photo/food-stand-and-waiting-customers-at-the-beach-bbq-festi val-in-bray-ireland-gm1439783283-479950611?clarity=false

Getty Images. January 14, 2023. Wild goats on the Slieve Gullion mountain in Northern Ireland. https://www.istockphoto.com/photo/goats-on-the-slieve-gullion-moun tain-in-northern-ireland-gm1455330199-490697248?clarity=false

Getty Images. January 30, 2010. Golf course in Adare – Ireland. https://www.istock photo.com/photo/golf-course-gm123662967-11791951?clarity=false

Getty Images. October 3, 2019. The St. Colman's Cathedral in Cobh is one of the most photographed cathedrals in Ireland. https://www.istockphoto.com/photo/impres sion-of-the-st-colmans-cathedral-in-cobh-near-cork-ireland-gm1175695879-327492164?clarity=false

Getty Images. December 21, 2016. Woman surfing wave on stand-up paddleboard in Kerry, Ireland. https://www.istockphoto.com/photo/woman-surfing-wave-on-paddleboard-gm624989358-109974033?clarity=false

Getty Images. September 7, 2017. Fit attractive couple cycling together through majestic countryside. https://www.istockphoto.com/photo/fit-attractive-couple-cycling-together-gm843871010-137993263?clarity=false

Getty Images. April 3, 2019. Road along the scenic coast of western Ireland. Slea Head, Dingle peninsula, County Kerry. https://www.istockphoto.com/photo/coastal-road-in-western-ireland-slea-head-dingle-peninsula-county-kerry-gm1132097821-299982224?clarity=false

Getty Images. December 3, 2019. Spectacular Tullan Strand, one of Donegal's renowned surf beaches, is framed by a scenic backdrop provided by the Sligo-Leitrim Mountains. Wide flat sandy beach in County Donegal, Ireland. https://www.istock photo.com/photo/spectacular-tullan-strand-one-of-donegals-renowned-surf-beaches-framed-by-a-scenic-gm1190164385-337273206?clarity=false

Getty Images. February 06, 2022. Carrick-a-Rede rope bridge in Northern Ireland. The suspension bridge built by salmon fishermen links the mainland to the tiny island of Carrickarede. https://www.istockphoto.com/photo/carrick-a-rede-rope-bridge-in-northern-ireland-gm1368328333-438337187?clarity=false

Getty Images. October 13, 2022. A man swims in a kayak in the summer on the sea against the background of rocks. https://www.istockphoto.com/photo/a-man-swims-in-a-kayak-in-the-summer-on-the-sea-against-the-background-of-rocks-gm1432224187-474550754?clarity=false

Getty Images. May 22, 2020. Ballygally Castle Hastings Hotel Co Antrim Coast Northern Ireland. https://www.istockphoto.com/photo/ballygally-castle-hastings-hotel-co-antrim-coast-northern-ireland-22-may-2020-gm1336766290-417911590?clarity=false

Getty Images. December 21, 2021. A sheep and lamb walking at the beach in County Mayo. Ireland. https://www.istockphoto.com/photo/a-sheep-and-lamb-walking-at-the-beach-in-county-mayo-gm1356127956-430379818?clarity=false

Getty Images. November 30, 2008. Young boy standing in the ruins of an Irish castle. https://www.istockphoto.com/photo/boy-on-a-hill-gm179076132-7882194?clar ity=false

Getty Images. January 3, 2016. Tourist white bus on mountain road. Ring of Kerry, Ireland. https://www.istockphoto.com/photo/ring-of-kerry-gm529665770-93295923?clarity=false

Getty Images. August 27, 2019. The George Bar in South Great Georges Street, Dublin's

LGBTQ bar and nightclub. Opened in 1985 it was then the only large gay venue in Ireland. https://www.istockphoto.com/photo/the-george-bar-in-south-great-georges-street-dublin-ireland-gm1170356532-323829521?clarity=false

Getty Images. May 16, 2019. The Panti Bar on Capel Street, a popular gay bar in Dublin City Centre. https://www.istockphoto.com/photo/the-panti-bar-gm1151750510-312226203?clarity=false

Getty Images. June 29, 2019. Participants of the Dublin LGBTQ Pride Festival hold colorful letters that form the word PRIDE. https://www.istockphoto.com/photo/people-in-dublin-pride-gm1440967213-480790264?clarity=false

Getty Images. July 6, 2015. Sun setting over the famous Giants Causeway, Northern Ireland. https://www.istockphoto.com/photo/sunset-over-giants-causeway-northern-ireland-gm479917040-68342641?clarity=false

Getty Images. December 26, 2013. Christmas market in Galway at night, panoramic view from high point. https://www.istockphoto.com/photo/christmas-market-at-night-panoramic-view-gm460094193-31443536?clarity=false

Getty Images. February 14, 2020. Northern lights as seen from Dunree County Donegal Ireland. https://www.istockphoto.com/photo/aurora-northern-lights-gm1205638000-347389218?clarity=false

Getty Images. March 17, 2014. Saint Patrick's Day parade in Dublin Ireland on March 17, 2014: People dress up Saint Patrick's at The Temple Bar. https://www.istockphoto.com/photo/dublin-ireland-saint-patricks-day-parade-gm507616207-43285968?clarity=false

Getty Images. March 8, 2021. Kilkea Castle is a medieval stronghold near the village of Kilkea, Ireland. https://www.istockphoto.com/photo/kilkea-castle-ireland-gm1305988598-396705571?clarity=false

Getty Images. August 6, 2015. Exterior of Rural Irish Cottage. https://www.istockphoto.com/photo/exterior-of-rural-irish-cottage-gm122343724-78247373?clarity=false

Getty Images. August 4, 2023. Colorful Decorated Facade of the Abbey Court Hostel. https://www.istockphoto.com/photo/colorful-decorated-facade-of-the-abbey-court-hostel-in-dublin-gm2089700212-565758592?clarity=false

Getty Images. July 5, 2022. Ireland detailed map with regions and cities of the country. Vector illustration. https://www.istockphoto.com/vector/ireland-detailed-map-with-regions-and-cities-of-the-country-gm1406899624-458286864?clarity=false

Getty Images. July 21, 2019. Thousands of spectators in Galway for GIAF2019. https://www.istockphoto.com/photo/thousands-of-spectators-in-galway-for-giaf2019-gm1163242009-319346935?clarity=false

Getty Images. November 20, 2019. The Metal Man. https://www.istockphoto.com/photo/the-metal-man-gm1186596484-334853026?clarity=false

Getty Images. February 7, 2023. People playing flutes at an Irish Traditional Music session at a pub in Northern Ireland. https://www.istockphoto.com/photo/people-playing-flutes-at-an-irish-traditional-music-session-at-a-pub-in-northern-gm1460463946-494638580?clarity=false

Getty Images. October 23, 2023. Aerial view of beach in Dogs Bay. https://www.istock

photo.com/photo/aerial-view-of-beach-in-dogs-bay-gm1750812068-543795320? clarity=false

Getty Images. August 10, 2018. World famous Cliffs of Moher, one of the most popular tourist destinations in Ireland. https://www.istockphoto.com/photo/world-famous-cliffs-of-moher-one-of-the-most-popular-tourist-destinations-in-ireland-gm1015452504-273276973?clarity=false

Getty Images. May 26, 2016. Dublin's Grafton Street. https://www.istockphoto.com/photo/dublins-grafton-street-gm527902804-92860423?clarity=false

Getty Images. November 26, 2019. Architectural detail of the old Irish whiskey distillery of the commercial brand Jameson. https://www.istockphoto.com/photo/architectural-detail-of-the-old-irish-whiskey-distillery-of-the-commercial-brand-gm1190182647-337287961?clarity=false

Getty Images. August 27, 2021. Beautiful sunset over the Atlantic Ocean with a small cottage house in Doolin, Co. Clare. Ireland. https://www.istockphoto.com/photo/beautiful-sunset-over-the-atlantic-ocean-with-a-small-cottage-house-in-doolin-gm1334432310-416554477?clarity=false

Getty Images. May 22, 2020. Ballygally Holiday Apartments Self catering Antrim Coast Northern Ireland. https://www.istockphoto.com/photo/ballygally-holiday-apartments-self-catering-antrim-coast-northern-ireland-22-may-2020-gm1472967560-503188381?clarity=false

Getty Images. March 5, 2018. Dromoland Castle in Co. Clare. https://www.istockphoto.com/photo/dromoland-castle-in-co-clare-gm923871748-253581931?clarity=falseIntrospectivedsgn. (n.d.). Retrieved from https://pexels.com/introspectivedsgn-4062559

Iso, Christian. (n.d.). Retrieved from https://pexels.com/pexels-christian-iso-538505

Jay's Photography. (n.d.). Retrieved from https://pexels.com/pexels-jaysphotography-15107517

Johns, Rick. (n.d.). Kylemore Abbey. Retrieved from https://pexels.com/pexels-rick-johns-145996356-18549172

Kamaji Ogino. (n.d.). Young Multiethnic Backpackers in Forest. Retrieved from https://www.pexels.com/photo/young-multiethnic-backpackers-in-forest-5064661/

Karlmphotography. (n.d.). Retrieved from https://pexels.com/pexels-karlmphotography-8221685

Kf Zhou. (n.d.). Retrieved from https://pexels.com/pexels-kf-zhou-609625381-19863222

Ludakavun. (n.d.). Retrieved from https://pexels.com/pexels-ludakavun-15350835

Marripati, Bhargava. (n.d.). Retrieved from https://pexels.com/pexels-bhargava-marripati-674798-4055521

Maumascaro. (n.d.). Retrieved from https://pexels.com-maumascaro-1154189

Matreding. (n.d.). Retrieved from https://pexels.com-matreding-10725912

Olsen, Barbara. (n.d.). Retrieved from https://www.pexels.com/photo/a-woman-with-a-horse-7882942/

Pexels.com (n.d.)-pexels-photo-2647936 Oysters

Pexels.com (n.d.)- pexels-photo-3566191-Irish bridge in Dublin

Pixabay. (n.d.). [Multiple entries, e.g., DJ with laptop. Retrieved from https://pixabay.com/pexels-pixabay-358129]

Pixabay. (n.d.) Temple Bar. temple-bar-2344400_1280 Temple Bar.

Ravier, Max. (n.d.). Two Men in Water. Retrieved from https://www.pexels.com/photo/two-men-in-water-3348392/

Selimkrdy. (n.d.). Retrieved from https://pexels.com/pexels-selimkrdy-19862479

Sharonang. (2017, December 26). Fish and Chips, Fried. Retrieved from https://pixabay.com/photos/fish-and-chip-fried-fish-chip-3039746/

Shylands. (n.d.). Retrieved from https://pexels.com/pexels-shylands-1649273 and pexels-shylands-3811712 Mourne Mountains

Spencer, Mario. (n.d.). Retrieved from https://pexels.com/pexels-mario-spencer-838155075-19840963

Shtefutsa. (n.d.). Retrieved from https://pexels.com/pexels-shtefutsa-

Vlaminck, Dirk. (n.d.) Pexels.com-pexels-dirk-de-vlaminck-473896557-15934817 Silver Strand Beach .

Weber, Timur. (n.d.) Pexels.com-pexels-timur-weber-9186160 Someone packing.

Printed in Great Britain
by Amazon